J R BILLINGSLEY

A Mind Full of Scorpions

Contents

1

INTO STONE GARDENS part one

Fayetteville, AR—

Cotton sheets scratched against my stomach and legs. Yellow luminescence, the shape of the sun, burned orange under my lids. Lumps poking and prodding against my back, my left hand caught in a vice of flesh, the palms sweaty. A voice. A hum higher up. A smell, something sweet and chocolaty and yet musky: cologne, my brother's cologne. My little brother.

I opened my eyes and winced from the humming fluorescent directly overhead, saw Chris smile at me, then the white cinderblock walls. The small lattice window on the other side of the room only revealed darkness, so I guessed it was night. I craned my neck and looked over my left shoulder. The door was solid and metal and had only the smallest of windows. If Chris were here then I was in Piney Ridge, in Fayetteville. Yes, I was, because I'd come home. Because...

Flashes: a man naked, sitting in a sea of a thousand magic markers, dressed in the runes and sigils that he'd marked over his flesh and the walls of his apartment, clothed only in the vest of explosives as we entered. He'd pleaded for me to help him. Pleaded, and then hit the detonator. Only, a moment before that, I'd seen something. A shadow – shadows – moved and shimmered. He was crying and then our world exploded.

Marion had gotten me out. Chris, here. With our mother. Me, with my partner.

"Marion," I said, trying to sit up, but Chris shushed me and said he was okay, it was all okay, and it was, yes, okay, all okay, and I'm okay. I'm okay. I'm okay.

"I was saying your doctor's hot, Adam," Chris said a minute or so later, when I'd calmed again. My brother knew I understood his fascination with the fairer sex. Only, I would call it an obsession. "Samantha, that her name? She's cute. Like the blonde hair. She's young, too, our age."

If I could have responded, I would have warned him against objectifying her, but they had dosed me up pretty good; at least the restraints were gone. To confirm, I lifted my right hand and stared at it, turning it each and every way. Restraints . . . might as well put a chain around a pumpkin.

He asked me if I remembered the bedtime story dad used to tell us. Some old fable about our grandfather on an adventure around the world, chased by bandits or Nazis or pirates, till he and his friends stumbled upon the mythological utopian city of Shangri-La, whose inhabitants were physically and spiritually superior to man, their location purposefully hidden to the rest of the world by the Tibetan monks in the Himalayas.

I tried to focus on a particular spot on the bed, my mind calm like a gentle surf rolling onto a sandy shore. As I focused on the one spot, my brother came in loud and clear and uninterrupted. Since the shot of Haldol yesterday evening, I hadn't seen the Shimmers, but then—

Like a reverse strobe, they were shadows that grew clearer when the fluorescent faded. There were seven of them. Lust, Greed, Wrath, Pride, Gluttony, Sloth, Envy—no, I knew their names—Asmodeus, Mammon, Aman, Lucifer, Beelzebub, Belphegor, Leviathan—and they each had their own faces. In their false faces, they looked like men, but they weren't men.

I tried to focus on the story, but Chris's words took a back seat to the dark figures shimmering around the room, smiling and taunting, flashing their false faces and every so often, flashing their real ones.

Lucifer wore a trench coat: a handsome man with dark hair slicked back and piercing brown eyes. He wore a tailored suit well. "You should really look at yourself. You're better than this, Adam. You could be a god, you know. With your knowledge—your wisdom."

The Marquis Amon was built like a man, but had a raven's head with a wolf's teeth, paws and claws and a snake's tail that whipped about. "Don't listen to him. You have nothing to be proud of. You are stuck here, your brother's chattel, he the savior of the family, your *little* brother, caring for you and for your mother. Remember when your mother showed you how to change his diaper? And now he is changing your diaper. How does that make you feel?"

"I'm not wearing a diaper," I said.

Chris paused and offered me only a worried look.

Another man beside the Marquis Amon, dressed all in purple, a wolf at his side; this was the demon face of the being called Mammon. "Take what is yours, Adam. Take it all. We can help you."

A beautiful young woman with dark hair and olive skin stepped out from the shadows, beside Mammon, her lithe legs carrying her forward. She had full breasts with perfectly shaped nipples. Her pubic hair was shaved. Her eyes glowed a deep red. I mumbled her name, "Belphegor," which gave Chris another pause in his story but didn't stop it completely. I felt him squeeze my hand and waited for the witch to speak.

"We are coming, Adam. Why fight it? We are coming and you are so tired. Just lay back. Take a nap." She morphed, then, into something hideous, just a glimpse of her real self, a demon with a beard and sharp claws. It smiled and Chris's words were all the sound in the room, hollow and echoing.

I averted my eyes and screamed out; Chris wrapped his arms around me and rocked me as Dr. Samantha Blake entered. A look passed between them, and I finally took a peek at the beast in front me. It was so rare that they'd all appear in front of me at the same time like this. Its most unnatural characteristic was its smile. The smile seemed normal on the lips, all the right muscles pulled back, stretching the skin, baring teeth. But a monster like this shouldn't smile.

Even with my most balanced meds, on my clearest days, could I barely comprehend what stood in front of me. There were three heads atop a serpentine, scaly neck. One was the face of a man, which stared at me with that horrible smile. The other two faces were of a bull and a ram. The body was a man's body, with a man's arms, but this morphed into a lion's trunk with four lion's legs and a fifth leg jutting out to the side, something that resembled a bird's talon. A serpent's tail flailed about behind, and around the torso a pair of dragon's wings flapped.

This, of course, is an imperfect description. In trying to rationalize what these things looked like, my logical brain assigned these physical traits the characteristics of animals I recognize. But in truth, these things didn't occur in nature. The serpent's tail of Asmodeus resembled a snake's like a leopard looked like a tiger.

Chris tried to continue the story about our grandfather and the Nazis and the race to Shangri-La.

"I can blow around the souls of the lustful like a hurricane," Asmodeus bragged, "so they can't gather themselves. And they knew that, coming in. They knew that when they kissed me at the door. She's pretty, your doctor. If but a taste of her you desire, I can help, with a bit of a price. Join me in this whirlwind, and I can make the rest of your earthly experiences so pleasurable."

I cried, "Why are they doing this?"

A serpent lay coiled in the corner, but it let out a hiss and began to unfold itself, stretching around the room, wrapping itself over and over until the walls seemed papered with its scales, and each breath it took threatening to collapse the room. It raised its eel's head and stared at me.

"Hello, Leviathan," I said.

"Look at what your brother has. Look at your old partner. They are coming, you know. To keep you down. But we are here to prepare you. We want to remind you." Every word he hissed, he slithered, and his scales flickered in the room. Chris didn't notice, but I did. The squeeze of the python's body jostled my brother's body as he tried to resume his story.

The snake vanished into the walls, and in its place squatted a large bug, height near six feet, a grotesque: half-wasp, half-fly. Its many eyes studied me as the head tilted this way and that. It echoed the hum of the fluorescent lights and amplified them when it spoke.

"Eat. We will come, and you should eat. Everyone should eat."

"You're the weakest of the Shimmers, Beelzebub," I said.

A handful of nurses joined Dr. Blake. There were syringes and hustling and Chris was pushed out of the way. I screamed. Beelzebub smiled.

"Eating's the best way to go," it said.

The dose of Haldol acted quickly, and with what was already in my system, I sank. Beelzebub shimmered away. Chris returned to my side, an arm around me, as the world blurred like I saw it through frosted glass, and my lids froze. Chris wiped the drool from my mouth.

"Keep telling him the story," Samantha said as the nurses left. Chris looked at her doubtfully but she only nodded. "Your words soothe him. He needs them now."

Chris squeezed my hand. The Haldol was working. His words melted into figures acting out the story in my dream, a cheap animation from the sixties where the background didn't change because the animator used the same cell over and over again, just changing the characters. "The Americans that had been wounded were healed," he said, his voice cracking, "and the La gave them all warmth and food and shelter. They imparted some of their wisdom, before the team slept. They slept for what felt like forever, awaking in a monastery to the south. Each of them had forgotten the way to Shangri-La, and for a while this upset them. Finally, after much arguing, our grandfather spoke:

"'That's their wisdom, y'see. We find peace in the journey to the perfect place. It ain't where we're going, just that we strive to stay on the good road and for all the right reasons. It isn't about being there but going there. The Nazis didn't understand that and will never find it.'"

I stood outside myself, staring down at my drooling, dosed up form, standing next to them as they studied me from their perch next to the door, as if I were a zoo animal.

"Nice story," my doctor said.

Chris shrugged. "I get what my dad was trying to say."

"You think your grandfather really found Shangri-La?"

Chris shook his head. "Don't know. I hope Adam can."

"It'd be nice if we all could," Samantha said.

~

Washington, D.C.—

Government offices were always bland, but Marion Case knew this was by design. This particular room had windows on one wall that looked out to another building, white-washed or off-white walls on three of the four, with one wood-paneled wall behind the row of officials . The fluorescents above helped ensure the coldness of the room. Again, by design. There was nothing warm or comforting in these offices, nothing to invite you in, welcome you or make you feel secure. They were cold and off-putting and meant to keep you on guard. Unnerved. This was exactly how Marion felt as he entered the room.

Of the faces in the panel, Agent Case saw familiarity and comfort only in our direct supervisor, Assistant Director Tom Builder. Marion, onetime officer in the Navy SEALs, athletic and barely thirty, found the tiny room hot and the sound of file pages turning annoyingly loud.

Five ADs looked down at him from their elevated judges' table. Each of them had a copy of the case file in front of them. While our boss was present, he was obviously not in charge of the judiciary panel. A middle-aged woman with dark hair who looked like Velma from *Scooby Doo* cleared her throat and looked over her OTC readers to Marion.

"Can you restate the facts of the case, for the panel, Agent Case?" She tapped her pen, a muted drumstick on a stack of papers.

"My partner and I—"

"Your partner's name," an older agent to the right of Velma said, a WASP, a classic cold government official, someone who'd probably made a career out of the mundanity of bureaucracy.

"—for the record," Velma said. Tap, tap, tap.

"My partner, Adam Richardson, and I were investigating interstate human trafficking and ritual sacrifice involving a cult in Virginia. We knew the principal members of the cult and the suspected victims, but the cult had been nomadic and hard to catch, despite their size." Marion shifted in his seat. He didn't sweat, because sweating indicated nervousness, and he had learned to control most such reactions. But the seat was hard plastic and painful to sit in one position for long. Still, shifting like this, he was sure, showed weakness or nervousness. Something they could feed on.

"What was the nature of this cult and how large was it?" Builder asked. The panel thumbed through the pages.

"Twenty members, large paper trails, including rap sheets for some. They were publicly representing themselves as some kind of new-age sect, but there is belief that they were involved in a darker branch of witchcraft."

"That's our first problem with this investigation," Velma said. "Wiccan is now recognized as an official religion." Tap, tap, tap.

"Adam is better at explaining this than I am." Wrong move. Don't let them see you get flustered.

"Agent Richardson isn't here," said another member of the panel, a black man in his fifties. He stared at Marion, a shark eyeing its prey, like he had something to prove.

"They aren't Wiccan," Marion tried. "They practice darker things."

"Satanism?" a panel member said. A woman, youngish, Hispanic, hair just above her shoulders. Only when she squinted did her eyes reveal she was older than she looked. "No evidence of satanic ritual or ritual sacrifice due to satanic practices. The case of the West Memphis Three forced us to launch an—"

"With all due respect, ma'am," Marion said, "I'm familiar with the investigation into satanic and occult practices. This case is different."

"This case took you in a different direction," our boss urged.

"Yessir. Somebody had massacred the cult. We found eighteen of their bodies at a farmhouse. We believed one or both surviving members were responsible. There was evidence at the farmhouse that supported the human trafficking charges, and signs of human sacrifice. There is evidence to support that the two dissenting members were breaking away from the cult."

"What was the manifesto of the cult?" Tom Builder continued. The eyes of the panel members ricocheted between him and Marion as though they were watching a chess match.

"They believed that the human sacrifices would resurrect their gods, or spirits they worshipped, or something like that." Marion knew I believed such things, but he felt ridiculous saying it here.

"You caught up with one of the suspects in Detroit," Tom said.

"Yes," Memories took over. Recent, traumatic, the kind that haunt you and make you forget where you are or what you were saying. Leaving you dumb and blind to the present, catching you up in the past. When he spoke, he narrated what he had seen, lost in that moment, lost to the panel before him. "We found him in an apartment with dynamite strapped to his chest. He said she wants the recipe that's in his brain. Said she couldn't find it at the farmhouse. He ranted that the Shimmers were there, then he blew himself up, with us in the room."

"The Shimmers. That would be their gods, that they believed in." Agent Builder said.

"Yes," Marion said, blinking. He took an unsettled breath and bit at his lip. Experts in body language might assume this stoic man showed a rare moment of doubt.

"Who was 'she'?"

"He never specified. We assumed the other cult member who escaped, named Pamela Jean Harlow."

"Your partner now subscribes to the same delusionary beliefs," Velma said. Tap, tap…she stopped the pen.

"He is currently hospitalized after being diagnosed with a schizophrenic break."

The panel exchanged glances and thanked Marion; the session was over. He left the room, found a plastic chair next to a potted fern similar to the chair he'd just been sitting in, elected to stand, replayed those moments again. We had just barely escaped. The building came down quickly, the smoke and dust so thick it suffocated us.

He paced. Was his career over? We'd gotten out, but other agents hadn't been so lucky. That was what this panel was for. Assigning blame for a botched assignment that left five FBI and three ATF agents dead, and another agent of the FBI hospitalized for a mental break. As the moments ticked by – five, ten, twenty – he convinced himself that he was unemployed. Someone was accountable. He couldn't hear them through the walls, but he knew that's what they were doing. Holding someone accountable. The only one left was him. Thirty minutes after he left the room, Tom Builder walked out. Marion tried to read our old boss even as Agent Builder invited him for a walk.

Outside, the sun shone brightly, forcing him to wince until he could get his Ray Bans on. They crossed two blocks and entered the park not far from the J. Edgar Hoover Federal Building. It was a warm day; Marion took off his jacket and looked up through the limbs of the maple trees to a cloudless, cerulean sky.

"I need to go see Adam," he said. As a rule, Marion didn't shuffle his feet or shift around. Like I said, he wasn't one to get rattled easily. Still, he said this looking at the nearest maple and not at his division boss.

"Of course," Tom said. "Take a few days." A pause. "They will find fault with someone, and they're questioning Adam's investigative methods as well as the SWAT leader's decision to withdraw the rooftop snipers after you entered the building."

"Adam—" Marion began, till Agent Builder cut him off.

"Is out of the FBI. Effective immediately. I don't like it any more than you, but they overrode me on that. If I can't save you both, then I can at least salvage your career. You don't have a clue how close you were to being tossed out on your ass."

Yeah, I do, Marion thought as he watched his boss walk away, the sun beating down, the hot day in this early fall a bit uncharacteristic. With everything to process, he walked the long way home.

~

Government offices aren't the only buildings meant to look cold; hospitals' bare interior design also rejected human comforts, warmth, or security. Odd, as these were supposed to be places of healing, but the coldness of the design, the white-hot lighting above, showed the bite in the connotative definition of "clinical." To her credit, Samantha Blake had tried to dress up her office. Picture frames showed her degrees and accrediting institutions; the bookshelf behind her desk held some of the titles one might expect to find as well as some novels by Thomas Pynchon, Jonathan Franzen, Marilynne Robinson, Iris Murdoch, and a short story collection for Flannery O'Connor with a bookmark two-thirds of the way through it. Her office was clean, carpeted, a Tiffany floor lamp by her chair, but the room smelled of antiseptic and bleach and could not hide the "clinical." No matter what she tried to do, nothing could detract me from the antiseptic room, and I sometimes wondered if anyone could ever get better in such conditions.

I scratched my left bicep because there was little else to do, and that's where they stuck me a lot. And it itched. She'd been careless laying my folder open on her desk, and I could read, though it was upside down, the clinical terms she'd used to label me. A nurse stuck her head in and Dr. Blake excused herself.

Journal, Dr. Samantha Blake:
AXIS ONE (*From the DSM IX)—
295.3—Paranoid Schizophrenia—F20.0
Patient Adam Richardson presented with audio/visual hallucinations and a paranoid delusion of beings he calls SHIMMERS stalking him and his friends and family. Source of delusions is environmental. Patient also suffers from social withdrawal and inappropriate affect.

AXIS TWO—

During initial break, patient exhibited catatonic symptoms at times. Current responses are minimal and sporadic, primarily due to administration of Haldol. Patient has high blood pressure, no familial history, likely due to job-related stress. Patient has no known personality disorders. Some characteristics can be attributed to Paranoid Personality Disorder. Patient believes he and loved ones are in danger, and the source of the danger is his delusion. No antisocial behavior issues at present. Patient feels at times he is the only one to stop "Shimmers" and that he alone is gifted enough to stop them. Suggests Narcissistic Personality Disorder but lacks other attributes of NPD.

AXIS THREE—

Patient's primary caregiver is brother, younger by three years. Patient's mother is in an assisted-living facility with degenerative kidney failure. Mother was older when she had children. Patient's father passed away five years ago. Never sought treatment but there is a record of forced hospitalization for schizophrenic behavior. Patient was close to both parents. Patient's parents divorced when he was twelve.

AXIS FOUR—

Patient is an ex-FBI agent. Patient worked as a profiler on a violent crimes unit. Patient and Partner encountered a cult practicing human sacrifice. Patient was introduced to delusion of SHIMMERS, spiritual beings, by cult, whose ultimate goal was to revive these spirits. In apprehending the cultists, one member blew himself up in front of Patient, nearly killing him and his partner. Delusional episodes triggered by this event began not long after.

AXIS FIVE—

Functional score for patient—50. Patient is violently reactive to everyone, especially when he says Shimmers are present. Patient fluctuates between near catatonic state and violent outbursts. Initial 5mg Haldol, then 30 minutes later 10 mg Haldol if patient is still uncooperative, 5 mg every 2 hours after second dose or 10 mg every 4 hours, depending on patient's affect and state.

~

Dr. Blake returned after a few minutes, handed me a bottle of water, apologized for the interruption.

Me: I still think about that day. I could have gotten us both killed.

Dr. Blake: You cannot blame yourself. Whenever you think about blaming yourself, you must refocus.

Me: I don't know if I can.

Dr. Blake: Marion is still alive. You are alive. Remind yourself of that. Why are you scratching your arm?

Me: Reflex.

Dr. Blake: You do it every time you come in for our one-on-one sessions.

Me: I'm pretty sure I scratch my arm in group.

Dr. Blake: That's where we administer the drugs.

Me: I don't like being dependent on drugs.

Dr. Blake: Now, remember our cognitive exercises. Say it.

Me: The drugs help me stay focused in the real world.

Dr. Blake: So, let's talk about why you scratch at that place on your arm.

~

I was still hospitalized when my old partner got to see my chart. Agent Case sat in the Denny's on Martin Luther King Boulevard in Fayetteville, Arkansas, opposite Dr. Blake. Marion, his back to the front door, glanced up and out the large bay windows to the street beyond. Two lanes of traffic waited as patiently as could be expected for the light to change, morning commutes to the university and the junction of the I-49 corridor that would take some of them north to the Tyson home office or the Walmart home office. Dr. Blake cleared her throat a couple of times, averted his eyes when he looked at her. Small talk didn't work. It was apparent she was ready to get this over with, that she wasn't comfortable with him, and that she'd rather be any place but here. At the light change, a new "arrest-me red" Camaro whipped into a spot, and Marion saw Chris exit and walk to the door. My brother sat down between them at the table, angled his chair closer to Dr. Blake and faced the agent. Pleasantries were exchanged frigidly and quickly.

"How is he?" Marion asked.

"I'm weaning him off the Haldol," Samantha said. "We've started on some basic therapy, and I'm going to try some medicines to help curb the hallucinations."

"What did the panel find?" Chris asked.

"They unanimously voted to give him a medical release from the Bureau."

"That's in his best interest," Samantha said, and she punctuated this with a sip of her coffee.

Chris slapped at the table, jarring them both. "He was your friend. You were supposed to take care of him. You knew our family history."

"How long have you known?" Samantha asked Chris, turning on him.

"Forever . . . years . . . our mother minced no words when it came to our father."

"And Adam?" Marion noticed how shocked Chris was that she'd confront him so publicly.

"As an undergraduate. An incident. He left school for a semester. We sent him to a family friend, balanced the meds. Concealed the records. He was brilliant. His future would have been—"

"He is brilliant," Dr. Blake said, "but you jeopardized his life and the lives of others by concealing this."

Chris shook his head. "How many lives has he saved, Doctor? How many people has he helped because we helped him, we encouraged him, and supported him, and we didn't let his illness define him?"

"I agree that his illness shouldn't handicap him, but he went into this profession without his supervisor's understanding who he was. And that was very dangerous."

"I understand," Marion said. The situation needed to be diffused. He looked at Chris and asked, "How is your mother?"

The waitress passed to fill their cups, and Dr. Blake emptied a creamer into hers. "I've got to find her a home, more than just assisted living. I can't run her to dialysis and cart her around, not anymore, by myself . . . with Adam . . . I've got a few places to visit after this."

"I'd like to see Adam," Marion said.

Chris and Samantha exchanged a glance before Samantha answered. "That isn't a good idea at this point in time."

"Y'all ready to order?" the waitress asked, flipping to a new page in her notebook. Marion smiled and motioned to his empty cup, Dr. Blake said she was fine. Chris ordered flapjacks, scrambled eggs, sausage, bacon, and hash browns, toast on the side.

"When in Rome," he said, as though that were some sort of defense. He was fit, so maybe he needed the calories, but Marion couldn't stomach all that grease.

Instead he nodded. What else would they say? He finished the rest of his coffee and stared at the bottom of the cup, the bits of ground beans floating in turbid liquid and thought, How appropriate.

"I have to get back to the office," Samantha said, standing and gathering her purse, her keys. Chris shrugged and dug into his food as Marion walked to his rental. When his name was called, he turned and found the doctor close behind him.

"I know he was your partner," Samantha said.

"He was my friend," Marion said. He wanted to correct that from the past tense to the present and wasn't sure why he didn't. The past tense made it sound like I was dead. Later, he told me that bothered him to no end.

"Give me your number," she said. "I'll call, keep you informed."

He fished a business card out of his inner coat pocket and handed it to her.

"He's my friend, Dr. Blake. I flew halfway across the country to see him—my *friend*, not just my old partner. And now you're telling me I can't."

"You should have called first." She offered him a consolatory smile.

"Goodbye, Dr. Blake," he said, not adding "for now," and got into the rental car. He drove around Fayetteville aimlessly a while. He drove the hills and saw the town, cruised up around the University of Arkansas, accessing as much of the campus as he could behind the wheel without having to get out and walk. It was around five o'clock when he returned to his hotel, dropped his coat off up at the room, and took the elevator down to the lobby bar. It served beer and a number of mixed drinks. Marion spent several hours there.

The actual, un-redacted case file had been classified Compartmentalized. All the information about the cult was now sealed, like the beings called Shimmers: those who saw them said that they never got a good look, that they seemed to shimmer in and out of reality like a mirage. The seven Shimmers were named for the demons that represented the Catholic Church's Seven Deadly Sins. Most saw human interpretations of the demons. Few saw the demons themselves, their real faces – those that did were said to go insane. Myths and legends, Marion thought, about a bunch of deranged murderers. So why compartmentalize it? This bothered him; it grew more bothersome the more he drank.

He went upstairs, struggled a bit with the keycard, and stumbled into the room. He checked his phone, swaying as he did so. No one had called. He slurred a request into the room's phone for a wake-up call at 6:30, then crashed onto the bed and slept, without undressing and without dreaming.

The next morning, five minutes before the call was to come, he awoke sober, alert to his surroundings. The night before still weighed on him. The thoughts, the knowledge that I had been broken—he wondered then what I'd seen, if I'd seen the real faces. He showered and shaved, dressed and caught his flight on time. He ordered coffee on the flight. Chris and my doctor didn't care about what I saw, that I saw *anything* was not good. But Marion couldn't shake the thought that had plagued him since the panel's inquest into the investigation. He had combed through the un-redacted file over and over. The only conclusion he could reach, the only reason that the file had been classified compartmentalized was the most disturbing one, as strange as it sounded. What if I hadn't seen a hallucination? What if what I'd seen was real?

~

Washington, D.C.—

A day later, Marion walked into ADA Builder's office, having not slept the night before. When he could sleep back then, he told me he often dreamed of that explosion. Our boss must have seen the weariness on his face. Tom waved Marion to the chair on the other side of the desk.

Was his boss going to give him a new partner or another assignment, forgetting the bond previously forged? Perhaps Tom didn't care about me and Marion's relationship.

"How you doing, buddy?" Tom asked, reaching into a desk drawer. "How you holding up?"

"Fine," Marion said. "What'cha got?"

Tom tossed him a manilla envelope; paperclipped to its edge were a plane ticket and an itinerary. Marion flipped through it, saw Chicago as the destination.

"Just an interview, to start," Tom said.

"For what?"

"Interdepartmental promotion, sent to all the ADs. Your name is high on the list."

"I like working here."

"But you need a change," Tom said. "If you stay, you'll be haunted. You need to work past this. You need a good place, a better place. A place that can challenge you; without reminding you. You need to put all this behind you."

"Like what they do for alcoholics, ship them off across the country for rehab. Fresh start for a fresh sobriety."

"Something like that. Do this, for me. For Adam."

Marion shook his head, but he was too tired to argue, "Okay."

He didn't really want to go, and in a way the trip made him feel like he was being punished, no matter that they were calling it a promotion. Being sent off the Beltway to Chicago felt like he'd been downgraded. He might as well have been sent to Siberia.

II

The video was played on an old VCR with the tab missing on the back of the video cassette. There was no introduction to the images, just the scenes unraveling. No background music, no dramatic dialogue, it was a documentary in the truest sense: cold, militaristic, official. The only words of warning came from a man in a pinstriped suit before the video started, letting Agent Marion Case know that this was official and highly Compartmentalized, above Top Secret.

"No facsimiles, no electronic copies, no photographs or extra videos. Eyes Only."

The first scene—

Date stamp: July, 1947, a desert, American southwest. Shards of metal scattered over the terrain, small fires in the brush. The sky is cloudless. Men in HAZMAT suits sift through wreckage. Men in Army Air Corps uniforms supervise. One such man with a bird on his lapel walks beyond the ridge of a dune where a HAZMAT stands, looking down. The camera doesn't follow; there is no sound. The colonel pulls out his service revolver and fires at the ground. With a quick hand motion, he signals four other HAZMAT men over and points first at the ground then to a covered jeep. Then he walks off.

The second scene—

Cottage City, MD, late 1940's. A boy lies in a bed in a bedroom. He is sick. A priest talks to a doctor and a man and a woman—the boy's parents. They look worried. There is still no sound. The screen goes snowy and then reveals a bare room with a hospital bed. The date stamp at the bottom of the screen shows that several months have passed, and the words assure the viewer that they are in St. Louis, Missouri.

The same boy now lies in the bed, surrounded by priests, murmuring prayers. Slowly the sheet falls away and the boy levitates over their heads. The priests look up to him and for a moment it appears they are praying to him. The boy's eyes look different, like someone has blacked them out with a marker. He stares into the camera and it looks as though he's staring through the lens to the audience. Like he can see whoever watches the tape.

The third scene—

August, 1985, a plantation just outside of New Orleans. Several men and women in suits scatter about the downstairs. In the dining room the camera spotlight shines on the table. A head—eyes open, they are blue and cloudy—lays in a soup bowl. Torsos sit upright in the chairs around the table. Arms and legs are scattered about. There is not as much blood as one would think.

The camera follows a man in a suit and a woman in a suit into the kitchen. Another man in a suit stands over a body. It flails, pinned to the floor by a wooden stake through the chest.

17

Woman: "I thought they were supposed to turn to dust when they got staked."
Man: "Hollywood. Myth. In truth, it's a lot harder to kill them."
The man astride the body reaches off screen and brings back an axe. The camera can't see the head of the body pinned to the ground. In a moment it doesn't matter. The axe swings down. The body stops flailing.

~

Wearing a polo and khakis, slouching in the chair, Marion sat across from a bald Air Force Colonel in dress blues in an unassuming office in the federal building in downtown Chicago while the man in the pinstriped suit stood in the corner, silently observing them. Marion caught a glimpse of a shoulder holster under his jacket.

"What are your thoughts?" the colonel asked.

Marion had never been one for the supernatural, and had this been a random office off the street or had there not been the credentials of government bureaucracy rubberstamping the operation, he might have thought it all a big joke. Even confronted with the officiousness, he still had his doubts.

"You stay busy, then?" he said.

"Busier than you'd imagine," the colonel said. "That is what we do at the PRI. The Paranormal Response Initiative. We're currently under the Department of Homeland Security."

"But older than the Department," Marion said. "And you're the head?" He leveled a finger at the bald man.

The colonel smiled. His badge read *Hamilton, USAF, Retired*. "Most days I'm in a suit or even just slacks and a polo. I've got a function this afternoon with the governor and mayor at the Hilton over on Michigan."

"The things on that video," Marion began.

"Bad. But you've seen just as bad. That last case you worked, where the guy blew himself up. How do you move beyond that?"

"You don't always."

"The PRI specializes in this. The things you'll see, the things you always assumed were myth or not real...it's important for us—here at the PRI—to

18

preserve that belief for the populace at large."

"Roswell," Marion said. "The boy. . . the demon possession . . . but I didn't recognize that third story."

"By then we had a handle on things," said the man in the suit, still leaning in the corner. "Roswell and the possession were leaked. That particular one we covered up well."

"So that's it," Marion said then. "We're what . . . the Men in Black?"

"We investigate these things and we cover them up for the sanity of the people of this nation. Globally there are agencies, corporations and organizations in almost every nation, dedicated to preserving these secrets." Colonel Hamilton spoke calmly.

"This is definitely not the FBI anymore, Agent Case," said the man in the suit.

~

Six months after I'd been delivered to the hospital, I finally left. Chris had found me an apartment. There was nothing startling in its design, layout, color scheme. It was a bigger version of the hospital in that the palate was neutral. I looked, but my books were all gone.

"You got my number?" Chris asked. I nodded, so he patted my shoulder. "We'll go see Mom in a day or two, once you're settled in. I'll check on you tonight."

He paused, unsure of how to respond next, then leaned in and kissed my cheek, then left. I stared at the closed door for an eternity until I heard a knock. When I opened it, the mail lady was walking away and there was a package for me on the mat: a thin manila envelope whose contents were a letter and a thumb drive that, when I plugged into my laptop, opened to digital copies of some of my old books and another file marked "Chicago Murder Case." I unfolded the note.

Hey Buddy,

Tried to come and see you but Chris wouldn't hear of it. I think he still blames me. I just took a new job that I'm going to need your help with, though, and I'm prepared to disclose certain pieces of highly classified information to your brother and doctor in order to retain your help. Information that I have acquired may shed new light on your illness. I don't want to say much more now. What I will say is that you will need your old books and probably more. So here. Oh, and you might get something else in the way of help. I'm sorry in advance.

Marion

~

The apology was out of place, as I wasn't aware of anything he'd done wrong. Marion was many things but was never contrite. That was because he was always upstanding and exuded high morals, so he never did anything to ask for forgiveness. I was left to wonder what he'd done as I made myself dinner, unpacked the groceries Chris had ordered for me from Richard's Country Meat Market. I read a bit on my laptop until the hour turned late and I was ready for bed. I brushed my teeth and took my pill and found that the bedding was Egyptian Cotton and of a high thread count. This mattered more to Chris and his tastes – I wouldn't have been as particular for myself – but it suited me just fine. The mattress consumed my form and the pillow fluffed just right, and quickly enough I was drifting off to sleep.

I awoke to complete darkness. A loud pounding came from the direction of my living room. I heard my front door open then a man screamed, "I'll back off. No. No. Please. Don't!" I was fully awake, roused to complete consciousness when a hail of gunfire drowned out the poor man's screams. I jumped out of bed and ran to the living room, only partly surprised to find a silent, dark room and my front door secure, locked, and deadbolted.

It had all been a hallucination. I returned to bed and tried to sleep, but the scene repeated itself a few hours later: the pounding, the screams, the shots. I rose to find nothing again but my full bladder, my heart pounding, my head spinning. I took a few breaths, calming myself, telling myself I'd had a nightmare and I had to pee. I went into the bathroom and flicked on the light, and my flesh ran cold. Scrawled in blood on the mirror were two words . . .

HELP ME

Fresh blood—some of the letters still ran. I backed out of the bathroom and lay back down, praying that this wasn't real, that I just needed more sleep.

I found it, although fitfully. I arose early, and crept to the bathroom to find the mirror clean, and so chalking it up to my illness, took my medication and readied for the day, spending several minutes running through my behavioral conditioning. It wasn't real. It was a waking dream. I recited these mantras over and over, finishing my coffee, mentally battling my schizophrenia.

Chris picked me up promptly at nine and took me to visit our mother, whom I hadn't seen since before my stint in the hospital. She looked so horrible, laying in that hospital bed, so unresponsive. I dared not enter the room as Chris sat at her side and caressed her hand. Her lips parted when he announced my arrival, but she made no other sign of acknowledging us. I'd asked him on the ride over if she were bad off, and he only grunted, chomping on another bite of his sausage, egg, and cheese McMuffin, cramming the whole of what was left in his mouth. Now I saw she was corpselike, unresponsive. He urged me to enter and I did so begrudgingly, afraid of her, of her condition, of what she might say that we'd hear, or that I might only hear.

In all her beauty, Belphegor hung in the darkest corner of the room, whispering. I heard her, of course, telling me there was nothing I could do for my mother, so I shouldn't even try, but as I sat and took my mother's hand in both our own, her head jerked to that corner and her lips worked soundlessly to produce a vocalization I could not hear, but made Belphegor smile. Had she heard her too? But that was impossible. She's just a figment, unless...

"I'm here, Mom." I cradled her right hand and took a deep breath. "I'm okay." One little lie shouldn't impact her. It was mostly true, after all.

Chris patted my shoulder. "I'm going to stretch my legs, get some coffee. You talk with Mom, okay?"

I nodded, but I'm pretty sure his back was already to me.

We were alone when she spoke.

"Don't trust her." Her voice but a whisper, coarse from disuse, cold, retaining only a shred of what I recognized.

"Who?" I asked. Belphegor? No longer in the shadows. Dr. Blake, who'd only cared for me? Surely not her.

When Chris asked me later what we talked about, I said nothing and dug into my grilled cheese. We were on the patio of Hammontrees off Dickson. The sun shone brightly. The air was tempered.

"You wanna go across the street to the bookshop, next?" he asked. I nodded, but that still didn't entice me to open up with him. I knew not to trust Belphegor, but I couldn't imagine she was talking about Dr. Blake. I trusted her. I believed in her.

"She's not just pretty," I said.

Chris furrowed his brow.

"Dr. Blake. She's smart. And she has heart."

"I get it," Chris said. He didn't like it when I admonished him.

"She'll be the heart of our team," I said. To be honest, I'm not sure why I said it at the time, though I am sure that I meant it, just as I'm sure she came to fill that role admirably in the years to come.

After browsing at the bookstore, Chris took me home, saying he had some work this evening, and I settled into what I hoped would be my nightly routine. I showered, ate a dinner of baked salmon, rice, and mixed vegetables, took my medicine, and went to bed a little after ten. That should have been the end of an eventful day because it was more than I'd normally done, but I awakened around three by similar sounds from the night before. I had thought about telling Chris about the sounds, but I knew what he would say.

The noise in the living room subsided as I opened my eyes and, though it was early, the sleep wore off as I became aware of a faint silhouette darkening the moonlit window. As the form and features became more apparent, I saw a bullet-ridden Black man in a dark suit, a badge pinned to his lapel. The blood had dried to a fine sheen, like it was still tacky.

I responded with what I'd learned in therapy.

"You aren't real. You materialized out of thin air, and real people don't materialize out of thin air. You aren't real people; therefore, you are a figment of my mind, so I will kindly ask you to leave."

The bloodied man said, "I'm not going anywhere, Adam. I want to help you, and I need your help."

"You can't need my help, because you aren't real."

He lowered his head and looked defeated. "Please just read the file," he said, before he evanesced into the shadows. The file Marion had sent me was on a thumb drive and marked "CHICAGO COP MURDER" and it stood out from the other files, digitized versions of some the books I'd lost. I clicked on the file and opened the first document, a photo of the Black man, labelled "Detective Leo Knight." The detective was a relatively young man in life, athletic, handsome, with the thin-rimmed spectacles that academics wear. Of the many questions left yet to answer, few were as pressing as the one I needed to ask when I picked up the phone.

"Your brother would shit if he knew we were talking," Marion said, his voice surprisingly awake despite the hour. I glanced at the clock and realized he was probably getting ready for his morning workout.

"Why not just email the information to me?"

"The disk is readable but not rewriteable," Marion said. "Too much information is corruptible online. There are security issues we must be mindful of, as well. I'm teleconferencing with your doctor and Chris in a bit to get you back on as a consultant."

"They won't like it. They won't go for it."

"What do you want?" Marion asked. It was a question I hadn't been asked in a while, what I wanted was of least importance. I had been too preoccupied with "getting better." And, in part, that was what I wanted. To get better. But I also wanted to prove or disprove the existence of the Shimmers. The fragile condition of my mind and soul seemed tethered to their existence. More than that, I wanted to work again, and this was what I told him.

"As long as you aren't delving into the occult or the paranormal, they shouldn't have a problem."

"I won't be, will I?"

Marion said we'd talk later and hung up. Out of the corner of my eye I saw the visitant sitting in my recliner, staring at me. As the sun rose neither of us moved, nor did we speak, until the daylight shone in tiger-stripes through the blinds over my living room floor and the dead detective faded from sight. I walked myself through my therapy again before showering, devoured a quick breakfast, and took my medications.

~

At the skype call the next day, with my brother and I in Dr. Blake's office, Marion hesitated as he described my job description of "consultant." As I suspected, Marion did not inform my brother or Dr. Blake as to the nature of my consulting job, only to say that my profiling and detection techniques could be called upon by law enforcement throughout the country on cold cases and those deemed unsolvable. He assured them that at no time would I have direct influence on the case, the suspects, or the victims. Still, I saw their skepticism.

"Adam," Dr. Blake said finally, "will you excuse us?"

I walked out into the hall, and saw the detective again. He appeared unnervingly normal, given that he was an incorporeal image of a deceased human. I had met so many diagnostic criteria to be labeled schizophrenic, but I was sure that not everything I'd seen was a hallucination. With the presence of this spirit, doubt had been placed in my unstable mind that, if he were real, how many other things had been real also, and what all would I now be subject to in this new role as "consultant"?

When they called me back into the room, I saw that they still skyped with Marion, who appeared visibly upset onscreen. The tension in the room was palpable, the stressful air raising the temperature substantially enough that I broke into a sweat as I entered. They waited as I sat and then waited a bit longer, looking at me and then to each other, until finally Dr. Blake spoke.

"Your brother and I are not fully convinced that this is the right move for you yet at this juncture, and so we are inclined to say no," she began. On the screen, Marion mumbled a curse and looked away. "But I also recognize the value of work, and I know how important it is for a patient to return to some semblance of their past life as quickly as possible. Work in such a capacity often does more good than a dozen therapy sessions. You'd be interacting with the world, with other people."

"You never approved of the work," Chris mumbled.

"But he'll be with someone who is now aware of his condition," Dr. Blake responded.

"You're worried about what I'll see," I said.

"Evil has an effect on us," Dr. Blake said. "The more we're exposed to it, the more it can damage the psyche, and quite frankly, Adam, yours cannot afford any more damage."

"I'll be careful," I pleaded. I sounded like a teen asking his parents to stay out past curfew.

"I have power of attorney," Chris said. This was as much a reminder for me as for Dr. Blake, who sighed.

"Your brother and I agree that right now it would be detrimental to deny you this opportunity to focus your skills, but Chris's point is that at any time should you backslide, we will have you hospitalized, which your brother has the legal right to do. We aren't threatening you, Adam. We are just concerned for your safety and it's with your safety and sanity in mind that we are going to be keeping a close eye on you."

I said okay, I understood, and Marion also accepted the terms, a smile creeping across his lips before Dr. Blake ended the call and we all stood. When Chris took me home, we didn't speak. At home the ghost appeared once to nod and offer me a grin before vanishing again, and I experienced my first full night's sleep in peace.

And that was how it was left, that I would resume my work with Marion, but Dr. Blake and Chris were going to watch me, that hospital and those meds only a signature away.

2

HECATE'S CRESCENT

I

Colonel Jack Hamilton's office was cool this early morning. The retired USAF officer sipped his coffee with a steady gaze on Marion while the man in the suit assumed his regular position in the corner. In Marion's hands a manila folder filled with bound leaves of paper, each page stamped with the words EYES ONLY.

The coven—Hecate's Crescent—had been founded three years earlier on November 1, and they met religiously in a compound owned by their High Priest on the outskirts of a small Dallas, Texas suburb. When the sheriff of Ellis County found the twelve bodies, he first called the Texas Rangers, who in turn called the FBI—fearing of an outcry of "Devil Worship" by the Evangelical population of the town—who then called the Department of Homeland Security, who redirected the call to the thirteenth floor of the Federal Building in downtown Chicago.

"Liver temps suggest that all twelve people were killed about the same time. Quickly. Efficiently." Col. Hamilton emphasized the last words.

"Coven rosters suggest there was a thirteenth member," the man in the suit said.

"Do we know which one is missing?" Marion asked.

"We do," said the man in the suit.

Marion flipped through the photos of the known members then through the autopsy photos. Outside the bay window to his left a torrent of snow blanketed the windy city, obscuring the lakefront and leaving Lake Michigan hidden behind a haze of white.

"There's a private jet ready at O'Hare to fly you down to Texas," Colonel Hamilton said.

"I'm not the expert in this," Marion said. "I tried to tell you guys this when you insisted on giving me the job."

"That's why we're sending you your old partner," responded the man in the suit.

~

Chris stretched out in his bed until another warm body blocked the way. He looked over to a swath of black hair and tanned, firm shoulders, but could discern little more of the woman snoring next to him. He rubbed her shoulder and when she didn't stir, he nudged her until she nearly rolled onto her side. She awoke with a "Hey!" like he was wrong for waking her up in *his* bed.

"You got to go," he said, chewing on cotton balls that tasted like tequila and beer.

"Later," she purred. "Comfortable. I'll show myself out."

"Bullshit," Chris rose with unbounded energy to his toes and began stretching beside the mattress. "I've got to go. So, you've got to go."

She rolled over, playfully giggling, smiling, and winking at him, hugging his pillow to her chest. "Fine. I'll shower and you can make me some breakfast and then—"

He stopped stretching and stood akimbo. "Get dressed and go."

"Coffee, then?"

"Get out! I'm late for work." Later, when he regaled me with this story, he admitted that he found her obstinance an indication of her lack of intelligence. Of course, he admitted this from the perspective of one who no longer objectified women, who had grown to respect them and, in turn, respect himself more too. That is perhaps why I'm including this episode now, to show where my brother started and how far he has come.

She gave him a go-to-hell look, gathered her things, dressed quickly and left. She mumbled a few choice words under her breath, which meant no never mind to him. He'd been called a lot of things and had received that look many times. A long time ago, he'd promised to call them but never did. Predating that, he actually did call one or two back, and they either clung to him like he was Velcro or thought he was clingy or thought he was interested in the chase, and so they'd start the games, as he put it. None of the above interested him, so rather than go through all of that, he'd sleep with them,end of transaction: quick and efficient.

After she left, he drank two cups of coffee and made his breakfast, high protein—a couple of eggs, today a piece of sausage—and carbs in the form of fruit. After breakfast, push-ups and some crunches and planks, then, sweat-sheened but not ready for a shower, he sprawled on his couch in his boxers to check email and a few porn sites; his appetites in those days were never satiated.

~

Dr. Blake sat at the table nearest the storefront windows in the coffee house on Dickson, sipping a pumpkin spice latte and reading the paper on her Nook. When the tall, pale man in the dark suit entered, the few other patrons seated in the coffeehouse looked up in awe, but Samantha paid no mind. The man bought a coffee, black, seeming befuddled when the barista offered him a plethora of choices in this seemingly basic order. Even when he took his seat across from her, she didn't raise her eyes, but simply sipped her coffee.

He removed his sunglasses. His hair under his fedora was blond, almost as chalky as the visible skin on his neck and face (everything else was covered; he even wore leather driving gloves that concealed his long hands and long fingers) and his piercing blue eyes stared wide as if with wonder. Still, she did not look up.

"Long time, Puck," she said casually.

"Thank you for meeting me, Samantha. It is so good to see you again."

She looked at him and smiled. "You too."

A smile came to his face with some effort and seemed alien once on his lips. "How are you?" he asked only after the smile dropped, in a solemn tone.

"Fine, but in all the times you've reached out to me since I was a kid, it's never been to chitchat."

"You're right," he said. He sat his coffee down and patted the tabletop with the palms of his hands three times. "You must go to Texas, Samantha, with your patient, Adam Richardson. He will be summoned there, and you must go with him."

"Why?"

"Do you remember how we met?"

She did. She was ten years old and had been playing at the park by her house when she saw the tall, strange boy emerge from the woods.

"I promised a long time ago that I would tell you about myself. I can promise that from here on out, you will see a lot more of me than you have recently. I'm sorry about my absence. Things are changing." He spoke slowly, seriously.

"And yet all these years and I still haven't learned your name, Puck."

"'Puck has served its purpose, and soon I will tell you more. I need you to accompany him to Texas. The woman he pursues is enormously powerful and has acquired some of that power from my people. In catching her, that will reveal some of the truth of who I am and where I come from."

So evasive, and yet so honest. There wasn't a lying bone in his body in all the years she'd known him. She lowered her eyes to take the last sip of coffee, and when she looked across the table again, he was gone. She looked around, but his ability to disappear had long since stopped amazing her. That was just Puck.

II

I awoke to no hallucinations, took my anti-psychotic cocktail of Abilify and Clozaril followed by a multivitamin and given that winter was coming on, a Vitamin C tablet. I fixed a pot of coffee and spurred my brain with another read-through of Detective Knight's homicide file. The poor man had been gunned down at his front door, just as my unrelenting dreams had suggested. Perhaps the violence of the story had made national headlines and I'd tucked the memory of the murder of this detective away into my subconscious till my illness could conjure it up.

Chris showed up at ten o'clock, looking equal parts sexually satisfied and jovial and generally disinterested in anything going on with me. Ma was cared for, and I was out of the hospital with a roof over my head and food in the fridge, so Chris could sleep at night with whatever trollop he found. If not for this weekly drive to Dr. Blake's office, I probably would not see my little brother as long as I stayed dressed and bathed and on my meds.

"You should try the bus again," Chris said. His Camaro felt claustrophobic to me, a tiny space for two grown men, and all the more dangerous as he pushed the car to its limits on the city streets, whipping around corners, speeding over the limit, breaking at the last so as to induce whiplash. He drove like he fucked, I supposed, with reckless abandon.

"You know what happened the last time." Even though his driving terrified me, the Razorback Transit — the city bus system that also serviced the university — had its share of sketchy characters, many of whom rode the Red Line, the route I'd have to take.

"That old lady did not have a gun." Tension in his voice, but he didn't take his eyes off the road, which was always a good thing; he kept both hands on the wheel unless he was shifting.

"It was a Desert Eagle."

"Jesus! She was ninety years old and maybe ninety pounds. She couldn't lift a goddamn fifty-caliber, much less aim it at your head. Are you ready?"

My phone rang the tune of Pearl Jam's "Garden." I struggled for it, stuffed into the inner pocket of my peacoat, which seemed tucked at odd angles around my body as I sat strapped in by my seatbelt. Finally freed, I found Marion's voice on the other end, explaining our first mission.

"I'm coming with you to Texas," Dr. Blake said as we walked into her office, before we had even settled into the chairs in front of her desk.

I asked, "How do you know about that?" I had just received the call, after all.

"Texas?" Chris wrinkled his nose.

Dr. Blake nodded. "When are you to fly down?"

"This afternoon. I have to go home and pack."

"Texas? Why?" Chris asked again. There was alarm in his voice. The status quo had been upset.

"I'm a consultant," I reminded him. "I consult. Today I have to go consult in Texas."

"I'm going with him," Dr. Blake assured Chris. "You go pack and I'll pick you up in two hours."

Back home, I studied my dresser drawers for what I could fit in my duffel. I opted for a T-shirt and some jeans, and then I set about with some toiletries. The hallucination stood in the corner watching me pack.

"I'm coming too," Leo said after a bit of silence.

"I doubt that's plausible," I rationalized.

"I can be of help to you."

"How so?" *Entertain the delusion to lead it to the inevitable conclusion that it is a falsehood.*

"Being a ghost is like being caught driving on one of those turnabouts, but you can't ever get off the rotation to get back on the road you need to be on. It feels like the exits are all closed off."

"Wow," I said as the metaphor sunk in. "How does that feel?"

"Dizzy," he said after a moment's reflection.

I continued to pack. Maybe a polo more than just the Tee. Or both. "So what do you think you can help with?" I asked.

"Aspects of the case. I was a cop, you know."

"The real you was a cop. I was in law enforcement also, so I suppose, as a figment of my imagination, you are too. Perhaps you represent that aspect of my psyche. The analytical."

"I'm real, Adam."

"You can't be," I said, pausing the packing. I closed my eyes and took several deep breaths, but he was still there when I opened them again. "Because I'm afraid of what that would mean if you were."

"How long until we're picked up?"

"About an hour," I muttered. As a part of me, he should know that.

"That's not much time to fashion a stang," he said.

I agreed. The thing was, after searching my mental files for occult topics,

I recalled the term and knew exactly what he was talking about and what I had to do. But he was wrong about a stang. What I really needed was a croomstick, and I had one in my closet. I'd been out shopping at a flea market a couple of Saturdays before and found one, and the fat, toothless woman selling it thought it was for sheep and swore to me with a horrible laugh that she had no sheep. Then again, she thought she looked good in that bikini top that was six sizes too small.

I'm not sure what was worse, answering the door to my psychiatrist while I held a wooden shepherd's hook or trying to carry the six-foot staff onto the private jet at XNA. I strapped myself into my seat, uncooperative when the stewardess asked if she could take my staff, and I said, "I'll secure it in the baggage handling above the seat."

Dr. Blake told me to relax.

Soon enough we were in the air and the flight attendant brought me a glass of ice water and Dr. Blake a Bahama Mama. I watched her, staring out the window, sipping at her glass, cradling it with both hands like it was a warm glass of cocoa.

"She's nice," Leo said to me. "Her heart, I mean. You're lucky. She's strong."

I started to respond but he shushed me, told me to just think it.

She's my doctor, ass. I thought he was as objectifying as my brother, but I was wrong.

She's lonely, Adam. She's tired of the humdrum crazies that waltz in and out of her office, and she's looking for something more. Oh, she'll never admit it to you; that wouldn't be professional. The shrink won't be shrunk, man, but she's intrigued.

So why is she here?

She wants answers. She's open to what we know.

And what's that?

That the shit in your head is real, buddy. Not all of it, but a lot. It's real.

"No," I said aloud. "It absolutely can't be."

The doctor paid me no mind. The plane pitched to the right, and I plugged in my headphones and played Pearl Jam repeatedly until we landed. I carried the croomstick down the tarmac and into the airport, where Marion waited for us. It had been months since our last face-to-face. The last time we'd talked, I was still struggling with my illness, and I was still one direction on the slope of recovery, mentally, in fact, although I couldn't tell if I were struggling uphill or gliding down at this point. But now, seeing him again was such a pleasant surprise, I could not contain my emotions. I rushed to my old friend and gave him a hug. My chin on his shoulder, I could feel him smile despite his outward professionalism.

Dr. Blake greeted him coolly and I half expected her to yank me back on the plane and return us to Northwest Arkansas, but I noticed he wore a bemused expression as she shook his hand. Her being there put him on guard and his questioning her presence put her on the defensive, and I attribute that initial state to our lack of progression from the gate's entrance.

"I have questions," she said. "About his position as consultant, about what he can contribute to a criminal investigation. I am here on behalf of his brother, and for Adam's continued well-being."

She's lying. The detective was in my head and standing over my shoulder. Across the walkway at another gate, a girl with Down's syndrome pointed at him and tried to tell her mother about the man with the gunshot wound.

"I rented a car," Marion said.

"Mommy! Hurt black man! Look at all the bullet holes!"

"What are you talking about, dear?" Her auburn-haired mother snapped her gaze from a pop culture magazine to scan the terminal. She, of course, saw nothing.

I was a detective, Leo Knight said to the girl. This silenced her to merely under-breath oohs and ahhs as he added, *And I was quite good up until I was murdered, Sally.*

"Who killed you?" she asked aloud, and this question concerned her mother, sparked her to ask who she was talking to. By now our little group was walking away, but I heard Leo tell her:

I wish I knew, Sally.

We must have made quite the little group: me with my croomstick, a tailored man in a dark G-man suit, a pretty blonde. I couldn't explain how the little girl could see the detective, and I couldn't ask Dr. Blake for fear of what she'd think, but perhaps I could have Marion ask her.

III

He drove us south from the airport in Dallas to the little town of Redmon, which we bisected to reach the compound where the heinous crime had been committed. Outside, the air was warmer, much warmer, than home, the sky cloudless and the sun bright. No one had told Texas that fall had arrived and was supposed to be cold. Aided by the Dallas field office of the FBI, the sheriff and his deputies did a remarkable job of securing the area as well as preserving the scene. The compound perimeter still taped off, we were greeted by two armed Texas Rangers as we parked, who said that teams of men worked in shifts around the clock to keep contamination low. Marion said that the FBI had acquired twelve mannequins to represent the bodies, had recreated the scene with the conditions and positions in which they were found.

"The entire cult was put down by one of their own," one of the Rangers said.

"Coven," I said, stepping under the tape, then holding it up so that Marion and Dr. Blake could pass under also.

"Pardon?" The Ranger pushed his ten-gallon hat up off his sweaty brow with one index finger. He had crow's feet from squinting in the sunlight.

"Hecate's Crescent was a Wiccan coven, not a cult," I said, and continued toward the house. I heard the Ranger and his partner snicker at my back, so I turned back to them.

"A cult is founded by a solitary leader who, by various means, sets out to enthrall and entrap his subjects, as many as he or she can attract, though most cult leaders tend to be male. The cult leader plays on religion or religious conviction, and is a master of psychological tactics that culminate in a kind of brainwashing of their subjects, who grow to such a level of devotion that they are willing to follow their leader no matter the cost or risk to themselves or their loved ones, even their children. When the devotion becomes great enough, cultists will even sever ties with their community in order to bend to the will of the predominant leader.

"A coven, on the other hand, is a preordained number of people—usually

34

thirteen, though that isn't a hard and fast number—who gather freely at set times while leading normal lives in an effort to worship a pre-Christian concept of dua-deities, a God and Goddess, and are generally led either by a woman or by a woman and a man, a High Priest and a High Priestess. But the purpose of the coven is not to serve the will of one megalomaniac, but of higher deities, and their meetings are scheduled without the inclusion of others, usually for a message of peace, a monthly mix of what you'd call church, a town social, a fraternal lodge meeting. There is also an element of instruction, and members, through testing, can advance through levels or degrees to gain prominence in the group." I then pointed to the squinty older Ranger. "You could be a Wiccan in a coven and other than that one time a month, no one who knew you would be the wiser."

The desired effect was achieved. The Ranger shifted his attention to his partner to plead his case that he wasn't, in fact, a witch, and satisfied, I turned back to the mission at hand. The scene was what I had imagined. Mannequins had been scattered about the compound where the bodies had been found; in various places, their appendages had been snapped off and placed in positions to mirror the original state of the crime scene. In the communal kitchen, a manila folder left for us contained files on the members as well as crime scene photos and autopsy results. Marion handed the autopsy results to Dr. Blake before beginning to pore over the rest of the files. He asked for my help, but I must admit I was too enthralled with the physical scene. The place had been trashed, tables upturned and desks scattered, paperwork strewn about. That the suspect was searching for something was painfully evident, but that drew out of me a slew of more questions.

"Marion!" I called. I had traveled down a hall past some meditation rooms, a few with sacred circles drawn on the concrete floor, some with mattresses, others with desks and books. The community must have secured this outcropping of stone buildings for more than just their Sabbats and Esbat meetings but also for the instruction and teaching and testing of the students as they passed from degree to degree. I hurried back down a hall to another room I had seen, a kind of office with a file cabinet, even as Marion met me at the door.

"The High Priest and High Priestess? What were their names on the coroner's report?"

He gave me their names.

"But the victim dressed as the high priestess on the coroner's report was not the High Priestess?" I said and showed him the coven roster I'd found in the file cabinet.

"The bitch didn't even bother with an alias," he said, but no shock washed over his face.

"You knew it was Pamela Jean Harlow before we came down," I said.

Marion shook his head. "I had a suspicion, but I wasn't sure. Not till now."

I had only seen her picture, and heard her name, but at night when the nightmares that weren't the Shimmers fell upon me, the face that tormented me was hers, the cultist I chased during my last investigation with the FBI, when I had been delivered to this condition.

"Why?" I asked. It was an emotional response, rife with meaning. *Why hide it from me? Why her? Why here? Why now?*

Samantha, still studying the autopsy reports, rounded the corner to the office as I searched the file cabinet. "Why what?" she asked, still staring at the reports.

"Why hide it from her?" I said. "She was the High Priestess, the leader of the coven, their spiritual guide."

"What were they hiding?" Marion asked.

"I don't know, but they saw fit not to include the head of their coven. Did you notice the yard as we walked up?"

Now Dr. Blake lifted her eyes off the page. "What about the yard?"

Glass jars had been filled with nails and shards of glass and buried in the dirt, I told them, but these had been uncovered and the contents spilled. "Once they've filled them with sharp objects, they fill the remainder of the space with urine, but the urine had been dumped out." The jars had been filled and buried as a protective spell, to ward off and defend a physical place against evil. But once the materials are spilled out, all bound power is scattered and weakened.

I brushed past them and walked to the communal room. Hanging over every window were shattered glass balls, jagged partial spheres. I told them even the Witch's Ball was meant for protection.

"These people had families," I said. "We need to talk to their spouses, their friends, their coworkers. They might have inadvertently revealed something about Pamela Jean Harlow."

"Like what?" Marion asked.

"You wouldn't hide anything to do with the coven from the High Priestess. She founded this coven. All of this is hers." The file said the coven was founded three years ago. I realized she must have been playing the coven against the cult we'd gone after for interstate trafficking. She'd been working both angles, searching for something.

"So, they didn't trust her," Marion said. "She murdered them all. Like she murdered that cult."

"They feared her. And she obviously ransacked the place, which means they feared her finding something," I said.

Outside, dusk was falling quickly, and with the approach of night, our long day was wearing us down. As we returned to the car, we found the two Rangers had resumed their post in silence, or at least they were silent when we approached. Marion said we had two rooms at the hotel, which posed a problem with Dr. Blake's insistence upon joining me, until she suggested that he and I take one room and she take the other. The room we were given smelled of mold and disinfectant, a kind of undercurrent of staleness, and had only one bed. Marion left to see if they had a room with two beds available, and I was left alone with the hallucination. Seeing him was better than seeing the Shimmers.

I peeked over her shoulder while she was looking at the autopsy results, he said. *COD exsanguination, from lacerations placed with surgical precision.*

"They were a sacrifice," I said, poking about the room. "I'm sure one was stabbed in the eyes, another through the side of the head, piercing the eardrums, another through the mouth, another through the chest." Logical guesses.

Yeah, all different, one through hands, one feet, and so on. How'd you know?

"A sacrifice of power. They didn't find the murder weapon because she took it with her. A knife, a special knife, called an athame. Who was stabbed through the hands and who was stabbed through the brain and who was stabbed through the eyes?"

"The High Priest, a Magus, and a Witch Queen," came the voice.

I spun to find Marion had returned with a folded metal cot which he dropped haphazardly on the floor. I stammered a reason for talking to myself but he waved me away and opened the little fridge, pulled out a tiny bottle of whiskey and took a swig. He offered me some, but I politely reminded him it didn't go good with my meds.

"The victims were religious practitioners of the New Age Religion recognized by Federal Authorities as Wicca. Pamela Jean Harlow is something else altogether. Adam, she's a witch."

IV

I have opted not to include names of the innocent, the victims, the bystanders and the local authorities as much as possible in the overall account, where it can be helped, strictly because this journal is for my eyes only, and will never see the light of day, but should others read it, no one innocent is unduly incriminated. Knowing what I know now about the government's desire to secure classified information, and specifically what the PRI is capable of, I will do my best to protect as many people as I can. People I'd already protected from the supernatural, now I must resign myself to protect from their own government.

The next morning, I stood in front of Marion, Dr. Blake, and the task force made up of local law enforcement and Texas Rangers in a boardroom down at the Dallas Federal Building. Shades were drawn across the broad bay windows that adorned one side of the room, and opened to the impressive Dallas skyline, and the lights dimmed, so that everyone could better see the presentation I'd put together the night before.

"We are primarily concerned with only three members of the coven for clues into the whereabouts of PJ Harlow: the High Priest, who was stabbed through the brain, one of the elder Magi, stabbed through the eyes, and the Witch Queen who had her hands cut off."

I explained the significance of their murders, along with what I had deduced the night before, that the coven had turned on its High Priestess. I said that we needed to focus on what these three were attempting to hide from Ms. Harlow.

"And what's that?" one of the deputies asked me.

"I believe it was a spell." This was of course met with laughter. Marion stood fast with me, though I noticed Dr. Blake hung her head. "I'm saying that that is what she believes. Whether or not we put any stock into the validity of spells and hexcraft is of little consequence to the investigation at hand." The laughter subsided. Marion took charge, organizing teams to investigate the family and friends of the three principle coven members. To some of these people questioned, it came as quite a shock that their loved one led this lifestyle. The Magus in question also served as deacon at his local Baptist church. The Witch Queen's parents protested vehemently her particular title. Our teams were allowed access to computers, personal files, at work, school, and at home, with little resistance. I, in the meantime, traveled with Dr. Blake and an FBI escort to various libraries and occult stores. I researched the nature of the coven in general and Wiccan traditions and discovered some disturbing facts that shed more light on PJ's mission, and what led to this senseless killing.

A specific spell had been discovered in the transcription of Latin-based *Wiccan Old Books*. In fact, the *Wiccan Old Books* were a secret library not currently in circulation, but witness reports and log-in sheets showed that it was the High Priestess herself who found some ancient copies during a European tour last Beltane. The trouble began when she stole these relics, along with a Fifteenth Century copy of the *Malleus Maleficarum*. She returned, ordering her coven to begin translating from the original Latin, but when the Three — the Magus, Witch Queen, and High Priest — stumbled upon this one particular spell, they realized her true intention.

V

Back at our hotel, I finished the summation for Marion and Dr. Blake, and Leo, out of breath from excitement.

"I think we should return to Fayetteville," Dr. Blake said. Outside, crickets or cicadas chirped, though I didn't know the difference between the two.

Marion chose to ignore her with his next comment. "Adam, we've come across this spell before. Remember the guy with the dynamite strapped to his chest, who almost killed you? He was looking for the same spell."

I had forgotten, in my zest for investigation again, what led me to this state. This spell had caused us trouble before, and I understood immediately the cause for alarm in those around me.

"If she believes she can control these—powers," I said.

"You called them *Shimmers*, before, not *powers*," Dr. Blake said. "Why the shift in tone?"

"If I called them that now you might have me restrained," I retorted.

"The debate isn't about the spell or Shimmers," Marion said, "but what *she* thinks a spell will do for her. From an occult standpoint, what does she believe will happen?"

"That all the Shimmers will fall under her thrall," I said. "That she could beckon them. But the spell isn't designed to work like that, I don't think."

"What would it do?"

"I don't know. I don't have the books. I don't know what they found or what they did with it." This frustrated me, not having all my resources at hand.

"This is ridiculous," Dr. Blake said then, but the anger in her voice wasn't geared at me. She turned ferociously on Marion, jamming a finger into his face, her cheeks flushing as she yelled at him, stayed on just this side of cursing.

"You promised — *promised!* — he wouldn't be exposed to things like this again."

"He's not been exposed to anything—"

"His mind is fragile. He can't take this!" She turned her back on him, pacing, then turned to me. "We're leaving, Adam. Pack your things." Then back to Marion, "Call the airport. You're flying us back tonight."

"Samantha," he said. "Come on. Let's talk about this."

"It's Dr. Blake," she corrected him. "I earned my goddamn degree, Agent. And you, my friend, will have no further access to me."

"Doctor," he tried, but she cut him off.

"You, the federal government, the FBI, whatever goddamn agency you work for now – all of it, all of you, expect a fucking lawsuit. You are liable for knowingly exacerbating Adam's condition, and I will make sure you pay for it."

"Now hold on a second. Adam is an adult, and you should treat him as such."

This unleashed a fresh tirade, and soon both were yelling at a fever pitch, nose to nose, spittle flying. I knew then they should just kiss and get it over with. But with their current state, I dared not say that for fear she'd dope me up to stupid levels for another six months. What I didn't appreciate was being talked about like I wasn't in the room, like I was a child who couldn't make decisions for myself.

Turn out the light.

Why?

I'm going to show her. It'll be easier in the dark.

They didn't even notice me as I crossed the room, but both directed their screams at me when I clicked the light off. Quickly they fell silent, though, as the room filled with an ethereal glow that captured their attention, a pulsating effulgence of light that slowly began to take shape, silently, until in front of them stood the Black man in a suit riddled with bullet holes, still stained with blood, blinking, opening his mouth, looking from one to the other, then finally to me. He gave me a thumbs-up, but I could see the fatigue in his eyes, the strain this put on him. He vanished quickly, and I turned the light back on.

Dr. Blake rested in Marion's arms, her cheek pressed against his chest. "Was that a Shimmer?" she asked finally. She'd collapsed nearly instantly, and I'd noticed that it was all Marion could do to catch her, as his knees nearly wobbled, and in fact he clung to her as much as she to him, both weak and needing support. Their mouths hung open, and their eyes trembled, staring agape. It took a while for her to even formulate her question, shaken as she was. Marion was still unable to speak.

"That was Leo Knight, a Chicago police detective," I said. "He was murdered six months ago. A little girl with Down syndrome saw him at the airport. You both saw him also?"

They sat on the edge of the bed together and only after I assured her many times that he was gone—an appearance like that took a lot out of him and he had to recharge—and after Marion found another tiny bottle of alcohol in the restocked bar, did they both finally begin to settle.

They had many questions for me after that, all of which I patiently answered as best I could. "How long have you been seeing him?" she asked.

"Since I moved into my apartment."

Marion looked intently at the bottle as I answered. "Might you've remembered him from your time at the FBI?" he asked.

"Even if I did, how did you both see him?"

"It's impossible," she said, but she couldn't deny her eyes. "Maybe that woman is here. Maybe we're drugged. Maybe ..."

"We aren't drugged," Marion said. "We really saw that."

"So I'm not just seeing things then," I said. Did this mean I wasn't really sick?

She took a deep breath and shook her head. "Schizophrenics whose meds are balanced have been shown to impart an intimate level of empathy, and have mentioned such insights and observations so as to appear precognitive. Perhaps this is another example of your shifted perception. It casts a whole new light on a lot of other issues, though."

I'd heard similar things before in my own research into the subject. Still, my next question came timidly, with my hands folded in front of me, nervously working the fingers into knots. "Knowing this now, do you still support your previous diagnosis?"

She released a great, exhaustive sigh and focused her gaze on nothing in particular. Marion continued to stare at the tiny bottle in his large hands. "What psychiatry may define as audio or visual hallucinations was not the be-all end-all to your diagnosis, Adam. You met a number of clinical criteria to be diagnosed paranoid schizophrenic that would still hold up even if this particular hallucination could be explained away. So yes, I still stand by your diagnosis, and I still plan to watch over you."

Several moments of silence followed. Marion moved to the table in the corner and continued to regard his bottle. Dr. Blake reclined on the bed, staring at nothing but the interiors of her mind, I'm sure still trying to process what she'd seen. Time crawled forward and she began to close her eyes, to drift off to sleep, I, watching her from a plush recliner just on the other side of my cot, suspected that she'd find no such answer. I covered her with the wool blanket from my cot as Marion sipped his latest scratch from the micro-fridge.

"You heard her," I said finally. "She is a link back to my sanity."

There was no sign of Leo. Marion didn't respond.

I heard a ringing in my ears and then a song that had not been introduced by my subconscious, though it was in my head and, I was sure, heard by no one else — the Hollies sing about a guy who met a woman in a black dress while he did some FBI field work.

I made sure Marion's back was turned, then eased the door open and shut it behind me. I had walked a few steps when there was a loud crunch. Turning, I saw that the door had been forced into the jam so violently that the wall around the doorframe had buckled a bit. I could hear Marion banging on the door and struggling to open it, but I knew it would take a greater strength than even he had to pry the door open. I knew I was alone.

I followed the sound in my head down the hall and down the stairs. If I turned the wrong direction, the song grew softer, but as I neared, it increased until it rang at nearly deafening levels, and I walked out the lobby and across the parking lot to the dark alley between our hotel and a self-storage facility, empty save for some wadded newspaper, a few cardboard boxes, and some broken bottles that had missed the open dumpster. There the sound cut out instantly, and I stood face to face with the witch: Pamela Jean Harlow. She had been the woman in my dreams, haunting my nightmares when the Shimmers left me alone, her image haunting me since the explosion. I had seen a photo of her in a file once, a blurry surveillance photo that didn't do her justice.

She was pretty, with long auburn hair and bright green eyes that glowed unnaturally in the dark alley on this starless, moonless night. She smiled at me as though she was studying me, like I was a Rubik's Cube she had to figure out. I feared that when she was done studying, she'd begin twisting and turning me until all my colors matched, and wouldn't I be a mess then.

"Where's your croomstick?" she asked.

I didn't answer. I'd left it in the room, where Marion and Samantha were trapped. With them, it was nothing more than a hook for sheep.

"I feel like I know you so well, Adam. This meeting has been long overdue."

I said, "Those people all believed something, and you twisted their belief to serve your own needs."

She laughed at this. "Those people? Those people had about as much faith as an Evangelical on a Friday night. With their 'blessed be!' and their 'purity' and their 'goddess' crap. Adam, you know the truth. You've seen it. The truth is, the only religion is power, and you know better than anyone the beings that hold the true power."

I had been right. She was after the Shimmers, then. And if she couldn't get it through the cult, then she'd try through witchcraft.

"You can't control them," I said. "No one can control them. No one is strong enough."

She glared at me and took a lurching step, twisting her hands into claws. I saw lightning at her fingertips and smoke billowing from her nostrils. Her hair whipped about her head and neck as though blown by a gale, though nothing else in the alley was affected.

"You don't think I'm strong enough," she said. "You don't think I'm strong enough!"

Her voice pierced my brain louder than the song had managed, and I buckled under the pain as her shrieks infiltrating every thought. It felt as though my eyes would explode from my skull, and still I chanced them open as I dropped to first one knee then both, my hands crushing my ears to my head in hope that would keep the sound out. I felt a flow of what felt like snot from my nostril, then tasted blood on my lip, and the witch leveled her hands in my direction, she directed the blast at me. It was all I could do to dive behind a dumpster, where I expected another onslaught. But the screams in my brain died away and when no such blast came, I peeked out from behind my cover to see her standing there, out of breath, her whole body trembling with each panting inhalation and exhalation.

"But a taste," she said. As her breath returned she raised her head and smiled at me. "My feeble-minded friend, if I wanted to kill you, I would have."

That was when I saw him, creeping up behind her from the shadows. Leo slid silently toward her, and when he was close enough, he lunged. To my surprise, he held her! An incorporeal being, what I'd heretofore imagined a figment of my imagination, latched onto a physical body. She felt him, screamed out and they began fighting. *Fighting!* Punches were thrown and she tossed him back against a pile of boxes that responded and crumbled under his imagined weight, then he was up again and grabbing her shoulder and her hair to fling her into the fence. He kicked her in the stomach and punched her and she howled with pain as blood sprayed from her nose. She knocked him away and recovered long enough to loom over me, panting, her whole body shaking.

"I thought we could be friends, Adam. I thought that if you had something I needed, we could be friends long enough for us to trade. Your sanity, your old life, for the Shimmers. But this!" She pointed to Leo who stood, ready to pounce again but not daring to yet. "Unacceptable."

With another enraged scream and a billowing of smoke, she vanished. Leo took a few quick glances around and affirmed my belief that she was nowhere to be found.

"You all right?" he asked.

"How could you touch her like that?" I was dumbfounded. I'd heard of poltergeists, spirits that could manipulate objects in the real world, but I didn't think the ability was accessible by most spirits.

He took a moment before answering me; his visual manifestation reflected the weakened state of his spirit. He doubled over at the waist and made like he breathed hard. "She has one foot in your world and one foot in mine," he said. "When I realized that, I realized I could hurt her."

"You did," I said, and only when I said this did he straighten and look at me apologetically.

45

"Look man, I ain't never hit a woman, if that's what you're thinking," he said. I wasn't thinking that. I was wondering if Dr. Blake's assumption was right, that with the medicines and my different way of perceiving the world, I might've tapped into another kind of sight. Or maybe there was a rational explanation for his appearance, and I'd infected others with my delusion. Or maybe, just maybe, he was real, and I wasn't sick at all. This wasn't the last time I'd question my diagnosis or my sanity.

I returned to the hotel to find Marion and Dr. Blake rushing down the stairs to the lobby. It seems Pamela's psychic hold on the door lasted as long as she was near. When she retreated, Marion was able to wrench the door open. He asked where I'd gone, what I was doing, and I told him without reservation.

"She found me. She was out in the alley."

"God, Adam, you okay?" he asked.

"I'm fine," I said. "But she isn't going to stop, not until she gets what she's looking for."

"What's that?" Dr. Blake asked.

"Power," I told her. "Absolute power."

The local authorities came and combed the area but found no trace of Pamela Jean Harlow, save some ash in the back alley, Tanis Root, used for relocation spells. We boarded the private jet at DFW and returned to XNA. Marion said that the local authorities knew who to look for now, and he'd pass the information along to the FBI and put as much information as he could in CODIS, but technically our job was done, for now. Before we landed, he turned to us and said, "When we locate her again, we'll need to stop her. I might have to call on you for how to do that."

"I don't like this," she said. "Any of this. And I've half a mind to tell your brother."

"Only half?" I asked.

She would look at neither me nor Marion. "If I tell Chris what happened, he'll want you locked up, and he's your guardian. Even if I don't think that's the best option, his word will outweigh mine. And if you get locked up, then we don't get to the bottom of all of this."

'All of this' being the ghost she'd seen, primarily, for I knew she had no solid answers yet. Still, she also must be referring to this whole world, and I remembered Leo's words about her and wondered what had set her on this journey.

I understood and thanked her; as we left the plane, Marion stood in the hatch until it was sealed again, and we watched the private jet taxi away down the runway. Neither of us spoke as we shared an Uber home, and for a few days I nervously awaited Chris' return. He was sure to have me committed, if she were to tell him, and it would be soon. When I didn't see him until our weekly luncheon a day later, my fears abated. He seemed disinterested in our trip and spoke little of it, only to ask if I'd had a good time.

"A blast," I said and stuffed half of my tuna salad sandwich into my mouth and filled the empty spaces with lemonade. I offered him a smile with my cheeks bloated like a chipmunk's, and he laughed and shook his head. The afternoon passed smoothly for my little brother and me as we sat on a park bench on Dickson Street and enjoyed the cloudless, cool afternoon.

For the moment, I was fine and happy. For the moment, we all were.

3

MISSING

J ust a few days after the events of Texas, Dr. Blake, Chris, Leo, and
I deplaned in Chicago, where I noticed my constant visitant grow
somber, as he'd returned to not just the city where he'd lived, but also
where he died. Marion met us at the airport with a car and PRI driver. My
brother bristled at the sight of my partner, refusing to shake hands with
him while Dr. Blake and I did so. As we rode in the car, Marion leaned in
and whispered, "Is he here?" and as I nodded, Chris seemed to take notice,
but didn't ask what we were discussing.

We were greeted the man in the pinstriped suit as we exited the car in
the parking garage under the federal building, who forced his cold, pale
hand on each of us whether we wanted to shake it or not. Again there was
bristling, this time from my partner. Though it was evident they already
knew each other, Marion didn't return the man's slick, reptilian smile.

"We're happy to have you, Mr. Richardson, as well as your brother and
your doctor. Please consider this your home away from home."

"Do *we* have a name, or are we to just call you the man in the pinstriped
suit?" Dr. Blake asked. He turned a leering smile on her for a second,
pausing as though trying to work out an appropriate response.

He settled on, "Follow me, please," and ushered us to the elevator, which
we rode in silence to the offices. The enigmatic Man In The Suit—Mr.
MITS, as I'd come to call him—whose blankness and plainness seemed an

overwhelming threat to any sane or rational being on the face of this earth (his dangerousness, I should say, would ultimately far exceed those initial observations), was easily identifiable even without a name, because others in the halls shared their names freely, approached us with pleasantries and salutations, and while most wore suits or similar attire, didn't seem to stand out as much as the former.

I was drawn to a small room down a short hall off the main lobby where most of the agents worked. An orange effulgence emanated from a caged room, where a cerulean-tinted woman worked at a computer and spoke to someone on a headset.

"Pythia," Mr. MITS said, appearing at my shoulder. She turned and nodded to me.

I commented with regard to her skin tone as he led me away. "That isn't due to a drug interaction."

"I should think not," he answered.

"You've an oracle for a switchboard operator," I said, amazed, but he ignored me and by then we'd rejoined the others. Her skin color was evidently a combination of inks worn by the oracle at Delphi and the effect the gasses had on her skin tone. Was she a descendant of a known oracle, or was this merely a strange PRI requirement for their operators?

That's ridiculous, Adam, Leo said. *Look at her. You know what she really is. This isn't a PRI thing and she isn't a descendent with a weird fetish.*

She can't be, I countered. *She'd be so old ... it'd be impossible.*

Like ghosts and demons and women shooting lightning bolts from their hands? he asked. I had to concede.

"Colonel Hamilton is in his office," Mr. MITS said, and we followed him through a set of double doors.

The colonel was a jovial soul, welcoming us all, busying himself with finding enough seating for all of us. My anxiety rose. As little interest as Chris had shown a couple of days earlier, his insistence in coming to this little meeting was a turn that left me sure he'd pull me from my duties once he learned of the case and my involvement.

"So," the colonel began. "The case in Texas. We still haven't found her, but that doesn't mean we've stopped looking."

"Colonel Hamilton," Chris interjected. "I'd like to know just what kind of work you do here at the PRI."

Leaning back in his chair, the colonel looked from me to Marion, then over to Mr. MITS. I wondered how privy he was to my condition and the conditional tenure of my employ.

"We are a subset of the Department of Homeland Security tasked with investigating domestic issues not handled by other departments. Unfortunately, the bulk of our work is classified compartmentalized, which means, until you and the doctor can pass security clearances, I am limited in what I can say in front of you. That being said, this particular case involves a young woman who has committed horrendous acts, and your brother's expertise has exposed her and provided us with insight which has brought us closer to her capture."

"I'm concerned for his health, Colonel," Chris continued. "His mental health has been compromised by digging into these kinds of things..."

"What kind of things?" Mr. MITS said.

"This, darkness," Chris answered him. "The occult."

"Is that what you think we do here?" Mr. MITS asked.

"We are all well aware of your brother's condition," Colonel Hamilton said.

"I'm in the room," I said under breath.

"Then you're aware that I am his guardian," Chris said. "So don't jerk me around, Colonel. I'm not a stupid man."

"No one said you were," Mr. MITS said. The look he gave my brother made me terrified for Chris' safety.

"No harm will come to him," Marion said to Chris. "I promise you."

He touched Chris' shoulder, an effort to ease him, but once my brother got wound up, only time would cool him off.

"As I was saying," Colonel Hamilton began again. "While we don't know the whereabouts of Pamela Harlow..."

"Who?" Chris said, looking at each of us in turn. "Who did you just say?"

He stood, the colonel sat back, obviously unimpressed with my brother's bravado, as Mr. MITS coiled, and Marion rose to match him. "Now hold on a second, Chris," he said.

"Back off, Marion," Chris said, pushing his shoulder. "I don't give a fuck if you were a SEAL or whatever. Don't give me a reason. That bitch is the reason my brother fell into this condition. You were chasing her last time, weren't you?"

"Sit down, Mr. Richardson," Mr. MITS said. Again with that scathing look.

"I'm going for a walk," Chris said, and pushed through the double doors back out into the office.

Marion started for him, but the colonel spoke up. "Come back, Agent Case. He'll be fine. The other agents won't let him get into any trouble out there. It's best you let him cool off." The man in the suit's eyes suggested otherwise to me. Chris didn't have the clearance Marion or I had, and after meeting Delphi, I knew there were things in this office he did not need to see, that he would not understand, and that could cause him a great deal of trouble.

As Marion returned to his seat, Delphi skyped into Colonel Hamilton's monitor and said there had been a kidnapping in Wisconsin, then asked if our team was ready. Dr. Blake, who had said little throughout, gave a nod when Marion regarded her, her silent acquiescence that I might participate in this case despite my brother's misgivings, but it was Mr. MITS who stepped forward and spoke.

"No. Get some rest. Agent Case, you need to keep monitoring official domestic offices for signs of PJ Harlow. I'll go. If it requires more than just my attention—if we need an official presence there—I'll let you know."

With that, he was out the door. Soon after, my doctor, my brother, and I all boarded a plane back to Northwest Arkansas.

II

The first twelve hours were crucial. When the boy wasn't found in the first twelve hours, the chances of him being found alive decreased by a factor of ten. When he wasn't found in the first forty-eight hours, the chances of him being found alive decreased by a factor of forty. When seventy-two hours passed, the numbers in the search party began dwindling. Ninety-six hours in, the immediate family and the police were the only ones still searching.

"This doesn't mean we're giving up," the Kewaunee County Sheriff — I'll call him Red Angus — told the mother, whose tears had fallen continuously since her boy vanished from his bedroom four nights earlier. When the family wasn't around, he said other things to his officers and the lead detective from Kewaunee Township PD. "Look into the family. A boy don't just vanish out of his own bedroom." As the time passed, he also said, "There's too much water around these parts," which was true. Lake Michigan was just to the east and the Port of Green Bay was just north. Sure, if a body was dumped in the Port, it might wash back ashore if not weighted properly, but a short boat ride into the middle of the lake and a weighted body might never be found. Chicago mob knew that well. Everyone knew that. He did not mention the calls he'd made, climbing up the chain of command, first through local and state contacts, and then to the federal level. He had thought surely the FBI would help until he gave them the particulars of the case, and then he'd been given another number, an agency he hadn't heard of before, located in Chicago. He talked to a woman with an accent—Mediterranean, like Italian or something—whose voice sang. She said she'd send help.

The nights were frigid, and while the dark and bitter cold that blasted unrelenting from the north for overshadowed days and pitch nights hadn't yet arrived, it wouldn't do to cost his men their health sifting through the underbrush in the cold dimness of the late autumn. With a county seat population of just over twenty-thousand, he hadn't been allocated the manpower to keep this up. His men were getting tired and were distracted from other duties. And if they were already getting the sniffles before winter hit, what good would they do the township and the county once the arctic blast really bore down on them?

"You need to get inside," Sheriff Angus said to the boy's mother, and looked to her husband to complete the Herculean task of reining her in. The boy's father only shrugged. The sheriff understood the tenaciousness of a woman searching for her child.

William "Red" Angus drove back to the county lockup, his headlights the blowing snow illuminated like stars speeding past the bridge of a spacecraft on one of those sci-fi movies he'd enjoyed since he was a kid.

At the station, he found the Kewaunee PD detective standing by his own vehicle, smoking an e-cig. The man's face refused to be illuminated by the sheriff's headlights.

"What is it, Vern?" Red asked, stepping into the cold. The temperature had dropped on the drive in. The sheriff shivered involuntarily. He glanced about. Silhouettes of pines swayed like hula girls. Something in the night air shifted.

"The parents didn't do nothing to the boy, near as I can tell."

"Didn't think so. We went to grade school with Margie and Paul. They one of ours."

"Yep."

They shared the silence, neither man wanting to say what they were thinking: someone snatched the boy out of the bedroom. If it wasn't the parents, then there was a sicko. Either a transient or a local. But not too local. Someone who had been here long enough to learn the comings and goings of the Kewaunee naturals. No, maybe they lived here five years, or maybe ten, or hell, maybe they'd been here twenty plus years, but they weren't from here. No one from here could do this.

"You got a visitor," the detective said.

"Who is it?" Red asked.

The detective shrugged and capped his e-cig. "Government man. From Chicago."

"Give his name?"

Vern wasn't telling him something. The detective stared at the swaying trees. "Just some man in a suit," he said.

The sheriff reached for the front door, paused and looked back at the detective. He was studying the tree line to the south and the stars just above as the clouds had cleared a bit from that horizon.

"What's wrong, Vern?"

"It's going to be a cold winter," the detective said.

For a native of Northern Wisconsin to say this, that was saying something.

~

The man in the suit had helped himself to the couch in the sheriff's office. Red could not remember leaving his office door unlocked. He opened the door to the smell of freshly perked coffee and saw a steaming mug placed on his desk in front of where he sat.

"Joe to warm your bones," the man in the suit said.

"How'd you get in here?"

"Really, you called me," the man in the suit said. "And that's your first question? Not who are you or why are you here or how are you going to help me find that missing boy?"

Red studied the stranger. No discernable scars, he was a clean shaven white male in his late twenties or early thirties, average trimmed hair tucked under a fedora, and nothing special about his eyes. His suit was a pinstripe, old-fashioned, with a vest underneath, and the hint of a shoulder holster.

"How are you going to help me find that boy?"

"I'm not," said the man in the suit, flashing a smile that did not ease Red. *'Cause the man didn't smile with his eyes*, he would think later. The smile was a mask, like the suit, like the indistinguishable features. "But one or more federal agents are coming soon. They'll help you get the boy back and investigate. You will report that you found nothing out of the ordinary to those agents that come, to the boy's parents, to the world. What you really find you'll report to me."

"How do you know I'll find something?"

The man in the suit shrugged. "Call it a good old-fashioned hunch. Cops like you get those all the time, don't you, William? Sorry. Red. If you find something, you tell only me. If you don't, then this whole conversation is moot."

"Who are you?" the sheriff asked.

The man in the suit, who stood an inch shy of six feet, took a final swig of his coffee. He upended the cup over his mouth and examined it for a second, then he shoved it into his coat pocket, the mug that the sheriff had received as an office Christmas gift the year before. He walked to the office door, paused and faced the sheriff.

"A strange little schizophrenic in Arkansas calls me Mr. MITS," he said, then walked out of the office. He had an ambling gait, unhurried, as though he hadn't a care in the world. Maybe he didn't have a care. He seemed awfully sure they'd find the boy soon enough, but Red recalled the man never said if they'd find the boy alive or dead.

Angus walked outside. His car was still there, but the detective's sedan was gone. He could recall no other vehicle in the parking lot, least not one he didn't recognize. He'd have noticed a rental or a car with government tags. Nothing. Vern surely didn't give the man a ride, and if he did, it wasn't back to the airport in Green Bay.

Flurries were still blowing, thicker and harder now, obstructing the view about ten feet out. The distant tree line had been obscured as had any stars; Sheriff Angus was an avid stargazer. So much for getting out the telescope, he thought. Hard to drive in this; not impossible, but hard. The detective would go home to his wife. To be sure, he'd call the detective an hour or so later and Vern would say that he left and saw no one walk out. In the meantime, the sheriff stepped out to the road and looked left and looked right. For as far as he could see, he could not see the man in the suit.

III

The next morning began bitterly cold, with the temperature dropping just after sunrise to nearly zero. The federal agent stood in the lobby outside the office as Red pulled up. He could tell this new guy was not like Mr. MITS. He was young, probably not even thirty yet, and fit. That's what he had in common with the man in the suit, but he smiled with his eyes and smiled easily, extending a hand as the sheriff entered. Red showed him in the office and fixed coffee and the two men exchanged pleasantries while the carafe filled with brew. The agent, like the sheriff, warmed his hands to the cup when it was handed to him, before savoring a long sip.

"It'll get colder," Sheriff Angus said. The two men looked to the window and saw crystals on the panes of glass.

"I'm from back East, and I'm not used to this," the agent said.

"It'll only get colder," Red repeated, this time a bit more defeatedly.

55

"I'm Agent Marion Case with the PRI, Sheriff Angus. I hear you got a missing boy."

"I don't think we'll find him." He put his cup on the desk and studied it like he was reading tea leaves.

"You consider the family yet?"

The sheriff waved him off. "Nothing there. It's like he up and vanished."

Marion slurped his coffee and nodded. "The heater out?"

"Working full force," the sheriff laughed.

"Can't imagine living in Canada," Marion said with a shiver.

"Not this cold in Chicago?" Red asked. He knew just how cold it got, because he'd been there numerous times. But after meeting that man in the pinstriped suit, he wasn't about to trust another government agent without sizing him up first. Catch them in a lie, even a small one, and the rest of the story would fall into your lap.

"Not as cold. But before today I thought Chicago was a damn icebox. Guess I was wrong."

The phone rang. Red was laughing when he picked up the receiver; banter relaxed almost everyone. Marion watched the sheriff answer the phone affably, saw his smile drop, the color drain from his face. He hung up and took a few deep breaths.

"What's wrong?"

"The boy," the sheriff said. "He's home."

~

The boy would not leave his mother's embrace. He would not look at anyone. He nestled into his mother's bosom but only shivered. He responded in the shortest of sentences when anyone spoke to him.

"How old are you?" Marion asked, knowing the answer.

"Eight," the boy said as drawn out as he possibly could while looking at the patchwork of the quilt.

"Did you know we've been looking for you?"

The boy nodded. Outside, an arctic wind screamed around the eaves in an all-too-human sound.

"Do you know how long we've been looking for you?" Marion asked.

"Two hours." The boy still wouldn't meet his eyes. He was frightened. Probably traumatized. Probably for life. The boy had no sense of time, Marion realized.

"Do you remember where you've been?"

The boy buried his head in his mother's chest and wept loudly, frightening everyone in the living room. The sheriff tugged at Marion's shoulder to reign him in, but he reached for the boy—gently—and made him meet his eyes.

"It's okay," Marion said. "We're here to help you. I'm not going to let any more harm come to you. Okay. I'm with the government and we help people. So it's okay to tell me."

The boy looked from his mother, who wiped at his eyes, to his father, who offered a nod of his head, to the sheriff, and then to Marion. "The gray men took me," the boy said. "They have big black eyes and little mouths and big heads and they come into my room all the time. They said we were going to play a game. They said it would be fun. They said Mommy and Daddy would like it."

Now it was time for the adults to share gazes. Gray men with big heads and big black eyes. Jesus, Marion thought. What have I gotten into?

"Did you like the game?" he asked.

The boy's lips quivered. "No. They scared me."

~

The cold air greeted the sheriff and my partner as they stepped out on the porch. Red blew into his palms and hugged himself vigorously, tried to stay warm. He stomped on the porch planks to stimulate circulation, wincing through clenched teeth. Still, he noticed something about my partner, who despite complaining about the cold earlier—and it was surely colder now—stood perfectly still with his hands in the pockets of his heavy coat, his bare head not trembling, his ears not reddening, his lips not quivering. Only his eyes squinted as he looked afar, off toward the arrowhead treetops. For all the bluster Marion had put on back at the office, why not now, unless it was a show meant to disarm the sheriff.

"What did you do before?" Red asked.

"I was a SEAL once," Marion said. "And I was in the FBI."

"And now this PRI?"

Marion stood silent, staring off into the distance. The frost of breath that escaped his nostrils was merely a thin plume, as opposed to the sheriff's great cloudbursts of CO_2.

"And do you believe him? That he really went there?" The sheriff asked. "Do you believe who he said took him? He's talking UFO's, ain't he. Little green men. Aliens."

"I do." The hesitance in Marion's voice wasn't due to a lie. I'm sure Sheriff Angus could read that well enough. I'm sure he wondered if fear had caused the hesitance, and if so, what was Agent Case afraid of?

"I need to make a call," the sheriff said.

~

Marion watched from the porch as the sheriff climbed into his patrol car and pulled out his cellphone. Two things bothered him, he told me later. One, the sheriff kept glancing up at him; two, the boy. He could have seen movies. Aliens were as common in media today as Dracula. But the boy had been missing for a week, and he was clearly terrified. Marion knew scared, what it looked like on someone's face. The boy was sitting on his momma's lap, scared. The sheriff was scared. Marion had inspected the boy's room after they arrived; he'd noticed things about the window and ledge. At the PRI, he'd been shown a file and told to memorize it. It contained telltale signs of what to expect from alien abduction cases. Scorch marks on the ledge, crystals in the pane of glass—in the glass itself—and the alarm clock ran ten minutes faster than the rest of the house. This detail had been catalogued by the local PD, but when asked about it, the boy's mother was surprised. She said that it should keep time with their other clocks. Marion's cell had some upgrades, apps and hardware that most people didn't have. He detected high infrared levels in the room that seemed concentrated at the window. Sonically, a murmur of electric noise, like the hum of a fluorescent, buzzed just under the range of the human ear, but was caught by the mic on his phone. All of this, the files at the PRI had said, pointed to one thing; because of this, Marion was scared.

He waited until the sheriff returned to the porch, then punched a button on his phone. Back in the SEALs, he had learned of another special programmer's app, from compatriots in the mercenary group once known as Blackwater. He had found occasion to use the app when he worked in the FBI's Violent Crimes Unit. The app didn't clone phones, exactly, but it connected his phone to another. It showed him messages and phone calls and gave him access to view the apps on the target phone. Civilians and white-collar G-men could not get this app. Probably Marion shouldn't have it either, he had probably just forgotten to delete it off his phone, but he was thankful he hadn't when he saw the number the sheriff had dialed. The one with the Chicago area code.

~

They walked back inside, Marion wondering, not for the first time, if they'd raided the LL Bean catalogue to decorate their home. The boy still sat on his mother's lap, the tears drying to streaks on his cheeks, his eyes getting heavy. Terror and trauma had exhausted him. This was to be expected. Marion thought the best thing for this family would be a long period of sleep. Still, he had to get a bit more information, so he knelt and offered a smile to the boy. He didn't return it, but at least he would look at him now.

"Where did they take you?" Marion asked.

"To the park by the lake," the boy said.

"We looked at the park and you weren't there." It was toasty inside. The boy's father had lit the logs in the fireplace, and the house heated nicely. Marion's voice was even and soothing and completely opposite what his pedigree might suggest.

"Not then. We saw you looking there. Except they weren't there, Mr. Marion, and neither was you."

"No," he smiled. "No. I was not. Where were you?"

"Up in the stars." The boy's words quivered with his lips and hung coldly in the air of the heated room.

The questions came slowly and easily and persistently for an hour or two. No one was sure how much time had passed until the sheriff and Marion stepped back out onto the porch together. This time they were followed by the boy's father who thanked them for coming. The man was trembling, and Marion knew it wasn't from the cold.

"He'll be okay," Marion said without giving the words much thought.

"Can you promise that?" the dad asked. Red looked at Marion, awaiting the answer. "What was all that talk about gray men and being up in the stars?"

"You two should lay off the Star Trek," Marion said.

"We watch Teenage Turtle Ninjas and read comic books. I don't let him near that other stuff, that scary stuff. So, you tell me what he saw. You tell me who had my boy!"

He grabbed Marion's shoulder and stood nearly nose-to-nose with the agent. Probably not many men would get away with bowing up on my partner like this despondent father. But to his credit, Marion didn't get hostile; he didn't get defensive. He put a hand on the father's shoulder and nodded. Red saw the lie pour easily out of the agent's mouth when he spoke.

"Someone coached your boy, is all. When they decided they were going to return him, they realized they wanted to cover up what they'd done, so they convinced him to fabricate this story. They—and we should be thankful for this—didn't have the heart or the stomach to ensure by other means that he wouldn't talk."

The father started weeping again, as the horror settled on him that something had been done to the boy in his absence from home, but there were no visible marks, or at least none they'd seen so far, so what that something was had to be left to the imagination. Marion suggested counseling, and said the combined might of the authorities would not rest until the kidnappers were caught. He said that the doctor who'd checked out the boy had found no visible signs of trauma.

"Go, be with your wife and son, now," Marion said in the gentlest tone he could offer, patting the man's shoulder. "Go be with your family, and get some rest."

The father nodded, thanked them, and closed the door on them. The sheriff gazed off to somewhere in the distance. The sky would be clear this night, perfect for stargazing. The snow had stopped while they were inside and the clouds were pushing eastward, reminding Marion of timelapse video.

"You lied to that man," said the sheriff.

Marion thought about the phone calls; the sheriff had excused himself to make two more during the questioning. On the way downstairs this last time, Marion had found a chance to glance at his phone.

He dialed, and when the case manager at the Federal Building picked up, Marion called her by name. He meant to do this in front of the sheriff. Marion did not appreciate duplicitousness from anyone he was trying to help.

"Pythia, sweetie, can you ID a number for me?"

The sheriff looked at him quizzically as Marion put the secretary on speaker and pulled up his Caller ID. As he recited the number, he saw the sheriff's face drain of color.

"Senior Advisory Number, government issue, not PRI. It's bounced off our tower a number of times."

"Could it be from another office in the building?"

"No. Tower records show this number connected to several office extensions, including...hmm."

The sheriff looked both interested and worried.

Pythia came back on. "Agent Case? There are a lot of calls from this number to the PRI Director's office. Colonel Hamilton speaks to this caller pretty regularly."

Marion sighed and said: "Pythia, I know I'm the new guy still, but can we keep this between us?"

"Of course. Anything for you."

Marion wondered aloud if he could trust her.

"Of course you can," she said. "I deliver only the truth. Some of it is meant for interpretation, but I cannot lie to you."

He thanked her and hung up.

Neither man moved. Marion watched every breath crystalize in front of them. He had several questions, and his time as an investigator told him in which order they should be asked to get the most effective answers.

Whether it was an interstate trafficker, a terrorist, or a small-town sheriff, they'd all answer the same way. You started with the most obvious question, the big question, possibly even reworded and skewed to trap the interviewee in a lie, about the elephant in the room, so to speak. And then you offered choices, depending on how they answered. Completely evasive, and you gave them a couple of different options on how they could provide a better answer, and then you gave them the consequences for answering wrong. And when you got the answer you wanted, when you got the truth, you asked another question, a little more specific.

"Why were you talking to my boss at the PRI?"

"I wasn't." He was evading the question.

"That's not what she just said. You and I heard her. She traced the call to Colonel Hamilton's office. Why is he following up on me? Why were you talking to him?"

"The man I talk to isn't old enough to be a colonel," the sheriff said. "And he sure as hell don't dress like one, in that suit of his."

Marion looked across the yard. The sheriff's car sat silent in the drive, the only avenue to deliver him back to his vehicle in town. Best not piss him off, Marion thought, and so he didn't press it. Mr. MITS had requested the case, then returned and was sitting in Colonel Hamilton's office when Marion had been called in and assigned to help in the disappearance. Before he'd left, Mr. MITS had said, "We here at the PRI are not just about solving the mystery. After we get to the bottom of things, we often have the unfortunate task of cleaning up the mess that's been made." And Colonel Hamilton had sat back and let the statement be made. He'd allowed Marion to hear that. To what end, now as he stared out at the Wisconsin wilderness, Marion wasn't sure, but this plagued him even as the sheriff started the car and drove them back to the station.

IV

William Angus stripped out of his uniform and put on sweatpants and a T-shirt. He filled up on a Hungry-Man frozen entrée of meatloaf and mac n' cheese and green beans and had chilled a twelve pack of Pabst Blue Ribbon for his dessert, which he'd just started in on. He finished watching

Nightline. It was a clear night, and a lot of star clusters were visible, but he had to put on a robe and slippers to step out on his balcony, for it was still unbearably cold. The sheriff was a man obsessed with astronomy, and after four beers, the cold wasn't as cold now. He turned his telescope to the sky to the south. If he tilted it down just a little, he might see the boy's house, if not for the trees.

The haze of the galaxy's arm was especially visible tonight. He readjusted the declination knob trying to spy a crab cluster till he realized that the haze wasn't from the stars. Then he could smell the smoke.

"On retrospect, perhaps the boy shouldn't have come back. He saw too much. You've heard too much."

Red turned and saw the man in the suit. He wondered if he had locked the door. "It's 'in retrospect,'" he said, and recalled he'd hung his gun in its holster on the coat rack in the front hall.

"I don't like to be corrected," Mr. MITS said. He pulled his gun and shot the sheriff in the stomach. There was little sound to the muzzled flash. Clutching his gut, the sheriff knocked over the telescope and sank into one of two Adirondacks. His eyes blurred as the fire in his belly flared and spread. He coughed and tasted blood.

"The boy and his parents didn't suffer," Mr. MITS said. "There was a chance secondary or tertiary evidence could have been linked, so we had to take precautionary measures."

"Burn...the house?" His vision was fading. Despite the fire in his gut, a coldness spread over him. A welcoming blackness pressed in on the edges.

Mr. MITS studied his own gun, seemed to marvel at it. "I did. It will be labeled an electrical fire. If the boy hadn't returned, I wouldn't have had to do this."

"How did you know...?"

"I tell a lot of sheriffs that the abductees will be returned. I'm wrong ninety-five percent of the time. The other five percent—well—we at the PRI have the unfortunate task of cleaning up messes, for the good of the people. Some of us are more capable than others at this part of the job description."

"Electrical fire...?"

"One of many possibilities."

He leveled the gun at the sheriff's head and pulled the trigger. I wouldn't learn of these events completely until we arrested Mr. MITS several years later. But that's another story.

V

Two days later, Marion deplaned at DC's Ronald Reagan Airport and met our old boss in the terminal. Tom and Marion shook hands and walked to an airport bar, ordered a couple of mixed drinks and sat at a corner booth in the back where every exit could be viewed. They ordered a second drink before they spoke. All in all, they spent four hours in that bar, their conversation coming in fits and spurts as they surveyed the other patrons carefully.

"He killed that family," Marion said. "He murdered that sheriff."

"Ballistics on that gun were traced back to a gangbanger who frequented Kewaunee but lived in Green Bay. Visiting an aunt."

A man sat down a few booths away once and stayed for thirty minutes. Neither Case nor Builder recognized the man, but he seemed to glance at them from over his menu. Marion shifted the conversation to the pennant race and watched him in the mirror as Tom watched the man over Marion's shoulder. Eventually, the man left.

"We know ballistics can be faked," Marion said finally.

"You don't have a name, Marion. You barely have a description."

A woman sat at the bar. She smiled a few times at Marion. She was pretty, and probably his type, but he didn't smile back. That might invite her closer.

"He's dangerous," Marion said. "And he's running around unleashed in a government office."

"Pay cash for a Tracfone when you get back to the city," Agent Builder said. "Call me from that number—here." He slid over a business card flipped upside down, a pen-scrawled number written on the back.

The bartender, a young Black kid, wiped down glasses, eyed them at intervals.

"This isn't too cloak'n'dagger?" Marion said, downing his beer.

"I was thinking spy versus spy. But if this guy is all that you suggested, then no, this isn't too cautious. We probably aren't being cautious enough. But I'm thinking on the fly and you are about to miss your flight back."

Marion shook his old boss's hand and boarded the plane. When he landed, he drove straight to his apartment and locked the door. That night, he couldn't sleep. Cradling his gun in his hand, he stared all night at the blank television screen in his front room. He wondered what he had gotten himself into. He wondered what he had dragged me into.

VI

Samantha had never seen Puck sip lemonade, but here he was, under a sunshade, enjoying the bitter beverage. Late fall/early winter was mild here in Northwest Arkansas, the temps barely getting above 70 or 75, a cool northerly breeze keeping the humidity down, so that outdoors was pleasant again. Puck wore his suit and fedora and had adorned some shades that more than covered his eyes. That the lemonade was spiked was no surprise to her.

"Enjoying yourself?" she asked. A young, tanned waiter with a ponytail approached and she told him that she'd like a Manhattan.

"Autumn is delightful," Puck said, sipping his drink.

They were silent until the drink came, and silent more until she'd taken her first taste.

"I saw a ghost, in Texas."

"I thought you might."

She set her drink down and studied him. His skin was chalk white, and looked like makeup, except it wasn't. Somewhere on Dickson or nearby, somebody was smoking beef or pork, the smell of charcoal rising on the air currents. Puck gazed in the general direction of the smell, his eyes concealed by the shades, a lazy smile revealing nothing.

"What do you mean?" she asked.

He didn't look at her, but continued to level his gaze skyward. "You should ask Adam."

"You urged me to follow him there."

"He has answers."

"He's a paranoid schizophrenic."

"Who has a ghost that you saw."

Samantha took another drink and rattled the ice cubes in her glass, thinking about what she had seen. "I don't know what I saw, really. I've thought of the possibilities. Hallucination. Trick of the light. Suggestive hypnosis brought on by trauma."

"But none of them hold water," Puck said.

"No," she admitted. "They don't. So what does that mean? That I saw his delusion. Does it mean I misdiagnosed him?"

Puck shrugged. "This is a conversation you need to have with him, not me."

She nodded, knew he was right. She picked up her drink and sucked an ice cube into her mouth, savoring how it melted and held the alcohol in its frozen cage, releasing just a bit with every lap of the tongue, with every inhale. "I like our visits again."

"I do too," Puck said.

"Look at me, Puck."

After a pause, relishing the weather, he did so, but his expression didn't change.

"I thought, when you and I were kids, that you were the love of my life. Is that weird?"

He studied her, then shook his head. "We can't. But you still have a chance."

She furrowed her brow. "With Adam?"

This elicited a laugh from him. "No. But love drives us all. I think it's something that drives us because it pursues us. Love wants us to feel it, wants us to exude it. It is what makes up the cosmos. It is what some of you call God, and it is calm and tranquil and when you see it, you sigh and realize in that moment your life can't get any better."

"And you think I'll find it?" Samantha asked.

"I think you have."

~

Our weekly session occurred at her office as per usual, the day a bit overcast and nippy. Chris drove me, still perturbed that I wouldn't take the bus, and though he didn't broadcast it, still up in arms about the visit to Chicago. What surprised me was that he didn't say anything, but grumbled something as he dropped me off, then sped away before I had the door fully shut. I knew Chris was angry, that he felt like we'd all misled him and so felt betrayed, but what that meant yet, I wasn't sure.

When she offered me a cup of coffee, I accepted, and drank it black as she sat and added cream and sugar to her cup. Her office smelled of vanilla, and I searched for the candle with futility.

"The brain is a transducer," she said finally, a statement that gave me pause.

"You mean it converts energy from one form to another?"

"Doesn't it?" she said. "Don't sound waves enter the ear, only for the brain to convert them to recognizable sounds, or light waves enter the eye which the brain then converts to recognizable images?"

I sipped my coffee, considering. "So touch might come from the nerve endings, enhanced in the appendages where we might use it, numbed in other areas where it wouldn't be common, like my thigh, or bicep. Enhanced in my fingers or palms or toes and soles."

She took a long drink from her own mug. "Yes, that's correct."

"So, reality is only how we perceive it through our senses. Our brains are the ultimate judge on what is real and what isn't."

"That's one way to think of it," she said. We finished the rest of our cups in silence, contemplating the mysteries before us. Without offering, she made us each another, and had set the full mugs down in front of us before I had the foresight to speak again.

"Do you think I'm crazy?"

Her tongue lapped at the coffee and considered the taste before she answered. When she did, her eyes were closed and there seemed to be a peace settling on her countenance. "I think you see the world differently than I do. I think that the world appears differently isn't a fault of yours, but is something misunderstood for the rest of us."

"Tomorrow I want to take you somewhere," I said abruptly, realizing how vague I sounded. She might have too, but acquiesced by not dignifying that with a response.

I left our therapy and had Chris drive me home. He didn't speak until we reached my door. I could see he was stewing.

"So what did you talk about?"

"Transducers," I said. I meant for my answer to leave him befuddled.

"Dude. You know I'm only looking out for you." He was being sincere, and I couldn't rob him of this moment.

"I know," I said.

"Jesus," he said, and hung his head. "You're the older brother. You're supposed to look out for me."

I reached up to his shoulder, the same one Marion had touched back in Chicago, but from this he didn't recoil. I said, "I always am, man."

He smiled at me. "I'm a piece of shit, dude. Womanizer. A drunk. I'm a wreck."

"You dress nice," I said.

He laughed a little, a chuckle.

"You're my brother," I said. There might have been tears in his eyes when he nodded at me. He told me he loved me. That wasn't common.

I kissed him and walked into my apartment. I shut the door on him and savored the darkness, the silence. I found the lounge and reclined easily. The darkness was inviting, eager to abide the temperament of the scene, like Goldilocks' porridge. Just right.

"Where does thought come from?" the dead detective asked.

I bolted up. "Imagination, which is why you are still alive. Why you are here."

"She saw me. So did Marion."

"You're an infection, then. A psychological virus I'm spreading to others."

"When she calls tomorrow, answer and respond with the affirmative."

He'd revealed to me the horror of his murdered condition, which no longer shocked me, then faded from sight not to be heard of for the rest of the evening.

VII

As we had prearranged, I found Dr. Blake at the rooftop bar on Dickson, gazing out at the western horizon as clouds amassed, sipping an amaretto as I took my seat.

"Transducers," she said, as though that word encapsulated all we had to discuss. She'd obviously been giving the subject as much thought as I had since we last broached it.

"You were saying the brain is one such function," I said.

"Sight and sound, and smell, even. You agree?"

I nodded. It made sense.

"So where does thought come from?"

At this question I frowned. "Some point in the brain?" I questioned.

"The Orch OR Theory suggests that quantum computations in brain microtubules account for consciousness, but if the brain's job is to convert energy from one form to another, such as the definition of a transducer, why would it ostensibly create new energy in the form of thought?"

This gave me pause. "What are you suggesting?"

She smiled. Her gaze never faltered from the horizon, the setting sun. Golden shafts of light streaked across the rooftop, but the arctic chill overpowered – for the moment – the weak rays.

"If the brain is a transducer, then perhaps thought doesn't generate from there," she said, finishing her drink.

"Where does it come from?" I asked.

To answer, she gazed skyward, a slight smile on her lips.

"Chris isn't happy with us," she said.

I sipped at the iced tea the waitress had just brought me. "He isn't happy in general."

"What can we do about that?" she asked.

I shrugged. I had no idea how to make Chris happy. He had been a miserable child for as long as I'd known him. He was never satisfied with his situation, and only seemed to grow more weighed down with every brick of responsibility laid upon his shoulders. But in the same vein, he relished in the torment, because it made him more human, casted him as more vulnerable when he was fishing for his latest conquests. One-night stands they might be, but they numbed him.

"We might just have to bear him," I said.

"That isn't good enough," Dr. Blake replied.

Leviathan appeared, coiling around the rooftop until he squeezed us all proper, then disappeared into a puff of smoke, leaving an angelic boy that knelt before our table.

"Do you see him?" I asked.

Dr. Blake looked right at him but shook her head.

"Your brother has you wrapped in his coils, doesn't he?"

"You don't scare me, Leviathan," I said.

Dr. Blake sat back, not appreciating this conversation.

"I am the creature of the deep. I am what you fear. The unknown."

I stood up from the table, knocking over the glasses and the tabletop fabric and all the stains and rings that came with it. Dr. Blake looked at me fearfully. I couldn't help that she couldn't see the monster before me.

"Say my name!" it screamed.

"I see one," I said. "A Shimmer."

"What do you want?" it asked. "I can get it ... we can get it for you."

"It'll be okay," my psychiatrist said. "Just remember what we talked about."

I took my seat and closed my eyes. "You aren't real. Go away, Leviathan." I counted, just under breath, concentrating on the numbers themselves, visualizing them beneath my lids, counting for as long as I needed with the touch of Dr. Blake's hands cradling my own. When I opened my eyes, the serpent was gone, the only other occupants of the rooftop bar curious onlookers watching at this freak have a nervous breakdown.

"Don't worry about them," Dr. Blake whispered, still holding my hands. I was shivering and my breathing was quick and shallow. She guided me to control it, inhaling and exhaling slowly, deliberately, breathing with me as I closed my eyes and focused on each breath until my heart rate slowed.

"You got an email," she said after another moment, my cell buzzing with a notification.

I checked it. A case file from Marion. "There was a boy, abducted."

"Is he okay?" Dr. Blake asked.

I scanned the file, then passed the phone to her. The boy wasn't okay.

Nor was his family, nor the sheriff of the little town outside of Green Bay, Wisconsin.

"The ghost. You and Marion saw him," I said when she set my phone down, her fist held to her mouth as she stared at the tabletop, as if the message had been written there. I wasn't just bringing this up to get our minds off the horror we'd just read, but to continue the topic Volac had so selfishly interrupted.

"I did see him," she said, as though it were a confession.

"Maybe ghosts are what we see when those thoughts no longer have a body or a brain to go to."

"Maybe," she said, still staring at the tabletop.

"Do you need anything else?" the waiter asked. Dr. Blake snapped out of her self-induced hypnosis to wave the young girl away.

"What if the Shimmers are real, too?" I said then. "What if they are things that have found a way to tap into my brain?"

She looked at me, tears in her eyes. "I don't know what we can do, Adam," she said. Was she talking about me and my damaged brain? Was she addressing the dangerous situation with the PRI, amped up to another level by the events described in Marion's email? I waited for her to clarify, but she didn't, or wouldn't. Or couldn't. She stood, taking up her purse, and I took the hint that it was time to go.

"Why did you want to bring me here today?" she asked.

Slow to the question, still focused on the assault to my sanity, I could only manage a "Huh."

"I've been here before, Adam," she said, smiling. "What did you want to show me?"

"Nothing," I said, returning her smile. "I just thought you'd like a drink."

When we left, she dropped me off at home, kissed my cheek at my door, and after I swore to her I'd be okay, she left. I worried for her wellbeing for the rest of the night.

VII

While we were having cocktails and seeing large serpents on Dickson, Chris later told me he'd walked up to the university campus when his own online search for answers had proven useless. He read the names carved on the historic Senior Walk on his way to Old Main, up the wide steps to the third floor, and was delighted to see a familiar name on the office door. At his double tap, a voice he hadn't heard in years told him to enter.

A computer science major, one of the few Humanities courses Chris took that he actually enjoyed was a course on mythology he'd taken through the philosophy department. His professor, a once-redheaded man with more white in his beard than ginger, had gone all white in the years since, but he still had the bright brown eyes and wore the same affable smile Chris remembered from so long ago.

"I do enjoy it when my former students return for a visit," the professor said, welcoming Chris into his office.

The office hadn't changed. Bookshelves lined one short wall from floor to ceiling. A few posters around the window behind the professor's desk, the blinds drawn so that the whole of the room was dim, only lit by a venetian floor lamp, the corner dark behind him. The professor closed the laptop on his desk and offered Chris a coffee.

"To what do I owe the pleasure, Christopher?"

Chris chose his words carefully. "Do you remember my brother?"

The old professor allowed the question serious thought, but ultimately shook his head. "I do remember hearing of him. He received such accolades at graduation, top honors, if I remember. I heard he was going to the FBI. What's the matter? Nothing serious, I hope."

Chris shook his head, deciding not to reveal family tragedy. "He's fine. I wanted to ask you about a lecture you used to give. It focused on the Christian religion, on demons and the use of exorcism in the Catholic church."

The professor smiled. "Yes, I still give a form of that lecture. I'm glad it stuck with you all these years."

He stood and poured a cup of coffee, offered it to Chris, who thanked him, then poured another, adding cream and sugar. Chris asked for a bit of honey, as he had back in the day, and the professor provided.

"I wish I could remember the specifics of the demons you discussed. I've been thinking about that lately."

Reflexively, the professor furrowed his brow. "Professional curiosity, or have you found God?"

"Professional," Chris said, sipping at his cup before placing it on the coaster before him on the desk.

"For your work at your computer company: Richardson Information Systems?" the professor asked, then nodded. "Yes, I keep up with all my students, especially when they stay local. Congratulations. Owning your own business isn't easy, and your name has been in the yellow pages for several years now."

"Thanks, though I didn't realize there was still a yellow pages to be advertising in."

"Old codgers like me rely on that more than the internet, I'm afraid. What was your question?"

Chris set his cup aside. "They were royalty, if I remember. In Heaven?"

The professor shook his head. "No, Hell. I remember you saying your brother was some kind of expert on this."

"He's away," Chris said. "On business."

The professor pointed to the shelf by Chris's head, and called out the name of a thick-spined hardback book, which Chris set weightily on his lap and opened. The pages were filled with all types of pictures of sculptures, paintings, and woodcuts, depicting spiritual beings from all over the world, from a variety of religions, all accompanied by descriptions.

"I have that goddamn text memorized by now," the professor said. "You can take it with you, if you want, just be sure to return it. The demons you're asking about start about midway through, around page five hundred and fifty, I believe."

It was page 578, but close enough, Chris thought, staring at their images. There were seven of them depicted in various mediums, each horrific in their imagery.

The professor continued. "A lot of people think Lucifer and Beelzebub and Satan are all different names for the same being, but in truth they are the names of different creatures. Lucifer was a favorite in Heaven before the fall, as the myth goes, but the others only rose to prominence once they found Hell."

Of the seven he saw in the engravings, only Lucifer resembled a man. Chris responded, "They're hideous."

"They are the princes of Hell. The rulers. These seven represent the seven deadly sins in Catholic faith."

"Catholics believe these things exist?"

The old man shrugged and supped loudly at his coffee. "Nowadays I think it's muddled. Metaphor for evil, but at one point they did believe."

"Beelzebub, Mammon, Leviathan, Asmo…" Chris mumbled. "Lucifer. No mention of Satan?"

"Satan is less a name and more of an office held by various entities, chief of which is Beliar. He's considered the chief adversary to God, and one of the most powerful to hold the office of Satan. What is your interest in all of this?"

Chris took his time replying. He closed the book and noticed the cover for the first time, an image of something like a traditional angel carrying a child in raised relief as it flew over the land. "I don't think you'd believe me if I told you," he said.

After he finished his coffee, Chris thanked his old professor and left with the book, promising to return it soon. He told himself this, walking home under the shade of the great oaks whose shadows seemed deeper, the sky a bit darker, though it remained cloudless. Still, he chalked the shadows up to the subject matter he'd just been discussing. Ghost stories always depressed the mood and the surroundings. TS Eliot had said something similar, Chris was sure. At least that's what he thought Adam had said.

At home, he put the book on his coffee table, studying the cover. He'd later tell me how amazing it was that my diseased mind could accurately formulate the images that were described within. Still, he couldn't waste time on philosophy at the moment; he was needed back at work. When he returned home that evening, he found it lying open to a carved relief of the very serpent that had just assaulted me on the rooftop, its body coiled, its head raised to strike. When he told me this, and what day it had occurred upon, he swore to me he'd left the book closed. I never revealed to him what happened on that rooftop.

bear him or bare him? If the latter, how so?

4

HOMESPUN

I

Marion and I arrived back in Texas as a frost settled over the Dallas area. We had been assigned to a case in which a local farmer went missing. I[1] knew, even before Dr. Blake had seen us off from XNA, who the suspect was in the disappearance we were investigating.

Mr. and Mrs. L— had lived all their lives in a small Texas town one hundred miles south of Redmon. They had combatted the recent central-Texas drought by transforming their land from angus-friendly to a big cat reserve. However anyone becomes a conservationist is a story not unfamiliar to Mr. L—. In truth, he was more an environmentalist than his wife, having introduced her and the community at large to the benefits of recycling back in the nineties, before it was commonplace everywhere and long before it was commonplace in the hills of central Texas. Where his story took a turn is with who it was that introduced him to conservationism. Long before the woman who would become Mrs. L—, a young Mr. L— dated a pretty young thing. This would have been in the late nineties. She went by a different name then and has gone by many names since, but I have known her as Pamela Jean Harlow.

After the events in Redmon, Texas, PJ had vanished from the map despite the fact that we'd assumed she'd pop up again soon after. . Having been

76

witness to her abilities, plus my own studies into the occult, I was aware that witches have a mélange of magics to disguise their movements and their features, I had lost hope in finding her conventionally. I knew that we wouldn't hear from her again until she made a mistake or she chose to show herself. As it stands, I was right.

I conjectured that she used a glamour to conceal her features to a more unrecognizable face, before she set in motion the second phase of her plan. She contacted her old boyfriend, the now-married Mr. L—. Local authorities were able to ascertain as much from his emails and texts. He had, according to his end of the correspondences, thought he was reuniting with an old friend, but it is evident that their initial meeting didn't go as he'd planned. Soon after, his texts seem emphatic to remind her that he was married, that he didn't want what she wanted. At some point, the texts indicated that he was aware of what transpired in Redmon and alluded to her culpability in those matters. Did she tell him? No evidence available suggested anything to the contrary. However he found out, things escalated quickly. The words of Mrs. L— best reveal what happened next.

TRANSCRIPT

MRS. L—

TEXAS

[Unnamed] Officer: "Just, in your own words."

Mrs. L—: "Um, okay. So, [her husband, refers to him by first name] never tried to hide the fact that he met up with this —Pamela Jean?—he called her something different. I've known him a lot of years, officer. He ain't that type. He ain't going to stray. I know my husband. So when he was up front about it even before he was to meet her, I know he thought he was meeting an old friend.

"But she wasn't satisfied with that. He showed me her texts, her emails. She didn't like the fact that he had someone. You could see it in the words she wrote. She said she wanted him. And when he tried to tell her that he was in love with me, well, that only made her more angry."

Officer: "How did it make her angrier?"

Mrs. L—: "She said he could do better. Said she was better than me and she didn't even know me. Said if I was gone he'd see that. So we took that as a threat and took it to the police but even though [her husband] had knowed the sheriff since they were both in grade school, the law said there was nothing they could do. I doubt that. I doubt that very much."

Officer: "So what happened then?"

Mrs. L—, snickering: "We began finding things. One of the first things we found looked like a doll hanging where my wind chimes used to be on the front porch. They'd made the best sound in the evening breeze. We'd set out on the porch and just listen to the chimes...

Officer: "Ma'am."

Mrs. L—: "It was a horrible thing, that little doll. Made out of this crappy, smelly material. Didn't have no face to speak of, just pale cloth and brown straws of fabric in its head like frayed pieces of shag carpet. But it looked ... lifelike ... nonetheless. After that doll, we didn't feel alone. We weren't alone."

[She takes a breath. She is shaken.]

Mrs. L—: "The worst though was when we found the cat. That was right before he ... I heard him scream. I ain't never heard him scream in all the years I've knowed him. Not like that. It was early one morning and he was going out to feed the cats and I heard this scream like bloody-murder. Heh. That's what it was. Bloody murder."

Officer, to the sound of papers shuffling: "This would be the rescued lioness—four years of age?"

Mrs. L—: "We called her Mildred after his mom, 'cause she thought she ruled the roost. She had gotten plump with us, and she used to purr, so whenever he or I walked up to the cage, she'd do that thing, like housecats do, and rub up against the cage like she's using her whiskers to spread her scent and if we happened to get in there for anything—real brief and we'd be real careful 'cause as sweet as they could be, we understood they were wild animals—she'd rub on our legs like that. He laughed at me once when I got her a ball of yarn but she looked like a big ol' kitten just a-playing with it. She was our favorite. I think that woman knew that."

Officer: "Take your time."

Mrs. L—: "He found Mildred that morning. She was a wild animal and I don't know how that woman could get that close to do that. She had to have help. To split her open like that in the night and hang her up. And you tell me why we didn't hear nothing. You tell me how a big cat like that didn't make no noise."

~

At the L— farm, Marion surveyed the scene for clues, and I did too, in my own way. I could feel her. I could smell her. He caught some things of importance, and I let him talk for a while. But then he stopped and he stared at me. We were upstairs in their bedroom. I'd found a second doll that neither husband nor wife knew about and the cops had missed; it had been tucked under his pillow.

"What does she want with him?"

I frowned as I looked at the doll. It was meant to look like the husband, in a crude sort of way, as I was sure the first was meant to look like his wife. It didn't have to be exact, just to embody the essence of the person. That's all she needed.

"I wish I had her copies of the books. *The Witch's Books of Magic* and the *Malleus Maleficorum*. I'm afraid my copies might lose something in the translation. I think he's a tool to summon the Shimmers. That's what she wants. But she can't use just anyone. It has to be someone who can exhibit passion. With her. Passion drives the Shimmers. Passion drives sin. Lust, Wrath, Greed—these are all sins because of the passion behind them."

"How can we stop her?"

I shook my head. I didn't realize how tightly I was gripping the doll until Marion gently took it from me. The books weren't that specific. The former was a book meant for the witch and would not offer up clues on how to restrain her, and the latter confused actual proofs with medieval hysteria so much that at times it was hard to differentiate between fact and conjecture. Even when the *Malleus Maleficorum* offered up proven techniques for subduing a witch, often its reasons were based in myth and Puritanical fearmongering. Most people might have missed it, but my high school and college undergraduate nights were spent reading these texts, studying the different translations, the various annotations from scholars on the subject of the occult. My years of study and expertise in this field is why Marion had recruited me to the PRI[2] in the first place.

"She didn't need help with that big cat," I said.

"There was nothing in its system to suggest she drugged it," he countered.

"She doesn't work well with others," I reminded him.

"Are you suggesting she put the cat under a spell long enough to string it up and flay it?"

My phone was ringing. I turned away and answered it. It was my doctor.

"Well, Chris knows you're in Texas," Dr. Blake said. "We can't keep lying to him, Adam."

"Is he pissed?" I asked.

"He didn't act like it. Just concerned. But you told me your brother can turn on a dime, and we both expected more after he blew up in Chicago. You're just as worried as I when he didn't. You need to be careful. Is it Pamela Jean Harlow?"

"Yes," I said, and thanked her, then hung up. I turned around to see Marion also on his phone, texting someone. When I asked who, he said it was Pythia.

"She can access various government files. Mr. and Mrs. L— didn't know PJ Harlow by that name, so I want to see if any new aliases are flagged in the system. Maybe we can see if she has a past after all."

We bagged the doll and headed for the local sheriff's office even as one thing nagged at me: the files the PRI had received were complete, the cops had done everything possible and, in the search for Mr. L—, had combed the entire house. So how could they miss the doll? If they hadn't, then when had the doll been left, and for whom?

II

Chris was used to wiping the spittle from people's mouths: mine, our mother's, our father's before he died. Someone entrusted to the servitude of others such as he was meant that, in Chris's mind, that person was actually entrusted with power. He was, by his estimation, the head of the family. He wrote the checks for our mother's assisted living home and for my therapy. He made sure the insurance was paid up, verified the deductibles had been met and the premiums didn't get jacked up. He filled prescriptions and bought groceries. He kept us fed and roofs over our heads. So, it could be assumed that when he offered his advice or opinion or stated what he wanted done or not done, he would be listened to. After all, parents caring for their children and living up to the responsibilities he'd been given are expected to be listened to, so where was the difference?

He wiped some crust from our mother's chin and stared into her vacant eyes. What she looked at, he wasn't sure. She hadn't spoken all day. She was getting worse; the nurses said she was more and more unresponsive. The doctor was concerned enough to call a meeting with Chris for the following Wednesday but wasn't so concerned to move the meeting up sooner. Perhaps, Chris realized, because there was no timetable for any decision they had to make. For his mother, there was the inevitable, and it was patient.

She opened her hand, and he took it. Her eyes shifted but didn't focus. Something in the blue, cloudless sky outside her window fascinated her. He didn't like that I had disobeyed him and went to Texas. He didn't like that I felt the need to associate with the things that nearly broke my psyche. He didn't like the fact that my doctor was complacent in my desire to commit mental suicide. And who would be left to clean up the mess? Not the doctor. She would move on to other cases. My partner wouldn't foot the bill for my hospitalization. No, he'd make some grand gesture like flying in to visit, but such ostentatious displays of concern would be too few to make any difference. Responsibility would fall to Chris, the consummate survivor. The rock.

"Careful." The voice was our mother's, a weak voice with unused, frayed vocal cords, harsh like gravel when crunched under tires. He searched her for any sign of awareness, but there was none—just her vacant eyes roving the featureless sky spread out on the other side of the pane of the glass.

"What's that, Mother?" He hung his head. With his anger bubbling just under the surface, tears threatened to well and burst forth, and he knew that he'd need to make some hard decisions. He'd talk to my doctor. He'd call the state psychiatry board; he'd report Samantha to her superiors and maybe someday, someday, she'd forgive him. He never cottoned to the idea of a beautiful woman staying pissed at him. But he knew I wouldn't want to go back. I'd fight. Chris knew he might need to notify the sheriff's department. He was physically bigger than I was, but he didn't want an exhausting confrontation. It would be better if I were escorted back by local law enforcement, would go smoother. He had to regain control of the family.

"Don't," our mother said, and her grip on his hand tightened and when Chris looked down he saw fierce determination in her eyes. "Don't trust her, boy. Don't. Adam, don't."

She squeezed his hand again then her grip lost all strength, and when her strength faded it faded from all of her. Her head lolled against the pillow and she resumed gazing out the window with vacant eyes.

III

I'd just settled into the office nearest the drunk tank at the police station. The whiff of vomit and whiskey blended noxiously with Febreze and the sheriff's overdone cologne, and I was ready to dive into the files when Marion entered and said we were leaving. He said he'd found Mrs. L— at a friend of the family's; she was ready to talk again.

With a deputy along, we drove to a white-washed, single-story ranch home, and entered to find the inconsolable wife and a friend beside her. Mrs. L— asked if there had been any word. I saw hope and desperation and fear in her eyes, all at the same time. The deputy said no and Marion introduced us as federal agents, here to help with the investigation. He asked if she would be willing to talk about the night he disappeared.

"After the death of our cat," she said, sipping on some iced tea, staring at the floor, "we found a note and then we noticed other things. Birds were dying on our property. The morning before he disappeared, a bunch of crows had up and died. Our field looked like someone had shook black pepper over the wheat."

"Murder," I said. Everyone looked at me. "A bunch of crows are called a murder," I said, and realized I hadn't helped matters.

"That day I noticed blood, a lot of blood. We'd walk in a room and there'd be blood. I'd go to turn on the faucet to clean it up and out would come blood. Then, just after sundown, we lost power. We went and got the guns. He took the twelve-gauge and gave me the rifle, and I also had the pistol he'd given me for Christmas the year prior. We camped out in the living room. We could hear her, calling to us. When we heard a door upstairs open and close, soft-like, and the creak of the boards overhead, we just knowed she'd gotten in.

"He said he was going to check it out, and I begged him to stay and he said we should go together. I didn't want to move. I was scared. There was something not right with this woman and I knew it. We had LED light apps on our cells and we used that to light the way, heading for the stairs. From the base, he tried to shine a light up but it wouldn't go all the way. But I swear, I swear she was at the top and looking down on us while we were looking up. I told myself I could see her outline up there, and when I close my eyes now I believe it to be true, but it was too dark. It was too dark and I couldn't see nothing and the lights from our phones just got in the way."

She stopped to take a long drink from a glass held by trembling hands. We waited patiently for her to finish her tale. When she finally spoke, her voice quivered.

"And then he was gone. He didn't even have time to scream. I caught a glimpse of him; it looked like he was just sucked up the stairs, and I was going to fire up the stairs at where I thought she was, but I didn't 'cause I feared hitting him. I turned in place, screaming his name, and I thought I heard her laugh from the kitchen, so I took the rifle and fired and then the barrels fell off. I pulled out my pistol and shot that into the living room because I heard her laugh there next, and then it sounded like her laugh was coming all around me. Then the lights came on, and I could feel it, I was alone. The house was empty."

We felt her words settle over us like a weight. No one said anything; there wasn't much to say. In such cases as missing persons, you didn't promise to find the missing person, and you never, ever hinted that the person could still be alive. False hope was worse than knowing their loved ones were dead. You didn't promise. You just delivered, if you could. But I wasn't sure we would; in fact, I wondered if she didn't take him for some type of sacrifice.

One of the deputies' wives had brought in some fried chicken, and Marion had helped himself to a drumstick and a spoonful of mashed potatoes and gravy. Poring over the files exhausted me, and I couldn't understand how Marion could eat. While the food smelled good, I was turned off by the putrescence wafting in from the drunk tank, the condition of which had been a source of contention for several hours. After the last of the night's drunks had been booked and discharged, the sheriff had given the order to clean out the cell, but two of the newest deputies couldn't agree as to whose turn it was to scour the walls. Royally pissed at their incessant bickering, by the time we returned from interviewing Mrs. L—, the sheriff had sent both men in with buckets of Lysol water and buckets of bleach and mops and scouring pads. They cussed at each other in Spanish relentlessly, and while I could hear the water sloshing around, I got the sense they were smearing the vomit and liquor and not actually getting any of it up, and my stomach turned at the vile smells now co-mingling with the cleaning agents.

My cell phone rang, and I hoped a call would help get my mind off the odor. Since I'd exiled myself to this office, no one had bothered to come in and talk to me, Marion choosing to stay out with the locals to talk strategy. I didn't blame them. I'm sure the smell of the chicken and fixings overwhelmed everything else once one was further away from the immediate area. On the phone at least, I'd be talking, so I couldn't breathe through my nose as much. It might cut down on the smell.

I answered it with only a cursory glance at the Caller ID: no name, and a number that had a 479 area code, so I answered, hoping it wasn't my brother. It wasn't.

"Ooh, that smell," sang the woman's voice. "Don't you smell that smell?"

"Who is this?" I asked.

"Shut the door to the office, Adam," she said. When she said my name, I realized who was calling.

"Is he still alive?" I asked, returning to my seat. I carefully followed the movements of Marion and the officers outside, making sure no one came to interrupt.

"He is, Adam," she said. "For now. For how long depends on you."

"You have the books. I don't know what passion spell you're after, but you have the resources. I can't..."

She began to laugh hysterically, so loud I had to pull the phone from my ear. "Adam, Adam, Adam," she said. "The passion spells aren't for him. He fucked like a cowboy, which is neither good nor bad, mind you, but...you still haven't figured this out, have you?"

I let my eyes roam around the office, and I settled on the doll in the evidence bag that I'd found earlier. "He's a means to an end," I said then. I knew what she wanted.

"You come alone, Adam Richardson. I'll text you where. If you are followed, I will kill him."

"And me?"

"You'll die a lot slower. Oh, and Adam?"

"Yeah."

"Did you bring your croomstick?"

"No," I said. I'd forgotten. And I hadn't considered my roommate, either. Where he was now I could only guess, but I could only hope that if he heard me call out, despite the vast physical distance, it would only be a brief hop ethereally from wherever he was.

"Good," she said, and hung up.

The door opened. I'd taken my eyes off it and jumped as Marion entered, closing the door behind him. He looked at me, concerned.

"What's up?" He glanced over his shoulder to the other cops, still enjoying their chicken.

"Chris is pissed," I said, motioning to the phone. I hated lying to him. "You got the car keys?"

"What for?"

I cocked my head a bit. "Come on. I used to drive all the time. I need my bag, is all. Want to get it out of the trunk."

"You put it in your hotel room."

"Well, I brought a book and if it's in my bag still, then I have to go to the hotel. But I think I took it out and it's either in the trunk or the glove compartment."

He tossed the keys to me. They slid across the desk into my waiting palm. I patted his back and said, "I'll be right back," and I smiled at him and left. I started the car and drove out of the parking lot and, glancing in the rearview mirror long enough to see that no one had followed me, I drove on.

I had, before this call, tried to research a few spells on the Internet and from some of the books — digitized grimoires — Marion had sent me. Most weren't of any help. The few spells that might help were in foreign languages and lost potency in English. I did my best to memorize them. On the flight down, I had excused myself to the bathroom to perform some protection spells for me and Marion, minor incantations that hopefully would ward off any unnatural calamity that could befall us. A weather-inspired strike, a plane crash, a car wreck, or a bullet might not be deterred, but those damn lightning bolts from her fingers shouldn't hurt. *Shouldn't.*

I plugged the address she'd texted into my GPS and was led to an old farm with a wood-slat barn and a rusted tin roof. She had mentioned the barn specifically, so I parked at the house and gathered my nerves, trying to remember what I'd read. But my nerves wouldn't abate, my fear unquieting my attempt at recollection, so my guard was down as I opened the door to the barn.

More of those lightning bolts fired from the tips of her fingers, fizzling out harmlessly a foot in front of me. That my protection spell had held angered her to no end. She chanted with futility, trying to command my destruction. She used her mind to hurl bales of hay, and slat boards from the wall and feed trough, and it was with all my energy that I dodged and deflected her assaults. Mr. L— sat, chained to the wall behind her looking frightened and helpless. Still, as a dried cow pie smacked me between the legs and brought me to one knee, I knew I could get no closer to Mr. L—.

"You think I wouldn't come a bit prepared?"

She cocked her head and studied my face until a smile slowly crept to her lips that looked more like a snarl.

"I can see it," she said, dreamily. "Your protective aura fades. You know they only last for forty-eight hours. When did you put on your armor, Adam?"

"You promised to let him go," I said.

"In what condition?" she taunted.

"You have me," I said. "That's all you need to get the Shimmers."

"But with him I can have fun, too. A girl can't have too much blood."

She raised her hands as if to begin conducting an orchestra, a victorious smile on her lips that faded slowly, her eyebrows knitting together slowly, her smile dropping at perhaps something she'd realized. No, it was something she heard, and I heard it, too: the wail of sirens approaching up the road, then the drive to the house, and down the pasture lane to the barn. Presently I saw the strobe effect of the blue and red lights through the slats. I had used the cruiser's GPS to direct me here. Now, at least a half-dozen cruisers sped down the pasture lane toward the barn.

"You lying, sniveling sack of rat shit!" she said.

I wasn't sure if she was right about the forty-eight hour time limit, but if she was, it was drawing near. Marion might still be too late.

She cocked her head again just as I was sure I was vulnerable, and then she swept her arms, catching up the loose straw that carpeted the stable into a whirlwind that concealed her and Mr. L—. Needles like splinters rained down, driving me back toward the door and preventing Marion or the local cops to press further. The slat boards rattled loose, now caught up in the twister, some with nails like hooked barbs that, had we pressed in, would have shredded our flesh and gouged out our eyes.

Marion grabbed for me, pointed to the walls in warning. I was already aware of the danger; too many boards had been pulled loose from the studs, and the whole structure threatened to collapse into the swirling vortex. I pointed through the dustbowl to the other side of the stable and Marion looked, really looked, before realizing what he had to do. He patted my shoulder, then gave me a shove, just enough to push me into the arms of two deputies before running headlong into the storm.

The twister settled instantly; straw and slat boards froze in midair briefly before falling to the floor. The barn exhausted one audible creak and swayed.

I could see clearly now—we all could—that Pamela Jean Harlow was gone, and on the other side of the stable Marion worked at the chains that bound the frightened but very much alive Mr. L—.

I started for them, but arms enveloped me, dragging me backward, as the plaintive sigh of the feeble structure elevated to a wail of rusted nails ripping through weathered walls and floors. I struggled, and cried out for Marion, but the deputies were too strong. They continued to drag me back on my heels as I reached for the barn, till we were out of harm's way. The creak echoed across the pasture, and the barn gave out one low groan and swayed once more, this time too far in the gentle breeze. It lost its shape as it crashed into a mashup of wood and iron, the rusted tin panels of the roof now entombing everything underneath, and all consumed by a great cloud of dust.

As the dust settled, nothing could be seen but a great mound of debris. As far back as we now stood, we coughed from the poisoned air and squeezed our burning eyes shut against the dust and dirt. As I'd buried my head in the crook of my elbow to shield my eyes from the flying sediment, I couldn't see when one of the deputy's shouted, "Look!" I had to rub my eyes vigorously just to see, and realized that, while I found an abundance of jubilation, I wasn't totally surprised. It had become old hat for my partner to escape crumbling buildings and to pull free another soul during his release. As Marion and Mr. L—, huddled together, their heads bowed against the settling debris, emerged relatively unscathed from the ruins of the old barn, I knew that I had expected this.

IV

Mr. and Mrs. L— were reunited and placed in protective custody, and their celebration became ours. The sheriff was convinced that PJ Harlow had died in the collapse of the barn, and that her body would be found soon enough. Marion and I stayed through the night, at first positive she'd resurface, then shocked and wary when she didn't. I didn't sleep much that night, sure as I was that she'd return. When dawn broke and there was no sign of her, the sheriff promised us that it was all over, and that the husband and wife were safe.

Seeing our invitation was rescinded in the politest of ways, we had no choice but to drive back to the airport for a flight back to XNA. As I unloaded from the plane, Marion appeared in the door, asking how I was.

I shifted my gaze away from his judgmental look. "Fine."

"That was incredibly brave, going after her by yourself."

A beat.

"It was also incredibly stupid." He sighed but didn't take his eyes off me. I felt like I was being judged. "Do you want company? I can stay a few days. Help ease things with your brother."

"Seeing you might piss him off more," I said.

"I can handle Chris," he said.

"No," I said after a moment. "That's okay."

The truth was, I was exhausted. I wanted to go home and go to bed. Once there, I could lock my door and not let Chris in, not answer his calls. I could even ask the ghost to watch over him. I would, as a matter of fact, find out why Leo didn't accompany me to Texas. He knew how dangerous PJ was, and he knew he could touch her, hurt her.

I caught a cab and shut my eyes as we headed south down I-49 to Fayetteville, and opened them to find the cab parked at the curb in front of my apartment, the cabbie's hand extended for payment. I shoved a wad of cash into his sweaty palm and shuffled upstairs, my overnight bag dragging behind me because I hadn't the energy to lift it. I thought I was tired because of the lack of sleep; that might have been a lot of it, but I also believe that the encounter, that as the spell I'd conjured to protect myself from her assault faded, it left me zapped of all my strength.

I dropped the bag just inside the door and called out for Leo. No response. I called again, loudly. There came a knock at my door, and when I turned to unlock it, it swung open, and I realized that I'd never locked it. Chris stood in the doorway. His face was blank and I could discern no immediate emotion, so I braced myself for what was to come.

"How was Texas?" he asked. His voice remained even.

"Good. We recovered the man that was kidnapped, unharmed."

A smile grew on his face, then he swayed and leaned against my door. I

89

realized that while I'd been fighting for my life and the lives of others, my brother had been passing time at the bar. He held up the door frame with his shoulder and grinned sloppily at me.

"Adam, man, I'm glad. You know I worry about you."

"You didn't drive here like that, did you?"

I moved to help him and he waved me away, then staggered into my room. I left the door open, following him closely, trying to help guide him to the sofa, till he collapsed on it, lengthwise but askew, with his shoes off the cushions.

"I'm good. I'll sleep it off here."

He was paying for it. He had the right. I stood over him, studying his features, making sure that, as drunk as he was, he was still breathing. With his eyes closed, he looked peaceful, but that didn't last long; he gathered his bearings and started to babble about the girl he'd met in the bar, and how intelligent she was and how pretty. Same ol' same ol' with my brother, I realized. Another day, another pussy; that's all they were to him. Something to use for a bit of fun and then toss aside like a dirty rag.

"No, she's different," he protested, even trying to sit up.

"Why don't you call her tomorrow morning when you sober up?" I suggested. Outside the sun had set and the day was drawing to a close, and I still wondered where the hell my roommate was. Often Leo made his presence known whether I wanted to be alone or not.

Chris frowned up at me and relaxed back. "But she's right there," he said, and pointed over my shoulder.

I turned. Pamela Jean Harlow—nearly unrecognizable with hair and makeup done, a little black dress clinging to her firm body—smiled at me from the open doorway, pausing long enough to present herself before strolling into my apartment.

She snapped her fingers and he rolled off the couch and thudded on the floor, motionless. I heard him moan; he wasn't lifeless, but he did not make an attempt to rise.

"Now, Adam," she said, and leaned in to me, her breath like black licorice. "Where were we?"

5

ADAM

I

Here comes Ira, the wolf with the serpent's tail, and she is angry, sharpening the blade on the palm of her hand the way barbers use a strap of leather before a shave. She says my blood will serve the wolf, will feed the wolf, and her voice is angry and she snarls and spits in my face. And then she slits my throat.

That was the first. I have died several times since she took me, with another crossing over every time I do. I feel her draw the blade across my neck, and I feel the blood gush forth, spill down my chest and into my lap as quickly as my flesh becomes unstitched. I have no voice to cry out. I wonder how I'll finish my story once I'm gone.

She heals my throat with a warm palm; her magic stitches my flesh and the muscle and the carotids and the jugular and the cartilage back together.

I hear the buzz of Beelzebub, and it is hungry, smacking its lips and humming, and makes the sound of a zipper when she draws the blade across my throat after she has stuffed me full of so much food.

"You were right, Adam," she said, healing my throat with her touch.

The pain is unbearable. I don't numb to it.

"To summon them takes passion. Passionate transgressions are deadly sins."

Garbed in purple, the athame in a purple sash on her belt, she carries dirt in her cupped palms, and when she gets close, she smears it on my face, in my mouth and in my eyes. In my ears and nose. She spits in her hands and rubs them together then smears the mud through my hair. She takes the blood-stained knife from her purple sash and lets the blade dip in the mud in her palm, then draws it across my throat so my new blood and my old and the mud of Mammon can mingle together.

She washes me in freezing water and says, "I must wait, you see, at least twenty-four hours before I can summon another, so that the previous Shimmer has time to cross."

"But none can cross if they all can't cross," I say, the sound of the blood pooling in my throat making me sound like I'm gargling. It hurts to talk, to breathe.

She straddles me and opens her mouth, and the head of a snake slithers out from between her lips, where her tongue should be. She opens her eyes, and they are snake's eyes, and the serpent in her mouth hisses its own name and bears its fangs to strike. *Leviathan.*

"I want what you have," she says, and draws the blade across my throat again, and the snake takes my blood.

She is on my lap and gyrates and thrusts and moans and groans. She kisses my neck and lets her tongue tango with mine. I can't close my eyes because I can see the abomination of Asmodeus, but I am a man and I can't fight how she makes me feel, when she thrusts and moans and gyrates and groans. PJ Harlow can be called nothing if not comely.

When I come, she slits my throat, and everything escapes me, into her.

It gets no better when she heals me. The pain does not diminish. "Don't fight it," she whispers. I pray that she won't heal me again. But she has two more times left, which means I've been in this hell for a week already. Maybe that last time she won't heal me. Maybe then I can find a medium to carry my message. Where was Leo? Why didn't that vision come? Why wasn't he there? And where are my friends? Where is Marion with his guns and his weapons and his military training? Where is my brother? Where is Dr. Blake, our moral compass? If she knew what I was going through, she would make them come. But what if this is real, and they were all the hallucination?

"They don't come because they don't feel like it," she says, and draws the blade again across my throat.

I have died, and I have been dead and felt the cold wash over me, and I've kissed death, who has appeared to me as a woman, her perfume necrosis and blood. She is sweetly rancid. I can't imagine smelling her for an eternity. I hope that one gets used to it, for soon I'll have no choice. Or maybe she's only there to help me transition, and when she goes so wafts away her perfume. Yes, I'll believe that.

PJ is dancing to Jane's Addiction. Now she dances to Fleetwood Mac. Now Pearl Jam. Now Tori Amos. She dances at odd hours, usually after she's fed me. She says I must keep up my strength. She told me before the first cut that it would only get worse. She was right. With every swipe, I feel it worse, and bound, I can't reach up to quell the blood flow. I can't scream. I have no tears left. It won't be long now, and I'll be able to escape this hell and find someone who can finish my story.

II

Marion rolled out of bed at the sound of a timid knock on his front door. He looked to the window. Christ, it wasn't even light out yet, though, this late in the year, that the sun had yet to rise didn't matter much. He rose and padded across the floor of his bedroom, then the hall, then the living room with catlike footfalls. At the threshold he hid his right hand behind the wall with his gun and used his left to open the door.

A rotund Black man with glasses, gray hair tied back in a ponytail, and a mustache smiled up at him. Marion's hand relaxed on the grip. He blinked, tired. The man began talking, quickly, like he was nervous. Marion asked him to slow down.

"I'm sorry. I'm Bob. Bob Link, if you will. I—well, my friend and I are investigative journalists, not that we're here in that capacity now," he said, chuckling.

Marion looked over the man's shoulder to the empty hall. "You're alone," Marion said.

Bob looked back and then laughed. "Yes. Yessir." He stopped and nodded. "I apologize for the time, but it is imperative that I talk to you. May I come in?"

"No," Marion said.

"I have news, Agent Case. Please, if you'll give me just a minute of your time."

"You've taken more than that just standing at my door."

Bob, flustered, stopped and tilted his head ever so slightly. "I'm trying," he snapped, his voice low. The man at his door wasn't addressing him. Reflexively, Marion tightened the grip on his gun.

"Are you okay?" he asked Bob.

"I am," Bob said, sweating. "I am, but Agent Case, Adam isn't. He needs your help."

Marion frowned. It was too early in the morning for all of this. Bob stepped forward, his hand on the door, stammering. "Look, Agent Case, if I can just come in, I will explain how—"

Marion stopped him. It was too fucking early for nut jobs. "Look, Mr. Link. I don't know how you know me or how you found my address, but I am not in the mood for games."

"Your old partner Adam Richardson is in serious trouble!" Bob pleaded.

Marion was too tired for this. One of the more interesting cases he'd been assigned had just taken him to Lake Louise in Alberta where he'd been hunting, of all things, a very aggressive Sasquatch. He wanted to sleep in, then run downtown, get an Italian Beef at Al's, and watch the game over several beers. The only thing he hadn't decided was whether he would drink at a bar or at home.

"I don't know you, Mr. Link. And I don't know any Adam Richardson," he said, and slammed the door.

Probably a panhandler, running some new door-to-door scam, he decided as he crashed back into bed.

~

After lunch, Samantha told her secretary to hold all her calls and reschedule her group session. She called a colleague and asked if he could take the psych evaluation at the Washington County Detention Center. She called another friend to see if she could cover her afternoon block at Ozark Guidance where she evaluated convicted DUIs on the sessions required for the reinstatement of their driver's licenses. Her afternoon freed, she drove home and pulled up the files of her sessions for the last six months. When she saw my file, my name, no face registered in her memory.

Still, here I was, given voice in one-on-one therapy sessions, speaking up voluntarily during Group. Here my brother—according to her daily journals—had talked with her at length about me. She should remember that. But instead, it was as though she were reading the case study of a colleague. She couldn't envision my face. All she had was her imagination and the word of the gray-haired hippie with thick glasses who'd just visited her, who insisted that she knew the name.

Except that wasn't all. Staring at the files, at her own words, a picture began to focus, and she realized she could *see* the face. She could *see* the name. She could see me.

III

After catching the earliest commuter flight from Chicago to XNA and calling the therapist on the drive down the interstate to Fayetteville, Bob Link exited the passenger side of an old Cutlass, nodded to the driver, and approached the front door of Fayetteville Computer Systems. The glass front windows gave him a preview of what was inside: Millennial hipsters in untucked shirts typing away on keyboards in their own cubicles, a few offices with vertical blinds halfway open, a fern behind one mahogany desk, and a front desk just to the other side of the glass double doors.

Bob entered the office to the sound of keys clanking, to the sound of an operator offering to send out a tech for a networking consultation, to the smell of coffee and the hum of the vent overhead. It had been cold outside. He'd cinched the coat around him when he exited the car. Now he found the office a comfortable temperature and relaxed his coat. He approached the desk where a young woman with short pink locks and a pierced nostril smiled to reveal too-white teeth and asked how she could help him.

"I'm looking for Chris Richardson," he said.

She crooked her mouth and looked deep in thought, then said, "I'll have to see if he's in."

He thanked her and stepped back, turned to look out the window and spied the Cutlass across the street. He felt unsure of himself and of his mission, but he knew there was no other way.

The front desk girl swooned involuntarily when Chris exited his office, the thew of his body accentuated by the tailored business casual attire he wore. Bob was sure Chris was sizing him up as well, a stocky man with a gray ponytail and coke-bottle glasses, a full mustache. Dressed in a short sleeve button-up Hawaiian shirt and a pair of jeans and a coat, Bob had wide shoulders and a substantial gut he'd slowly but surely been trimming down with walks on the treadmill every morning.

Chris offered a hand and introduced himself, though Bob needed no introduction. He'd seen Chris's face many times. He'd almost memorized it.

"Would it be possible to have a word?" Bob asked.

Chris's brow instinctively furrowed, and Bob prayed this would go differently than the others.

He sat in the extra chair in Chris's office, espied the fern he had seen from outside, and smiled at a motivational poster with more buzzwords than sense. Chris offered him a cup of coffee, which he accepted. Through the window, he could still see the Cutlass.

"Now, how may I help you, Mr. Link?"

"This is your tech firm?" he asked.

"Two friends and I have been working to build it up. It's cost me some sleepless nights and some relationships, but it's what I love."

Bob looked around, sizing up the office. "It pays for your mother's nursing home bills."

Chris leaned back. "Yes."

Bob said, "And your brother?"

There was no response. Bob noticed a twitch. Outside, the Cutlass pulled out of the parking spot and pulled around the corner. Bob touched his chin and dropped his eyes and heard a voice—not Chris's—say, *Not him too.*

"Are you responsible for taking care of your brother, Adam? Your older brother?"

He'd heard Chris had a temper. It was best to tread lightly in such cases.

"I don't have a brother," Chris said. A vein in his temple was thumping. His face was reddening.

It's too late, came the voice only Bob could hear.

"Are you sure about that?" Maybe the voice was right, but Bob saw the signs of anger and frustration manifesting themselves inwardly. Whatever spell she cast, it was unnatural. They couldn't just be made to forget.

"Am I sure?" Chris mocked. "I know my family, Mr. Link. I'm aware of my life growing up. I don't know how you know about my mother, but I am damn sure I know who grew up in my house with me. There was me and mother and for a while, my father, until he went batshit crazy and blew his brains out in front of me and Ad—"

He caught himself mid-word. His eyes narrowed. By degrees, his face paled till the red was nearly gone.

"I think it's time for you to leave, Mr. Link," he said.

Without argument and without further discourse, Bob stood and laid his card on the desk, then showed himself out. Around the corner from the entrance, he found the Cutlass and his old friend behind the wheel.

If Bob was short and stocky, Ernie Quill was tall and lanky. His cheeks hung off his jowls in great aged wrinkly sags, but his gray-blue eyes were sharp and saw everything. With their day jobs, the two men made an odd-looking pair, but they'd made a name for themselves as investigative reporters. Within a dying industry, they were the last of a dying breed: twenty-first century's Woodward and Bernstein. They dug and dug, but no one would believe them if they revealed Bob's secret gift. Hell, Bob knew his buddy didn't always believe it either, that Bob Link was psychic: he could see and speak to the dead and sometimes, just sometimes, had insights into information that he couldn't have known. Call it precognition or some form of telepathy, but Bob had been right too often for it to be intuition, coincidence. Like with this Adam Richardson character. Something more than just the ghost of Leo Knight had drawn Bob to this missing man. While Bob didn't know what, he did know that the man was in trouble, and no one seemed to remember him.

Bob slammed the door, and Ernie pulled away.

"Nothing," Bob said. "Like the others. It's like he didn't even exist."

"Past tense," Ernie cautioned.

From the backseat, the voice in Bob's head now materialized to a form only he could see. A Black man wearing a shield on the lapel of his wool coat shook his head in disgust. "They're trying to remember," Leo said. "She won't let them. I can't believe she's that strong."

"She was strong enough to keep you at bay, from what you said," Bob replied.

"Bitch," the detective said.

"All these years," Ernie said. "That creeps me out to no end when you talk to the dead like that."

The detective: "What do we do now?"

Bob: "I don't know."

Ernie: "Don't know what?"

Bob: "What we're going to do."

~

St. Louis, MO.

Bob was not a drinker, but a beer every now and then proved beneficial in clearing out the cobwebs from the corners of his mind and settling his troubled thoughts. He felt he knew me from all the detective had told him. He'd become an investigative reporter because his talents allowed him to be profitable at something he enjoyed, but he'd often used his psychic abilities to help others. A naturally caring man, Bob Link found empathy as innate as talking with the dead, or maybe it was because he could communicate with the dead that he could also empathize with the living. Seeing what was in store for everyone made all their earthly sins seem trite.

The dead detective stood in his apartment, refusing to leave. Bob wasn't a trained medium, and had no idea how to force the man out even if he wanted to. He popped the bottle cap from his Michelob Ultra and, sipping it, reclined on his couch as though he were going to watch television.

He didn't turn on the TV. Rather, he stared at the black screen and sipped his beer and imagined the television was on, imagined he was flipping channels, imagined he had the guide on and he could see what was playing. Ernie's doubt and Agent Case's secret files each played on their own channels. Dr. Blake's channel played a mystery, a resilient heroine vigilant in the search for the truth. Chris was a study in denial. He wanted this life. He wanted to not have a brother. He embraced the spell.

"If we can't find him," the detective said, "I need a favor."

"No." Bob said, and sipped his beer.

"No? What you mean, no?"

"I won't help you solve your murder. I'll help you find Adam."

"You sound sure of yourself. That we'll find him."

Bob shook his head, frustrated with his own inability to articulate what he felt. He wasn't an expert, but what he could see on the imaginary channel guide as he flipped through the stations and landed on one for the witch was that her magic was a glamour. It changed reality like a mirage, the road ahead warped by the heat, and it was just as substantial.

"She has to exist," Bob said. He was scanning ahead, trying to find a program. When he found it, he'd rewind it, searching. "She has to have a trail. She had to come from somewhere; *everyone* comes from somewhere. That's Investigative Journalism 101, Detective Knight. We need to find her."

"If there are records on her," Leo said. "She can manipulate people's memories, but can she erase all records of someone existing?"

"I would think that would be too hard," Bob said. "She might block memories, but to hide such a paper trail—she'd more than likely bury it."

"Bury it where?"

Bob thought about all the white-collar infractions he'd uncovered, all the crimes and schemes where the evidence had been buried and hidden. Once, he'd investigated a CEO who had embezzled from the company retirement plan, then faked his death and picked up another identity. Bob and Ernie had tracked him all the way to Venezuela. Why Venezuela? The man's great-grandparents had been from there. He'd run as far as he could but to a place he could still know. People always ran to where they knew and were generally afraid to venture outside their comfort zone.

"I want to know where she's from," Bob said.

As if on cue, the doorbell rang.

Though it was late at night, Bob wasn't that surprised to see his partner at the door with a deep scowl on his face. Or that he strolled into the apartment without being invited. What surprised Bob were the three who entered on Ernie's heel.

Samantha Blake smiled at Bob and asked if she could sit down. He could tell she was tense. When she sat, her back was as straight as a board and she placed her hands primly on her knees. Chris asked for a drink. He made his way to Bob's kitchen, then helped himself to a beer from the fridge. Agent Case was ready to get down to business. He sat down beside Bob and would not break his gaze.

"We remember him," Marion said. "But it's all fuzzy. How long has it been?"

"A week."

"How do you know about all this?" Chris asked. "Did this witch block our memories of you too?"

"No," Bob said.

"He talks to ghosts," Ernie said.

"Then Adam is—?" Samantha started.

"It's not Adam. It's a ghost you sent him," Bob said, looking to Marion. Chris and Samantha turned venomous gazes on the agent.

The look on Marion's face was like a deer caught in headlights. His cheeks flushed and all he could manage was a blink for a second before he met the angry gazes of Samantha and Chris. "A detective. Murdered in Chicago. He...he was going to watch over Adam, and in return ask Adam if we could solve his murder."

Chris, the fog over his memories still lifting, wanted to focus on this betrayal, but Marion waved him away. He wanted to know why the ghost wasn't there to keep me safe. Bob explained that PJ's spells had kept Detective Knight away long enough for her to abduct me, and then she clouded their memories. Weakened from her spell, Leo had to find someone with whom he could communicate.

100

"How did you all figure it out?" Bob asked.

Agent Case was the first to answer. "A man at the—the agency I work for—I don't know his name—he struck me as being immune to certain things. And there were case files missing. When I confronted him, he said that there was someone missing. I found Chris and Dr. Blake from what we had on Adam. They both had your card."

"My group therapy files," Dr. Blake said. "My memory of those sessions had filled in the gaps, but those were inconsistent with my files. And along with them, I found research. Marion here had asked me to consider PJ Harlow's history. I found some information out about her. Who she is. Where she came from."

"You can't forget a brother that's been a pain in your ass for all your life," Chris said. "No matter how bad you might like to."

The talk shifted to Dr. Blake's research, which she'd brought with her. She laid the paperwork on Bob's coffee table, revealing that PJ Harlow had shifted through many aliases over the years before returning to her original name, an identity of a person long since believed deceased. What better alias to use, after all, than one's own name? It was like hiding in plain sight. If anyone researched the name they'd find Pamela Jean Harlow had died fifteen years earlier in the house fire that also consumed her parents and her sister. But that she'd survived, changed her name again and again, always running, always searching, only to finally settle on her identity again—who would suspect that?

"So who were the Harlows?" Chris asked.

As she began speaking, Samantha zipped a file over to Ernie Quill's email, who began typing away at his laptop. Bob knew his partner was accessing old police files, real estate records, financial records. Over his shoulder stood Chris. When Ernie happened upon a page that had been encrypted, Chris was there to hack through the techno bramble blocking the path, until all was discovered.

Mr. Harlow, Samantha explained, originated from Detroit, a descendent of Midwest robber-barons whose family had another chance at success when his grandfather became lead engineer for Henry Ford. But Mr.

Harlow's father squandered the family fortune and lost the family estate in a fit of partying and gambling. Mr. Harlow moved his wife and two little girls to Texas, and then fifteen years ago was killed in the fire.

"There's an unclaimed deed here," Ernie said, his fingers dancing on the keyboard, his gaze unbroken from the screen. "It's for a warehouse. It belonged to a dummy corporation for a while until it went into the hands of—someone who didn't exist until two years ago, the CEO of another dummy Corp that hadn't existed since the grandfather worked for Ford. A woman... Morgan Le Fay?"

Bob laughed. "Christ, she didn't try very hard, did she? There are more obscure witch names throughout history, but she had to go right to the Arthurian legend."

"Where's the warehouse?" Marion asked.

"In Chicago, on Lake Michigan," Ernie said.

"Why would he hold on to that? Why would *she* hold on to that?" Dr. Blake asked, as Marion asked them to pull up the specs and address, then stood to make a phone call.

"It doesn't say," Ernie said. This was an unsatisfactory answer, but it was the only answer they got. Within the hour, Bob was flying to Midway Airport with his partner, the PRI agent, the psychiatrist, the brother, and the ghost of the detective who'd brought them all together.

IV

She kneels in front of me with the blade, and she smiles at me. I'm too weak, too exhausted and in too much pain to be fooled by her glamour. She draws the blade across my throat and I can't remember how many times now my blood has spilled. The pain comes, and my mind spills down my chest and into my lap. The Shimmers are almost all there. Six of them, spinning around me in the darkness, calling my name. I can't even see which one is missing. It doesn't matter anymore. I've failed: myself, my friends, my brother.

There he is, come to collect, wary of the Shimmers and of the witch. She doesn't feel him, probably because he is smaller than the Shimmers, and when they are around everything else feels small. Her back is to him. I open my mouth and blood bubbles up to my lips. She draws her hand across my neck and I feel the flesh seal, my throat tightens, the fibers of the muscles and tissue lace back together. But the pain is still there; it doesn't subside.

I hear a door open. I hear screaming, like cops or soldiers, mini points of light dart through the darkness. She turns with a hiss. My friend attacks her, knocks her to the ground. Men in urban soldier-wear swoop in from all areas. She is screaming to them, laughing. The knots that bind me to the chair begin to loosen.

"We found you, buddy," the voice whispers in my ear. It isn't a soldier—I don't know the Black Ops team—and Mr. MITS, who leads them, is on the other side of the room. He has a bead on her. It isn't the ghost either, for he has her pinned and is pummeling her. Only she and I can hear the names he's calling her, the curses he's delivering on her with each blow. Her blood is splattering, and while the members of the Black Ops team have seen a lot of combat, a lot of violence, they are afraid to approach, because to them she is being attacked by an invisible force. I know the voice is Marion's and he shouldn't have come in. I know what she has planned. I saw her set the drums of oil and gas against the walls of the warehouse.

"Hoawk—," I try. I meant to say *Hold her hands and her mouth shut*. I think it, and the ghost looks at me, but it's too late. Pamela Jean speaks something in Latin and flicks her wrist, and Marion lifts me to his shoulders as a fireball sparks off her fingertips and missiles toward the drums. I want to scream, but I can't. Marion and I are just far enough away. We make it into the offices in the back as the warehouse explodes. I see two Black Ops soldiers catch fire and scream. I see black. Maybe Mr. MITS got it too. I—

V

Chris refused to leave my side. He kept apologizing to me. There was more there, but he didn't explain. I could tell something gnawed at him. My throat bandaged, the tenuous wound muting me, I had no inclination to respond.

I met the two reporters. They seemed nice enough. They had a lot of questions for Marion, but he refused to answer any of them. Inviting them in opened a Pandora's Box that we weren't ready to contend with. I understood that the public didn't need to know. No one needed to know about this stuff.

Chris spent a few nights on my couch. I awoke a few times to the ghost standing vigil, sometimes over my bed, sometimes in the living room, sometimes on the landing outside my front door. All he would tell me was something was different.

Marion returned five days after we came back to Fayetteville. Chris had just made me some more green tea—I was sick of the shit—when Marion and Dr. Blake walked into my apartment.

"How's your throat?" Marion asked.

I nodded. He dropped some pictures on the table, the burned-out shell of the warehouse, a blackened corpse at the center of several of the pictures.

"DNA came back. Enough to confirm. Pythia has a certain skill — we had her look in the morgue, and she confirmed that this wasn't magic."

My worried look drew the ghost to my side.

I knew she was weaker, Adam, Detective Knight said. *It's 'cause she dead, man.*

"She's dead," Marion said, deaf to the ghost.

The news relieved my brother from his watch, but I could see something had changed in him. Though it wouldn't be until later that he'd tell me what, exactly. He realized at that moment that these things — ghosts and demons and witches and monsters — would seek me out. He hugged me before he left, a voluntary action he hadn't conceded in years. I thought a question to the dead detective, asking him what had happened to Chris. He said it was up to my brother to tell me; when I was able, I should ask Chris what she did to them to conceal my kidnapping.

I slept soundly that night—perhaps more peacefully than I deserved—and for many nights after that. Weeks passed before my dreams took me back to that warehouse, the Shimmers skulking in the shadows, muttering how close they'd come. I was drawn to the blackened body in the middle of the floor. I knelt and saw that some of her hair still topped her seared scalp. I felt the strands, thinking fire is a fickle bitch with what it eats and what it leaves.

Her eyes opened. Her jaw unhinged. Her eyes seemed perfectly alive, the scleras white and clear and the pupils pinpoints in the green pools of her irises.

I told her she was dead.

Her jaw worked up and down; her voice said "Good." A blackened, scarred arm reached up and the scorched claws of her fingers raked across my chest, bringing a horrible pain that awoke me from an otherwise sound sleep, clutching at the spot on my chest that she'd scratched.

I looked down, the raised abrasions on my chest stretched from my right shoulder to my left floater ribs, fresh burning welts that seared and reddened as I watched. Panic set in. I tried to call out but, my throat still too sore, I thought as loud as I could till the ghost materialized with concern on his face.

I thought— I struggled with how to proceed.

I'm here. It's okay. What's wrong?

"Are you a manifestation of my subconscious?" I asked, my voice caught between a grunt and a susurration.

"Does it really matter how I answer that?" I hate questions as answers to questions.

I looked down. My tee didn't appear to reveal the welts. Perhaps during my nightmare, I'd scratched myself.

"Yes," I said. "What do you want?"

"To help you."

"Why?"

"So maybe you'll help me. Death is traumatic, Adam. I don't remember who killed me. I don't know why. But I want to know."

He promised he wouldn't stray away from the apartment, then vanished from the room. I could feel him in the residence, my visitant guard. I lifted my shirt for the mirror only and stared at the abrasions raking my flesh. Perhaps I scratched myself, and perhaps he's just a manifestation I'd conjured. Perhaps. But what if—perhaps not?

6

THE SHADOW FOLK

I

Stone Avenue in Reeder, Arkansas doesn't technically exist anymore. The house of ill repute is still there, though, hidden behind brambles and thorns and overgrown flora and some pines and maples. It's dilapidated now, the clapboards worn of whitewash and gray and buckling, the windows smashed in with shards of glass like grains of sand peppered about the molded floor, the tin roof rusted, its panels loose and flapping in whatever zephyr decided to mottle through the South Arkansas landscape.

I brought them all here. The dead detective, my psychiatrist, my brother, my old partner; I picked a weekend when the weather wasn't supposed to be excitable, and we drove down to the southern part of the state. We filled up at the gas station in Reeder before heading out toward a county road that abutted a stretch of the Missouri/Pacific long since abandoned and entombed by weeds and overgrowth, her segments fractured by rusted rails upended by storms and mudslides, till they intersected an extinct road. We drove slowly; I watched Leo, his ghost eyes particularly keen, like he could see through all the overgrowth better than us, and when he gave the word, I spoke up and Chris stopped the car.

"Here," I said, exiting and looking first up one stretch of the track and then down the other. "Here was where the train conductor died." Marion found a place to pull off in a small dirt alcove just off the road.

"How can you tell?" Dr. Blake asked. To her credit, there was little to discern this desolate stretch of road from any other on this two-lane highway, either side lined with pine and oak for as far as the eye could see in either direction.

I shrugged like that was an answer to her question. "Chris tells it better." I looked at my brother. What I needed was to bide some time while I helped the detective search for the path. Around us all was silent, not a car for miles, and the tops of the pines swayed in a late-afternoon breeze. We had to get moving. It hardly ever snowed in South Arkansas, but the nights could be brutally cold. We took turns at the trunk of the rental. Marion and Samantha carried overnight bags, but, in addition to my overnight bag, I also had a bag full of other things, and Chris' second case held a myriad of electronic equipment I'd asked him to gather for the trip. All that any of them knew, up to this point, was that I'd found a place secure from the prying eyes of MR. MITS and the PRI, and we'd be staying the night, and that Chris, who was as familiar with the area as I, would need to provide us some rudimentary electrical power and a secure internet connection.

Chris said, "He wasn't a conductor. He was a signal maintainer on the Missouri/Pacific line that ran down here to the old logging camps. One night the tracks were washed out—a bad storm had come through—and he caught word of a train speeding along because it was late for a pickup. He walked out at the switch-track, swinging his lantern to notify the conductor, signaling that the train needed to stop till he had the chance to switch the track, but the conductor maybe didn't see him, or maybe he just didn't care.

"The mud was still slick, and as the signal maintainer reached the track, swinging his lantern, he slipped. Just then the train rolled over and decapitated him." Chris paused and looked around to gauge the response of his listeners. Dr. Blake looked aghast. Marion stood stone-faced. I had heard the story enough that I was now desensitized to it, though hearing a good old-fashioned ghost yarn always brought a smile to my face. It might have been my brother's penchant for storytelling—one of the few good things he inherited from our father—that got me into studying the classics and literature and mythology, and then brought me here. Still, smiling may not have been the best response.

I glanced over to our ghost. Leo stared down the track and saw something I could not see. There was sympathy in his eyes. I reached up to him but he brushed my hands away. A tear rolled down his cheek. I followed his gaze but saw only the swaying pines, the lonely, silent track. It wasn't until I looked away that peripherally I saw the headless figure strolling along the track, swinging his lantern.

"They say you can see his lantern on certain nights, swinging back and forth as his spirit walks up and down the track," Chris said, "searching for his missing head."

"It's probably swamp gas," Dr. Blake offered.

"The house," I said, drawing all their attention, "should be just over this rise," and I pointed over my shoulder into the woods. Without a word, we hiked over the red-clay ridge into the forest. The path threatened to vanish beneath the overgrowth, and at times, not trampled for ages, weeds obscured our way, but our ghost resumed his lead and pointed me through the flora. This enabled me to lead the others until we stood under the shadow of the two-storey farmhouse with pitched roof and multiple gables.

The shadows were already long and late, the day waning. The front yard, probably once seeded with Kentucky bluegrass, was now overgrown with chest-high blades of swaying dead fescue, and knots of crabgrass like giant dun spiders wriggled their limbs in the evening breeze.

I gave them a moment to take it in: its whitewash now gray and peeling, its wraparound porch, a steepled roof with dormers.

"I know this one as well," Chris said, stepping forward to stand shoulder-to-shoulder with me. "There was a cowboy back around the turn of the century who stepped in on a card game here, once. It was his first time here, but other wranglers and outlaws had used this place before. Our ... what was it ... our great-grandparents ... must have been kids here then. Anyway, he sat in on this card game and was winning most of the night, and as he won the others began to get privy to his machinations."

The trees swayed in a cool breeze and Dr. Blake shivered, which Chris answered by offering her his coat, then draping it across her back. In the gilded light of sunset, the pines loomed over us, tall and menacing. The shadows promised only mysteries and horrors.

Chris continued. "They accused him of cheating. They strung him up with chains and drug him downstairs and dropped him on the floor and shot him full of bullets, and when he was dead, they drug him outside and buried him ..." Chris turned and pointed behind us to the tree line "... there.

"The card game continued on into the night. The pot shifted hands. Laughter. Joking. Someone had brought moonshine and whiskey. The mood lightened more. Around two a.m., as the game got serious again, a new sound could be heard on the stairs. It was the sound of chains rattling on the risers, and heavy footsteps slowly ascending to the second floor."

Chris looked around. His audience stood in awe. I always loved this part of the story. Usually someone asked, and this time it was Dr. Blake who spoke up.

"Was it the cowboy?"

"The men wouldn't talk about what they saw," I said, diverting all their attention to me, finally. "Those that survived, that is. Several of them were gunned down. The bullets came from the one cowboy's gun, and that gun was still chained up with his body when it was recovered out in the mud."

Overhead, a thunderclap hollowed out our cores, and pellets of rain assaulted our outer garments. To the east, a bolt of lightning flickered dangerously close to a copse of pines. A wall thundercloud had ambushed us.

"We best get inside," Chris said.

As we rushed up the porch steps to the front door, I bit my tongue. The house's other story was why we were here.

II

The last rays of light filtered in through the dusty screens of the windows. From where I stood in the foyer, I could see the living and dining rooms, the cracked walls and peeling wallpaper that helped reveal the age of the edifice.

A shuffle upstairs drew our gazes, as though we could see through the ceiling.

"What was that?" Dr. Blake asked.

"Nothing," Chris said, a bit too quickly.

I said, "We have another story to tell."

"Then tell it," Dr. Blake said. "Before it gets too late and we can't leave."

"We have time. We're spending the night here." I said this a bit too gleefully, to the shock of my entire party. While they knew it was to be an overnight trip, none expected that we'd be anywhere other than a cozy hotel, especially not at an abandoned farmhouse.

Our first priorities as the sun set were to establish light and warmth. We unpacked flashlights and candles and scattered them about the ground floor. I returned to the car and unpacked a cord of firewood from the trunk, which Marion and Chris lugged back to the house. A fire roared in the fireplace less than ten minutes later; luckily the flue wasn't clogged. Only after the fire had knocked off the chill in the room and the candlelight flickered in defiance of the sunset shadows did I tell them what we were doing in this house.

"I had an ulterior motive for bringing us here," I said. I looked out the window to the lengthening shadows. Night seeped in from between the trees, encroached on the house like an invading army. The storm provided the necessary ambience befitting a stay in a haunted house. "I bought this house. Got it for a song, some would say. Not me, I wouldn't say that, but somebody might."

"Why in God's name would you buy this place?" my brother asked, and he looked to the others as if to say, *See? Look how mentally unstable he is.*

"There's a Wi-Fi tower on the outskirts of town," I said. "Did you bring your laptop?"

A bemused expression on his face, Chris nodded slowly. I suggested he turn it on, log on.

"I can check my service," Marion said, but I stopped him, raising a hand.

"No," I said. "They know your phone. We don't want them to trace us here. Chris has ..." but the techspeak to accurately describe his computer skills evaded me, so I just said, "... camouflage for his presence online."

"I can reroute my known connections through several LAN connections stemming from this local tower. Each of those LAN connections will also be dispersed. By the time anyone can trace us back here, we should be long gone. Why, though?"

"What's the other story?" Dr. Blake asked, and hugged herself. "I feel like I'm the only one out of the loop."

I was the only one *in* the loop, however. "The ghost is with us," I said.

"The dead cop?" Chris asked incredulously from over the rim of his laptop.

"Detective Knight, yes. He knows that I asked him here for his keen insight. It seems the dead, more so than the living, are able to peer through the flotsam and jetsam of life to get to the truth. But he doesn't know why Marion doesn't trust his new boss, or why Mr. MITS is dangerous. Marion doesn't know that either, but we know that our residences aren't safe. They could have them bugged. Our most frequented places could be bugged. This place isn't; it's safe from Mr. MITS."

"And that's why you need me?" Chris asked. "To give us a secure line here that they can't bug."

I nodded.

"Adam," Dr. Blake said, reaching for me, with eyes that were consoling, sympathetic, but horrible, because she looked as though she pitied me. "If you don't trust them, we need to know."

What she meant was, if I was that delusional or paranoid, they needed to know. I bit my tongue. It would not be prudent for my case if my illness proved to be overwhelming me.

"He's right," Marion said. "This PRI is something different. They use a Black Ops team, and that man in the suit—"

"Mr. MITS," I corrected.

Upstairs, something shuffled. Chris gave a start and cast his eyes up. Reflexively, Dr. Blake grabbed my arm. Detective Leo Knight vanished then reappeared and shook his head. Marion, in this short spurt of time, reached for his gun.

"Someone is in the house," Chris said.

"No," I said. "We're alone. I should probably tell the other story now, before the night—before it gets worse."

"Worse?" Dr. Blake said.

"There is more than just the ghost of the murdered cowboy in this house," I said.

III

I told the story as our father told it to Chris and me. I found the story's rhythm metered by the flickering candles and by the flames in the fireplace. The shadows retreated and advanced, tangoed with the light. Far off, lightning flashed.

"A family moved in not long after the cowboy gained his revenge. They were Black, a mother and a father and their three kids. The one daughter was older, older than her brothers by five years or more."

At this, I stopped and looked around to the encroaching shadows and I looked to my friends who stared at me, even Chris.

"They were scared of the shadows that moved without bodies. They were tormented nightly, and no one in the area knew. Not until one day when the father brought his two boys to town, to Mr. Runyan's general store down in Crossett. He brought them in and bought them each an ice cream cone and sat them on the front porch and had Mr. Runyan call the sheriff. And then he confessed. They boys just went on eating their ice cream cone, oblivious to what their father had done."

"What did he do?" Marion asked.

Three deep breaths, slow, gave me time to look them all in the eye. "His wife, the kids' mother, was found in the cellar, slumped on the dirt floor, a pickaxe buried in her skull. One quick, swift blow."

"Where was the girl?" Dr. Blake asked.

I knelt and ran my hands over the wooden slats until I could feel the loose boards. After all these years, while I was afraid that the house had been torn down or someone might have bought it and remodeled the ghosts away, I was more afraid I would not be able to find the loose boards. More dust had settled over the years, and at first, I couldn't jostle them, but with some prying, the boards gave way and I lifted their bellies to the beam provided by Chris' flashlight. Faded and dried as they were, we could all easily see the scratch marks against the underside of the boards, the dried blood that had stained streaks of black into the faded gray slats, the bare dirt floor underneath and the mealy crawlers and earthworms slinking and lurking under the house.

"He buried her here," I said simply.

But the scratches revealed were more than just frantic struggling and clawing to escape the makeshift tomb. Samantha knelt to look closer. I gave her time to discover the faded words.

"Shadow Folk," she said finally.

~

I had three plans for the night. First, I wanted our dead friend to patrol the perimeter of the grounds and the house. It would be great if he could communicate with any spirits, but we needed a guard against the ghosts. We needed him to keep away any visitants while I enacted the second phase of my plan. As comical and stereotypical as they were portrayed in popular media, Ouija boards served as an important direct communication tool. I had studied the use of the board for years, its history. I knew the kinds of things that could be summoned whenever the ignorant cast a wide net. I did not need the Shimmers tonight.

Our third plan was to go hi-tech, and Chris helped immensely with that. He had brought a bag of tricks, some mini cameras, some microphones, a router. He hooked up wireless eyes and ears around the house and recorded everything to his laptop, monitoring this continuously while Marion, Dr. Blake, and I began the Ouija board. The candles we placed at twilight were enough to give some definition to the living room, but not offset the night vision capabilities of his cameras. Then we began:

Are you with us?
YES

Are we talking to the Father?
NO

Are we talking to the daughter?

NO

Who are you?
S-H-A-D-O-W-F-O-L-K

"There was something," Chris said, staring into his monitor. "Up in one of the bedrooms on the second floor. Like a blur. A dark blur."
What do you want?
L-I-F-E

Whose life?
Y-O-U-R-S

"Dear God," Dr. Blake said. "Adam, it's a trick. These things are tricks. You manipulated it somehow."

I shook my head. She looked to Marion, who shook his head as well.

"What are Shadow Folk?" she asked.

I took my time to gather my words. I knew they might—probably would—think me insane. "Shadow Folk are different from most other spirits. First, they don't haunt places, but people—in particular, children. Legends spoke of families espying the Shadow Folk hovering over the cribs of babies. It's said that the Shadow Folk devour familial spirits until they are strong enough, and then they go after children. A lot of times parents back in those days would find their kids dead in their cribs, and what we'd call SIDS now was attributed to the Shadow Folk."

"And you think they're here?" Chris asked me.

Looking around the room, I saw Marion and Chris, and Dr. Blake, but Leo had already vanished, presumably to begin his search. "They are," I said.

IV

As Detective Knight patrolled the grounds, a figure of impenetrable darkness blotted out the night, the shadows, and the grounds. It swirled around him, a jet whirlwind in the still of the South Arkansas evening. There was a menace to the indistinct features, though he could discern no scowl on its blank face. It was more of an echo of the entity, whose indistinct silhouette shimmered into and out of existence.

"You are brave coming here, Casper. You are helping those people?"

"I am," Leo said.

"You know what we are?"

"I do," Leo said. "But we have no children. What we do have are questions about this house."

"You want this house." It hissed the sibilants like a snake; Shadow Folk were just as trustworthy.

"We need a place to operate away from prying eyes."

The shadow man growled at this then swirled again, consuming Leo like a hurricane. The detective hadn't even had time to react. "Unacceptable," it whistled.

~

We separated to investigate the house and grounds. Flashlight in hand, I walked slowly through the downstairs, my narrow beam illuminating the hall, the floor. I could hear the footfalls of the others scattering to other levels and rooms. Chris sat near his gadgets in the living room, monitoring the cameras and microphones from his computer, while Marion found the cellar door in the kitchen and descended the rickety steps. Dr. Blake began a slow and careful ascent upstairs.

I entered the back bedroom. Now furnished only by dust mites, cobwebs, and rat droppings, I imagined a queen-sized frame and a dresser; there wouldn't be room for much else. I guessed this had been the parents' room. Shining my light around all the floorboards, I turned in place, listening. I opened the closet door and peered inside, aware immediately of a presence behind me; I felt something watching me, the hairs on the back of my neck raising. When I turned, however, the darkness revealed nothing. .

"Leo?" I said. No. "I know you don't want me here," I said. "We want to help you, and we need your help. We need to hide here from time to time—"

The bedroom door slammed shut. My cell buzzed. I glanced down to find I'd received a text from my brother. It read, "Get OUT now!"

Movement caused me to tear my gaze from the phone. I was surrounded by black figures like animated silhouettes dancing in the moonlight, cascading through the window. They probed my mind, flitting in and out through my body, violating me. And then as quickly as they were in the room with me, they were gone. The door opened on its own, and I hurried back to where my brother had been perched in the living room. Except he wasn't there.

~

The upstairs consisted of a dark hall with several doors leading to other rooms. The silence stood nearly impenetrable. Samantha saw Chris's webcam and a microphone. She flashed the light around the hall, praying silently that it only illuminated the walls and the floor. But then why was she up here, if not to catch a glimpse of something, like that night in the hotel when she saw the ghost of the detective? Perhaps, she realized, to prove to herself that there was nothing, or that what she saw in Texas was an aberration, for there couldn't be ghosts and witches and demons fluttering about. There was no room in her worldview for such things. She tried to tell herself this before she considered her old friend Puck.

Puck was odd. Puck was an aberration, like the ghost detective. He was tall and strange and did not comprehend normal ways. But what he was she did not know, only that he made her feel safe when he was around. But he didn't come around much, and he wasn't here now.

Footsteps from behind. She turned, flashing the light back toward the stairs. The heavy thump of boots on risers, slowly ascending, the rattle and clank of chains and—spurs? She backed away, her light never leaving the stairs, but the beam trembled where it fell, like an oscillating strobe powered by fear.

"Adam?" she tried. "Chris? Marion?"

Nothing but the slowly rising footsteps. Her back hit the wall. She could not tear her eyes away from the other end, from the sound. She'd counted thirteen steps when she climbed to the second floor; she'd heard nine footfalls. Ten. Eleven. She swept the beam around the top of the stairs. Twelve. And saw—thirteen—nothing.

She closed her eyes and sighed, relief as embarrassment flushing her cheeks. She became aware of sound again, of the patter of rain on the tin roof above and she opened her eyes to the dark hall. Just in the periphery to her right, an opened door exposed movement, and she swallowed a scream.

The cowboy stood next to her. Nearly a century of rotting in the peat had worn away his features, though he wore his clothes and his hat and the chains still. He leveled a pistol at her head and pulled the trigger, and this time she did scream, sure she was dead.

But she still stood, and in the second that she had blinked at the gunshot, the cowboy had vanished again.

Without hesitation, she bolted for the ground floor to find only me in the living room.

"I saw Shadows," I said.

"I saw—" but she couldn't finish it. She looked around. All the equipment was still set up, and it seemed to be functioning. "Where's Chris?" she asked. It didn't seem likely he'd leave his gear unattended.

"I don't know," I said.

The cellar door exploded open.

~

"Shimmers," the Shadow Man hissed. "Casper's friend is plagued by the Princes."

"This bothers you?" Leo said. He was weak from his encounter with the spirit, slick as oil and squirmy as he imagined an octopus might be.

"We are just as worthy as the princes. We have delivered more damned delicacies to the ovens of Hell."

"The Shimmers—the princes have all the power," Leo said.

"You give them power!" The shadow man was enraged, and Leo took a quick step back. "You sstudy them and their namess, and you fear them because you ssee them. But we are nameless. We can sslink in quieter than the tromping hooves of Greed or Avarice or Lust or the Crown-Prince himsself. We sspawn in the corners of the ssoul till a man hass to listen to uss. Like the loving and doting father—do you believe that such a ssolicitous man would do what he did, unless we prodded and prickled and fiddled and fondled?"

117

So, they were manipulators, Leo realized, and never gave something for nothing. They were demons of the deal. The question was, what did they want?

~

When the flashlight flickered and died, Marion slapped its bottom, but nothing. Removing his cell phone, he found the LED light app and, turning on the digital light, shined it across the cellar's dirt floor, mealy earthworms turning in the loose soil, something squishy squirming in one of the many dark corners of the room. Down here, the rain echoed hollowly, and thunder was but a grumble, and the smell of something festering permeated his nose.

Maundering something intelligible, Marion wondered if this was necessary, not the goal to learn what haunted this house—he understood that before they could use this place as a safe haven, they would have to conquer and own whatever resided here. No, he wondered if they could ever have a safe haven. It seemed wherever they went, Mr. MITS could find them. But there was something else about this place, something dark that they may not want to uncover. What had happened to that little girl buried here by her father? He turned in place, trying to get his bearings. If he were under the living room, as he thought, then the little girl couldn't have been buried under the floorboards, because the light shone boards above. Perhaps the living room was there, he thought, shining the light on a dirt wall.

From behind he heard a shuffling, a rustling, and he pivoted as the LED light clicked off. He fumbled with it until it turned back on, and he saw, huddled in the corner, someone with their back to him. But the door hadn't opened or closed, and no one had descended the creaky, frail wooden steps.

The figure stood and turned, a short Black woman in a flower-patterned dress, her head split open wide, her skin faded to ashen gray, her eyes appearing to look in different directions, but both still seeming to focus on him. Her mouth (the split in her skull hadn't reached that far down) worked like a goldfish, the lips soundlessly forming words or searching for breath. She regarded him with sadness, and as she stepped toward him she vanished.

Marion couldn't take his eyes off the spot; he stared for a moment, expecting her to return. When she didn't, he turned to leave. She stood on the bottom step, blocking his egress.

"Leave," she said. "Before the shadow folk get you too."

He didn't move. Couldn't. He hadn't expected her to talk.

Around him the shadows swirled and the ghost screamed as the darkness washed over her, pulling and clawing at her and tearing her image away in bits and strips until there was nothing left. When her scream faded to a whisper, the shadows swirled again, and Marion saw a blackened phantom, featureless save for two red eyes.

Marion ran up the steps, busted through the door back into the kitchen. More screams erupted, this time from the living room. Screams for him, living people he recognized, his companions calling his name, both Adam and Samantha afraid, possibly they'd seen what ran in the darkness also. Bright lights blinded him as the screams stopped, and to save his vision, Marion shielded his eyes with a forearm from the flashlight beams that assaulted him. Samantha and I lowered our flashlights once we recognized him.

"We have to get out of here," Marion said. "I don't think we should come back here anymore."

"We can't leave yet," I said. "Chris is missing."

"We'll find him," Marion said. "Then we'll leave."

~

"What about the cowboy?" Leo asked.

If the Shadow Folk had lips, then this one smiled. "Avarice came that night. Said he could make a bigger story than us. What do you think? Do you think a dead cowboy back for revenge is as potent a cautionary tale as a father who pickaxes his wife's brains and buries his daughter under the floor?"

"And which of you were responsible for creating me?" Leo asked. Waking up to learn that you are dead and not understanding why is like going to sleep in your bed and waking up on a park bench on Mars. He advanced and the Shadow Man took a step back.

"Another demon, not a Shimmer and not a Shadow Folk. But a demon nonetheless that…your word is 'possessed,' but that is too weak, too temporary a word…*hijacks* the bodies of men and women to complete its work. You had caught on to it in your cases; it knew that, and it had to kill you. Self-preservation, as you humans say."

Had Leo's ghost a mind? If so, then it raced to fill in the blanks. What cases? Did it mean he knew his killer? Had it been a suspect he was chasing? One look at the Shadow Folk, though, and he could read enough to know those were all the answers it would divulge. If it was even telling the truth.

"You didn't like it when Avarice was here," Leo said then. He smiled because he could smell the hate the Shadow Folk wafted when one of the princes was mentioned. Perhaps he could use that to get more answers.

"The Princess aren't welcome here. They taint our 'here' and make our work meaninglesss. But you want to use our 'here' too. Cassper wantss uss to protect his kith and kin and bloody friendss from the Princess."

"Just while we're here, on this land."

"But we are ssso bored," it said, and the featureless silhouette seemed to mope and pout; this shadow man paced.

"What do you want?" Leo asked.

"A deal," the shadow man said.

V

There came another flash across the screen. Not a flash of light but a shadow, whizzing across the camera in the bedroom where I had stood. In the upstairs hall, Chris saw Samantha's heel, but in the far corner, was that a figure? He wasn't sure. The corner appeared blacker than the shadows upstairs—or perhaps that was a trick of the light—and what looked like two red eyes could have been a glare on the lens.

There came a sound like a footstep. Chris's head shot up, his eyes darting around the darkness. The candles that had been placed around the living room only teased at illumination. In actuality, they made the shadows that much more opaque. And while the fire warmed, the firelight gave life to the shadows, allowing them to roll over the walls.

He checked the living room camera feeds and froze. He saw his own back; behind him, moving slowly, was a young girl with red eyes. His hand trembled, hovering over the mouse. He was afraid to move and clung idiotically to an idea that she wouldn't see him if he stayed still. She stepped closer, and closer, and when she was almost to him she raised a hand to his shoulder.

Out of the corner of his eye he could smell her death, he could see her hand, the fingers she'd raked across the underside of the floorboards in a desperate attempt to escape her tomb, peeling off her nails and flesh in strips that now hung from her digits like strips of old cloth.

Chris screamed and turned and ran for the door, then down the steps, then out into the yard into the rain. He spun in place, unsure where to head as the rain came down, drenching him, sheets of it blinding him to his surroundings. He thought about the car; when the lightning flashed, he saw an old barn behind the house. But then he saw *them*, the cowboy and the girl and her mother with her head split open and their blood-colored eyes. They approached from different paths, joined by featureless shadows with blood-colored eyes, and as all closed in around him the three ghosts lost their details until they too were featureless shadow-figures with blood-colored eyes. Chris bit into his fist to stifle a scream, looked frantically over his shoulder to back away but he was surrounded. He removed his fist and screamed out, his voice drowned by the roll of thunder as the shadow folk encircled him, and then another figure was next to him, a Black man with a badge on the breast of his coat — the dead detective he'd heard me talk about. That he could see my delusion only served to unnerve him more, and Chris sank to his knees, to the mud, and let the rain wash over him as he screamed again. He was either going insane or he was going to die, and he was prepared for neither.

A flash of lightning, then thunder rolled across the clearing. The pines swayed in the torrent, and then the rain slowed to a drizzle and the wind died down. Chris jumped as he felt a warm hand on his shoulder. He looked up. He was still surrounded, but only by us. Rising to his feet, Chris looked first in my blue eyes, then Samantha's turquoise, and Marion's green.

"Is it you?" he asked.

It was my hand on his shoulder. "Yes," I said.

"Was that the shadow folk?" Marion asked.

"Yes," I said. We finally felt the rain as our hearts settled, and we filed back inside to the light and warmth of the fire in the fireplace.

"We can't come back here," Dr. Blake said.

We can, the dead detective said. *I made a deal.*

"What deal?" I asked. While the others questioned what I meant, I listened to Leo recount vaguely what the shadow folk had suggested. Finally, to my brother, doctor, and partner, I said, "No, we can. The Shadow Folk wanted us to know they were here. But they're working against something, something that might make Mr. MITS an enemy, and they'll ensure that neither he nor his will come close. They won't reveal themselves again." But at this I frowned, a look Chris knew all too well, with my furrowed brow and crooked mouth; I'd been forced to tell a lie for the greater good. But for the moment, it satisfied everyone.

Chris said, "Get your electricity turned on here, and I'll make sure the lines and connections are safe. We'll set up a permanent network that this Mr. MITS won't be able to hack."

I wanted to know the specifics of the deal Leo made; when he refused to tell me, I worked off my suspicion. When we returned home the next day, I subscribed to the *El Dorado Tribune* and watched the stories closely. Most were yawn-worthy. A few of the less boring stories involved hitchhikers, either passersby or passers-through. All of them had stopped near the house but no one made a connection. When the hippie family's van was found near the tracks and their bodies were found scattered on the grounds of the old house, the police went after some escaped convicts. Ripped to shreds all of them, from the twenty-five-year-old patriarch to the two-month-old daughter, they managed to gun them down before the cons could be questioned. That was not the end of the deaths; whatever deal Leo made, that was what we got: a safe haven. In return, some people vanished and some more died.

For myself, I knew that Leo was not an evil creature, but this was the moment I really saw him. I've long believed that our motivations define our actions as either morally just or morally bankrupt, is, and I was sure

122

that Leo's spirit was still working for some sense of justice. But sometimes, despite the purity of our motives, sometimes our actions are so black we cannot justify them. I was sure he'd crossed a line and that loss of trust worried me.

What had he compromised to secure our safety from Mr. MITS, from the Shimmers, and from the shadow folk?

7

ZEITNOT

I

Three o'clock one random morning a week or so later: blustery winter winds whipped about the eaves of the Chicago apartment. Marion sat up in his bed, alerted to a sound on his nightstand, his room dark and cold because he slept more soundly in colder temperatures. His tours in the SEALs had trained him to awake clear-headed no matter how soundly he slept. Recognizing the caller by the tone that played, Marion skipped the formalities as he answered.

"I'm here." Still, he rubbed his eyes. The voice that responded was muddled and cold, alien at first, like it spoke under mud.

"You have forty-five minutes to get to O'Hare. Even then you'll just make it through security to catch the flight."

"Where am I going?" Marion asked. He rose and inspected himself in the mirror. There might be time for a quick shower.

"You still want our mutual friend?" ADA Builder didn't need to ask the question, as Marion was sure his old boss knew him well enough. Whoever the man in the suit was, he was up to something. He was in a dangerous position in the government—mid-level with a lot of power, easy to disappear if things got rough, with little apparent accountability—Mr. MITS could cajole and intimidate and even kill, then vanish into the labyrinthine halls of bureaucracy. But all Marion had, for right now, was just a hunch that the man in the suit was up to something more than just a midlevel power grab. He had positioned himself, a knight disguised as a pawn ready to topple a king or—if not yet so brazen—perhaps a bishop, a rook. He was up to something. E4 to G6.

"Yeah." He pulled his suitcase from his closet and, opening drawers, began slamming underwear and socks and trousers into his carryon.

"Gate A8. O'Hare. Clock's ticking." His old boss hung up. His phone signaled he'd received an email, and he viewed the e-ticket, the itinerary, and finally the destination: Brandenburg Airport, Berlin.

Marion took a sailor's shower, dressed, and rushed out the door. The cab picked him up promptly and drove him to the airport, a ride just long enough for him to contemplate what he was doing. He knew nothing of his mission but rode on a promise that information was forthcoming. Instead, he followed the crescent moon hovering just above the skyline, and thought about what awaited him.

Nothing. Darkness. The cold touch of horror. That's what he felt as he passed through security and took his seat and sipped his coffee on this transatlantic flight. He'd known the assistant director long enough to trust his information, but his time in the SEALs and his time on the Washington Beltway watching the Machiavellian political moves of seemingly everyone working for the government had reinforced his own desire to confirm all information, no matter the source.

II

By the time Marion landed in Berlin, he'd had the opportunity to twice review the encrypted file sent by his old supervisor before deleting it. The target Marion had been sent to protect was a Bavarian business mogul. Simon Zeitnot was the thirty-three-year-old heir to Zeitnot Industries, whose father had passed away six months earlier after a long battle with prostate cancer. Among Simon's inheritance were an energy research think tank — The Hanz Zeitnot Institut fur Deutschland, a medical research facility — Deutsche Institut fur Fortschritte in der Medizin, a state-of-the art German cancer treatment facility, and the pockets of several Deutsch politicians, a UN ambassador, and a couple of Washington lobbyists. Those were the big, publicized pieces of the Zeitnot fortune. What was well-known but never discussed was the Zeitnot Airfield in Austria. Situated on the wide mountain plateau, shaved of its trees, the airfield might have been visible from space if it could be detected by satellites, but rumor had it that state of the art cloaking technology, developed in house at the airbase, helped shield it from prying eyes. That's because Zeitnot Airfield was known, in quiet, clandestine circles, as a research facility in its own right. It was the only privately-owned military research airfield in existence in the world, and its late owner enjoyed Top Secret privilege, thanks to his government contracts. Simon, according to the now-deleted dossier on Marion's laptop, had inherited his father's clearance when he inherited the airfield.

The dossier offered up a lot of evidence pointing to Mr. MITS' interest in the young heir. In fact, much to Marion's surprise, someone was secretive as the man in the suit proved highly visible. Airline tickets and military flight manifestos to Germany and Austria matched up with stills from security footage that, blurry as it was, showed Mr. MITS traveling to the country. More stills showed the man in the suit meeting with various Zeitnot allies and players, almost all of whom were nervous about handing the keys to the kingdom to this young, unproven heir. It wasn't unfathomable that a clandestine figure like Mr. MITS could be positioned to stage an industrial coup. This wasn't some hare-brained conspiracy theory. The Zeitnot bigwigs had spokenvocally spoken[1] out against Simon's placement at the head of the country, thinking that someone more familiar with the goings-on of the business should have been put in charge. The dossier contained numerous articles showing their outrage. It was all but a given that these players wanted Simon gone. But Marion couldn't see what Mr. MITS had to gain. A hunch told him this man was more than just a gun for hire, but he couldn't figure out the man in the suits' endgame because he didn't know enough about the man behind the suit.

"It's obvious he wants to reveal something," Marion said. He spoke to his old boss in generalities and revealed no names over the Bluetooth call as he drove down the autobahn. "Who's set to inherit the company should he not make it through the day?"

"It's a consortium of corporations that own minority shares in Zeitnot Industries," Tom Builder said, "set to divvy up the financial estate while leaving the home and personal belongings to his wife and kids."

"So *he* has a stake in that consortium," Marion said.

"Or he works for someone who does."

"Supplemental employment? That might be considered treason."

"You and yours don't exist anymore, friend. Everything you do for the government might be akin to treason."

"Do we know how?"

"High profile. There must be proof of death."

"For an unquestionable ascension by his successor?"

"Or a message to anyone else who might want to be transparent."

"I'm ten minutes out," Marion said, and hung up.

III

Simon Zeitnot had stayed up most of the night preparing his speech, but he was not tired. The truth of his father's business — the scope and totality of which he'd learned over the past six months — energized him, for the truth was life-altering. What he had understood as his world had been expanded by light years. Before learning this truth, despite what science class had told him, the stars were merely sparklers in the sky, tiny princess cuts that glistened when the sun went down. Now they were a place, an address as tangible and reachable as the Caymans, as Munich, or New York, the Guggenheim or the Empire State Building. Space-time, he realized, was merely an expansive autobahn, and now he had access to the best technology to drive that autobahn.

It was Simon's desire — nay, his responsibility to share this truth with the world, a truth that contained revelations. It would advance mankind two centuries, at least, just in the time it would take him to hold this press conference, and that was a conservative estimate. This truth would lead to much faster growth than if he stayed silent and let the current, exponential, evolution of knowledge continue unabated. He was going to kick growth in the ass, as the American COO of his research hospital liked to say. If current technology and scientific knowledge were a ninety pound weakling, Simon was about to inject that weakling with steroids and HGH and turn him into a three hundred pound ripped behemoth.

The office door opened and closed. There wasn't enough of a reflection in the window to show him who entered, but Simon recognized the cologne, a musky scent preferred by his attaché and long-time friend Pietro. He turned as Pietro poured himself a glass of vodka and savored it. The poor man, uncomfortable in a three-piece suit, was more at home in a polo and golf pants, or a bathing suit and his Russian mistress on his yacht.

"Are you sure you must do this?" Pietro asked.

"Relax, old friend," Simon said, and turned back to look out the window. "After today, the world will know the truth."

"Or think you stark raving mad."

Simon chuckled. "Is that what you think of me?"

"No." Even not looking at him, even with that single, short, one-syllable word, Simon could hear the quiver in the voice of his boarding school roommate. "I have seen too much to not recognize you are telling the truth."

"Yes," Simon said. "There is but one truth, now."

He could see enough of himself in the glass to adjust his own tie, and then he turned and patted his friend's shoulder. He walked out the door.

~

Now alone, Pietro felt like his spine was going to crumble. How he had held it together so long was beyond him; he grabbed for the table to brace himself. He felt heavy, weighed down, and so removed a single shot pistol from his coat pocket. The man in the pinstriped suit had been so persistent just this morning. He said that it would be neater if Pietro did it. It would be understood. For payment, he promised security for both Pietro's and Simon's wives and children, and for Pietro he offered a swift death.

"No suffering," he said. "You won't feel a thing."

"And why would I do this thing?" Pietro had asked. "Hurt my friend, as you ask."

The man in the suit sneered and spoke in a flawless Austro-Bavarian dialect. "My dear sir, I said kill him. I never asked. I told you. Would it not better serve the world that Caesar be stabbed by his Brutus?"

And that was to be his role, to which he was condemned. He was Brutus. He was Judas. Which told him just what his life was worth now.

~

Even as the day pressed towards the afternoon for Marion, the dawn was just breaking as Dr. Blake strapped on her running shoes and set out from her house on the Razorback Greenway, an asphalted trail stretching thirty-plus miles from South Fayetteville to the Missouri state line. Samantha set out on her little section, prepared to tackle five miles, round trip, a smidgeon of a section of the trail. Runs for her were times of reflection something akin to prayer or meditation for the religious. She used the time to clear her mind and let her thoughts wander, to reset. The early morning exercise served her as much as a cup of coffee or a bowl of oatmeal, or morning mass.

There were few people out on the trail this morning. She ran, unencumbered by traffic or fear of aloneness. A low fog settled over the path but didn't restrict visibility, and the air was autumnal cool, the dew of the grass adding a bit of humidity to each intake of breath, a refreshing spritz urging her on.

Alone with her thoughts, Samantha considered the case in Texas, from the appearance of the dead detective to the witch's arrival. She thought about the Shimmers and about what happened to the little boy in Wisconsin. Most of all, she thought about my diagnosis.

Now, before you get ahead of yourself, dear reader, I can tell you now, so many years later, that she wasn't incorrect in her diagnosis. Nor have I misspoken, for the most part, of the events that have transpired, that I've recorded in what looks like will end up being five volumes, of which you are reading just the first. If you are hoping for some happy ending where I am relieved of my mental health issues, you are sadly reading the wrong story, just as if you are hoping that the Shimmers are a figment of a diseased brain. The unfortunate fact is, both are true, but still I have found some closure with this diagnosis, and we that have survived have mourned the dead, not limited to my visitant investigator, whose murderer we finally revealed several years later.

No,[2] Samantha took stock on her run of where we all stood at that moment. It is an imperfect analysis, mind you, metaphoric as the morning forced the fog to lift around her, but still shielded so much. Presently she saw a cyclist or two; an old shirtless man jogging at the pace of a power walker, his muscles sagging; a coed out walking her docile Mastiff giant, subservient on his tiny leash.

The ghost, she decided, was real. She still wasn't sure how, as the "brain as transducer" definition lacked experimental validation, though it felt good as a workable hypothesis. There was more than just a mental conundrum to unravel there. As complex as she realized the ghost and my psychosis proved, including things like the Shimmers and an all-powerful witch only further exasperated the questions. So she ran, prepared to solve all the mysteries, but familiar enough with the mysteries of consciousness and the mind to not just excuse all that was alien with scientific hubris, and while not accepting of a hard and fast definition yet, Dr. Blake was open to resolve the possibilities, however they presented themselves.

IV

Marion recognized the possible assassin, and he felt sick. He discerned another chess move (I was the chess player and had won every game we've ever played). D2 to D4: expose a pawn by moving him out front. Suddenly he understood what ADA Builder had meant, that by working for the PRI he was now an accessory to treason. The man he saw, strolling through the crowd, whose eyes focused on the podium where soon Simon Zeitnot would stand and deliver his truth, was one of the men from the Black Ops squad that often accompanied us on our missions, or followed soon after to clean up. Nudging his way through the crowd, desperately trying to remain inconspicuous, Marion tailed his target right up to the front steps. A crowd gathered as Simon Zeitnot emerged from the building, bundled in a tight wool coat, smiling and raising his leather-gloved hands as though to embrace the world.

"The world has assumed for many years," Simon said, his smile dropping just a little, "that they have known my father's business. But I am here to tell you that you do not know everything about Zeitnot Industries."

Marion's target lifted his left arm to block out the sun and adjusted the dials on his wristwatch. Marion thought the man should have an umbrella or be wearing sunglasses and looking toward some grassy knoll (unlike Dallas, this area of downtown Munich had no such geographic feature nearby), and then thought that was too on the nose.

"Zeitnot Industries. Our motto, our stance, has always been to make the world a better place. Now we have that opportunity. What I must share with all of you will change your perceptions of reality itself. It will ensure that humanity will transcend war, and disease, and crime, and addiction. It will allow us to finally reach up to Heaven itself."

"You call for transparency," one reporter said. "Does that mean you're calling out your competitors?"

"Please," Simon said, "hold all questions till the end."

Marion stepped up behind the man he recognized and held his own service pistol tightly in his coat pocket as he pressed the barrel into the small of his target's back.

"Please," Marion whispered. "Hold all questions till the end. Did the man in the suit send you?"

The man made a move but Marion shook his head and said, "Tsk tsk. I was a SEAL. You should've known that."

"I do. You should have known that *Mr. MITS* always sends the whole Black Ops squad." There was a chuckle in his tone. "Isn't that what your retarded friend calls him?"

Just as Simon was describing the cancer hospital's miraculous advances, a shot echoed through the concrete canyon of downtown Berlin. The crowd, stunned frozen for just a second, included Marion, who watched helplessly as Simon Zeitnot collapsed behind his podium mid-word. A second later, chaos began. People screaming, and Marion, fully aware that his target hadn't fired a shot, let go of the gun in his pocket and knocked him out anyway.

Marion quickly scanned the countless windows that overlooked the plaza, searching for a figure or a pane of glass opened or removed. All around him the crowd devolved into panicchaos[3] . Security guards had their guns drawn and police were arriving in patrol cars and scattering about as civilians ducked for cover. Medical personnel rushed out of the hospital to attend to Simon Zeitnot, but Marion knew it was too late. He focused instead on the man at his feet. He rolled him over and was dismayed to see that he now foamed at the mouth. Still squatting, Marion lifted the target's but found only the scleral white of eye, and a quick pulse check revealed no heartbeat. He hadn't hit the man that hard. He opened the mouth now, and saw, in the froth, hints of a white substance. Apparently, the Black Ops team came with their own self-destruct button: a cyanide capsule. To verify that, Marion thought of shipping the body back to Quantico, to an ME Tom trusted, but when the cops surrounded him with their guns trained on his head, he realized that transporting the body might not be an option.

~

At the local precinct, stripped of his street clothes, badge, wallet, passport, and his gun, Marion sat in a poorly lit cell, handcuffed to the table. His German was poor and it had been a long time since he'd used it, so he wasn't sure what he'd said at first to the Inspector. In a moment of linguistic confusion, he may have said *federali*, which was why the German laughed. He might as well have said, *I am a hotdog.*

The door opened and the Inspector poked his head in, looked back and then ducked away. Marion was not surprised to see Mr. MITS appear. He walked in and sat down across from him, smiling. In this semi-lit room he seemed a small, smug, little man.

"They say," he said to Marion after a moment of silence, "that too much time in a room like this robs a man of his cones and retinas. His sight becomes little better than cave-dwelling animals. Blind as a bat, they say, eh?"

Marion had just enough length in the chain around his wrist to fold his arms across his chest. This was not the time to reveal his hand, what small hand he had. Two pair of shit and Mr. MITS sat there with a full house. Mixing metaphors, or games, he thought; he'd been checkmated.

"I vouched for you, Agent Case. They were curious what a US federal agent was doing in Germany, and they thought your arrival seemed a little coincidental given what transpired, but they know you did not assassinate Simon Zeitnot."

"Did they question what you or the Black Ops team were doing here?"

Mr. MITS extended his arm and perused the freshly manicured nails of his right hand, then curled the fingers and blew at dust he imagined still clung from the filings. "Agent Case, neither I, as you know me in this incarnation, nor our Black Ops team, that aids you and yours on occasion, exist, as far as they are concerned. I am merely a visiting aid to the US ambassador stationed here in Berlin, and the man who died was an American tourist whom you were unfortunately close to when he suffered from his heart attack."

"Heart attack?"

"That's what their ME will find. Agent Case, I don't want to frame you. I don't want to hurt you. I want you to be a part of the team. That's why I vouched for your hire. I really hoped you'd be a team player."

"And if I'm not, what? I rot here? Or maybe you go after my team. Maybe you want Adam gone."

A flash of anger washed over Mr. MITS's face. He leaned forward and slapped the table in one swift move, quick like a rattlesnake strike. "I pushed for you. And I pushed for him too. Even Colonel Hamilton wasn't sold. He thought Adam Richardson was too unstable, but I sold him. I knew the two of you working together again would be what our department needed to get the job done. And when his brother and his doctor wanted to come along for the ride, it was my acquiescence that gave them clearance."

He leaned back, breathed, and took a moment to straighten his tie and his suit and settle back into his skin. "But their clearance can be revoked. Maybe you and Adam are needed to get the job done, but his brother sure isn't. And there are plenty of shrinks in this world. And as for you? This place? In two hours, you'll be back on a flight to the US."

"Someone stands to gain from Simon Zeitnot's death," Marion said. "There is something more going on here."

Mr. MITS stood and readjusted his suit and knocked on the door. When it opened, he considered what else he had to say, but did not turn around to face Marion when he finally said it. "Agent Case, there is always more going on than meets the eye."

~

"Isem R. Smitt, Esquire," Tom Builder said as Marion boarded the plane, phone to his ear.

"Who?"

"His name keeps popping up on signatures of these different conglomerates that are taking control of the Zeitnot estate. For some of these companies, the only thing that connects them is their Zeitnot holdings and his name. Marion, I told the German authorities that you were working there on a hunch that Zeitnot was in danger, and they've given me authority to look into the Zeitnot holdings. We have a team on it . . ."

"But . . ."

There was hesitation, an audible sigh. "But there's a lot that's redacted. Even with their cooperation and a subpoena, I don't know how much we'll get."

"Looks like Simon's truth dies with him," Marion said.

"We know that truth."

"Do we?" Marion asked. "I want to bring him down. He's dangerous. That's all I know. Or think I know. The question is, how did you come by this information, Tom?"

"I shouldn't have sent you," Tom said. "You're going to make this personal."

"This sonofabitch is dangerous," Marion reiterated. He dropped into an available leather seat and smacked a fist on the armrest with no real authority for fear of damaging the private aircraft. The *why* nagged at him. Mr. MITS was a positioner, a chess player, but why position himself in a clandestine agency? Yes, it gave him above Top Secret clearance, even compartmentalized access, but why this particular agency? The CIA and other departments in DHS, these could provide more information. Was he hiding something within the PRI? Had he positioned himself in the agency to guard a secret? No, probably not: too passive, too defensive. While he obviously had secrets to protect, Marion was sure Mr. MITS had another angle: he was after something. And if what he was after was in such an agency as the PRI, then this man was even more dangerous than he'd already assumed.

As the plane ascended, Marion considered all he'd uncovered with his security clearance. But another question had taken hold of his thoughts and wouldn't let go—how had ADA Tom Builder learned of these things? Just as importantly, why was his old boss trying to insert himself into Marion's new job?

V

While Marion was losing a real life game of chess in Munich, Chris had picked me up in a Camaro and had steered us out to Highway 23. Leo had asked me if I wanted him to tag along, to which I said no, hoping for some private time with my brother. This wasn't the same sportscar I had been in several times already, red with a moon roof. No, this Camaro was a Hennessey Exorcist Convertible, a black car with black top and black interiors, and a bit of white trim. He put the top down in the parking lot in front of a racetrack abandoned for the day..

"There is a modified Charger that's called the Demon," Chris said, pulling onto the track. He shifted to first and engaged the brake and the clutch, sending the car into a restless idle, the car shaking and trembling and itching to move. To do what it was called to do. To deliver us. Chris stared hungrily at the stretch of pavement before us, its arc and curve, and I cinched up my seatbelt and gripped a space on the console and also the armrest on the door. Pearl Jam played on his iPod through the console, "Lightning Bolt."

"Not too fast," I whimpered.

"Like you," Chris said, "That car needed an exorcist. That's the nickname the Hennessy Company who modified the Camaro ZL1 gave to their creation — the Exorcist. It can race down and beat that modified Charger and just about everything else on the road. I have wanted this automobile ever since I first heard it came out. And now I have one."

Within two seconds, we hit sixty, the Gs pushing us back into the seat, the hurricane-force winds stretching smiles on our lips. We hit the first curve at 100, topped the next stretch at 200, finished a full lap and squealed out of the gate, angling the car towards the Scenic Pig Trail, Highway 23, where he strived to straighten the curves and break the sound barrier on land.

How far we traveled, how long we were out, I could not know. The car, with us in it, left behind all concept of time and space. I'm sure it shot us into another dimension full of laughter and 70s and 90s punk and alternative. Pearl Jam was followed by Green Day's "Welcome to Paradise" and "Sabotage" by the Beastie Boys. We heard the Cramps and the Misfits and Nirvana and the Dead Kennedys. The day tried to catch up to us but failed because he never put the top up and we didn't slow until Chris found a gas station. He pulled up to a pump like he was going to gas up, but I was surprised to see that he hadn't used much of the tank of gas. He shut the engine off.

He gripped the wheel tightly and nodded at it, then looked at me. "You were always there for me, you know it? With dad's shit."

"You were my little brother," I said. He turned the radio down. On the other side of the tank, a motorcycle idled loudly. "I had to protect you."

"I know," he said. His hands fidgeted on the wheel. There were few places my brother felt unconfident, and behind the wheel of a sportscar was never one of them.

"What's wrong?" I asked.

He took a deep breath. "You don't really believe in all that, do you? Ghosts and demons and monsters? Do you?"

He looked at me desperately, like it was essential that I told him, no. I thought about doing so, in fact. His look so desperate, I thought about just telling him it was all a big goof, that I was putting it on. But I faltered, or something, or maybe I just stumbled in my words, or took just a little too long.

He dropped his eyes and shrugged his shoulders and sighed heavily.

"Chris," I tried.

He shook his head.

"Let's go," he said, cranking the radio again. He peeled out of the parking lot, squealing between vehicles on the city streets, ribboning the car through traffic, beating lights. I tried a few more times to reach out to him, but the traffic noise and the music was too much.

Chris pulled into the parking lot where Dr. Blake's office was located, and I realized that our afternoon drive had been a diversion. Soon enough, I found myself in my psychiatrist's office, staring past the potted plant out the window to the temperate winter day. I felt ambushed, betrayed. Samantha had offered us both something to drink before we settled into our respective chairs: Dr. Blake behind the desk and my brother by my side.

"Adam." The way he said my name. I knew that tone. "Dr. Blake and I have been talking, and we have come to some conclusions." I saw them exchange a look. "We believe this PRI, and especially Mr. MITS, are very dangerous."

The words settled in the office, worthy of their weight, before my doctor added, "Neither of us fully trust Marion, either."

The pain in my chest flared up despite the fact that last I'd looked, the scratches were healing nicely. I hadn't had any trouble in a number of days, so I rubbed at the spot absently.

"I'm just not convinced," Chris continued. "I just think the "shadow folk" and this detective could be a hallucination. Like mass delusion or something."

"But you saw Leo," I said to my doctor. I had scanned and uploaded key elements of his file to my One Drive that I could access on my phone. I pulled it up now and passed it across the desk. I watched her scroll through it; I could tell by the expression on her face she'd seen his photo.

"That's him," she said quietly, and passed my phone to Chris who studied the file with the eye of a skeptic.

"And you met PJ Harlow," I said to Chris. "You picked her up in a bar. You can't ignore that, or the fact that she cast that amnesia spell and abducted me."

"You say magic spell," Chris said, "and I say she drugged my drink."

I looked across the desk. "Is that true? Are there drugs that can make you forget someone existed?"

"There is a category of depressants that can affect consciousness and memory—"

"For a week?" I said. "Without the administrator present to continuously apply the dosage?" She didn't answer, but she was conceding my point with her eyes.

Finally, she said, "I've dissected the spell repeatedly, and while I can't reconcile it yet with what I know to be true, I can't deny it."

I rubbed my chest again and tried to remember if I'd dreamed of the witch the night before.

"Bottom line," Chris said, "this new job is dangerous, and that strange man is dangerous, and your old partner is keeping you in danger, and so he's dangerous as well."

I rubbed my chest again, and this time Dr. Blake noticed. She asked me what was wrong. I stood and lifted my shirt, revealing the scratches that marked up my torso.

"I didn't have these when I was rescued. Didn't have them until a few weeks after, when I dreamed about the witch, and she reached out and scratched me in my dream." I let that sink in as I recalled something PJ Harlow had said to me once. "I'm afraid, whether I'm involved with the PRI or not, that these things will keep coming after me. And if that's true, then shouldn't I be prepared?"

"Adam," Dr. Blake said remorsefully.

Chris leaned in to look at the scars. All he could say was, "What did you do to yourself?"

I pulled down my shirt, and sat down, deflated. I hadn't the words. How dare he blame me for this, but before I could say it, he stood and loomed over the doctor.

"As his guardian, I've made up my mind. He is not to interact with Marion Case or this PRI anymore. And if you can't help me enforce this, then I will call the State Psychiatric Board and bring to light your encouragement in these actions."

Dr. Blake stammered.

"I swear to Christ I will have your medical license yanked. How dare you!" and with that, he slammed a fist on her desk. "How dare you keep that trip to Texas from me. Goddammit, I can't forget that. If I'd have known, none of this would have—"

She rose, trembling, and raised a finger to his face. "How dare *you* walk in here and call into question my professionalism, and how dare *you* raise your voice and threaten me and disrespect me in my office."

"I'm concerned," Chris tried to backpedal.

But she'd found her courage. "You want to be blind to what we've seen, then you have that right. How you choose to reconcile your beliefs and your senses so you can sleep at night is between you and your higher power. But you don't get to dictate the beliefs of others no matter how much you might disagree with them."

"I wasn't trying to—"

"Get out."

He stood, dumbfounded.

"You slammed your fist on my desk! Well, know this. I videotape all my sessions. You go to the State Board, then I will show them how you physically tried to intimidate me."

Chris's face reddened. I knew his anger. I wished she would stop because this was going to bite me in the ass later.

"You may drop him off for his sessions," she said. "And I think we should all plan to revisit the PRI soon, you included, Chris. But you are not to step foot back in my office again. Are we clear?"

My brother said nothing, but straightened, jammed his hands in his pockets, turned and walked out, banging the door shut behind him.

The fading echo of the slamming door gave her time to collect herself. I watched her hands cease to tremble before she spoke.

"Adam, schizophrenia is about perception. Your perceptions manifest inappropriate behaviors and emotions in your day-to-day life. Even if the ghost is real and the witch's powers were real—let us even concede that she reached out from beyond the grave and scratched your chest—and we saw the Shadow Folk, how *you* process this: that is still your diagnosis."

"You think I scratched myself?"

She shook her head. The confrontation with my brother had exhausted her. The way she rubbed her temple, I imagined a massive headache was building behind her skull. "As your psychiatrist, I must evaluate your symptoms as they manifest. Given what we've seen, I can no longer write off all your perceptions as hallucinations, but it would be dangerous to assume that everything you experience is real. We must move forward carefully, evaluating each case individually, and you need me more than ever to help determine what is real and what is false."

The session was over. She scheduled our next appointment and gave my shoulder a brief squeeze, and with her eyes said I shouldn't worry about my brother. But I was concerned because Chris controlled my fate. I worried about her diagnosis, and I felt defeated. I'd labored with the hope that either my hallucinations were part of my disease or I had been misdiagnosed and what I saw was real; I'd hoped for the latter. I never imagined that both could be true. This would make my climb to sanity that much steeper and that much more treacherous, and I wasn't sure I was ready to scale such cliffs. I walked outside to see Chris leaning on the hood of his car. His arms were folded across his chest and he stared off to the distance, and as I neared he unlocked the car with a beep. He drove me home without speaking, and dropped me at my door just as wordlessly, squealing the tires as he sped off just as I shut the door.

VI

The man Marion and I knew as Mr. MITS walked into an unassuming office building in downtown Chicago after debarking the flight from Germany. He walked through a door with a frosted glass pane with a name in gold lettering: ISEM R. SMITT, Esq.

"Hello, Mr. Smitt." His secretary was pretty, and wore a floral print dress. She'd worked for him at this office for exactly a month, just long enough for it to appear legitimate, but this alias had been in use for a little longer. He waved to her and smiled then walked into his own private office. It was a room he'd contracted off the books with trusted government construction contacts. This {4} unassuming office had been remodeled with soundproof insulation and a secure line that was virtually untraceable. He had a large desk and a leather chair that was comfortable. He sat in it, propped his feet up and fished his alias's cell out of the drawer. He dialed the only number in the contact list.

"Reinhold," he said. He did enjoy trying out new accents, and this one he'd been practicing for the man on the other end of the phone for quite some time. "Dear boy, Reinhold, how are you, old chap? Yes, it's Isem. How are you, old bean? I'm well. Right well. Feeling good, they might say. And how is Marge, and how are the kids? Smashing! Well, old chum, it's not all cookies and cream with me, this call. I'm checking on our holdings. We've been dabbling, correct? You spread my investments as I asked? Wonderful. Have you looked?"

Mr. MITS could hear him typing. The man on the other end was a nervous, balding and middle-aged Jewish man with a ruddy complexion and an astigmatism, constantly pushing his glasses up his nose. The typing stopped. His silence told Mr. MITS everything.

"I...you read about Zeitnot? You...how did you know? You made out like a bandit!"

Mr. MITS smiled. "No, old boy. *We* made out like bandits. Take your usual fifteen percent and give yourself a ten percent gratuity on the top."

"Thank you, sir."

"For your financial acumen and your personal discretion. Remember what we discussed?"

"Yessir," Reinhold said. "Isem R. Smitt doesn't exist." Mr. MITS hung up. He smiled. Checkmate.

VII

Sunset was beautiful to behold, with all its desert colors fading into the eventual night, warm to cool, orange to indigo.

I sat in my living room, my blinds open to the north, so that the sunset came in the periphery, the light fading as my new roommate materialized. I'd made some hot chocolate for myself after a dinner I'd prepared from a Food Network recipe. Only Beelzebub joined me for dinner, but I wasn't disturbed, and ate ravenously.

"You aren't scary," I said, not wanting to miss the sunset, the colors, the dipping below the horizon which existed behind Old Main and the university campus.

"I don't want to scare you," the dead detective said. He sat in my recliner as I sprawled on the couch.

"What do you want, then?" I asked.

"I want to know why I'm like this," he said after a minute. He sighed, as if ghosts could sigh. How much energy had he to expend now that, in life, was so available?

"You're like this because you are dead," I said. The marshmallows were melting quickly into the chocolate. The consistency was perfect – just enough milk and not too watery.

"Why am I dead, Adam?"

I could feel his eyes on me. Still, I was afraid to answer. Afraid, because I wasn't sure I was prepared for the journey. I could barely care for myself, and I felt, daily, that I was broken. And here was this other presence that, if he weren't just some figment of my broken mind, was an entity that needed me to be stronger than I was.

"I can't help you," I said, mimicking Leo's sigh as though I were catching a yawn. I let out my weakness, my frailty, my helplessness. Still, this didn't deter my phantom.

"You can," he said. "And I'll help you. As I promised. I need you, Adam, and you need me."

My cup now empty, I set it on a coaster on the glass-top coffee table, then reclined on a couple of throw pillows, and closed my eyes. The nighttime was sweeping into the apartment at an alarming rate.

"I need sleep," I said. My arms folded over my chest in repose.

"Rest, my friend," the dead, Black detective said. "You need your strength to help me solve my murder. You'll rest more when I'm finally at peace."

"You're a figment," I muttered, but without conviction, and I soon slept on the couch as night poured through the blinds. He let me continue peacefully, without the usual interruptions like the violent moment of his death to rouse me. When the dawn came, I awoke more satisfied than I'd been in a long time.

One or the other, or choose a different adverb!

Dear reader - if you keep this aspect, I'd better see it in other places. If not, this paragraph doesn't fit.

Chaos already began in the prev para. Suggest "panic" instead?
you used unassuming in the prev para. Please replace one.

8

INTO STONE GARDENS part two

I

She had asked me if it would be safe, but I could only shrug as an answer to my brother's deepest motives. I reminded her that the meeting would occur in public, but that did little to assuage her. For a few minutes, she fumbled with the paperweight that held down nothing.

"He was really a bastard to me last time, Adam. I really shouldn't acquiesce."

She always grew pretentious during high personal drama. The traffic outside interrupted the stillness of her office, and so her analysis of the idea of meeting again with Chris.

"Still," she said, and bit her lower lip, an indication that she was thinking.

"Chris isn't dangerous," I said. I was thinking of him as my brother, whom I'd known for decades.

To this she nodded. But there was a flicker of doubt in her eyes, a little golden flame that suggested, when you looked right at her, that her eyes were less blue, than tinted with a gild that suggested more of an emerald. Like that tint, under a particular light believed true, her smile weakened as she offered it to me.

"What did you call me here for, Chris?" she asked, sitting in the restaurant on Dickson, again smiling politely though weakly. Outside, winter had finally arrived in Northwest Arkansas with a polar chill carried by a northerly wind that was, for the moment, deterred by the east/west line of brick buildings that made up the various eateries and bars and venues. Inside, the buildings were large, old, and not well insulated; most people, including Samantha and Chris, left their coats on.

He looked tired, his eyes swollen and darkened. They darted around, never settling. If she'd not known better, she'd have thought he was on drugs. She offered a sigh, then dropped her head and reached over the table to him. He didn't pull away.

"Am I going crazy?" he asked.

She shook her head. "What's going on, Chris?"

The bar around them was in the process of shifting from lackadaisical afternoon slosh to techno-driven co-ed. Outside, the afternoon light was giving way to the winter solstice with a promise of shadows.

"I read about it, the things he sees. Apparently, they're real. Or, his delusions are based in reality."

"Maybe that's it," she said. "Maybe he read about them too."

He shook his head and squeezed his eyes shut. A fist pushed against his cheek.

"But the detective is real, isn't he?"

She pulled back and bit her lip, a physical sign of her doubt casting on what she'd come to believe. That's what it comes down to, kiddoes. Doubt is physical and belief is spiritual, and so doubt will win out every time.

"I saw something," she said.

"And Marion saw it too," Chris added.

Slowly, considering her next move, Samantha nodded. When the waitress approached again, they both ordered more drinks.

"I visited an old professor who gave me this book," Chris said. He was toying with the silverware to his left and eyeing them just as heavily. "It was full of the... things he's talked about. The pictures of the ones he calls the Shimmers look exactly like what he's described."

"You are wondering if Adam had access to these references prior to his manifestations, and yes, it is possible that he had."

"The pages turn," Chris said. The tabletop wasn't as interesting as his gaze

145

afforded it.

The words hung in the air, even as the waitress returned with their drinks. Absently, Chris stirred his coffee and stared at the tabletop, and Dr. Blake thought about my diagnosis and my delusions. And about what my brother had just said.

She considered the ghost we had seen and wondered if I were sane, and quickly, on the heels of that, if she were. Then there was the fact that Chris might be burying some delusion all his own. Among the toys in the Richardson family's attic, perhaps the lone, sane mannequin was also possessed.

"What do you mean?" she asked.

Chris sighed heavily, and when his shoulders dropped, it was as though a great weight had slumped off them. Still, he couldn't raise his eyes. "This book, a demonology book, my old professor gave me."

"Okay." She wasn't sure where this was going, but her fear for him increased.

"I took it home. I shouldn't have, but I did. Can you forgive me?"

An odd question, one she chalked up to him being completely unsettled. She didn't know what else to do but nod and offer him a smile. "What happened when you took it home?" she asked.

Chris sighed, leaned back, regarded his place setting, the half drunk cup of coffee.

"The pages turned. I found a demon that Adam talked about, and the pages turned. I thought of a demon that Adam talked about, and the pages turned."

"What do you mean they turned?"

Chris sighed. "I mean if the book was left open to page 138 when I left it on my coffee table, when I returned it was on page 160, and on page 160 was some Succubus or some Incubus or some demon that I'd just been thinking about."

She took a moment to look him over. He was distressed, like he hadn't slept, and he was evidently bothered by this revelation. Might he have left open a window, or been running a ceiling fan? She cast these two ideas away instantly, given the temperature outside. Still, she asked and was not surprised that he shot them both down.

"How many times did this happen?"

"Five," he said, and downed the rest of his coffee. "So far," he added.

She ticked off a few explanations, each of which he shot down. No, he hadn't been mistaken. No, there was no chance of a breeze either from an open window or a vent. The binding allowed the book to lay flat, so the pages wouldn't turn on their own. He didn't know what could be doing it. "I would get the book back to your professor, then, as it's causing you this discomfort."

He could only shake his head at this. "The source of my discomfort is that my fucking nutjob of a brother might be seeing monsters that are real."

She considered this and remembered that I was being called back up to the PRI in another day or two. What she had to suggest, he would not like.

We all hopped a flight to meet Marion in Chicago as soon as Dr. Blake and Chris could get time away from their jobs. For me, it was a much-needed change of scenery; despite my meds, I could feel the Shimmers encircling me. They were closing in like a storm building off the coast of my sanity, with roiling thunderheads that broadcast their arrival long before the torrent. I said I wanted to investigate the detective's murder, but I did not tell them that I had to go for my own sanity. It wasn't till we were taxiing to the terminal that I realized, in my haste to pack and in my anticipation for this flight, that I had in fact forgotten to take or pack my medication. What's worse, I feared the Shimmers knew this too, and were biding their time.

We found a cloudless though windy day when we landed in the city, with arctic gusts from the lake topping forty miles an hour. As we walked across the breezeway from the terminal to catch our ride, we always seemed to be against the wind. And though our trip was merely from O'Hare to downtown, to the federal building, we found ourselves confined to the leather seats of the PRI Lincoln for almost two hours.

When someone else has a say in your quality of freedom, based on your mental health, you find you can afford few secrets. I told them I'd made a promise to discover who murdered the detective who now visited me. Chris scoffed. Still, I knew it was for my stability they were concerned. Not justice.

We were in a nice ride; the Lincoln had been converted into a stretch limo. I sat, looking out the window, across from the two people currently in control of my freedom, who faced the rear of the car. Beside me, but not too close, sat the detective whom only I could see.

"I exist," Leo Knight said. I questioned my own mental state, as one with my diagnosis is prone to do, but I'd also been questioning his existence in case it weren't tied to my sanity. There are a lot of people who claim to see ghosts yet haven't been diagnosed with some mental illness. He had to have picked up on this, a fact that made me feel, not in the least, violated; that, if he were real, meant someone could penetrate my thoughts at will.

But I also felt bad for him. "I know you do," I said aloud, which confounded my corporeal companions. "I just want to ask a few questions." Then I resumed staring out the window.

Marion met us at the federal building and led us up to the PRI offices. The cubicles had been abandoned for the day by the time we arrived, but Col. Hamilton still worked on paperwork and—like a fly on the wall—Mr. MITS watched us.

Marion tossed me a file. I opened the manila folder and read the scant but familiar pages, copies of the files he'd sent me once before. A refresher.

"Scenes from the murder of a Chicago detective," I said when Dr. Blake asked me what I read. I handed her the file so that she and Chris could peruse it. Leo seemed extremely interested in what it contained and leaned over their shoulders to read the file also.

Detective Leo Knight, out of the 53rd on the Southside, had been gunned down one night several months earlier at his brownstone apartment, where he lived alone. He was survived by a wife but no kids. His father was in Cook County. His mother's whereabouts were unknown, and his caretaker when he was a child, his grandmother, had passed five years earlier.

"I remember that," Leo said. "I remember standing at her hospital bed.

I remember I held her hand. I remember she squeezed it and she tried to smile when I told her I made detective."

I said, "He lived alone in the apartment, but the file says he had a wife."

"Don't go there," he said. He had squared off to me and stared at me without blinking. He was a few inches taller than me, or maybe as a spirit that's what he wanted me to believe.

"I have to go there," I said. "If you want me to solve your murder." I don't think he agreed with me, but I think he understood. This exchange alerted the whole office, and all eyes turned on me, nearly all activity stopped, something that might have been comical if not for the looks on the faces of those around me, especially those worn by my brother, doctor, and friend. At a nearby desk, a phone rang. Mr. MITS cleared his throat, then leaned over and picked up the receiver. He mumbled something, placed the phone back on the cradle, and ambled over to our little group, smiled, and looked to my doctor.

"Dr. Blake. Would you be so good as to accompany me? It seems we have a case, and I would certainly appreciate your expertise on the subject at hand."

"I'm afraid I'm not an agent of the PRI," she said. "I'm here merely to assist Adam... Agent Richardson."

"I need her," I said, and he looked at me and blinked and smiled, looking a bit like a toad.

"I am only asking, Dr. Blake. I am not in a position to order you, but your expertise is sorely needed. We have, it seems, a serial in Seattle, responsible for a dozen deaths; and while most of the suspects are in custody, some of the most dangerous are still at large and the local PD is afraid more deaths will come."

"'Serial' suggests a single killer," Marion said.

"I don't see how I could help," Samantha said.

"My apologies for not being clearer," he said. "The suspects are all recent recipients of organ donation from the same donor, who was a known pedophile and serial killer. The recipients were all blood matches, in desperate need of his gifts. Rare blood type. They received his organs just after his execution."

"They got more than they bargained for," I said.

"You're talking cellular memory," she said. "It's science fiction."

"But you've heard of it and you are aware of it, so you can help me," he said.

From the inner pocket of her light jacket, Dr. Blake's phone buzzed; she excused herself saying she had to check her texts. When she returned, she looked as though she was about to say something she didn't want to say.

"I'll go."

Chris and I were both pretty vocal against her going, insisting that someone we trusted go with her, like Marion, but then I felt an icy hand on my shoulder and realized who must be touching me. Mr. MITS had turned his Cheshire grin on me.

"She's important to you. I get it. I'll protect her." The smile was not reassuring.

II

After Samantha walked out the door, Chris and I spent several minutes blaming each other for letting her go, scolding each other that she was unprepared. Our voices were raised, and I was sure Colonel Hamilton could hear us, but we argued, nonetheless. It wasn't until we both received a text that we both noticed that Marion had backed away. We quieted. The text was from my partner.

"I think we should go for a walk," the text read.

The three of us—trailed by the ghost—walked out of the building and into a nearby alley. We waited in tense silence as Marion scoped out the area. He pulled out his cell, dialed a contact with a single button and spoke into the phone.

"Secure South, three, East, one through three, and West, one, two, and five, near escape routes I49 and two West near Dan Ryan and Halsted, twenty clicks. Jam all electromagnetic frequencies at 620 kilohertz and below."

"I don't trust Colonel Hamilton," Marion said, approaching us. "I don't trust Mr. MITS, either. I trust you two, and I trust your dead friend, I trust your psychiatrist, and I trust our old boss."

"ADA Builder?" I said. I thought we'd left him in D.C.

"He has looked out for us," Marion said. "Here's the deal. I texted Samantha. I told her to go with Mr. MITS."

Chris exploded. He jumped up, grabbed Marion's collar, and slammed him against the brick wall of the federal building with such force that he nearly lifted Marion off his feet. Not fazed, Marion glowered down at my brother as perturbed as a bull bothered by a fly. My brother's gym physicality was no match for my partner's muscle and military training.

"She has the best chance of all of us of getting him to let his guard down. If any one of us can learn anything, anything at all from Mr. MITS, it's Samantha."

"And what if he kills her?" Chris asked.

To that Marion pulled up his text history and showed Chris what he'd written.

"It's up 2 u," the text read. "U r the best chance @ learning who MRMITS really is. If u go w/him, learn wh8 u can. If u don't want 2 b put in this position, then say NO."

"She didn't say no," Marion said.

Chris let him go.

"You two, work with Colonel Hamilton and your ghost and start investigating this murder."

He straightened his suit jacket and adjusted his tie, then turned to exit the alley, when Chris yelled out to him and asked where he was going and what he was going to do.

Marion did not turn around to face us to tell us of his plans. "I watched a man get murdered because he owned a special company, a company that had a lot of fingers in a lot of different projects. I want to see just what all Zeitnot Industries has been involved in."

I wanted to tell him that the correct syntax was: "… and I want to see in what all Zeitnot Industries has been involved," because you shouldn't end your sentence in a preposition, but by then he'd walked out of the alley and Chris and I were left alone.

III

151

Captain Morris Planter, a fat Irishman with curly red hair, was a cop from the South side—specifically, from Behind-the-Yards. He'd been made Captain of the Bridgeport precinct ten years prior to Detective Knight's murder. We waited ten minutes to see him, while the dregs of the neighborhood paraded through to greet us. Chris's ogling suggested that he even found the hauled-in, drug-addicted and scantily clad prostitutes attractive, which told me that my brother had a serious problem.

When we finally walked into the captain's office, he greeted Chris and me as my ghost silently retreated to the corner. He took his time to return to his seat behind the desk and smiled amiably at us. I noticed he had one green eye and one blue-grey one.

"Well, gentlemen, how can I help you?"

Chris and I exchanged a glance. We'd rehearsed this many times, but previously Marion had agreed to accompany us. Now that he was gone — that is, now that we were without his badge — we'd appear a lot less official and amended our rehearsed story on the fly. My brother was always good at amending his story.

"We're government consultants," Chris said. "I'm an expert in computers and my brother here used to work for the FBI. His old partner is now part of Homeland Security and has asked for our support in a case."

"Computer specialist, eh?" Captain Planter said. He opened the top drawer of his desk and pulled out a can of salted pecans, walnuts, almonds, and cashews. He dug his paw into it, pulled out a handful, and popped them in his mouth. He studied us both for a moment, crunching loudly.

"I love this town, boys. I love everything about it. I guess that's why I became a cop."

"Christ Jesus," Leo said. "He gave me this same damn speech the first time I met him."

"I love the architecture of this town. I love the history of this town. That's what's allowed Chicago to grow and prosper. Architecture. History! It is a story that no other city in this country—hell, in this world!—can match. Perhaps it's either its story or its architecture that defines a city, but rarely it's both. LA has a great story and a pretty good skyline, though from a distance it looks like any other metropolis. New York! New York has both. But think about other cities. Think about Memphis, or Dallas, or Little Rock."

As he paused to munch on more mixed nuts—the can promised each serving was heart-healthy, but this wide girth of a man had already exceeded the daily serving with his second fistful—I began to wonder why he'd pick cities so near to my home. I hadn't yet told him where I was from.

"Memphis has the Pyramid," I offered.

"I said Beale Street," Leo said, "and we argued for a bit over whether recognizable features meant skyline or landmarks…"

"And there is a story for Memphis, sitting on the River, but in Sweden or in Bangkok they might recognize another Memphis—more ancient. But Chicago, a city built back up after it was burned down by a cow, built on so many industries, a city with a skyline recognizable by anyone traversing Lake Michigan, is a city that the world knows. Her history, shrouded in dark, in mystery, is a history known to everyone.

"But I didn't join the police force to turn this city into Mayberry. No, I'm far too world-weary to believe that could happen. But tranquility could still happen. Do you boys believe in tranquility?"

"I'd like to," Chris said. He seemed transfixed, almost hypnotized.

"I said that too," my ghost said. I looked over my shoulder and saw solemn remorse in Leo's eyes.

"You will, Leo," I said. Throat clearing, harrumphs, and nudges righted me in my seat, where I found both the captain and Chris stared at me.

"Leo?" Morris Planter said. His brow was furrowing. His face was paling with the loss of blood.

"That's what we're here to investigate," Chris said. A lot of people looked at me like he looked at me now, with equal parts revulsion and fear. Didn't mean I was used to it.

"The Department of Homeland Security is interested in the death of Detective Leo Knight," I said. "We think a terrorist cell that has been suspected in the area was responsible." Story amended.

"And what would you like from me?" Captain Morris Planter asked.

I grinned at the motivational wall art behind his desk by the oversized street map of the city and her suburbs. Chris answered, "Case files. That's all. We would appreciate all pertinent files concerning the death of the detective, including any active cases he was working on at the time of his murder."

The captain considered our option with a nod and another fistful of nuts, then stared at his desktop for a while, still nodding.

"Give me your address," he said finally. "I'll send you what you need."

As he ushered us out the door, I turned to prod for one more question. "His wife?"

"Laura," Leo said.

"Laura?" Morris Planter replied. "What about her?"

"What's her address? Where does she work?"

He paused a breath, and retreated to his desk, where with pen and sticky-note he jotted down the answers to my questions. Handing me the tiny yellow square, he smiled, and slammed shut his office door.

~

Chris steered our rental into the parking lot of CVS on Halsted and Fifty-First. I noticed the bars on the windows and wished again that Marion was with us, or that I was still certified to carry a firearm. Near the entrance, a lean Black man bulked up by his dirty, muddy rags begged for change.

We found her in the health and beauty section, straightening the perfumes. Leo tensed as we neared, and he lagged back for Chris and me to take the lead.

Laura Knight was stunningly beautiful, with high cheekbones and her own natural hair falling straight to the middle of her back. She seemed to keep herself in shape. She smiled at us with a row of bleached ivory circumscribed by full crimson lips. Her dark skin and features contrasted her eyes, wide and blue-green like Caribbean waters.

"Can I help you find something?" she asked.

I wished I had a badge to flash to set her at ease.

"We work with the Department of Homeland Security," I said.

"We're interested in the murder of your husband," Chris said.

154

She took an instinctive step back and raised a hand to her mouth, as though to stifle a scream.

"Leo?" I allowed the horror to settle on her face and rest in her soul. Her face settled into indignation, into anger; her brow furrowed, and a frown aged her ten years. I could see in her eyes that she no longer trusted us.

"Leo? Let me tell you 'bout Leo," she said. "We was separated when that son of a bitch got himself shot!"

I studied her. "I mean no disrespect, but you've received an education above and beyond high school. You are a smart woman, and yet you work at a menial job stocking shelves. Why?"

"How you know that?" she asked. Ferociously, she wiped away a tear and took another step back. She would not meet my eyes. Chris eased his arm around her and led her away, and I turned to see my ghost, his eyes on the floor, his hands in his pockets, his shoulders shrugged.

"It's in the file," I said, and though it might actually be, I'd heard it from Leo himself.

I looked back. Chris was hitting on her now, rubbing her back, smiling at her. I couldn't hear his voice but I *could* hear it, soft and smooth. She seemed entranced, but her head snapped up and she arched away, staring back at him with black, venomous eyes. I quickly looked back to my dear, dead friend.

"I couldn't protect her," Leo said.

"What do you mean?"

"She was hurt. I don't know. *I don't know!*" I reeled from the volume, the force like a punch to the face, staggered back and knocked an endcap display into the aisle.

"You couldn't protect her?" I said. From behind, Laura had torn her tear-filled gaze from my brother and approached me, a delicate hand raised to my shoulder.

"I was raped," she said, a whisper meant only for me.

"She hated me, I couldn't protect her," he choked out.

"You hated him," I said.

"No," she said.

155

"But we couldn't work through it," he said, and turned away from me bitterly, biting his own fist. The emotional range of the tormented spirit must stretch longer, thinner, more violently than anything the living can experience.

Her eyes glistened. She reached up to my cheek. "Leo? You... you see him? You know him? How?"

I nodded. "He said you couldn't work through it," I said.

"I wanted to," she said.

We'd reached her. And there was my validation. More than the file my old partner had sent, more than Marion and Samantha seeing the specter in the hotel in Texas, this was proof that he was more than just a figment of my imagination. He was real. He'd been known and he was loved. And that meant I had to find his murderer. But that would be the only breakthrough we'd see that trip.

Laura Knight's manager kept us from interviewing her further. He didn't like the mess I'd made in the aisle and said we should leave before he called the real cops. I told him he could call Captain Planter and he did, standing between us and Laura like a shielding parent. It didn't take long for a couple of uniforms to arrive on the captain's orders and escort Chris and me off the premises. Had Laura wanted to talk more? I wasn't sure. Maybe all she wanted was to commune with her husband like I was a medium, so he could use me like I was Whoopi Goldberg.

~

We spent that night in a Chicago hotel, a nice one downtown on the PRI's dime, and I convinced Chris that I needed my own room. The Shimmers had been flitting around my head all evening, biding their time, I assumed, for the remainder of the medication to seep out of my system. I didn't want Chris there when they came. Finally, alone except for the detective, I watched him pace, his gaze focused on the floor till I screamed out.

Around me, the Shimmers fluttered and spoke. They poked and prodded at me like I was a mole and they were inquisitive, mischievous children who'd just discovered me, and laughed when I cowered from them, me this timid little creature who'd wandered onto their playground. They whispered, then screamed, occasionally both at the same time; the seven Shimmers threatened and promised all in seven breaths. They called my name angrily, and they called it seductively. They called my name softly, they screamed it and pleaded and mocked.

All the while Leo sat by my side, his arm around my shoulder, and I allowed him to rock me gently, not that I could feel him, but I knew that's what he was attempting, and so I allowed myself to rock and to pretend to put my head on his shoulder. He said, "There, there," in soothing tones that were overpowered by the Shimmers' voices. He said, "Don't listen to them," like it was as easy as that. Like I could just tune them out. If I could tune out the voices when I heard them, or the things I saw when I saw them, I wouldn't need the medication. At one point in the night, I heard a banging on my door, and I heard my brother call out for me. He sounded panicked. By then I had tears rolling down my cheeks.

I tried to sound upbeat, but it was hard to fight through the sobs, so I faked a smile and said, "Sorry, Chris, I was just having a nightmare!"

He knocked again. "Unlock the door, Adam."

"I said I'm fine. Go back to sleep."

I'm sure he stood at the door, contemplating, before I heard his door the next room over slam shut.

The Shimmers silenced after that, instead deciding to show themselves to me. Before, the disembodied voices had been bad, assaulting my ears even when I tried to block them, but when the visions came, when the Shimmers decided to dance in front me even when I closed my eyes, to reveal their various forms to me, I felt myself slip into a new level of horror, for if you can't trust your mind, your own soul seems in doubt. This was how I felt in the hospital, before Dr. Blake found the proper balance of medications to calm my rambling and dubious mind.

Now, the danger of forgetting my meds weighed on me, too afraid to let my brother know. I sat in my bed with my covers pulled up to my chin, staring—because closing my eyes didn't help—as the Shimmers revealed to me their human forms and then their other forms, one after another, two at a time, the whole damn legion, appearing over my shoulder, or next to me, or across the room. For his part, Leo kept his visage by my side.

At dawn, inexplicably, the Shimmers faded and their voices did not return. We checked out of our room for our return home.

III

Marion had caught an evening flight out of Chicago. Thirty minutes after his flight landed in DC, he sat on the couch in his old boss's apartment. Tom Builder poured him a chardonnay and joined him in the living room.

"How are things?"

"Busy," Marion said.

Tom set his drink down and leaned forward. His wife had allowed them their privacy, was finishing up a patchwork quilt in their den, but Tom still dared not speak too loud.

"Zeitnot Industries is paramount to your understanding of the PRI and Mr. MITS. Where is he, by the way?"

"Took Samantha off to Seattle," Marion said.

Tom raised an eye. "Samantha?"

"Adam's shrink. Dr. Blake. You know."

Tom shook his head with a smile and said, "Samantha." Then, sobering, "Was that wise?"

"She'll be fine. He plays things close to the vest. He won't let someone close to Adam get hurt. It'd raise too much suspicion on him. He doesn't want to do anything to get investigated."

"Jesus!" Tom said. "You don't even know his name! How do you know what he's thinking?"

"Tommy!" his wife called. "Everything okay, dear?"

"Fine!" he yelled back.

He removed a thumb drive from his shirt pocket and placed it in Marion's hand. Standing, he turned on some baroque chamber music on the turntable by the door. Croce's *Triaca Musical* filled the room as he poured another glass of wine. He sat back down next to Marion and leaned in close.

"Zeitnot's old buddy was named CEO. I learned this last week while touring Wright-Patterson with an old friend; he showed me an interesting mainframe. Seems Zeitnot had defense contracts with the US government and let the US back up a lot of their encrypted research files under Top Secret classification. I don't know any good computer hackers that could break the encryption. Do you?"

"He's not my biggest fan," Marion whispered back. "But I think I can convince him."

Tom Builder stood and turned the volume down but not off. He sipped from his glass.

"How'd you manage to piss him off?"

"He blames me for Dr. Blake leaving with Mr. MITS. He... has a crush, I think, on her. But I wouldn't... I won't allow her to get hurt."

"You gotta crush too?"

"It's because I don't know his name," Marion said, checking his voice. He leaned forward and gulped down the last of his drink. "Mr. MITS is Black Ops or Intel. A spy," he said. "And I know spies. Samantha—Dr. Blake's—death would draw too much attention to him, and that's the last thing a man with no name wants."

"Bed, dear?" Tom's wife said from the doorway. ADA Builder stood and looked at Marion apologetically. The younger agent understood. The conversation needed to be cut short by a wife's inquisitiveness into her husband's reunion with an old friend.

"This couch still fold out?"

"Yeah," Tom said. "One sec, dear." Then, to Marion, "We'll talk more tomorrow, but be prepared: Zeitnot Industries is the key to everything we are seeking. They have their hands in everything. Whatever case you're working on, take a look how and if it could relate somehow to one of Zeitnots' primary focuses. There's medical research and research into military and industrial energy applications, including fringe divisions."

"If you know, why can't you just tell me?"

"What makes you think I know?" Tom asked. "I've told you almost everything I know, but I haven't had the luxury of the PRI's case files to go further."

"Almost everything?"

Tom nodded. "Like I said, think about fringe divisions, especially what could be derived from extraterrestrial sources."

And with that, he flicked off the light switch and left Marion in the dark, still listening to chamber music. Marion left the next morning without alerting his host to his departure. By the time Tom realized his houseguest was gone, the former SEAL was already boarding his flight back to Chicago, thinking about spies and ghosts and aliens and even witches and demons, and trying to connect all of it to Zeitnot Industries.

~

We were at the airport when Marion arrived, hoping the security at the airport would help keep out prying eyes. He dropped the thumb drive in Chris's hand while we awaited Dr. Blake's arrival. He sat and spoke hurriedly, his eyes wide. I hadn't seen my partner this excited in a long time.

"It has everything," my brother said, after inserting the drive into his laptop and flipping through the files. "Zeitnot Industries has their fingers in freaking everything. They're working on cryostasis and stem-cell therapy, genetic manipulation, lysosomal nanotech, biomechanical merging therapy.

"GMT — Genetic Manipulation Therapy — utilizing ideas from these other projects, has led to an increased spread in cancer and a development of a super-soldier formula. They only offer vague details here and a lot of scientific jargon. We need Dr. Blake for that stuff: she could make sense of it."

"We need proof," Marion said. "This file only posits how Zeitnot Industries is involved. It gives us copies of files, file transfers, and research data, but nothing from a source. Nothing actionable. For all we know this whole file could have been forged."

"And yet," I said, still shaken from the horrors of the night before, "you were so excited about it a minute ago."

"I am." Marion sighed. "It's a fucking tease," he said, dropping his head. "It's a kind of holy grail, a promise on the one hand and in the other, a rabbit hole we have to scurry down."

"This particular rabbit hole leads to Wright Patterson Air Force Base," Chris said, scrolling, ever scrolling, his eyes glued to the screen.

"What?" I said.

"The US government issued a lot of those grants to Zeitnot Industries directly," Chris said. "But the weird thing is, Zeitnot isn't saving anything to the Cloud, nor on any commercial data server mainframes. Their contracts with the government stipulate that they must only keep hard copies of all contracts and research information. One copy is kept at Zeitnot Industries' Headquarters overseas and the other copy — the government's copy — is kept in a secure file at Wright Patterson."

"Does it say where?" I asked.

Chris sighed. "No," he said. "Just at the base."

"Then, when Dr. Blake gets here," Marion said, "I know what I've got to do."

As it was, we wouldn't have long to wait for her return flight from Seattle, and we'd hear all about the case Mr. MITS needed her for.

IV

Dr. Blake and Mr. MITS exited the airport to a cloudless Seattle day. An FBI field agent met them at the gate and drove them south out of the city, where Samantha was greeted with her first view of the magnificent Mount Rainier. The agent was up for small talk, and she engaged while Mr. MITS remained his stoic self in the rear passenger side seat. The agent asked what she was a doctor of, and she answered.

"You've experience getting into the minds of the criminal?"

"I am a scientist," she replied. She motioned to the enigmatic passenger and nearly called him Mr. MITS but caught herself. "He thinks I'll be of some help," she said.

"You briefed her on criminal investigative procedure, Agent Lawson?" the field agent asked, and Samantha raised an eyebrow. Later, after they'd left the car and were walking into Port Wesley's police station, she took the opportunity to pull Mr. MITS aside, catching him by the arm.

"'Agent Lawson?' Do we know your name?"

The look he shot her made her blood run cold. He yanked his arm away and rubbed where she'd held it, as though her touch burned him.

"In this business, I'm required to have many names," Mr. MITS said.

He then stepped around her and walked inside.

A manhunt was in progress for the last two suspects. A criminalist began to give his behavioral report, until a local cop asked about the connection.

"But these last two," the cop, a petite Latina, said, "have no history of any kind of criminal or behavioral issues. Upstanding citizens, except he needed a kidney and she, a piece of a liver. Same with most of these recent suspects."

"They may have seemed like good people, but they had to have been harboring some deep emotional trouble," the criminalist retorted.

Another officer spoke up. "But we were able to link all these suspects to a donor list and their MO follows..."

"It is a coincidence," the criminalist said.

"It's a coincidence that six previously-upstanding citizens have all exhibited traits of the known serial killer who donated organs and tissues to each of them after his execution?" Yet another speaker, this time the field agent who'd picked them up. Mr. MITS looked to Dr. Blake and nodded. She stepped forward and cleared her throat.

By now most of the room had been made aware of her arrival, and most had questions as to what a clinical psychiatrist from Arkansas was doing in the suburbs of Seattle. Hoping that some of those answers might be forthcoming, the entire room silenced, including the profiler after the field officer introduced her.

"My name," she said again for emphasis — since she'd been introduced, there had been a lot of discussion — "is Dr. Samantha Blake. I am a psychiatrist. I'm aware of the profile and mental workup you've been offered, but it fails to take into consideration these things you now question." She looked around. She had the room.

"There is talk among some scientists about an unproven idea that memory and thought begin at certain cellular levels. In particular, memory involves specific organelles of the cell that are found not only in neurological cells but are common in all cells in the body."

"You're talking about junk science," the profiler said.

"It wasn't too long ago that people said the same thing about criminal profiling," she retorted. "But it does lend to another theory. Whether or not it is true, it lends to an urban myth, and a pretty popular one at that. Countless horror movies and stories have been told about the recipient of an organ transplant seeing the murderer of the donor. I suggest these people were aware of that myth and their behavior lends to that. The simple explanation, and the one that explains why they're linked and why they're acting out of turn, is that even though the hospital records should have been sealed, these recipients knew who their donor was. Once they received the transplant, they believed they'd received a part of an executed killer. And they believe, we can extrapolate from all that's happened, that they have *become* the killer."

This, the precinct bought or seemed to. Several officers congratulated her as a game plan was mapped out around recent intelligence that suggested where the suspects were holed up. Down a state road and a two-lane turn-off sat a cabin that had been marked, but it had gone unnoticed during the heat of the manhunt discussion. Samantha pointed to it and once again captured the room's attention, including that of Mr. MITS, who had not prodded her to rise.

"As I said," she began, stepping to the image of the map on the wall, "if they believe they've become the killer, then wouldn't they go to the killer's home?" She jabbed her finger to the location of the family cabin, not far from the shores of the Sound.

Dr. Blake told us that, as the cars pulled away to race toward the cabin, she once again caught Mr. MITS' arm and yanked him back. This time she was less afraid. His icy stare did not intimidate her.

"What in hell!" she snapped. "You could have pulled anyone up here to deliver that cellular memory crap. Why bring me?"

He smiled that godforsaken toothy grin. "Because you are the only person I know in this field who would be in a position to believe it."

To this she scoffed and retreated a step, letting his arm go as though she'd been the one burned this time. "Why in hell would I believe that?"

"The PRI, Dr. Blake. You are in a unique position. You don't seem to grasp the fact that as Agent Case was promoted to our humble unit, your patient—young Master Adam—was dragged along and, by hook or by crook, it would seem, so were you and Adam's brother. Or so you'd have everyone believe. But you've come willingly. To see what the PRI is. And what have you seen so far, Samantha?"

She thought two things. She thought of all she'd seen, of ghosts and witches and monsters and things that defied conventional science. And she thought how absolutely corpse-like she felt when he called her by her given name.

Over his shoulder, she saw the Seattle field agent waiting at the car, leaning on the open driver's side door. He was a handsome, ambitious young man, and his face suggested that his patience was wearing thin. They were losing the police convoy; the three of them were the only link to the Fed's claim of partial credit on this local authority bust.

She brushed past Mr. MITS to climb into the passenger seat, and the three departed. The field agent was ready to turn right with the rest of the convoy when Mr. MITS called from the backseat, "*No!* Take a left."

"But—" the young man started to protest.

"She was crafty, our Samantha, our good doctor, with the cabin. But I'm craftier. How quick can you get us to Tacoma?"

The young agent from Seattle gassed the sedan and hit the dash-mounted light.

~

Mr. MITS instructed Samantha to wait in the car, then he and the field agent drew their guns, hunkered below the hedges, and made their way toward the house. The sky outside was a light gray, overcast with swift winds that carried the front from the Pacific onto the mainland.

Something nagged at her, so she exited through the passenger side door and crept along the hedgerow to the front gate of the Colonial with the detached garage. She unhitched the latch and crept up the gravel path to the front porch steps. Ascending, she pushed open the door.

She could hear them inside, scurrying and talking. Breathing. She looked around but saw neither Mr. MITS nor the field agent. She stepped into the entry hall; no one in the house seemed to notice her, but she could hear their words, and the aggressors sounded exhausted.

"Mom, believe us!" a woman said.

"We're your son," a man said. They both sounded weary, and their voices, while sounding alike, didn't not seem to belong to either man or woman standing there. It came from within them, a tonal match between the two, a voice she'd heard before when she watched the final interview of the serial killer before he was executed. She'd watched the video on the flight over, headphones channeling him straight into her ears, and when they spoke, it felt the same way.

Samantha had no idea what to expect, but her step into the room disturbed the home's inhabitants, and as they all turned to face her, she froze. The old man and woman from the file, the killer's parents, bound and gagged with duct tape, sat on a bench in front of an antique grand piano. Their pleas were muffled and ineffectual. A younger man and woman stood in front of them, each holding a handgun. Dark bags surrounded their red eyes, their hair messy.

"Who are you?" the man said, his gun quivering.

"How many children do they have?" Samantha asked, nodding toward the old couple.

"One," he responded.

"Me!" Both the man and the woman spoke at once, and looked to each other, apparently shocked that the other had answered.

"We... are his son," the woman said in the son's voice.

"How is that possible?" she asked, and with a trembling hand, she held up her cell phone. On screen, she'd pulled up a picture of the original suspect. Both stared at it, and then both looked to the mirror hanging over an accent desk. When she followed their gaze, she nearly screamed; from under their gags the parents made what horrid noises they could, for they all saw within the reflection not the man and the woman who spoke with the son's voice, but two images of the son staring back at all of them, one dressed as the man and one dressed as the woman.

Were they finally of one mind when they raised their guns at my doctor, or had they finally accepted their duality? This mattered little as gunshots rang out, and Samantha fell to her knees, cowering, her eyes closed. As the gunshots faded, she heard two thuds, and opened her eyes to see Mr. MITS standing over the young man and young woman as blood pooled underneath them. The field agent entered, gun drawn, but seeing the suspects dead, moved quickly to untie the elderly couple even as Mr. MITS helped Samantha to her feet. She was still shaking, her ears ringing from the gunshots, as she stared at their bodies.

"They looked like him," she said, her voice low and trembling. "Even sounded like him. For just a moment."

"You okay?" the man in the suit asked. When she nodded, he said, "They're dead now. He's gone." Shaken, Samantha walked out to the car, and rode in silence back to the airport, not saying much even on the flight back to Chicago.

V

When her flight landed, we met her at her gate and all caught a flight back to Arkansas, Marion booking a hotel room before we boarded. It had been decided, given the sensitive material Chris had acquired, that we'd travel commercially rather than taking the PRI's jet. A day later, we gathered together as Marion packed a hefty duffel.

I said, "The case files from your most recent investigations are on the way, but I asked for something else. I asked for the file on your murder, of course, and also, I asked for the file on your wife's attack."

The ghost flinched. "Why?" Leo asked. "You looked at it all at Morris' office."

"I want copies in hand," I said. "It's all connected. I felt it, when I talked to her. You were murdered right after your separation from her... and right after her rape."

"I had a suspect," he said, looking bitterly at the floor, the tiles of the room's kitchenette the only thing that wouldn't look back with reproach. "But I couldn't convict. I didn't have enough evidence, though I know the S.O.B."

"We'll have to work on your suspect," I said, "and we'll have to investigate and document your leads and evidence, or the lack thereof."

Leo nodded. I looked to my psychiatrist and my brother and explained

166

the legalities and the rights of the presumed innocent. We all looked over to Marion, who'd nearly finished packing.

"I've got to get overseas," he said, slinging the satchel over his shoulder and facing us. "I have to fly to Europe. I need to visit Zeitnot Industries again."

"Can you trust the source of this file?" Chris asked. Marion assured us that the source was irreproachable, but I only found assurance later, when he finally divulged to me who gave him the thumb drive. "Because if you can't, you should maybe try and get into Wright-Patterson and verify the files for yourself. See if what's here corresponds to what is on the hard copy."

Marion shook his head. "More heavily guarded, too dangerous. Besides, that I trust the source should be enough for you."

"Well, there might be something there that could help with the encryption," Chris said. "The drive doesn't give me much."

"I'm sure you'll manage," Marion said, and then he was out the door, and he was gone.

9

EVERLONG

I

Chris peeled the blinds apart. He stared down the street at the black SUV that was parked just out of range of the streetlight, under the old elm. For the fifth night in a row, the man in the suit sat in the SUV just down the road. The first night Chris had seen the vehicle, he had dismissed it as belonging to a neighbor. But then the next day, coming home from an office network install, he saw the SUV and saw the government tags, and then he saw the driver. He remembered those eyes. The man wore the same suit he'd worn in Chicago.

When the SUV showed up again the day after that, Chris called the police. The patrolmen performed a cursory glance of the area but saw no signs of the vehicle; however, Chris saw it had returned not long after they left. At one point during that week, Chris watched a patrol car cruise down the street, passing right beside the SUV. And Mr. MITS was still in the SUV, behind the wheel.

He was sure they wanted him to see them. Why else park in the sightline from his home office window? They were broadcasting their location, keeping him worried, sleepless; in fact, he hadn't slept in several nights. He contemplated calling me, but Marion had been the one who had asked Chris to dissect the contents of the thumb drive. Marion had told him he was the best, had appealed to his vanity, but my brother didn't especially like my old partner. He blamed him for a lot of things, not least my condition, but he believed that what Marion was asking of him was incredibly important. It was linked to something he'd seen in the news about that assassinated billionaire, and Marion had said something about Mr. MITS' involvement. He had given him a starting point and no leash. Dig and turn up and break into whatever coded sites he had to break into. Find whatever he could on the name Smitt R. Isem, Marion had told him. He had trusted Chris with the thumb drive, after all.

So, Chris had investigated, and he dug and he slipped past firewalls and passcodes, and learned all he could about Mr. Smitt R. Isem. He'd found his way into some major corporations, some tax records of a few board members; right after that was when he first saw the SUV. His work was slow, deliberately so, for fear of alerting the wrong people, fear of setting off the wrong bells or too many digital tripwires at once. He investigated Smitt R. Isem's past, his known residences, the addresses and the bank accounts. What he found terrified him. That the SUV had arrived, and Mr. MITS was so obviously surveying him only elevated his fear.

Just a few hours earlier, Chris had reached a dead end, but he knew all there was to know about Smitt R. Isem. He catalogued the information and backed up his files, then set up a few fail safes on his own laptop. He installed several firewalls and plugged in a reverse counter that would wipe his hard drive with the stroke of a few keys.

He looked out the blinds again. From the position of the van tonight, he couldn't see if anyone sat behind the wheel. He had finished his research, and if Mr. MITS hadn't come before he was done, that only meant he was waiting for Chris to finish.

Chris tucked his 9 mm into his jacket and put the flash drive under the Dr. Scholl's arch support of his left shoe. He'd been so sly — he surprised himself that this was in him. Once he realized exactly what he had, he'd copied the information to a second flash drive and mailed it to me.

He shut off the lights to his apartment and walked out into the hall, where the fluorescents glowed a dim yellow from brass fixtures high above. In the apartment next to him, the widower Barnes had his television on too loud. Chris couldn't hear if anyone was on the stairs. He jammed his hands into his coat pockets, felt his right hand close around the handle and his finger on the trigger guard. He inched to the stairs and looked down. He was three floors up; the stairs went up to six and if he had a key, he could make it to the roof. But he didn't have a key. The window at the end of the hall was painted shut, denying him easy egress to the fire escape. He could bust the window, he thought. If it came to that.

Glancing around, and down again, he gripped the gun tight in his pocket and descended the stairs. A figure emerged, shrouded in shadow, and Chris tightened his grip on the gun. When the figure stepped into a pool of light, Chris paused. "Marion?" he asked, his grip relaxing.

My partner said, "Hello, Chris. We have a problem."

"They're after me," Chris said, looking around, then taking the last few steps to stand beside the agent. "I thought you were in Europe."

"I was, but when I learned more about Zeitnot, I knew you were in danger. I had to get back. Chris," he said, capturing my brother's attention. "I don't think I can stop them."

Chris swallowed hard. "They're going to kill me."

Marion shook his head. "I don't think so. I think that would cause too much attention. They want me, and Adam. Killing you would expose them. But they do want you. They'll probably take you somewhere. Keep you drugged."

"But I could learn some things too. We could stop them. Stop this guy, this man in the suit."

Marion nodded. Around them the air grew palpable. They were coming for Chris, whoever they were, whoever Mr. MITS employed for this little mission. They were coming, and time was up.

II

The catalyst, it turned out, had not been the murder of Simon Zeitnot; rather, Dr. Blake's foray into cellular memory had spurred Marion on to Austria where now he faced two pressing issues. There was no heat in the villa. That was problem one. He'd started a fire in the fireplace and had since stepped up his reconnoiter around the perimeter of the house, scanning the back alley and the gaslit posts that lined the cobblestone street out front. The second problem had not moved from the corner, and he had not spoken in some time. He had not been able to speak, and, truth be told, he would not make it through the night. His death would be on Marion's hands.

His hand pressed to the gunshot wound in his gut, Simon Zeitnot's friend almost glowed in the dark with sweat, his bloodless flesh the color of marble. Marion inched to him, checked his wound. It was bad, bloody and infected, but the blood had slowed and the pulsing under the flesh had slowed as well. Marion looked in the bucket for more ice chips and found only frigid water, so he splashed some on the man's forehead then returned to his place by the window.

~

It hadn't been hard for Marion to find him. His friendship with Simon Zeitnot was public knowledge, as was his place of employ. His schedule easy enough to decipher, Marion simply followed him for a couple of days before cornering him in his office. Pietro had told him the man in the suit had approached him to kill his friend Simon, but must have understood that this would be impossible for someone as loyal as Pietro. Simon had made Pietro the man he was. They had been friends since childhood. The new CEO of Zeitnot confessed all of this as though the gun Marion held could offer communion.

Marion had led him to the research hospital owned by the company, and so had access to basement level three research. Marion had a thumb drive with enough memory to copy the files of their active projects. He'd had enough time to download them all before sirens wailed through the hospital corridors, before the heavy fire doors slammed shut and locked automatically. This was no fire drill, Pietro assured him. His eyes had narrowed, and he looked as though he wanted to spit in his captor's face.

"Because I set off the alarm," he said.

Marion led him at gunpoint out of the research department, up the stairs and through double doors to the parking garage. He heard footsteps closing in and once outside, heard sirens. The hospital guards closed in with the local police outside, as Spezialeinheiten (SEK — Germany's version of SWAT) landed on the roof. Marion, gun in hand, pulled Pietro to a crouch behind a windowless white custom van, kept cool. There was always an extraction point, he knew; he also knew that, if caught, the German authorities wouldn't be so forgiving this time.

"You are tough, American," Pietro said. "Are you tough enough to take on all these men?"

But Marion had memorized the hospital blueprints. The nonmedical waste disposal unit in basement level four fed right into the sewer system. The main pipe, he recalled, was just large enough to crawl through, and if they could make it to the open sewage system, they could make it out of the city. It was blocked by a filter, which was replaced every night, with an hour and a half break between its removal and the installation of a new, clean replacement. The time of this operation varied from 1 a.m. to 4.

It was three o'clock.

Marion led Pietro back inside, where four guards impeded their path, each with a semi-automatic pistol. He hadn't a lot of time, so he dispatched them quickly, disarming them as he went. From the SEALs, he had learned self-defense and hand-to-hand techniques, and since his youth he'd been a student of many disciplines, from Krav Maga to Jeet Kun Do, to American boxing and Aikido. He'd studied Savate and various forms of Kung Fu, including weapons fighting. It didn't take him long. He was happy to see that Pietro hadn't tried to run.

They hurried past the research level and into the maintenance hall, and quickly found the waste disposal unit. They also found new pursuers, the sight of which left Marion dismayed. He recognized them, these armed men in black, as his Black Ops team at the PRI. They toted M-16s and gave no sign of recognizing him. They took their shots and with no apparent concern whether they took down Marion or his captive.

Marion barred the door to the waste disposal unit on level four and worked quickly to disengage the machine, unplugging it and then disabling its override features so that the walls wouldn't accidentally power up and crush them as they made their way down. He stopped long enough to explain the facts of life to Pietro, his voice elevated over the banging of the SEK on the door, and someone barking commands in German.

"Those men outside don't care if I kidnapped you. They now believe you know too much, and if they capture me, they will kill you."

"I know nothing," Pietro stammered.

"You saw those research files like I did. Now, you may not like this, but if you want to live, you'd better trust me. You'd better follow me and do what I say."

~

His prisoner coughed. Marion looked across the room, away from the window. Even in the dim light he could see Pietro's eyes flutter. The man's head rolled on his neck, and he seemed to regard Marion for a while before he spoke.

"You could have told me," Pietro said. "You could have… told me it was for Simon. You didn't have to abduct me."

"I should have told you," Marion said.

Out of his periphery, there was movement in the shadows along the street below. The tiny Austrian village should be quiet and still. But somewhere in the darkness a dog barked, alerted to another presence.

~

They had made it through the waste system… barely. They were nearly free when the Black Ops team smashed through the door and restarted the machine; and Pietro's left foot snagged in the grinding gears designed to pulverize refuse into a paste before sloughing into the sewer. Marion had pulled him free, only to notice they'd missed their window, and he had to kick out the newly placed filter so they wouldn't drown as the holding tank filled with water. Soon enough, they were in the sewer line, and not long after that, they were out of the city.

A few miles out, they had found an all-night gas station and a car Marion could hotwire. As dawn rose, they were thirty miles away and gaining distance. Pietro said he had an aunt in a village not too far away, so they drove there, hoping for sanctuary.

They had entered the aunt's house to find a disheveled mess. The cushions had been ripped open and the furniture busted. Upstairs, in her bedroom neat and tidy, Pietro's aunt still knelt in prayer, the blood from the bullet hole in her forehead dried like a red scar from her brow to her chin.

Pietro sank to his knees, uttering a mournful wail. Marion indelicately rifled through her clothes, pulling out a set of keys, then yanked Pietro to his feet. That was when the gunfire had started. Dodging bullets, the stucco and drywall exploding around them, they raced to the back of the house, found the aunt's car, and screamed out of the drive, bullets smacking the metal body, nearly rocking the tiny Opel Adam off its wheels. Somehow, they evaded their attackers, but not without cost. Gut shot and screaming in pain, Pietro sat doubled over, clutching at his stomach.

Marion had driven to another village, one of three only a short distance away, but the one with the least ties — that he knew of — to Pietro. There, he had found an abandoned villa. There, they had holed up.

Another flash of movement below. It was the Black Ops team. Marion's cell went off. He examined the caller ID and then begrudgingly answered. Pietro, when Marion began talking, livened a bit and turned his head to listen.

"Agent Case, you know it would not behoove us to sacrifice such an esteemed member of the United States government, but we cannot allow this to proceed further." The voice on the other end was a smooth bass with no hint of accent.

"My friend needs medical attention," Marion said.

"He isn't your friend, Agent Case. He is the man you abducted to procure information. I am not sure who sent you on this fool's errand, but I can assure you, this not within your purview at the PRI."

"He's dying. Will you help him?"

"Will you give me the thumb drive?"

Marion looked over to where Pietro lay. He hadn't meant the man any harm. He had only meant to coerce him into giving him answers. He had thought, stupidly, that because he had forced the man against his will, when they were pursued, the pursuers would go easy on Zeitnot's new CEO knowing he was a captive. But he knew that wasn't true; he'd known all along that they would not let Pietro live.

As for him, he was an agent working in a clandestine office, which meant one of two things: he was either too valuable to kill, or the office was covert enough that he was expendable. If it were just him, he'd keep running. He could take at least a couple of the Black Ops guys, make a hole to squirm out of. He could run. But he'd leave those he cared about vulnerable. And if he ran with his information, and if they realized they couldn't reach him, then what would stop Mr. MITS or the Black Ops team from going after those he loved?

"Well," the man on the other end said. "What's your answer?"

"I'll call you right back." Marion hung up and dialed another number. He thanked a god he'd never stopped to consider except in moments of duress, when the call went through and his old boss at the FBI picked up.

"Jesus, Marion, where are you?"

"Somewhere in Austria," Marion said.

"Secure line?"

"I don't have time for that, Tom. I need an extraction."

"I don't know if I can do that."

"Then they need to understand that I've got a dying man here who needs medical assistance."

"Do you know who's on your ass? Other than the whole Austrian and German police force, that is."

"Yeah. Call Adam. Have him call Colonel Hamilton at the PRI."

"Will do," ADA Builder said.

"And Tom? Please hurry."

He hung up. Of course, he could not know that Tom would not bother with me, that he would call the colonel himself, because even Marion's old boss had a few secrets. One of those was that he knew Marion's new boss.

Marion held his gun tight and put a finger against his lips for Pietro to see, and the wounded man nodded in understanding. The creaking, the near-silent ascent of boots on the stairs outside the door had grown steadily closer.

Marion slid back over to Pietro. Wounded as he was, Zeitnot's CEO didn't have much time left. Marion might be able to escape, but he would have to turn the wounded man over if there was a chance for him to survive. Marion put the back of his hand to the forehead, checked the pulse. Pietro, slick with sweat, coughed up a spherule of blood. "We don't have much time, Pietro. Soon they will be here, and they'll get you to a hospital, but I need to know, as quickly as you can tell me, just what you have learned about Zeitnot Industries. I've had someone trying to break through a file encryption I've found, but I need more answers. Pietro, I'm trying to stop some bad people."

The man nodded in understanding, closed his eyes, winced. Outside, more sounds. Shuffling and susurrations. There wasn't much time left. "To start," Pietro said, "whoever is hacking that encrypted file… they are in danger. But yes, I will tell you, if you are truly trying to find who killed my friend Simon. Then I will tell you all I know."

III

One morning I was awakened by the scream of the ghost. Leo loomed over me, yelling for me to get up. I shot out of bed and dressed, realizing that he wore not anger but fear. I called Dr. Blake, who came immediately to pick me up. She drove me to Chris's apartment, where, after a few tense moments of banging on the door with no answer, I took the spare key and entered.

The furniture was in shambles. Papers were scattered about the place, tables overturned, and cushions ripped open. Dr. Blake shook as the ghost moved through the walls from room to room only to return empty handed. I knelt and dipped my finger into a puddle on the floor, deep red and already tacky. It had been there a while. I looked up: another smear of the same red across the wall.

"Adam?" Dr. Blake was looking at me, wanting— needing answers.

I had none, save only the most obvious, and the most disturbing. "Chris isn't here," I said.

She took me home once the police arrived, but Leo continued to haunt the apartment, unseen by the living, overseeing their investigation and engaging in his own.

"I have a subliminal effect," Leo said later. "If they miss something, I can speak directly into their head. They had overlooked a fingerprint on the handle of the sliding glass door, so I mentioned it to one of the investigator guys. He walked back over like he forgot something and found it."

I said, "What did you find out?"

"Nothing much. They've got some work to do at the lab. I'll keep checking in. In the meantime, we'll wait and keep our ears to the ground. If I learn anything, I'll let you know."

But we didn't learn anything.

I tried to call Marion, and when I was unable to reach him, I tried our old boss at the FBI. The assistant director would not accept my calls, or else he was always away from his office phone and his cell. I slept fitfully, and mainly just laid in bed listening to Dr. Blake toss and turn on my couch, awaking the next day resolved to find answers, and so I called the last person I knew to call.

Colonel Hamilton answered on the third ring and listened as I spoke. I dare not tell him my theory, just that my brother was missing and the search for his whereabouts had been called off.

"Maybe it was called off for good reason," he said. "Maybe they found him."

"He left his laptop," I said. "It was broken."

He sighed heavily into the phone. "I'll look into it. Make a few calls." And with that he had to dismiss himself to something more of his station, something made up, I'm sure; anything to get me off the phone.

Resigned, worried for my brother, I sat in silence until I heard the mail carrier downstairs, and tired of waiting and tired of sitting, I walked down to greet her. Dr. Blake had said she'd be back to check on me when she left earlier, that she had to get some work done at the office. I arrived in time to say hi to our postwoman as she left. From my slot, I removed a single box wrapped in brown paper, with only my address printed in block lettering. There was no return address.

Returning to my apartment, I felt the need to lock my door before I opened the package. Inside there was no note; it contained only an unmarked flash drive.

I tried to open the flash drive, but whenever I inserted it into my computer, my screen filled with only gibberish, which converted Windows back to DOS—that much I recognized—but could make neither head nor tails of the information on it. I knew only one man who could break such an encryption, and as he was the subject of my search now, I figured I had no one to rely on but myself, unless... I asked the ghost if he knew computers. He scoffed at me invisibly. I tried my best to read the lines of code, in the hopes that something intelligible would jump out at me, but the gobbledygook stared back indifferently, mocking me with its alien runes.

Still undeterred, sure that the whereabouts of my brother lay hidden in the lines of code, I ignored everything else and continued to focus on the flash drive until a knock came at my door so vehemently that I had no option but to let the visitor in, especially when I saw that it was my own psychiatrist.

"I can't find him," I said simply.

She said, "The police will find him."

"You've seen what I've seen. Do you really think they'll make a difference?"

"No," she answered quietly. She placed a call and cancelled her appointments for the rest of the day, and as she hung up my phone rang. I answered to a man asking for me by name, who introduced himself as the detective I'd met at my brother's apartment.

"Yes, I remember you," I said, and told Dr. Blake who was on the phone.

"Mr. Richardson, I was hoping you could come down to the station. It seems we've recovered a body, and I need you to identify it."

Somehow, I thanked him and mumbled a yes then hung up, but as Dr. Blake asked what the detective had wanted, I couldn't answer her. I was numb, and I could not stop the tears from streaming down my cheeks.

IV

The air was thick; the time passed slowly. The car ride lasted forever. Dr. Blake's voice carried platitudes timed over the drive, assuring me all was going to be okay, but I could hear the doubt in her voice. We reached Washington Regional's basement morgue, all of it passing impossibly fast and impossibly slow, as time has a way of doing in times of stress, of life and death, when all you can do is wait and the fates of you and your loved one rests in a stranger's hands.

The curtain was pulled aside, and the sheet was lifted. I nearly collapsed.

It wasn't Chris. We left—I was relieved but felt like I'd been punched in the gut at the same time—when I received a call on my cell phone as we climbed back into her car. The number was blocked.

"Hello?"

Dr. Blake looked at me, a brow raised, and lips pursed: every woman's unasked question about who a man is talking to, Chris told me once. I nodded and said "Yes, but probably four to six hours," and then I hung up.

"Who was it?" she asked.

"Marion," I said. "He asked if we could meet at the house in South Arkansas."

"The house," she said. "Like, the house you bought, with the things... the shadow folk?"

Without a signal and barely slowing for the turn, she headed west through the turnabout at the next intersection to take us to the interstate.

When the night began to wear on us, she put on the radio, but till that moment it was easier to ride in silence. She interrupted the radio a couple of times to ask me what Marion had said. I told her, and she asked if I was sure that was all. Chris always said it was a woman's way of sounding helpful and doubtful at the same time.

"I know he was disappointed in me." I had to watch that. I couldn't think of him in the past tense.

"Your brother has a lot on his plate," she said after the briefest of hesitations. Making excuses for someone so insufferable must be an exhausting occupation.

"Detective Knight said that you were all made to forget, when *she* had me."

"That's the ghost, right?"

He sat in the back of her SUV, quiet and still. If she could've seen him she

179

might've screamed. I said, "He told me that Chris didn't want to remember. That he was perfectly happy not having a brother."

"Adam, he…" but the words failed her.

"I get it," I said. "I'm a burden. I know what I put people through. I just want to tell him I'm sorry."

I felt myself getting choked up, so I had to stop talking, and bless her heart, the good doctor didn't press. We rode without speaking the rest of the way until we reached the abandoned house on Chester Street in the small South Arkansas town. We shut off the headlights and got out of the car. Dr. Blake turned on her flashlight. I looked around at the stars and the Shadow Folk, who danced at our return, hissing and laughing.

The front screen door opened, and heavy footsteps clopped on the wooden porch. A silhouette lurched off the steps into the yard. Dr. Blake turned the beam of her flashlight to reveal Agent Marion Case, bruised and a little bloody, but none the worse off. He looked around cautiously, then silently motioned for us to follow. He led us into the house and into the living room, where he'd lit a few candles and, with the aid of the mirror hanging over the fireplace, we could see enough. A fire burned well, warming the house. Our greetings were cut short as Marion sat down cross-legged, staring at his gun, and said, "I failed." We rushed up to him. He looked haggard, his hair disheveled, his clothes torn and dirty and wrinkled, fresh cuts and bruises on his face and his knuckles bloodied. When he looked at me, his eyes glistened. "I failed, Adam. Twice."

We took some time to gather ourselves before Marion told us what happened.

"The Black Ops team had wounded Pietro, and so I wasn't able to escape with him. He told me a lot about what Zeitnot Industries was involved in, however, there towards the end, before they made their way inside. I knew the thumb drive I'd given Chris could benefit from what I learned this time around, so I fought my way through the Black Ops team and caught a transport back to the US, but Mr. MITS and the team had beaten me here. Chris was under surveillance and I knew it wouldn't be long before they executed him — I was nearly too late. A two-man shooter team had been dispatched. I took care of them, but the rest of the Black Ops team and Mr. MITS were on us. Your brother is a solid fighter, but they were too much. I tried to keep up, but they'd taken him. I came here because I knew the Shadow Folk were camouflaging this place and would safeguard us until you arrived."

We passed the night in the living room, listening to the Shadow Folk scream about the eaves, the detective staying close to me. Dr. Blake drove to a nearby town and found a McDonalds and brought back some cheeseburgers. I think she did it just to escape the confines of the old, dilapidated home, where glimpses of shadows and an undercurrent of whispers constantly reminded us we weren't alone. None of us really ate.

"We need to let Col. Hamilton know," I said. "I don't think he'd like what Mr. MITS is using the Black Ops team for."

"He's a figurehead," Marion said. "I think the key to finding Chris is going to be through Mr. MITS, but all we have on him right now is his obsession with Zeitnot Industries."

"So what do we know about the company?" Dr. Blake asked.

"Zeitnot Industries has three areas of research," Marion said, "a chain of hospitals with headquarters in Germany, a military facility on a small plain in the middle of the Alps, and an energy think tank in Geneva. I only found files concerning research at the medical hospital, but some of the studies could be game-changing breakthroughs."

Marion pulled out his laptop and powered it on, and I handed him the flash drive I'd received in the mail. While his computer skills were not on the level of my brother's, Marion could still break the encryption. I commended him on that.

"I didn't do it," he said. "It's Chris's computer. He broke the encryption on some of these files." I was about to say I thought his computer had been destroyed before remembering that my brother normally employed at least two laptops. The free files sprang up on the screen and we all pressed in to read.

"This is impossible," Dr. Blake said.

"Research on the fringe," Marion said.

"More like science fiction and the most obvious of conspiracy theories," she replied.

The science was over my head. She snatched the laptop away from Marion and flipped through file after file, reciting the research grants for the hospitals, a list of highly covert projects.

"Some of this is the basis for the cell memory case. Incredible. Cryogenics as a viable restoration process and a preservative... lists a patient, Isem. Experiments documenting cellular memory in transplants, and lysosome and nanotech cellular repair."

"Isem," Marion said, like the name haunted him.

"I've found another file," Dr. Blake said, reading. "I can't, Marion... I can't believe this."

"There's more," he said. "There were experiments in gene manipulation therapy, biomechanical therapy, and explosive claims in stem cell research." Dr. Blake frowned as she moused through the files. There was a single file that, once opened, proved heavily redacted. "We can't break the encryption," Marion said.

"The file's titled Project RH Mobile Men? What the hell is that?" she asked.

I sat back. Something clicked in the darkest recesses of my mind, and as I processed what they'd found, I realized I knew where all of this was heading. "BACH," I said.

Marion frowned at me. "The composer?"

"The quartet," I answered. "It's an acronym, and it stands for the four pioneers to twentieth century science fiction: Ray Bradbury, Isaac Asimov, Arthur C. Clarke, and Robert Heinlein. Heinlein wrote a book called *Starship Troopers* that featured 'Mobile Men,' or 'Mobile Infantry.'"

"And you think these infantrymen are the subject of this research? Why would a world-renowned research hospital concern themselves with fictional soldiers?"

"The name is an identifier on a file that probably couldn't be found by most people," I said. "The Mobile Men were super soldiers. They aren't working on this for medical research. They're designing super soldiers."

"Christ!" Marion said. He pulled out his cell phone and dialed a number, waited and didn't introduce himself when he spoke. "We got Black Ops and Mr. MITS on us, what can you do?... and if I come to Chicago, how can I guarantee..." He listened. When he hung up, I knew he was leaving.

"You'll be safe," he said. "I'm going to Chicago."

"If you leave, you can't ensure our safety," Dr. Blake said.

He removed a gun from the holster on his belt, a fresh clip from his pocket, slapped it home and handed it — a 9 mm — to me.

"I can't," I protested.

"You were a great shot," he said.

I took the gun, though he was a horrible liar. I wasn't a great shot. Anytime we had to draw our weapons, he'd cross himself like he was Catholic. It was meant to relieve the tension some, but it was also because he knew my qualifying scores were some of the lowest in the Bureau.

"Mr. MITS knows that we can't unlearn the information Chris sent you, and without Zeitnot's CEO, any conspiratorial information we have is unsubstantiated. We might have these digital files but they can get rid of the real files before we move in. They no longer need to kill us. They've castrated us."

Kill a man, create a martyr, but devalue his evidence and all you've created is a crackpot.

Marion stood and stared out the window, then turned to face me. He motioned for me to follow him out onto the porch, into the predawn light. I could feel the Shadow Folk press in to hear what we were discussing, or perhaps they could already read what was on his mind. Also present, the detective's ghost stood over my shoulder.

"You have this," Marion said to me.

"If you go back up there, they'll kill you."

"In Violent Crime, before you and I met, I worked on a case with a serial bomber who hid the explosives in and around his victims. In their house, in their car. And he made the trigger something common. If they depressed the brake right after the gas, it would arm the bomb. Flip the turn signal to indicate right..."

"Boom," I said.

"In the house, in the office, even more common: pencil sharpener, electric toothbrush, iPod dock station, microwave, George Foreman grill."

"It must have been hard to catch him."

Marion nodded. "His victims never knew when or how it would go off, but he always warned them of what he'd done. I think it was fun for him to watch them try and figure it out. And us."

"What are you going to do?"

Marion looked around like he could see the Shadow Folk too. "You said these things here, they haunt people, right? Not places. Meaning they can go elsewhere."

"The Black Ops team…?"

Marion shook his head. "Replaceable, each and every one of them. But Mr. MITS — I'd like to watch him try and find the bomb before it goes off."

It was my turn to look around. "I think they're ready for you to go."

V

They met in the parking garage of the federal building downtown. Marion arrived alone in the predawn hours, when the garage was only half full. He saw Colonel Hamilton and next to him, Mr. MITS, looking dangerously dapper. Marion glanced around; he spotted the first sniper rifle under a white SUV further down the row. Still behind the wheel of his car, he dialed the saved number on his cell.

"The Black Ops team is here."

"No," Col. Hamilton said.

"I see them."

From behind the wheel, he saw the colonel cover the mouthpiece and turn to Mr. MITS. Mr. MITS seemed unperturbed.

"He says you threatened him," the colonel said. "He says they are merely here for security. You'll be safe."

Marion got out of the car and approached the two men. He could feel the weight of the barrels on his chest, his head. He could not see the Shadow Folk, but he hoped they'd found their target. As he neared, Mr. MITS began looking around as if he was being swarmed by mosquitos.

Marion drew—slowly—his badge and held it aloft.

"He's under arrest. If the Black Ops team tries to stop me, they will be killed on sight. I've got an FBI tactical unit positioned on the levels immediately above and below ready for my call. If anything happens to me, no one will walk out of here alive."

"We can discuss this like professionals," Col. Hamilton said, holding his hands up, his voice calm, his eyes locked on Marion's.

"He kidnapped Adam's brother," Marion said. "He assassinated both CEOs of Zeitnot Industries and sent the PRI Black Ops squad after me."

"Is this true?" Colonel Hamilton asked, stepping back from Mr. MITS, who had begun thrashing, looking around to a force unseen by the others but that must have been encircling him. Finally, down on his knees, sweating profusely and trembling, he looked up to Marion

"And you thought, what, you'd infect me?" he asked. "Sic your dogs on me?"

"I might call them off if you tell me where Chris is."

"You can't call them off," he said, then grabbed at his ears and screamed. "And we were trying to save Chris. Zeitnot Industries didn't like him prying into their affairs. The men you went after — the shooter teams you engaged and the men chasing you in Germany — were not the Black Ops team. We were there, but we were trying to help you. It was Zeitnot's security force that was after him, sent by their CEO. They took Chris. I don't know where they have him."

"Pietro Olikov is dead."

"What's wrong with him?" the colonel asked.

"Shadow folk," Marion said. "I'll explain later, but we thought it was time to fight fire with fire."

"Pietro wasn't the CEO," Mr. MITS said. "He was a pawn, like Simon. The CEO was appointed by the new board after the assassination of Simon Zeitnot.

From their various hiding spots, one by one, the Black Ops team revealed and stood by Col. Hamilton and Marion as Mr. MITS pulled himself up, looked at them all, then walked off into the shadows. That the Black Ops team held their weapons, albeit loosely, only reinforced for Marion that they were more for deterring him from following the man in the suit than standing in unison as the PRI.

"What did you set on him?" Colonel Hamilton asked.

"Shadow folk. Spirits. Demons. They haunt people."

"You did that to him, and he was trying to help," the colonel said.

"No, he wasn't," Marion said. "He's lying."

"So are you," said another of the Black Ops team. "There is no FBI tactical squad waiting in the shadows."

Marion took a few steps for his car before turning back to the colonel. "So, am I fired?"

"No," Hamilton said after a moment. "At least not yet. Not till you wrap up your current caseload. Including your most pressing assignment."

"And what would that be?" Marion asked.

"You've got to find Chris Richardson."

Marion returned to his car and drove away. He didn't return to his apartment, however, but drove around the city until he found a place to park near Oak Street Beach. Night had settled in, and even the city lights could not illuminate the waves crashing into the sandy shore. Marion took a step and felt something crunch under foot. A pebble. But knowing what he knew about the beach, it could very well have been a syringe, too. His coat pocket buzzed and vibrated.

What he would confess later was that he knew Chris would be taken. He knew Mr. MITS wouldn't draw attention to himself by killing my brother, but he needed Chris out of the way, so when Chris called him, panicked, Marion gave him unexpected advice. "Let them take you."

Now, where Chris was, Marion still did not know, but he'd given him a transmitter to hide on his person. When his phone rang, he wasn't too surprised; in fact, he'd expected it.

"Hello," he said calmly, his other senses shifting and scanning the darkness. The call had come at eleven, just like he and Chris had planned. That was a good sign. Not a true cell, not even a burner cell, but a piece of PRI tech.

Something undetectable unless its presence was already known.

"They brought me to a hospital. I'm in a regular room. There's a bed next to me, but it's empty."

"Do you know where?" Marion asked.

"We rode for about twelve hours without stopping, but no flying. I was in kind of an ambulance. I couldn't see out."

"Are any of them there with you?" Marion asked. Movement out of the periphery.He glanced over sharply, but it was just a torn page from the Sun Times. The wind was picking up.

"I don't know. But I don't think this hospital does just medical. I think there's research here too."

"Can you tell if any of the employees work for Zeitnot Industries?"

"No, I don't think so. Does Adam know? What did you tell him?"

"I told him I couldn't get to you, and I told him that we'd find you. You up for this?"

"It was the only other name on file. We have to follow this through."

"They'll be watching you. You remember the safe word?" Marion listened and nodded to the lapping lake. There was no one else on the beach. He said, "Be careful," and hung up, then stared out across the lake hidden by the night. He looked up but could only see a star or two. Not like the stars in northern Wisconsin, or like that one time he was out in the desert. He hated to lie to me, at that time, but he had little choice. Chris was right. This was the only lead.

VI

Afternoon debriefing went longer than expected due to the fiasco in the parking deck. Colonel Hamilton spoke to the final agent, as the hour pressed late. The city had already settled into nighttime. Normally, Hamilton would be home by five; now he'd be fortunate to make it by ten.

"It was a residual haunting," the young agent was saying. She had joined the Department just prior to Marion. "They thought it was intelligent because of the mannerisms, but each family member caught only part of the haunting."

"How did you decipher the type?"

These briefings were especially important for the newer agents. Veterans only spent a couple of minutes detailing their mission, leaving the report to fill in the details. With the newer agents, Hamilton wanted to hear the particulars of the case before they were committed to paper and filed away by Pythia — wherever she put them — never to be seen again.

"We used a combination of video and audio equipment to record the nightly activity, spaced out over three nights. It was while I watched the footage on a loop that I discovered the repeating pattern and determined they weren't dealing with something intelligent."

"So, your final determination?"

"They aren't in any danger, sir. I'll keep following up with them for one month, as per the guidelines, just to make sure, but my belief is that they'll learn to live with it and eventually not even notice it."

He nodded and offered the young agent a smile. She was eager to please and a good worker. Kept her nose to the grindstone, and all that. "Good. Write it up in your report. Submit by the morning to Pythia."

"Yessir," she said, rising. "Sir," she said, looking around the room. "I can't help but notice your number two isn't here, and that you are here very late. Mind if I inquire…"

"Goodnight, Becca. You've done good work. Go home and get some rest."

"Yessir," she said, finally, and walked out of the door.

The office was quiet, dark. The whole floor empty now, save for Pythia in her little cubicle, monitoring the phones. She never slept, as far as he knew. Never went anywhere, not that she could without being noticed; she stuck out like a sore thumb. And that was all he knew of her. If she had an apartment, he wasn't aware of it, nor if she had friends or family.

Her cage-like cubicle was always so hot, a dry kind of heat. He followed the orange glow to her little spot and poked his head in.

"Goodnight, Pythia," he said. Some people might be startled by the appearance of another in an otherwise empty office, but she didn't blink.

"Good night to you as well, Colonel. And Colonel?"

"Yes, Pythia."

"You know he'll be back."

She swiveled in her chair to meet his eyes. A deep breath issued from him before he offered a response.

"Did one of the Black Ops guys tell you what happened?"

"No. I know..."

"Right, right," he said. "You know all. What do you mean?"

"The man in the suit is an enigma to everyone, even to me, but I do know that this unit is his... and he won't like being displaced. He won't stand for it, for long, and he *will* find a way to retaliate."

"Marion thought of that, I think. Agent Case sent him... something... to keep him preoccupied."

"Shadow folk," Delphi said. "They will try and torment the man in the suit, and they will succeed for a time, but he'll find a way to best them and to return. You'll see."

"You know this?" Hamilton said.

"Yes. Because he always succeeds. This world is his for the taking."

"You chronicle everything, don't you?"

"Yessir."

"If anything happens to me, I want you to tell Agent Case. Marion. And his friends. They don't trust the man in the suit, and probably for good reason. So, if something... tell them, okay? What we talked about, what you know. Will you do that?"

"Yessir," she said. "You trust me. You don't believe I'd consort with that type."

"Your job has always been about illumination. Sometimes you speak in riddles, but that doesn't imply deception."

"Deception is a tool for the Machiavellian, and power – human power – earthly power – it doesn't interest me."

For some reason, that made sense to the colonel and brought him a bit of peace as he bid her goodnight again and left the building.

Still, he couldn't forget about what she said as he walked through the parking deck to his car, the winter wind whipping through the levels, forcing him to cinch his coat tightly around him. He looked around as his footsteps echoed on the concrete, sure with each reverberation that someone was following, lurking between vehicles or in the dark recesses of the corners. Surely Mr. MITS might appear, holding a gun, ready for retribution, the shadow folk Marion sicced on him merely a temporary distraction. He started the car remotely while he was still a distance away.

He checked the back seat before climbing into his SUV and didn't feel totally safe until he was out of the parking deck and deep in traffic. It was then that his phone rang.

"Hi Camille," he said.

"You sound exhausted," she answered, then got right to it before he could respond. "Kyle's yearbook photos are this week, and we still need to get his class ring."

Jesus, his youngest was already a senior. "Let me know how much," he said, pulling onto the Dan Ryan as fresh snow began to fall. "I can bring it over Saturday, maybe. We can talk."

"Use the Cash App." Her voice as chilly as the Chicago winter, she hung up.

He pulled into his apartment and fumbled for his keys, his mind now completely off Mr. MITS and settled more on missing his wife and kids and wanting a drink or two to unwind. He opened the door thusly preoccupied when he spied the man in the suit sitting in his leather recliner in the dark, becoming illuminated only when Hamilton flicked on the light.

"What the hell are you doing in my room?" the colonel asked, drawing his gun.

"They are effective," Mr. MITS said. "The shadow folk. It's been all I can do to suppress them. Kudos to your agent."

"You need to leave," the colonel said, drawing his service revolver from his coat and leveling it at the intruder's head.

"Now, John, is that a way to treat a guest?" He stood, but Hamilton kept the barrel aimed at his toad-like face.

"Guests are welcome. I don't even know your real name."

"Your abode needs more protection. I hesitate, you notice, to call it your home. Your home is with your estranged wife and your boys, miles away in the suburbs: a single-family two-storey home." He walked to the kitchen, pulled a glass from the right cabinet on the first attempt, and poured himself a whiskey, neat. The smell, he savored before taking a gulp.

"If I have to ask you again, you'll find a bullet between your eyes."

Mr. MITS offered a chuckle. "Your home needs such protection as well. You'd be surprised who can just walk in, upsetting your wife. Your kids."

"What do you want?"

"Nothing," Mr. MITS said, sipping his drink. "Just to remind you. You aren't safe. From me, from this world. If you side with Marion Case and Adam Richardson, you are on the wrong side. I'll best these shadow folk, Colonel."

He finished his drink and set the glass in the sink, then strolled past the colonel, toward the door.

"You come here again," the colonel said, "and I'll put a bullet between your eyes."

To this, Mr. MITS smiled, offered a wave, and shut the door behind him.

Only when he was sure he was gone did Hamilton reach for the door and engage the deadbolt, the doorknob lock, and the chain. He shut off the porch light and retreated to the kitchen, his weapon still raised and aimed at the door. Finally, he tucked the revolver away, and reaching into the same cabinet, he drew out a glass and poured himself a drink. And then another. And another.

Eventually he sat in his recliner, facing the front door, and sipped at the drink he kept refilling, his service weapon resting locked and loaded on the arm of the chair, just within reach. At some point, he sat the glass down. At some point, he palmed the weapon, and laid his head back, and slept fitfully. Dreams of me and Marion and Shimmers and shadow folk and Mr. MITS left him uneasy until the morning came and he found his apartment just as alone as it was the night before. And just like the night before, prior to discovering his intruder, Hamilton found his thoughts occupied by the wife and kids he missed desperately.

10

HILBERT'S SPACE

I

We had been experimenting with different antipsychotics following my diagnosis so that I could achieve maximum cognitive function and social interaction, with minimal negative side effects. For a time, Clozaril had been working, and I'd managed to avoid agranulocytosis, a potentially debilitating condition often associated with the drug. After Chris's disappearance, however, I got very sick. Dr. Blake thought it best that I switch to Abilify, with a small intermediary dose of Risperdal to help manage symptoms. This helped me manage the more negative symptoms like mania; to take my mind off of Chris, I had dived into my work with the PRI and needed focus now more than ever.

Specifically, I focused on Mr. MITS. While I had verbally opposed Marion using the Shadow Folk as weapons, I rejoiced in the idea of Mr. MITS suffering from their relentless haunts, their tortures on the mind, their unabated attacks on the psyche and soul of any living individual. Perhaps he now understood how it felt to be me, and oh, the repercussions of such an act! Should he be locked away! Should he go certifiably insane from their attacks! In a moment of desperation, surely, he'd return my brother to me unscathed. But more than that, with him experiencing such aggravated torrents from unseen forces, perhaps a compatriot in these experiences might finally give some validation to my own experiences.

Dr. Blake continued to maintain a healthy dose of skepticism despite all she'd seen, but hers was not from being obtuse, but rather, a desire to understand the unknowable. She was a true scientist. She no longer doubted the Shimmers or my dear, dead roommate, or some of the horrific things we'd seen during our time at the PRI, but as a scientist she desired to relate those things in context with the observable world. Modern mainstream science had become, she said, as closed-minded as a Protestant preacher, the latter eschewing anything not biblically sound and puritanically dogmatic and the former unwilling to consider anything that, in its hubris, it could not explain away. If it didn't fit into their narrow world views, she said, then it wasn't real.

But she still insisted that I was sick. That the bombardment of these tormentors had given me a different kind of post-traumatic stress disorder that manifested more along the lines of schizophrenia, though, since my symptoms focused on the hallucinations, she had been prone by degrees to lessen my diagnosis to a kind of residual-type schizophrenia. I took this as progress but longed for the day that my brother could return and see me no longer afflicted. If he came back, he would not have to care for me anymore.

But the first step for any of this was to take down Mr. MITS. Marion, for his part, was examining the file for any clue about the connection between the nom de plume of Isem R. Smit and Zeitnot Industries, the projects and business affairs of which seemed to be directly related to most of the cases we studied at the PRI.

I buckled down with work. Now, I have long believed that everyone listens to music when they get ready in the morning. Music of all types (save country, death-metal, and most hip-hop) soothes my condition. I asked the detective what his favorite music was, and he said he couldn't remember, then mumbled something about it being a curse of the dead, to not remember music. I hoped fervently upon hearing this that he would not be stuck here forever but would end up some place where there was music again. The record player in my bedroom played Pearl Jam on vinyl while I shaved and shimmied in front of my bathroom mirror in preparation for our flight back up to Chicago.

From behind me, the ghost laughed.

"You goofy-looking bastard," Leo said.

I turned to him thoughtfully, mid-stroke up my neck and half my face still left to feel the razor. "Can you hear this? The music?"

He was just as thoughtful with his response. "Sound is different on my side. Anything melodious sounds... muffled."

"Like underwater?" I asked.

"Like it's in mud," he said. "But no emotion—no joy, no sorrow. Just flat. Not just songs, but voices, sounds in general. Except..."

He looked away. As a clump of shaving cream dripped onto my shirt, I wiped it away and turned back to my refection, to continue shaving. I could see him in the mirror, which wasn't always the case, so I figured he must allow such things at times. I gave him time to work the words out on his own.

"The shadow folk," he said finally. "And the Shimmers. I can hear them. Really hear them. Not like you do. They sound..." and this was another thought he couldn't vocalize, save for the shiver that visibly shook his image. He looked at me, frightened, this tremulous ghost.

"What about other ghosts? Angels?"

He shook his head. "I don't meet enough of the first, and I ain't never met the second. Angels might have been a myth invented by demons to give a false sense of hope."

That unnerved me on so many levels. I finished getting ready and took my morning pills, and let the conversation die. What curiosity I'd had about insights into the dead had been satiated for the moment. I finished packing my bag as the doorbell rang; Dr. Blake stood on the other side, offering me her most comforting smile. She saw all I'd been through with Chris. She might not have agreed with me over everything, but she served as my support.

"Ready?"

I nodded. I hitched my bag strap to my shoulder and tried to smile in return.

"It'll be okay," she said. "We'll get him back soon."

For us, that was all that was said of importance as we traveled in the plane north from XNA to Chicago. We arrived unceremoniously and, greeted by Marion, we rode to the PRI headquarters in the Federal Building in downtown Chicago. In the boardroom, Colonel Hamilton stood waiting. Pythia sat at her laptop, ready for transcription and a few other agents sat in chairs. But Mr. MITS was nowhere to be found.

Pythia spoke up: "Dell Labs called again."

"More gremlins," said one of the agents.

"Who's going to take it?" she asked, and that agent raised his hand.

"How is the Romani case?" Colonel Hamilton asked.

A few days after returning from the house in South Arkansas, Marion and I had been sent out to Oregon on a case involving a migrant camp being overrun by law enforcement and retaliating with hex magic. I announced: "We went to Oregon. We found the source of the curse." That was all I cared to say on the subject.

"We eradicated all potentially dangerous subversives," Marion said. He shot me a look that said I should play along. Our discord came from our individual understanding of the situation in Oregon. I believed the Romani weren't totally at fault, but Marion still believed that the PRI was the law, and that black was black and white was white.

The colonel looked at me specifically. "And that's all?"

"The curse was lifted," I answered, lowering my eyes to the tabletop.

That answer seemed to satisfy the bureaucratic minds, and our meeting was adjourned for a break that was long enough to allow me to stretch my legs. I hurried to the lobby and stepped out into downtown Chicago to breathe in the industrial air. That was when I saw him: a strange little man with a potbelly and a five o'clock shadow, a nervous little man whose tics extended beyond the constant adjustment of his glasses to glancing over his shoulder at every beep of a car horn and every yell of a pedestrian, and every sound produced by the city.

He studied me, and I studied him; he smiled and I frowned. He crossed the nearest crosswalk and approached me, extended his right hand, and cocked his head like a curious Labrador unsure of its owner's behavior. I shook his hand and cocked my head to the other side.

I said, "Hello."

"I've been looking for you," he said, his voice timid, a bit high pitched and nasal. "I knew you'd be here."

I had a million questions. Who was he? How did he find me? How did he know who I was? Why did he expect to find me here? But, "How?" was all I could vocalize.

"I know where you are always," he said. "I know all your locations."

"Who are you?" I asked.

"I'm Hilbert," he said, as though that were all the answer I needed.

I did not see a threatening individual, but a man, slight of stature with a sadness in his eyes, like he was trapped or in mourning. I didn't understand then just how perceptive that was. Hilbert asked if we could get off the street, but when I offered sanctuary at the federal building, he cried out like a beaten puppy and said that was the worst place we could go. With all that had happened lately, I sympathized with his distrust.

So, I phoned Marion, who offered up his place, and an hour after meeting him, we stood in his downtown Chicago apartment with my partner, the ghost, and Dr. Blake all accompanying us. Hilbert looked around shiftily and asked if the place was bugged.

"These are my friends."

He looked at me and at each of us in turn, even pausing to turn his face where the ghost stood, which gave Leo and me pause, and said, "A possibility— one of the possibilities I see is that Agent Case's apartment has been bugged with technology he cannot comprehend."

This presented our first problem, even as the timid little Hilbert clutched his hands together. I had yet to introduce anyone to him, and I hadn't called Marion by name when we spoke on the phone. Marion ordered Hilbert to identify himself. Hilbert flinched away and raised his bare, empty hands over his head. He shied away, nearly weeping.

"I'm a doctor," he repeated three times without a breath.

"Fine, doctor, how did you find—?" Marion began.

"I'm a physicist, a theoretical physicist. May I please have some water?" Marion pointed to the cups and Dr. Blake fetched some water from a pitcher in the fridge. Hilbert collapsed on Marion's loveseat and buried his face in his hands till the water was brought to him, and then he drank noisily. He took several deep breaths before continuing. I could see the carotid jumping out on his neck. "Do you know Quantum Theory?" he asked of an ignorant room. I'd heard about it, but I was no physicist.

"I can see into every possible multiverse that exists and I can see everything that can or should happen."

"How?" I asked. I meant how was it possible, but I also meant to question what series of events occurred that would give a man such an ability.

Hilbert glanced out Marion's window and cried out, pointing, saying that that woman shouldn't cross the street. A bus whizzed by, and he began to weep. We all saw the woman jaunt into a shop and Hilbert, doing a double take, dried his eyes. "In another space, she... didn't make it," he said. "I see all outcomes unless I concentrate really hard, and even then, sometimes it isn't enough."

I felt immediate sympathy for him; I glanced over to the dead detective who appeared to me whether I asked him to or not, and I thought of the Shimmers. Then I remembered Hilbert had seen the detective as well. I mentioned this, surprising both Dr. Blake and Marion.

"I see him," Hilbert said simply, and then he looked again at Leo. "You're dead here, right? Yes. No, don't answer that. You are dead in a lot of space. But one or two, you weren't murdered. You survived the murder plot and are wearing a captain's badge and... on your lapel..." He squinted as though reading something, took his glasses off and cleaned them. "CPD special liaison to the PRI. That's the office you wanted to take me to?" he asked me.

"Do you know who killed me?" Leo asked. I started to translate for him to the living as I often had to do, but Hilbert was already shaking his head.

"I'm sorry, I don't, Detective. I just see what I see right now. The woman who just got hit in one of the other spaces, I didn't know her name or her parents or where she's from."

"This is impossible," Dr. Blake said. "You're talking science fiction."

"Actually," Hilbert said, "physicists are finding more and more that this is science fact."

"Yeah," Marion said. "You mentioned quantum theory?"

"We've toyed with the idea of a multiverse for a number of years, now, and the math is playing this out in several possible ways. One is that our universe—our galaxy and all the billions of galaxies that make up the known universe—is just one bubble in a swath of bubbles, each filled with billions and billions of galaxies. Another theory is that the multiverse is a series of parallel universes layered side by side and is based on Heisenberg's Uncertainty Principle. That states—"

Dr. Blake spoke up. "You can know either the speed of a quantum object or its location, but you can't know both."

"Precisely!" Hilbert beamed.

"But it also suggests," Dr. Blake went on, "thanks to the two-slit experiment, that an observer can indirectly affect the system he's observing."

Hilbert frowned. "That is my hope. But I thought you didn't understand quantum mechanics."

She blushed. "That's the sum-total of my knowledge."

"You're talking small, like atoms," Marion said.

"And smaller," Hilbert said. "The two-slit experiment was conducted with electrons."

"But you're talking universes," Marion went on. "Women walking out in front of buses. People alive in one world and dead in another. You're talking big."

Hilbert nodded. "For years that was the problem, that we couldn't rationalize what happened in the quantum world with what happened in the big world. In the big world, gravity is one of the strongest, most impactful forces, but in the quantum world, gravity is a lightweight, pushed out by the strong force, the weak force, and the nuclear force. But we postulated that what we saw on the quantum level had to carry over into the big world, and we've searched for a unifying theory that could forever link the two worlds together: the elusive *Theory of Everything*."

"That sounds—" Dr. Blake began.

"Arrogant," Hilbert said, hanging his head. "Time-consuming. Petulant. I think we started out with the best of intentions. We said at first that there had to be an explanation because God is not a magician. Along the way, we even forgot that God was on the stage."

"What do you need from us?" I asked.

"In another space, the PRI are lauded as heroes. You are all so well known. I thought you could help me, protect me. Teach me not to see the other things."

We were ready to discuss just how we could help him when Hilbert and Leo both alerted us to sights and sounds that the rest of us couldn't sense.

I heard Leo say, "You're being followed!" at the same time Hilbert said, "They are coming up the stairs," as the door flew open and armed men in black entered the room. Marion dispatched them quickly, shot a couple of them, then led us down the stairs, and we hurried into the bustling streets of Chicago to find refuge in the Windy City.

We walked without direction, only to keep moving, and after a few city blocks, I took stock of our group and saw that Dr. Blake was missing. Leo blinked out of sight for several tense minutes, only to reappear and say she was safe.

Still, I was afraid. We hadn't seen Mr. MITS in a while, and he seemed to have his hands in everything. What if he was involved here too?

"Those men weren't Black Ops," Marion said, and placed a call. Hanging up, he steered us to his car and then drove us toward the airfield."

"We're taking the PRI jet," I said.

"We're getting out of the city," Marion said. "Until we can regroup and find out exactly what's going on."

"We can't just leave Dr. Blake," I said. No one had called her, attempted to retrieve her.

"I don't think those men were after us," Marion said. "We're collateral damage. I think they're after him." I looked at the sheepish, timid Hilbert, the theoretical physicist who had displayed such an amazing and traumatizing gift and watched him nod to me. He had, after all, asked for our protection.

II

Dr. Blake had received a text from an old friend, so she broke off from us and walked to a nearby diner, where Puck sat in a booth, sipping coffee. He was dressed as he always was, in basic black. He smiled but did not rise as she walked in, took her seat, and ordered a cup of coffee. He asked how she was, and how her father was, and she said he was well; they waited until the waitress delivered her coffee before delving into the meat of the conversation.

"It might not have been wise invoking the shadow folk."

She gaped for a second before saying, "I've always felt you had a tracker on me, Puck." She sighed. Took stock of the room. It wasn't too busy at this hour, the smattering of patrons too consumed with their own problems to notice the tall, thin pale man. He had a knack for finding places not too busy but near enough to her location. She wondered if he really did have some kind of tracker.

"You are important to me," he said, sipping his coffee.

She leveled her gaze at him. "And you to me. So, what is this about? Really?"

"You and your friends have been visited by a man, very recently. I saw him talking to your friend, Adam."

"What do you know about this, Puck?"

He took a sip of coffee, then made a bitter face and regarded his mug for a moment.

"I think it's time I meet your friends."

"This man. I'm having a hard time wrapping my head around…"

He smiled. "Your people are so adorable. You are stuck in that infant stage of intellectual evolution where everything is still considered irrelevant if it can't be observed. Have you ever wondered why we became friends, Samantha?"

She nodded.

"Because I see something in you, and I have known all our lives that you and those you'd associate with are capable of rising to the next level. Your physicist is telling the truth. He can see the various universes, as scientists can observe the conflicting movements and behaviors of various electrons. But there is something else to that equation, more pertinent than the ramifications of the observable world realizing quantum behavior."

"That the very act of observing can affect the outcome," she said.

Puck nodded gravely, and he took a sip of bitter java. "He's observing a merging of universes, Sam. Eventually, the universes will collide and cancel each other out."

He didn't need to explain the direness of that statement.

"How do we stop it?" she asked.

Puck had an answer that she didn't like, and soon they parted ways; he disappeared into the throng of Chicago pedestrians, and she hailed a cab to Midway, where Marion stood guard by the plane, his gun drawn to make sure that the airport security kept any and all intruders at bay.

III

St. Louis, Missouri—

In a refurbished brownstone in a gentrified neighborhood, we took shelter with Bob Link, the psychic journalist. Why I felt the need to introduce more people into this plot seemed foolish, till I reminded everyone that we couldn't know if Mr. MITS was involved and, assuming he was, we couldn't know if our own homes were safe. Those mysterious armed men in black had found us at Agent Case's apartment, after all.

The short, squat, and ponytailed Bob Link fixed us all drinks and tried to put the nervous Hilbert at ease. He offered us the standard finger foods to eat and, when his journalist partner Ernie Quill arrived, the latter filled in everyone on what he found. Hilbert's research department held a government grant funded by the Department of Defense. Ernie Quill was just as curious why a military contractor would be interested in a man who could see parallel universes and alternate realities.

I realized that another question remained unanswered. I poured a cup of water and sat next to him. Above us, the others argued. Marion was concerned with intelligence, with this armed team coming. Ernie Quill and Bob Link debated the importance of a man able to see other realities. Samantha told us what she'd learned but not how she learned it. This stopped us all.

"You're saying he can destroy our universe?" Marion said.

I offered him water, and Hilbert took it and drank voraciously.

"I don't know." Samantha said. "I don't know how."

"Who told you this?" Ernie questioned.

"How can we stop this?" Bob asked.

Dr. Blake shook her head.

"When did you learn this?" I asked. It was my question that would get answered, however indirectly.

Hilbert's sigh captured the room. "We postulated, acting on what we knew of quantum theory, that multiverses would not be set eons apart, but would act more like electrons. We could know either their speed or their location, but not both; still, the math bore out that they were past a flimsy membrane but lay basically in congruence with our world. If we could but peer through the veil, we could see other universes, the other possibilities.

"I became obsessed with this idea. After all, there might exist another world where an intrepid physicist better balanced his time at home and at work, and his wife didn't feel abandoned... and he with all his knowledge might have caught the early symptoms of his little girl's leukemia. And he might have sought treatment sooner, before she was symptomatic, and would have thus saved her life."

Dr. Blake put a hand to her lips as tears welled, while Ernie stood stoic and speechless, and Bob's mouth gaped silently. Marion looked deflated; Leo paled. I listened to the silence in the room.

"I obsessed over the idea after her funeral," Hilbert said. "And sometime after, I saw another world — a flash really — where she was okay. In that world, the intrepid physicist existed, and knew how to balance work and home. In that world, they existed happily and eventually welcomed another child into their little family."

"At least you have that," Marion said.

Tears streamed down Hilbert's face. He shook his head. "No, no. That was the other space. I can see it, but I can't be there. My wife blamed me. I couldn't have known. And the cancer, it was fast-acting. She went so quickly. Too quickly. And then my wife went too."

"But you get to see her," Bob Link said. "In some way or another, she still exists."

"It's such a shame," Ernie said.

"I think," Dr. Blake started, "we need to go see my friend. We can find him—"

"Back in Chicago?" Marion added. "We aren't prepared. We have—"

"He's our only hope!" she responded, and I understood how much she trusted this source.

"We don't know him!" Marion said. I got it. I saw Marion's doubt and Dr. Blake's trust, because I saw both positions in me as I looked at the poor, sad man hunkered down before me. .

Hilbert tugged at my shirt sleeve. "Maybe you aren't sick," he said to me. "Maybe you see other realities too. Like me."

Bob Link said if there were answers, perhaps they should seek them out, and Ernie Quill said that he was tired of all this discussion. They all began to bicker, disagreeing about what should happen next, and I wanted to speak up — I tried to though I was shushed — and then I heard the door close. I pointed toward the door and for the second time, the room quieted.

Hilbert had left.

IV

Marion was the first physically out the door, though the ghost had beaten me (and most of us, and I assumed Marion) to the street. I arrived to see Marion sprinting down the street, losing ground on a white panel van that was speeding away. Bob revved the engine of his convertible, the first to catch up to Marion, as the rest of us piled into Ernie Quill's Escalade. We raced through the streets of Bob's neighborhood, winding our way through the city streets, headed for the river. Bob's sports car caught up to the van before losing them in the traffic of the causeway, while we struggled to keep up, no visual line of sight of either Bob's car or the van, but in constant phone contact. Leo, meanwhile, would flash intermittently onto the seat next to me in the back, reporting in before he vanished again.

I slapped the back of Dr. Blake's seat. "Leo says they are losing him."

"How could he lose him?" Samantha asked.

Leo said there were two paths he could have gone, that Hilbert's aura extends down both of them. "Can't you see if one of them doubles back?" I asked the ghost.

"One of what?" Ernie Quill asked me, swerving through traffic. "Why is there always traffic during a car chase?" he asked Dr. Blake.

Leo snapped at me: "I ain't a fucking dog, man!" and I turned away; he knew I didn't like to be yelled at.

"There!" Dr. Blake uttered. Obediently, Ernie Quill pulled over, joining Bob's car on the shoulder of the causeway. I saw her look at her cell phone as we exited. The significance of this I didn't realize until I saw a tall man in dark clothing emerge from an alley near us and wave us over. He caught our attention, his arrival and appearance distracting us as she slid into the driver's seat of Quill's SUV behind us and sped away. Marion turned, directed Bob to follow her, but the tall man spoke.

"My name is Puck. I sent Samantha on after Hilbert, but we both thought it was imperative that you understand the inherent danger of the scientist's ability."

"Can't you explain it after we get Hilbert to safety?" Marion asked.

"String Theory dictates," Puck began, ignoring the question, a strange calm in his voice, like he hadn't a care in the world, "that all the dimensions are tied together. Your science can't understand it yet, but the uncertainty principle can be solved and will help explain what Hilbert is seeing. That he can both know the location and see these other realities in spacetime means that he is inadvertently drawing these realities together. "It would be best for our world, for all universes, if he doesn't live."

"You sent the men after him," Marion said.

"I assure you, I didn't. But I don't think, in this instance, they should be stopped either."

"Who are you?" I asked. A secret she'd kept from me. Her own darkness, when she forced me to expose so much of my own.

"I have been friends with Samantha for a very long time," the strange pale man said, "and while I will probably divulge more at the appropriate time, that time is not now."

As though his words were a portent, Marion's cell rang, identifying Dr. Blake as the caller. He answered with clipped responses; we piled into the convertible as Puck retreated back down the alley despite my calls to him to join us and sped the two blocks to the riverfront. At a warehouse by a dock, we found first Ernie's Escalade, parked and unscathed. Then, we saw her kneeling by an office door, cradling something in her lap— Hilbert's head, his body lay prostrate on the ground. Dr. Blake crying over the broken, bloodied body of the physicist.

Law enforcement swarmed. Sirens blared. An ambulance and two fire trucks showed up, too late, futile. It was all futile. Hilbert was dead, shot between the eyes. We gathered around Dr. Blake, putting as many arms around her as we could, but it was Marion's shoulder she chose to cry on. We asked her what happened; she said men in black came with guns. We inspected her for injuries and found where a bullet had sliced through her right triceps—grazed her, really; the poor thing must have been in such shock, she had blocked out the pain. She made no motion, just stood mutely until Marion led her to the ambulance.

V

The man in the suit met another man in a suit in a sun-soaked Chicago park, several days later. The other man hailed from a consortium. He identified himself as a physicist to everyone he met. He'd already met Mr. MITS. The two sat on a park bench under the sunshine, a soft breeze blowing in off Lake Michigan.

"We were right to be concerned," the man said. Mr. MITS nodded.

"It could have meant the death of countless worlds."

"Still, to understand what he saw. To get to catalogue and witness for ourselves."

"It is no longer our concern," Mr. MITS reminded him, "and the ability is no longer ours to control."

"I can dream."

"Not on my time," Mr. MITS said, and stood and walked away, for now, pushing away his acquired demons so that no one else could see the torment he consistently felt.

~

Chris slept. When he awoke, he received more meds that put him back to sleep. He was only vaguely aware of tests, of poking and prodding and X-rays. The only person he really saw was his nurse, a blonde built like a porn star who coddled him.

One night, after she fed him the pills, he pretended to drift off and waited for her to leave. Sure she was gone, he spit the pills into his hand and climbed out of bed. He opened his door, scanning the hospital halls. No sound. No movement. Pulling the door shut behind him, he padded over the tiles till he reached a corner. He peeked. A woman in seafoam scrubs sat at the nurse's station. He dared not move, for he saw another figure walk up to the station.

"Excuse me, ma'am," Mr. MITS said. "I need to see Dr. Green immediately."

Chris darted down a hall as the doctor emerged from a nearby office.

Dr. Green said, "I am a very busy man."

"You have your funding now," Mr. MITS said. "Zeitnot Industries."

"How—?"

"A lot of interested parties bought up the company when the CEOs were murdered; they all had stockholders, and there was a primary stockholder."

"You are peeling again. I warned you this was a side effect of the cryonics process."

"Where?" Mr. MITS seemed rattled. Chris couldn't imagine him rattled.

"Here. Behind the ear." The doctor reached up and pulled away a transparent flake of flesh.

They walked away. Afraid he'd be seen, Chris ducked back to his bed. He pushed the button behind his earlobe, waited for the signal, then left a voicemail for Agent Case. Then he dug into his pocket and found the pills he had pretended to take. He swallowed them now and slept dreamlessly.

VI

Morning came, dewy on the screens of the windows, a chill in the air, a low fog hugging the grounds. The colonel rose as the first rays of sunlight penetrated his blinds and his Keurig provided him the means to continue with the morning.

The fact was, his bed wasn't uncomfortable. His neck pain and upper back pain which had subsisted in the marital bed had all but disappeared with this new mattress and pillow. He turned on CNN and sipped his coffee, flavored now with Half 'n Half and a bit of sugar. The news played in the background, with him barely attentive to it. The world was malleable. His thoughts were concerned with this Hilbert guy and his own family.

"I can't download the app," he said, the phone pressed to his ear. "I'll swing by, Camille."

"Whatever."

"What happened to us?"

She responded with a sigh. The phone call had gone on too long.

"What do you expect me to say?" she asked. He hung up. The apartment lived in brown and neutral tones, sanitized, cold. He slept here comfortably, but he didn't feel at home.

He missed them.

He missed his wife and his children. He missed that his boys were growing up. He missed his wife's full lips, her widened hips, the way she carried a blouse, but more than that he missed her thigh against his after sex, the door shut to their dog or the outside world, just the two of them cuddling. A lover's embrace.

"I love you," he whispered to her in such moments, and she had echoed the claim.

She had, until one day.

Sex had become as ritual as washing the dishes, and it had been a bright and sunny afternoon when she rolled away from him, sighing after he came. His cock well lubed, he reached around her waist, still hard and hoping for more.

"I said I love you."

"Yes, you did," she responded.

And that was it. He moved out soon after, after their talk, and their talk with their kids. He hadn't been there for her, and that was the main issue. She saw that his work came first and responded appropriately.

He walked to his new bathroom and rubbed on the stick of antiperspirant, then sprayed on some cologne, and shaved and dressed like he was going to the office, though that was never his destination.

The car started efficiently, warming the seats. Above, the sky was cloudless and the air was cool. The winter chill invigorated him. Might there be another reality where he still woke up next to his wife and kissed her good morning? Perhaps, but not here.

The flower shop was but a few blocks away. He parallel parked and broached the entrance, smelling the inviting aroma of the neighborhood florist. Camille's favorite had always been irises, so he ordered a dozen. He toyed with adding baby's breath to the bouquet and a signed card, but nixed those ideas, figuring the simpler the better. The bouquet, wrapped in plastic, was tucked into the passenger seat next to him, riding shotgun until he arrived at the all-too-familiar drive.

Snow had begun to fall as he pulled into the empty driveway, the garage door closed. Was that fascia leaking over the garage still? Silently he admonished her, getting it out of his system as he rang the doorbell, the bulge of irises tucked behind his back.

"It's too early," Camille said, punctuating her exasperation with a sigh.

"Might I come in?" the colonel asked, producing the bouquet from behind his back, shrugging humbly. "Just to talk for a few minutes."

She seemed transfixed in the flowers for a spell unmarked by time, broken only by the fluttering of her eyelids and an exasperated gaze turned his way.

"Why do you do this to yourself?"

"I miss you," the colonel said. "And I miss the boys."

"We are gone," she said, shaking her head. Her eyes conveyed such sorrow for him. I've seen that look too, offered up to me by my brother, my doctor, the nursing staff, when I was insistent in seeing what couldn't possibly be there.

"But the prom pictures...?"

The door opened, and a haggard Black man with a beard stood in the frame, looming over him. He rubbed at his eyes, hadn't even changed out of his sweats, shirt, and robe.

"Prom pictures?" the man said.

Did the irises wilt in the colonel's palm?

"My family," he offered weakly, confused.

"Can I help you, sir?" the man at the door asked. Colonel Hamilton stepped back, regarded the structure. Sure, the basic outline was the same, but the colors were different. And when he stepped back for another look, he saw the landscaping was all wrong. The flower bed off the porch didn't follow such a curved path, and he'd never use red mulch.

"I'm sorry," the colonel replied. "I'm at the wrong house."

The man shut the door and Hamilton returned to his car. He tossed the flowers into the passenger seat and masked his face with his palms, dragging his nails against the flesh, screeching a mute scream until he looked up and — for a moment — again saw the house the way he remembered it. Then, just as suddenly, it wasn't.

I'm at the wrong address, he thought, and pulled out of the drive, and found landmarks and guides back to the home he'd purchased so long ago with Camille. A block from the elementary school, three houses down from the intersection on the left.

The same house. He pulled into the same drive. The same colors. The same landscaping. His, but it wasn't his. It was different now, alien. Because someone had *made* it different, alien. The man at the door. He'd changed it. But why?

Perhaps to make Hamilton doubt reality. Perhaps this man was in league with Mr. MITS, and this, finally this, was his revenge. But what this man nor the man in the suit had anymore was the full power of the federal government behind them, and exiting his SUV, Hamilton intended to rain that power down on this block, at this hour.

The front door of the house opened again, and Camille walked out, wearing her slippers, her silk robe cinched tightly around her body, the man of the house keeping pace behind her.

"Where are the flowers?" she asked.

Her eyes were silverfish scales that reflected the moonlight. She didn't blink. Didn't react.

"Tucked away," the colonel said, motioning back toward his ride.

She sighed, in that her chest and shoulders rose and fell, but her eyes never wavered.

"I'm sorry for all I did wrong. I'm sorry I let you down."

"Forever and ever and ever," she said.

He looked past her. "What have you done to her?" he demanded.

The Black man shrugged. "This is your trippy fantasy, bruh. I'm just along for the ride."

In the front seats, the heat blew from the vents and the flowers crunched under the Black man's weight. Hamilton clutched the wheel and stared at the bloody body of his wife, prostrate in the spotlight of his vehicle's headlights.

"So, where is she?" the Black man asked.

"I couldn't afford the house," Hamilton said.

"You could afford it," the Black man said. "Where is she?"

"They weren't there at the house," Hamilton said.

"No, but I was. I was at your house."

The night unfolded before them. The stars rolled passed their windows, and the landscape whipped along, appearing and vanishing just as quickly, hinting at the world around them.

"You have no business at my house," the colonel said.

"You don't want to be there."

"I do!" Hamilton said, slamming his hands on the wheel, from which his passenger recoiled.

"Sorry, dude. Really." The Black man pulled the lever that helped the passenger seat recline. "But *do* you want to be there? I mean, your job has always taken precedence. First the Air Force. Now this PRI."

Now gripping the wheel, staring out into the starry, desert night, the colonel cast a menacing glance sideways at his passenger. "Reclining isn't safe."

The hands went behind his fellow traveler's head. "Yet you've been reclining, settling on procedure, hoping that the normalcy of reality will coax you beyond this horror. You can't escape it."

His passenger seemed quite complacent, eyes nearly closed, breathing easily, when a horn alerted the colonel back to his driving. Though he jerked the wheel, it was too late. The oncoming sedan's driver's side bumper clipped his SUV with a spark. As the former spun into the opposite field, his vehicle careened over the curb, jumped the median and nosedived into the trunk of a small oak.

A deep breath, eyes closed. His ribs ached. His arms were stiff and his back felt immovable. If he turned his head more than forty-five degrees either way, his spine might crack open like a lobster shell. When he managed to glance at the passenger seat, there was no sign of his companion. What was going on? he muttered.

He forced his left arm to stretch beyond its socket, to snap the button for the seatbelt that strapped him in. With its release, Hamilton let out a great sigh. His door opened, and he tumbled out, tasting the dirt and grass of the median.

Cool. The air was cool and the sky was bright and cool and the stretch of highway was cool and bright. Cool and naked. Cold. He had had a passenger. The passenger was cold. He knew something about Camille. Something cold about her.

A slight explosion drew his attention back to the ditch on the other side of the road. It was muffled, not intended to destroy the other vehicle, but to draw his attention. The Black man stood next to him watching the artificial flames.

"You never even learned my name," the man said.

"You answered my door," Hamilton said.

"I wasn't drinking, but you know that. I had a family too. Wife. Kids. I was a computer programmer."

Bodies poured from the wreckage, engulfed in flames. One called out his name. The others cried, "Daddy!"

"I'm sorry," the man said. "For what you lost and for what I lost. She shouldn't have run that stop sign and I shouldn't have been arguing with my project leader and speeding."

"Daddy, help us," the voices said.

"And now your wife is dead, and your kids are dead, and I'm dead."

"Honey, help us," the burning driver said.

"And this is how you spend your free time. Dreaming a messed-up dream like this that's the best hope for some kind of inner peace."

The colonel sat back in his recliner in his apartment, sipping his eighth beer.

But the colonel's sobs weren't enough to absolve himself of the guilt that drove him to sell the house he'd bought with his wife, and so lose the home he'd built with his wife and kids, to move into his own apartment, to imagine that his family had abandoned him rather than the truth.

The truth was, he was all alone. The only ones that spoke to him were the ghosts of the past.

VII

It is interesting to note that the apartment, while furnished, was uncluttered. You'd think a man of the world would clutter his living space with things of this world, but the man I'd named Mr. MITS, aka Isem R. Smitt, aka who *knows* his real name, while he was a prince of this world, was not entertained by this world. He wasn't hypnotized by the trinkets or objects. The latest tech didn't entice him. He led, by all accounts, a simple life. But this didn't mean that he wasn't interested in this world; no, he was engaged in politics. Every book that came down the pike, whether it were a grimoire or history or a biography, or political science or a piece of historical fiction, he bought it and read it. He thrived on these books, and he thrived on these stories, because they were stories of the powerful. This was what cluttered his otherwise meager apartment.

But to reduce him to a Machiavellian sycophant doesn't do him justice. Sycophants are followers, and Machiavelli was limited to human flaws. Mr. MITS had spent years, for example, examining the spiritual. This night, he'd just returned from a séance at a reputed medium's house, where he'd been cast out violently, though he'd only arrived with the most innocent of intentions. He was no follower.

Now, you might ask yourself how I come by this information. I'll answer by affirming how I came by all my information: from the source. I had a chance to talk to Colonel Hamilton at length about the things he saw — about his life — prior to his death, just as I had a chance to squeeze out the little bit of information this man in the suit would provide. Once we had him, he was quite talkative. That story doesn't occur in the timeline of this book's chronology, but I will cover it later. For right now, just be aware that I am confident in relating the story of Mr. MITS and the shadow folk.

They'd weighed down on him since Marion had set him as a target, and so the man in the suit had fallen depressed. His world now darker, colder, he slumped his shoulders and returned to his apartment, plagued with two ideas: how he could defeat these entities and how he could rise above this setback. The PRI was his key, and he had to get back involved in the intricacies of the agency. He felt out of control, powerless.

In his bed, curled in the fetal position, intoxicated by a dose of melatonin and a shot of bourbon, the man — now devoid of his suit, sleeping only his boxers and a Tee — tried with futility to sleep. The whispers came from the darkened corners, the deepest shadows. This is what first roused him from his rest.

He breathed in deep and kicked his legs. And saw the corner move.

"So, you're here."

Now turning his back to the door, the man squeezed his eyes shut and cinched the sheets around his body. The walls began, as an answer, to breathe. Hypnotized, eyes now wide, he watched them, realizing only as he followed the movements that what he mistook for exhalations was really a sliding motion, as the shadow folk painted every wall and the ceiling above in a kind of liquid black that undulated as though they were waves in a pool of oil.

Then the voices started.

"We are legion. We know your thoughts." Thousands of them echoed through his mind. Unrelenting, speaking in rounds so that the words became muddled sound. They were in his head, so he couldn't shut them out. He couldn't just bury his head in the pillow, though he tried. No matter which room he was in, the shadow folk followed, incessantly singing their hellish requiem.

This went on for a week: the man in the suit locked in his own apartment, tormented all day, every hour, by these creatures. When the voices finally quieted, he looked up and around, to see that his walls had returned to normal, that it was daylight, and that only one, a red-eyed being wearing a hat, now stood by the wall. It had no face, but the man thought it was grinning.

"You don't know who I am, do you?" he said to the hat man.

"We do, actually." The figure's voice, oily and slick as the black waves had been, slithered into his head. "We've seen your secrets and your desires. We know why you are here and from where you came."

"Then you know you shouldn't be trifling with me. Is that why you stopped?"

"We think you could help us. We think you want to help us. The Seven torment the boy. Your feelings about the princes are as ours."

"A truce? But if we align against the princes now, we only help Adam Richardson, and his little band will be all the more dangerous."

"Not... if we wait until he's broken... and they are strong enough to return."

"If they are strong enough to return, will they be too strong for us?"

"No," the hat man hissed. "They only think they will be too strong. But we will best them, in the end, and then hell and earth will be yours, and heaven won't have the might to withstand such a combined assault... from man and demon."

So that was the plan. Too grandiose for Mr. MITS to hope for, but still within his reach. This shadow man could just be telling him what he thought he wanted to hear, but if it meant a truce, an end to the incessant haunting, the man known as Isem R. Smitt felt a truce would be prudent at this point in time.

VIII

Joined by a stout youth instead of his lanky, aged partner, Bob Link rose to hug a boy that shared his eyes, nose, and general build. He ushered a chair to him and sat back down, the cuffs of his coat dragging along the cement floor as he pulled his seat back up to the table.

Removing his coat and gloves and scarf, Warren said, "You look good, Dad."

"How ya been?" He couldn't help but beam at the boy. Warren was his pride and joy. When he was an infant, he looked just like Bob's baby pictures. Upon first seeing the swaddled babe, and cradling him in his arms, it had been just the three of them, for forever (in that time, Bob also had a black Lab—Bear—who followed him like a shadow).

"Good, Dad. School's going well. How're you? How's Uncle Ernie?"

"Good," Bob said with a smile. "I'll tell him you said hi."

He ordered beers for each of them, which were delivered after Warren produced his ID. They each took a sip before speaking again, and it was Warren's turn.

"So what's up? You call and say you want to meet up, and you never just want to chat."

"I was thinking about you, with this last case. And I wanted to see you."

The appetizer came: modestly spicy boneless chicken chunks slathered in hot sauce and sides of ranch and blue cheese. Warren jammed a forkful into his mouth.

"What's wrong, Dad? What happened?"

Bob shook his head and jabbed the tines of his fork into a couple of chunks, dowsing them in blue cheese before cramming them in his cheeks.

"Nothing." His moustache lifted on his smile. "Possibilities. Alternative futures. I... I did right by you, didn't I? I mean, you have no regrets? You don't hold any hostility toward me, do you?"

Warren smiled as he sat back and sipped his beer. "Of course not, Dad. Why would I?"

Bob fiddled with his silverware, averting his eyes. "I know you have questions about your mom."

To that, Warren shrugged, nodding. "I know you'll tell me in time about her. And you've told me some. You told me you met her on assignment."

Bob took a healthy swig of his pint, still staring at the salt and pepper shakers abreast the napkin dispenser. "That stuff I've told you, about the disabled man and the government agent and the stuff I see sometimes. How do you feel about that?"

"Dad, what's wrong? You're all over the place."

Bob shook his head. Their platters arrived, burgers and fries. "You think I'm a quack, huh."

"Dad," the boy sighed. "You've always seen things. Remember Nana's house. She died there. And the shadow that your ex, Rachel, saw?"

"But the stories?" Bob persisted.

"You mean about how this ghost found you and drew you and his friends to him, and he was held by some violent woman."

"A witch," Bob said. "She said she was a witch."

"I mean, it sounds fantastic, but Dad, you've never been one to embellish, near as I can tell. Like when I had my tonsils out. You could have told me it wouldn't be that bad but you were honest. It hurt like a bitch, just as you said. And when I've asked about mom, you said someday."

Bob nodded, as if agreeing with himself. He downed the last of his beer and flagged the waitress for another. Two was normally his limit, but tonight it might have to be three. Or four.

"Someday is today, son, and I should start by admitting something. That ghost didn't seek me out randomly, picking me out of the six billion other people in this world. He saw my connection to that young man."

"What connection?" Warren asked.

"I knew his mother," Bob said, and both took a sip of their beers.

11

TALITHA CUMI

I

I awoke to a recording of The Who, to which I'd set my 5:15 alarm. I took my Abilify, ate a piece of toast and drank my OJ.

It seemed I was waking up with scratches nearly every day. I'd come to expect it was something subconscious, that I was doing to myself, until I conducted a little experiment where I trimmed my nails down to the cuticle yet still woke up with what looked like raised, inflamed welts. They didn't hurt, and I didn't even seem to notice them until I saw them. I was inspecting the fresh scratches across my chest when my cell lit up; hoping it was news of my brother, I didn't bother to pay attention to the number, but swiped to answer.

"Hello? Mr. Richardson?" I didn't recognize the voice, though I placed the accent as Italian. Moving to my coffee maker, I prepared the Keurig. "Mr. Richardson, I would like to speak to you for just a moment, if you can spare the time." Thick Italian, broken English. Probably selling something.

I excused myself and hung up, readying the rest of my breakfast: oats, two scrambled eggs, and a banana.

Not much later, Dr. Blake and I were on the regional jet ready to pull out from the terminal to fly to the Kentucky hills. Unlike the PRI jet — a Gulfstream G700 that had been outfitted with sleeping quarters, two bathrooms, twelve seats with foldout tables, and a small kitchen area — we had boarded a narrow plane with a single aisle with two rows of seats on either side. The plane was packed full, something else I found discomforting.

"You didn't have to come," I told her, as the plane taxied out to the runway.

"Marion isn't available. We don't know where Chris is yet."

"I'm not helpless. I did this for a living, once." And I'd remembered my meds, this time.

She focused on the case file in front of her, the one that had been overnighted to my apartment from the PRI. "Things have changed, Adam. You know that."

"I'm taking the meds. I do the therapy."

The eyes of a few other passengers raised to see who'd said that. I was always aware of the eyes of others.

"We'll have about an hour layover in Atlanta," she said, "before our connection to Louisville."

"Do you want to talk about Hilbert?" I asked.

She closed the case file and looked at me. "Not here. Not now." More eyes: I could feel them, like I was a leper. I tried to tell myself that it was the paranoia seeping through, even as a well-dressed woman across the aisle looked my way.

To her, I said, "Hi. I'm a schizophrenic," which, I could tell, instantly raised her hackles. "But it's okay. I remembered my meds…"

"Adam!" Dr. Blake snapped.

"… Today," I added, and winked at the lady, who now looked like she was going to cry.

Serves her right, I thought. Eavesdropping. Though, to be fair, this was a small plane, packed full, and I wasn't trying to keep my voice down. Still, most people think a schizophrenic plays the role of villain. They certainly don't perceive us as heroes. Even those closest to me saw me as handicapped, I realized, as I tried to reassure my doctor with a smile that I would stay silent. She returned to the file.

We rented a sedan at the Louisville Airport and drove the thirty miles to the next town, up and down and around some hills — an indirect path that took nearly an hour. The only thing of real relevance that was said came from the ghost. "Can't they just cut a damn hole through the hills?"

I laughed; Dr. Blake thought I was laughing at nothing.

We stopped at the police station and met the sheriff du jour — we meet a lot of law enforcement in our line of work, and after a while they kind of blend together — and his trusty sidekick. Since I've promised myself to not disclose names unless absolutely necessary, we'll call them Mutt and Jeff, because the sheriff resembled a mangy mongrel, and, well, the deputy introduced himself as Jeff, with a firm handshake.

Mutt and Jeff took us into the police station, believing from the outset that we were from a special investigative division of the FBI. As a tease, I tried to introduce Dr. Blake as Scully, but she interjected with her real name.

"You right pretty," Mutt said. When he smiled, his teeth were brown, stained by the coffee he drank and the bits of chew in his teeth. I took him then for just a figurehead and asked Deputy Jeff what we were looking at. He opened a set of blinds so that we could look into one interrogation room, then crossed the small office and opened another set of blinds, revealing another room.

In the first sat a man, his head in his hands, his hair frazzled. His face — when he raised his head to look around, as he did every few minutes — was flushed, his eyes were red. In the second room, a woman with long dark hair sat perfectly upright, motionless, and stared at the one-way mirror as though she could see through the pane to all of us. She cocked a half smile on her lips. Her build, frame, and hair were not dissimilar to the witch that haunted my dreams, but her face was not the witch's in the least.

It wasn't odd that she was on my mind. She'd been haunting my dreams almost nightly ever since I'd been rescued. The last dream came the night before last, with the witch raking her nails across my chest, and saying she'd see me soon, before vanishing. I stood somewhere dark, that smelled like burning fuel, but I could see no features. Then, from the darkness, a little girl emerged wearing a checkered-cloth dress and carrying a teddy bear.

"My Pawpaw need you, Mr. Adam. Please come." Something reached out of the darkness and snatched the little girl away, her screams waking me.

When I was sent the case file, something told me the dream was related.

The case had evolved thusly—

The town to which we'd traveled, nestled deep in the Kentucky hills of the Appalachian Mountains, was a mining community, and the local company had been owned by the same family for generations. The head of the company and of this family was an old man of substantial wealth who'd built his fortune on the coal mines and on the backs of the locals. A lot of people had worked his mines over the years — families had slaved in the tunnels, sweat and bled for the coal, even suffered and died from breathing in the poison day-in and day-out for years. Lawsuits had been filed and dismissed and settled, but never won against the progenitor.

He had never allowed his immediate family to work in the hills, especially not the women, but neither his three sons. His youngest sat in interrogation room one. One of his brothers ran the mine now that their father had retired, and the other was a surgeon somewhere up north. All of them were married and all had children.

"What does he do for a living?" I asked, pointing to the despondent man behind the glass.

"Investment banker out of Memphis," Deputy Jeff said. "When his father got sick, he returned home, and his wife and daughter soon followed."

"What about his brother — the one running the mine? His mother? Didn't his dad already have people here?"

"Dead," Sheriff Mutt said. He was working on a plug of tobacco with his peppered teeth and spit thick, black juice into a Styrofoam cup. "His wife died last year from the black lung, and no, she never set foot in those mines. Sometimes it hits the loved ones, like second-hand smoke."

"And the brother?" Dr. Blake asked.

"Some say that's what started this whole mess," Deputy Jeff said, and then he explained.

There had been a massive cave-in at one of the mines a month ago, but even before then, miners were sick, coming down with coal fever, and he explained that sometimes breathing in that crap every day, all day can mess with the head, cause hallucinations. Dr. Blake asked if there weren't safeguards put in place, and he admitted that, while OSHA had its standards and there were signs posted everywhere, when the inspectors left, so did the rules. There were oxygen tanks and rebreathers, but oxygen — especially down in the mines — proved dangerously flammable, and the few tanks that were up to spec, on display for OSHA when they came around, weren't enough for the men, just like the rebreathers and the filters. Most of what men had was worn and used, dirty, and provided little if any real protection.

The miners who suffered from the fever in the days prior to the cave-in began speaking of visions, specifically, a woman. She appeared a ways off, seemingly floating down in the tunnel, beckoning to them. At first, they were still in their minds enough not to follow; the deeper you go, the more dangerous the shafts become. The air is thicker, and the support is weaker. There is a greater chance of being buried alive, cut off from the outside world and from oxygen.

At first it was only one or two coming forward at a time. Everyone assumed it was a kind of suggestive hypnosis. One guy sees it, so then other people think they saw it. If it would have stayed like that, one or two at a time, then fine, but it got worse. More men suffered the fever first, then the hallucinations. Some were worried about toxic fumes, but their concerns fell on deaf ears. Then one day, three miners all saw her at once, realized they all saw her, and thought some lady had gotten trapped in the shaft. So, while one went back to report to the foreman, the other two chased after her.

The deputy continued after a pause, looking at us both to make sure we were still following along, saying that word a woman might actually be in the mine sent a flurry throughout the camp. The boy who'd taken over for his father went down — no one is sure why — with the foreman and a bunch of other men. "And then..." the deputy trailed off.

"Cave-in," I said.

"We was on our way," Deputy Jeff said. Sheriff Mutt spit more black juice. Both men stared off at nothing. "We heard it, like a roll of thunder over the hills, 'cept it didn't come from the sky, but down below. It felt like an earthquake. I had to pull over; I thought the ground was going to split open under us. When it didn't, when it all subsided, we sped on to the camp."

"Twenty men died at the camp. Another thirty was injured," Sheriff Mutt said.

"Why weren't we called then?" I asked.

"It was a tragedy!" the sheriff answered, a bit angrily. "Worst one we seen in a while, but it wasn't the first cave-in we dealt with. At that point, we still didn't believe they saw no woman. We just thought—"

"It was a portent," Deputy Jeff said.

The cave-in proved costly and extensive. Bulldozers worked to retrieve the bodies, but the process was slow. In the end, everyone who had been in the mine that day died; few of their remains could be salvaged. There were no open caskets.

The old man came into the sheriff's office a week after the funeral for his son. He said he dreamed of a woman. He said the woman claimed she knew his dead son, that she'd visited him as well, that he'd gone to the cave that day because of her. Grief-stricken and feverish, the old man was hospitalized, and soon his youngest son and his family — his wife and daughter — came to care for him.

"We began to get called out to their house on a daily basis," Deputy Jeff said. He indicated the ravaged-looking young man in the cell. "The son and his wife had hired nurses, but none would stay long. The nurses we interviewed said they heard things in the house cackling and laughing, and disembodied voices."

"They heard the voice of a woman," the sheriff clarified.

"And the old man was getting sicker by the day," the deputy continued. "But the little girl," he said, and trailed off into his own thoughts. I asked what he meant, but it was the sheriff who explained.

"Unbothered by the comings and goings of the house. Off playing with her little dolly, singing to herself. Talking to… herself" — his pause gave me pause — "like she didn't have a care in the world. Just her and PJ," he said.

"PJ?" I felt my stomach roll. Dr. Blake put her arm around me, patted my shoulder. I could hear my heartbeat, a steady pulse in my ears, as I felt the blood drain from my face. She said, "Just a coincidence," as I sat down, but I knew, sickeningly, that it was no such thing.

"Her doll," the deputy said. "Her mom said she named her doll PJ when they got out to the house."

"And that's her mom in the other room," I said, looking back at the woman who still sat perfectly still, and now sang to herself a little song none of us could hear. "I want to talk to her."

"I don't think that's a good idea, Adam," Dr. Blake said. She did not explain her consternation, except to say that it might be better if she, as a woman, and specifically as a trained psychiatrist, questioned a female person of interest.

"I'd like to talk to the little girl, then," I said. "And the old man."

Sheriff Mutt grumbled and the deputy hung his head. "That's why you were called in," the deputy said. "That woman in there killed the old man, and the little girl up and vanished two days ago."

II

Of course, there had been a search party. Though the county had blamed the old man for the years of repression, the years of hardship, and the recent tragedy, the good Christian folk couldn't abide a missing little girl. They couldn't let that rest on their collective conscience, so the local police had assembled a search party but had so far come up empty.

"We was out looking too, but someone had to greet you here, and someone has to watch over these two," the sheriff said. He looked back and forth with vile contempt to the man and woman in their respective interrogation cells.

The deputy unlocked the door and ushered Dr. Blake to the woman's cell, and the sheriff turned on the speaker so we could hear what was being said. Dr. Blake had read the case file as they had filled us in, so she knew the woman's name, but it was not that name to which she answered.

"What should I call you, then?" Dr. Blake asked.

The woman smiled at the one-way mirror. "Adam knows. He's out there. Hello, Adam. How've you been sleeping?" She doubled over for an instant, wincing, and in a flicker of a reflection I glimpsed the face of PJ.

The sheriff and the deputy looked at me and asked me what she meant. I told them she was delusional, but their stares remained fixed on me for a time longer. They were starting to sense my uniqueness.

"Where is your daughter?" Dr. Blake asked.

The woman didn't respond.

"Did you murder your father-in-law?"

"How've you been, Dr. Blake?"

The question unsettled my psychiatrist. She hadn't introduced herself formally to the woman. I saw Dr. Blake take a breath and another and then sit up straight and offer a faux smile. "I'm fine."

"I'm sorry about messing with your head. That, admittedly, wasn't nice, but I knew if I didn't, then y'all would've come for Adam."

Another breath. Steady. Steady. "You didn't try too hard," Dr. Blake said. "We found him, after all, before you could kill him."

The woman laughed. "No, no, no, my dear lady, my goal wasn't to kill him. Killing him would have been a release. No, I had to bleed him. The Shimmers appreciated my effort, Adam, and they respect my resolve."

The deputy asked me: "Do you know her?"

"Not like this," I said, transfixed by the woman. Despite her dark hair and her frame, she had looked nothing like PJ Harlow when we entered, but now, as she spoke, the facial expressions rippled flesh and furrowed her brow, twitched the lip; all permitted her countenance to change in a glimpse to something more familiar and vastly more terrifying. I gasped. The look on my face must have worried the two lawmen. I think they were beginning to realize the gravity of the situation, as I rubbed absently at my scarred throat.

"How did you facilitate the cave-in?" Dr. Blake asked.

Again, the woman laughed, and now she looked almost exactly like PJ Harlow, so much so that I thought they'd switched seats.

"Wasting time with all the wrong questions. You really want to know how you can find the little girl?"

"How do we find the little girl?" Dr. Blake asked.

The woman shrugged and looked in my direction. "Hello, Detective Knight. You know, for a dead man, you've proved almost as resilient as me. Well, I haven't forgotten about you. We'll have some good times yet."

Dr. Blake slapped the desk. "Hey! Where do we find the little girl?"

"In every way—" the woman now looked uncannily like PJ Harlow, so much so that the sheriff and the deputy now stumbled back, startled, "—she is still at the house. And the longer she is there, the more complete I become." There was a hiccup, a slight bump in her speech. Like she didn't believe her own words. And in that hiccup, I saw the conflict under the skin.

"Deputy," I said, "take me to the house." He and the sheriff both wore the same expression, like they wanted to ask who that was that sat there, or how the mother had changed, but their words faltered to dumb syllables that tripped off their tongues. All the deputy could do was glance over at me and nod.

We arrived, fifteen minutes later, at the drive of an old plantation home, cracked and weathered, and not all of that did I believe happened with the return of the witch. It sat on a street filled with dilapidated edifices that had once been grandiose, but like the rest of the Old South, they were crumbling icons of a ready to be forgotten era. These homes, their beauty... the lipstick on the pig that was the Old South. Many today, unwilling to separate the beautiful from the ugly, would be happy to watch it all burn, themselves unable to admit that every culture — not just the Southern White — has its beautiful and its ugly. So, what then? Should we burn the whole world, or just pick and choose who pisses us off this week? PJ would attest to this — and I'd be remiss not to agree — that you can't have the one without the other, because it is ugliness that makes us appreciate beauty. Anyone who suggests otherwise is delusional.

Deputy Jeff let me into a house with long shadows and an unsettled stillness. Everywhere stood evidence of prestige, on display for any visitor to the old home, furnished as an homage to splendor and to a bygone era, but now covered in a thick layer of dust and strung together with cobwebs. Silence vibrated like the hum of a fluorescent. I glanced back to see the deputy had drawn his gun.

"What now?" he asked.

I searched the ground floor, not sure of what to look for, save it would belong to PJ Harlow. When the ghost detective motioned for me to follow him upstairs, I obliged, followed closely by the deputy.

Leo led me to a bedroom decorated for a child. On the bed sat a stuffed doll, brown straw-wire hair jutting out from its cloth scalp, clothed in a blue plaid dress with a white apron. Sensing the deputy at my shoulder, I held it up so he could get a better look.

"PJ," I said.

"I'll be damned," he said. "That thing went missing with the little girl. We combed over this whole house."

"She's here, Deputy."

We started in the attic, and after tossing boxes aside and sweeping the room from corner to corner, we made our way down, floor by floor, room by room. Once, when separated from the deputy, I asked my dear dead friend if he had any sense of the little girl, and, somberly, Leo responded with "No."

We stirred the dust in the house till we were sneezing, shuffling through every room, examining every nook and cranny for any sign of the girl other than the doll that she'd disappeared with, that 'goddamn doll' as Deputy Jeff said, like he wanted to spit a curse at the infernal thing, but the dust settled and the air stilled and the silence quit vibrating as we descended the stairs into the basement. We shined our lights — the deputy had a Maglite, and I had the app on my cell — but the darkness stood resilient, impenetrable. Even Leo remarked that it was too dark. I paused before we reached the dirt floor.

"What's wrong?" the deputy asked me.

I could feel it; I could sense her. Before the ghost and before any evidence to reveal the truth, I knew.

"She's here."

III

The Interrogation:

Room One: Sheriff Mutt sits across from the despondent father, who is still weeping.

Room Two: Dr. Blake sits across from the mother.

226

Sheriff Mutt: "Now, there ain't much time left. You know we'll find her."

Dr. Blake: "They're all gone, now. They can't hear us. Tell me the truth. Who are you?"

Mother: "You know who I am, Dr. Blake."

Sheriff Mutt: "Why'd your wife do it? You help her?"

Mother: "You can't understand what is really going on because you still refuse to believe."

Dr. Blake: "So tell me. Help me believe. If you are who you claim to be, why did you come back? *How* did you come back?"

Father: "I could never. We're haunted. We've been haunted ever since we came back."

Mother: "Which question would you like me to answer first?"

Dr. Blake: "Why did you come back?"

Sheriff Mutt: "You hate your father? That why she did it? Tell me, you hate your daughter too?"

Mother: "I came back because I'm not done."

Father: "I never asked her to do what she did. She said she had to. To make sure it all went okay."

Sheriff Mutt: "What went okay?"

Mother: "There are rules. You can't just steal life. You can't just intrude. The rules prevent it. Sure, they allow for hints and suggestions. *God* doesn't like such things unless he approves it, but we can tinker, can make noises. But to come and live again? That isn't permitted. Not without a price. Can you imagine the price I had to pay?"

We found the body, buried in a shallow grave in the dirt floor of the basement. Deputy Jeff called the county's ME first, then we knelt side by side, each of us looking over the body with a cursory examination "We would have saw this before," the deputy said, assuring me again they searched the house top to bottom.

"Bruising," I said, raising her arm with a gloved hand, just enough to get a look. "Suggests lividity. Indicates hours or days."

"I'm telling you, we didn't see nothing." I nodded.

Dr. Blake: "That was your little girl. How...you...?"

Mother (smiling): "Not my little girl. Hers. I told you, there is a price if you want to live again. And it is *steep*."

Sheriff Mutt: "The deal is, your little girl wasn't just killed. You aware of the stuff done to her? You had to be. We swabbed your DNA... that cheek swab we did. It will match you, you sick fuck. And when the ME gets here, she'll confirm it all for us."

Father: "Oh, God!"

Mother: "God isn't here anymore."

Dr. Blake: "Where did He go?"

Mother: "He ran when He got a load of me."

Father: "When I saw her, when I really saw her... I couldn't. I couldn't say no. I wanted to, but I was scared. I couldn't... I... Sheriff, Sheriff! Listen to me! Sheriff! She'll kill us all!"

Mother: "Dr. Blake, you should really think of leaving soon. Real soon. [pauses as though listening to something]... Oops, too late."

We drove back to town in a storm, a real torrent that had blown in from nowhere, and fought through the deluge and thunder and lightning to reach the police station, where even as we pulled up we could see the damage. The front door lay in the parking lot, ripped from its hinges. The front office windows were shattered, bits of the blinds jutting through like white splinters.

Deputy Jeff got on the horn; I heard the other deputy say she was almost back to town, when the ME pulled into a spot. I exited with my gun drawn and headed for the entry, despite Jeff trying to call me back. I hadn't taken two steps inside, however, before Dr. Blake rushed into my arms, crying.

I led her out, put her in the care of the ME and I followed Deputy Jeff back inside. We found the sheriff and the youngest son, the man that had been her husband. Their blood painted the room. The whole of the office was silent save for a far off drip, the buzz of an unseen fluorescent. Neither of these sounds were sufficient to mask the arrival of another car: tires crunched over the broken pavement and loose gravel of the parking lot outside. When we walked back outside, the ME was talking to the other deputy, who'd just pulled up. I looked around, befuddled.

"Where is Dr. Blake?" I asked.

The ME was trembling, her face pale. "That's what I was telling her," she said, motioning to the deputy. "As soon as you walked inside, that woman vanished."

IV

A blood sacrifice wouldn't be enough to satisfy her demons; most people don't realize that for elemental beings like witches, it has to be a perfect union between the sacrifice, the time, and the place. Weather conditions have to be right. Planetary alignment (including lunar phases) have to be right. So she couldn't just kill Dr. Blake like she killed the woman's husband and the sheriff. She'd have to take her to a place of significance. I asked Deputy Jeff's partner if she'd had anyone stop off and get the girl's body, and she said yes, that the local paramedics had just radioed and were heading this way. I asked Jeff to take me back to the house, and I said a slight prayer for the paramedics. I'd learn soon enough that it wasn't answered.

The rain had lessened some as we — nearing the house — saw the wrecked ambulance. We slowed, surveying the scene, the late afternoon light sufficient for us to see that there was no need for us to stop. The gurney was tossed in the ditch and empty, and one paramedic lay half out of the busted windshield; the other sat slumped on the ground by the rear tire, a syringe in his eye. Neither man moved, both were bloody.

Deputy Jeff called it in, asking for state troopers to the scene, before we pressed on, not waiting for their arrival. We slowed down as we approached the grounds, past the oaks and perimeter fence and stonework covered in Spanish moss, dripping from the rain that had, by now, ceased. The manor house stood back against the circular drive, cold and in shadow. It seemed as though it were under a spell, darkened by the incantation that had brought so much death under the roof. Fitting then, atmospherically, that the landscaping was caked in spider webs and browning from disrepair, the blossoms withered from neglect.

"Stay outside," I said, drawing my service gun. The black windows seemed to shimmer, beckoning me.

"Hell, no," the deputy said, drawing his own service revolver. "Whatever is in there, it killed my sheriff."

We took the steps in unison, reaching the porch at the same time. But as I reached for the knob, the door swung open, and the darkness invited us in. Our second time in this house, we paused in the front hall to consider the doors to either side, the grand staircase in front of us, the halls leading to the back of the home. Where might we start? Perhaps with the upper floors, working our way down, searching every room? Exhausting. God, we really needed a whole force combing this home, not just two guys.

But they were easy to find. Upon entering, we heard them in the basement; I could just translate the Latin chants from a voice far too similar to PJ's now for it to not be her. The old stairs gave away our position, but PJ was expecting us anyway. I didn't see her first, but Dr. Blake struggled against the restraints that bound her to a dust-covered newel post and screamed a muffled cry through her gagged mouth. The body of the little girl now lay, curiously, under a sheet.

PJ's voice echoed through the room, her form hidden still by the shadows. "Welcome back, Adam. You brought your cop friends, I see."

"Friends? What's she talking about?" Deputy Jeff asked. I looked over his shoulder to the dead detective.

"I have a ghost," I said. "A cop."

His look of disbelief at me passed quickly as the figure stepped into the light, looking like PJ Harlow. This was all too much for him, I could see. He pulled his gun and called her by the mother's name, and said, "You just halt now. You under arrest, ya hear!"

PJ laughed. She was really amused by the stalwart deputy and stopped in her tracks to laugh for a considerable amount of time. She muddled through, "He has no idea what we're doing here, does he, Adam?" in between hard guffaws, then doubled over to grab her stomach. Tears began to stream down her face.

"Why is she covered, PJ?" I asked. This question prompted Dr. Blake's eyes to widen and struggle harder, while Leo whispered that I should remove the sheet.

"You touch that goddamn sheet," PJ barked, "and... I love you, Adam, but you touch that sheet, and I'll kill you where you stand."

The mention of the sheet prompted a curious thing. She doubled over again and screamed out in such a piercing tone that I winced from the pain of her screech. Her hair fell forward over her eyes as she thrashed violently and collapsed to her knees. I grabbed for the sheet, managing to toss the cover away. It revealed the body of the little girl, pale and shining as though she'd become a porcelain doll in death, which seemed to send more violent convulsions through PJ's body. Finally, she stopped, ever so briefly, and raised her eyes. The face we saw was no longer PJ's, but the face of the woman she had possessed.

She reached out for me and said, "My daughter! Please. Help me!"

That was all she had time to do before PJ regained control, and the face morphed once more to the face of the witch — now struggling with every breath — and she rose to her feet, sweating profusely.

"Adam," she said, "I have to get rid of her. I can't... share..."

I realized that was why she wanted Dr. Blake. She wanted to expel the woman's force into another body, an act that would probably destroy the spirits of both the woman and my dear doctor. But as I've said, for these kinds of things to work, it is all about doing the 'right' things at the 'right' time, under the 'right' circumstances and with the 'right' words. The setting sun signified that time was growing short, and PJ knew we weren't going to give any ground. She might focus her energies on one of us, but we both had our guns drawn and anyway, the ghost detective was there to keep her occupied as well.

"Can you do it, Adam? Will you shoot and kill this woman's body just to stop me? Because that's what it will take. You know I'll never stop."

So I shot her. She fell back against the far wall, and looked up at me with shock and surprise, and anger. Her shoulder began fountaining blood and we watched the color drain from her face as her features flickered between woman and witch. Aware that she'd lost this round, she fluttered away into the shadows, vanishing impossibly from the whole of the room.

As Deputy Jeff worked to untie Dr. Blake I searched the basement, but the woman had completely vanished, and I had no idea which personality was in charge of the wounded body. I helped Dr. Blake up the stairs as he called the Kentucky State Highway Patrol for backup to come and secure the scene. We didn't speak until we'd arrived back at the station. Even then, Dr. Blake and I huddled together as the state police and the deputies buzzed around us. Orders and commands were shouted. It wasn't until hours later and things had started to level out that we had some time with the deputies again. And though Dr. Blake and I had been comforting each other, I wondered about the deputy, who'd seen some unbelievable things.

"I guess I'll serve as interim sheriff until we can have a runoff," he said. The bodies had been cleaned up and removed, and the state police had investigated and left. We all sat in near silence in the ruined office, sipping coffee.

"I'm just as qualified," the female deputy said. Her haughtiness sounded deflated.

"We'll keep an eye out," he said, "for when she comes back."

"She won't come back here," I said. This relieved him. I saw the fear in his eyes, heard the tremble in his voice.

The time had passed on the elementals of this place, but I knew PJ had other options she could explore to solidify her state. But first the woman's gunshot would have to heal; as long as the body was weak, PJ wouldn't have the strength to keep the other soul at bay. And that's what I was counting on, I told Dr. Blake as we later flew home.

"If she'd remained Incorporeal," I explained, "we'd just go through all of this again with another family, but now she's trapped and tied to that woman, and too weak for a while to cause any more damage. It gives us time to regroup and consider our plan."

"So you meant to wound her?" Dr. Blake asked.

I really needed to get recertified.

V

Agent Case, a brace on his arm, pulled into the parking lot of the VA hospital in Boise, Idaho, next to a Volkswagen driven by a short old man in a fedora. Marion smiled at the driver, who grumbled and offered a wave. The sky was cloudless, and a northerly breeze chilled the air. Entering the hospital through the double doors, he approached a young woman behind a plexiglass window, who handed him a clipboard stacked with papers. He sat down to fill out the needed paperwork, and soon found himself in an exam room, in front of a middle-aged doctor with a fake tan and a paunch, who smelled like cigar smoke.

"Since the IED blast, I have no feeling in my right arm," Marion said, holding up his braced arm. He had a high tolerance for pain; when the doctor tested the nerves, Marion didn't react. The doctor left the room.

Marion removed the brace and, after a few seconds, cracked the door open. The nurse's station was unoccupied, and he saw no one else in the hall. He stepped out and hurried to the third door on the left. The code from the flash drive — 387 — got him inside, where he found floor-to-ceiling shelving along the wall to the left. Each shelf was filled with test tube racks, each of which held dozens of test tubes. Agent Case picked up one corked vial; to his eye, it was just filled with a clear liquid, but the flash drive suggested something else was contained inside.

From his blazer pocket, he produced a small roll of duct tape. With it, he efficiently sealed the cork to the vial, placed the vial in a plastic bag, and inserted it into his brace, before strapping it to his arm again. He exited that room and made it five steps back toward the exam room when he heard the name he'd given them. He turned to see the over tanned doctor coming out of another room at the other end of the hall.

Marion smiled pleasantly. "Bathroom?"

"We're almost done," the doctor said, a bit suspiciously, "then I'll have the nurse show you."

Marion followed him to the exam room and the doctor examined his arm again.

"There are treatments," the doctor said. "We have access to experimental treatments here that not all VAs have access to. If you're interested, we can restore the feeling to your arm."

"Is there information I can take with me, think it over?"

The doctor smiled, produced a syringe, and jabbed the needle in Marion's thigh. Marion, of course, picked the man up and thrust him against the door, then dropped to his right knee, wincing in pain. He grabbed at his thigh; it burned like acid had been injected into his veins, and for a moment Marion thought that was what was in the syringe.

"You were in my clean room," the doctor said. "Why were you in my clean room? Did you take one of my vials?"

"I..." It was all Marion could get out. His throat burned, and he clutched at it.

The doctor held up his iPad and touched a button. Marion's pain subsided, but weakened, he could not rise off the floor. "I was just looking for the bathroom," Marion tried again.

"Whoever you are, I can push a button and you will feel the pain again. I saw you coming out of my clean room. Did you take one of my vials?"

"I took pictures," Agent Case said. "That's all."

The doctor smiled. "Well, that's easy enough to verify. You wait right here, and I'll go look... if I see that everything is in place, then we'll discuss your options."

The former SEAL knew his options, so when the doctor turned, Marion was at his back; even in his weakness, in one swift move he rendered the doctor unconscious. He removed two zip-ties from another pocket and bound the doctor's hands and feet. Marion knew he couldn't get the man out of the building without being seen, so he shoved him into a cabinet. Decisions needed to be made with no time to spare. There might be others with iPads that could deliver the pain. He dialed a number. ADA Builder answered.

"He injected me," Marion said.

"Do you have the thumb drive?" Builder asked.

"His iPad controls whatever was in the solution I was injected with, whatever Zeitnot was experimenting with in these treatments. If I use the drive..."

"Take the iPad and shut it down — down, as in power off, not sleeping — then insert the drive into any desktop for five seconds. You'll have approximately ninety seconds to exit the building." The drive, Marion knew, delivered a virus that did three things: (1) it attacked the power center of the building, sending out a kind of EMF charge that fried the system and killed all power to the building, as well as shut down any active electronics in the vicinity that were powered directly by the building's power supply or by battery; (2) all electronics connected to the system's router either directly or through Wi-Fi would be susceptible to a second virus upon turning back on that would wipe their hard drive; and (3) it would search out and disable any long range signals coded to the specific frequency of whatever now drifted through his body.

Ninety-five seconds later, Marion sat in his car, wondering if his exhaustion was due to whatever he'd been injected with. Buildings like this usually had backup generators, but none kicked on. Must've disabled that too. He sped away, rubbing his throat, imagining the pain was trying to return.

~

St. Louis, Missouri—

Bob Link hovered over a microscope and Ernie Quill poured Marion another cup of tea. Marion had needed his old boss to reassure him five times over the phone that turning on the iPad would be okay, and now, sipping his tea, he and Ernie examined the apps one by one, careful about which icons they pressed.

Bob said, "Unbelievable." It was the fifth time he'd said that. He didn't offer up more, and he didn't share the microscope. Ernie told Marion that it was useless to try to get more out of his partner until he was ready to share. Still, Marion was growing more worried.

He said, "Will you just tell me what the fuck you're seeing, Bob?"

There came a knock at the door. Marion drew his gun and asked if either was expecting anyone; when they said no, he hoped it was the one person he could trust. When he saw his old boss on the other side, the tension between his shoulder blades relaxed some.

Bob looked up from the microscope. "Nanotech!" he said.

"Why am I at the St. Louis home of an investigative journalist?" ADA

Builder asked.

"They're Adam's friends. I needed their help."

Ernie said, "Seems the iPad is outfitted with a program that controls the nanotech he injected you with. That's what was causing you pain."

"What about the Zeitnot files?" Marion asked. "They referenced treatments that could restore mobility to paralyzed limbs."

Two weeks earlier, an ex-soldier had approached ADA Builder in DC. He had showed him doctors' files and pictures of his amputated arm — and then showed him his new arm. Smooth and hot pink, hairless and featureless, it had the texture of lizard skin. He said he'd been to the VA in Boise, Idaho, and that the pain to regrow it had been great. But it was worth it.

ADA Builder had asked him what he could do for him. The soldier had been asked to do questionable things, and the first time he had refused, he'd felt pain worse than what he felt after the accident, worse than when his arm had regrown. He had learned quickly, from some man wearing a suit, that you didn't say no after receiving such a gift.

There were technical specs on the iPad. Marion planned to show them to Dr. Blake; perhaps she could explain to him how these tiny robots could do such things. It appeared they worked at the cellular level, even at a mitochondrial level, and possibly at a genetic level, cleaning out trash and initiating repair sequences that rebuilt tissue one molecule, then one cell at a time, eventually able to regrow damaged nerves, even missing limbs.

"If they're in me," he said, finally, "we have to get them out."

"I don't know if we can," Bob said. He stepped back and allowed each of them a look. The nanotech on the slide had begun to duplicate. Exposed to oxygen, Bob surmised, it had a new directive: replication at an unprecedented rate. Injected into a body, they replicated, then monitored and repaired body systems. Or, if otherwise programmed, they destroyed.

"So, what do we do?" Marion asked.

And then he collapsed.

V

The office colors were neutral. Not government neutral — all white with bland white trim — but calming neutral. Government offices weren't calming, in their glaring white with fluorescent lights humming above. The ceiling light here was a fan with four bulbs; it spun silently, cooling the room. A Tiffany lamp cast a soft yellow luminescence over a bookshelf lined with self-help books and religious texts on love and self-ownership.

He didn't much appreciate those, as each of their theses presumed some higher power was responsible for everything. Where was this god when his wife had skidded the SUV, braking to avoid the oncoming car?

"I saw them. I saw her. And the guy that killed them."

"What do you mean, you saw them?"

His therapist was youngish, definitely younger than he, and wore a trimmed beard and moustache; he was perhaps of Persian descent. Today he wore a Cosby sweater and a pair of khakis.

"Penny loafers?" the colonel noticed.

"You're deflecting."

Hamilton sighed. He seemed to be gathering his courage. "The other night, I left my office, and I drove home."

"Home?"

"Home. Not the apartment. I pulled into the drive and a man answered my door."

"The man who killed your family?"

Hamilton nodded, his head bowed. The carpet was made of colorful squares, laid seemingly at random. He followed the reds with his eyes.

"He'd remade the home."

"And why do you suppose that is?"

"I know why that is! I know what I did. I know what I saw, and I know it wasn't real."

"How do you know?"

The blinds were bamboo and shielded the office from the world. As he was trained to, Hamilton took a few deep breaths and studied the shadows.

"Because I woke up."

"Where?"

And there it was. "At home. At the apartment."

The therapist drummed his fingers. "Are you afraid you are forgetting them?"

The cadence of his speeches rang with an English accent.

"I don't want to forget them, but I have a job to do… but I'm also worried that my dealing with them will affect my job."

The therapist sighed. "This is true." His fingers were steepled. "So, we must figure out how you can compartmentalize these two issues, so that you can later process them individually, and wholly."

"Compartmentalizing is such a cold word, isn't it? It's a type of forgetting."

"It can be about order. Arrangement. You tuck away files neatly so that you can find them later."

"It reminds me too much of what I do, the things I've seen. I don't want my job to be my life."

"What is it that you want, in your heart of hearts?" The therapist didn't wait for an answer but rose, fished a bottle of water out of the minifridge by his desk, and handed it to the colonel. Saving his answer until after the bottle was empty and crinkling loudly in his hand, the colonel hung his head and began to weep.

"I want them back," he said blubbering, his hands folding tightly into fists, the tears streaming down his cheeks.

"That isn't possible," the therapist said. "We must contain our wishes to reality and not the fanciful."

Oh, but how wrong he was, the colonel thought, because of the things he'd seen that he could not divulge, even in therapy sessions. It was possible to see them again. It was possible to have them again. He could be reunited with his family, and that was what he most desired.

There were resources. He could start with Pythia, check with one of the agents under him. Perhaps Agent Case, perhaps further reaching out to me. Ending his session early under the pretense of an emergency, the colonel did just that, and soon enough we were Skyping from our respective confines, me in Arkansas and Colonel Hamilton in his office in Chicago.

"I should have my report up by tomorrow," I said. The PRI's Intranet system had been programmed especially to not save any documents on the cloud but delete their contents as they were emailed through the server and delete them fully after printout at the office. This ensured confidentiality even in this technological age. One of Pythia's duties was to monitor this server, and given the lifespan of her experience, she had been unhackable.

"That's fine," he said, waving me off. "Do you have time to research a topic for me?"

"Sure," I said. I would never have told him no. I don't possess the kind of gumption to reject a boss's request.

"Please understand, Adam, that this requires the utmost secrecy. Even more than our job usually entails, I'm afraid."

"Yessir," I said, but I couldn't help but frown. I got the impression, even before he specifically said so a moment later, that this was not to be known by anyone in my group, either. "I understand," I said. He paused for effect, and in that brief instant my mind raced with the possibilities of what all I just agreed to so blindly.

"I don't want to limit this inquiry to necromancy necessarily, but I am interested in learning about the various ways one might communicate with or even raise the dead."

My lip quivered. He was talking about dangerous magic. Dark magic. "Might I ask why, sir?"

"That isn't important," he said then, and ended our call.

I took it upon myself, after exiting our protected server and turning on my own VPN provided to me by Chris, to search for more information about the colonel. He had a less than extraordinary military career, at least what I could find through Google, but given his current position, that couldn't have been entirely accurate. Information on his personal life was a bit more forthcoming, and I quickly discovered a major mistruth he'd allowed the office to believe, which was that he was separated from his wife and kids. I read about the tragedy, my heart breaking for this man, even as I deduced the reason for this odd request. I then grew fearful for him.

12

THE FAMILY

I

Mom wasn't doing well. She was unresponsive except for touch; I think she squeezed my hand a couple of times that day. Outside, it was bright and sunny and warm — the temperature pleasantly nestled in the mid-sixties this early spring day — but the room was dark by design. I still didn't know where Chris was, and I hadn't heard from Marion; even the ghost, it seemed, had abandoned me. I could only assume he was off searching for PJ, reconnoitering the location of the witch — or more accurately — the body of the woman she now inhabited, so he could more accurately update me of her status. Wherever she was, she was probably nearly physically whole, now. My scratches had nearly healed, and I had been inflicted with no fresh lacerations since our last encounter, and my dreams were — for the most part — peaceful again. Even the Shimmers had seemed to have lost interest in me, but I could not allow myself to forget them, lest they ambush me while I was otherwise preoccupied. I would not let them stray far from my thoughts.

Just before I arrived at the nursing home, my phone rang. Dr. Blake said she'd be unreachable for a few hours, that a colleague from Washington County Human Services Division had asked her to accompany him on a wellness call to a family in a rural area. I wondered if she informed others, if she paid this much attention to her other patients, or if I was special

240

because of what she knew about me and my situation. I decided there weren't enough hours in the day for her to devote this much attention to all her patients, and felt a strange mix of smothering, coddling, and warming comfort from her attention — conflicting emotions that waxed and waned depending on the day and my mood. Today, isolated from everyone else important in my life, I was comforted that I had heard from her.

My mother made a groaning sound. Her most recent TIA had left her speechless. I fetched the pitcher of water and put an ice cube between her lips. Her pale, cracked lips moistened just a little. I thought then it would be best if she died, and I felt horrible. Perhaps, since my brother was gone, it fell upon me to adopt his cynical view. But it *would* be better. Since Chris had gone missing, I was drained (caring for her had already worn him down). Every day she lingered on was a tax on us, like her continued existence depended on satiating herself on our very souls.

I watched the ice melt on her lips and dribble down her chin, and I thought, *We're like the chips of ice, hydrating Mom with each morsel of ourselves we allow her. As she hangs on, she devours us.* I contemplated all of this as, over the loudspeaker, an instrumental of "Hotel California" played softly.

"Mom. Mom!"

She made like she looked at me. Leo had said once that her soul was tethered with a fraying thread to the body, which whipped in the astral wind like a kite in a hurricane. He said she was already interested in the other things to be seen, and unlike him, when she left she would not come back. I wondered then why he stayed and — if the other side was so fascinating — why she stayed also.

"I'm no longer with the FBI, Mom. I work with another agency now — the Paranormal Response Initiative, part of the Department of Homeland Security. I still work with Marion, but..." I paused. *Would this do more harm than good?*

"Almost a year ago, I was diagnosed after a schizoid break. I saw things that everyone said weren't there, and I heard them too. I was diagnosed paranoid schizophrenic, and I was released from the FBI. I was hospitalized. You might remember that time. I didn't come and see you." Did I think this admission would be good for her? For me? Did I feel her grip tighten?

"When I was released, Chris helped set me up in my own apartment. Not long after moving in, my old partner from the FBI, Marion Case, sent me — in an effort to recruit me to this new agency — some case files and a ghost." I let those words sink in. Her head flopped to the side; her sightless eyes roamed over my face, and she gasped.

"I can see things, Mom, now that I'm like this... like Dad was. I wonder if Dad could see these things too. But you never told us what he went through. I see spirits, and I see the Shimmers. The Shimmers are why I was diagnosed. Can you see them?"

"She can," came the voice, and her head flopped toward the sound. I looked up to see an old man standing in the corner, leaning heavily on a cane. He looked much better than Ba'al's other incantation — a fly/wasp hybrid.

"I haven't seen y'all in a while," I said.

"You have misconceptions about us," the old man said. "We know who we have to torture and we know who can help us, and you, Mr. Richardson, can help us."

"You... why would I help you?"

"Ba'al is the lord of Gluttony, my boy, and your mother's continued existence — feeding on your well-being, your livelihood, your soul... her hunger for life calls to me. She's seen the other side, Mr. Richardson, and it terrifies her. Your world is the closest any of you will ever come to heaven. All that awaits you is ugly."

"I refuse to believe that," I said.

"Why do you think your detective friend refuses to cross over? Why do you think your mother refuses to die? She sees your father. She's scared for what awaits her."

"Is that your role now?" I asked. "Are each of you to come in turn and sit on my shoulder like a devil and pretend it's help?"

My mother squeaked. I looked down and saw I was squeezing her hand, her knuckles a bundle of pale wrinkles crushed in my fist. I looked back up to the old man and said, "You need to leave now. I don't want you here."

He laughed, a derisive, joyless noise. "Mr. Richardson, we're always here. We aren't going anywhere." He evanesced and I looked down to my mother and patted her hand.

My phone buzzed, but I ignored it. I was with my mother and despite my earlier misgivings, nothing else was important. "You have always been a source of strength for us. Are you scared, Mom? You shouldn't be." I was speaking on faith, not fact, and I wasn't sure if she heard me. She opened her mouth and she sighed, a sound of relief, of contentment.

I stayed with her all day, holding her hand and feeding her ice chips, and I regaled her with stories of my exploits at the PRI. I told her about Mr. MITS and PJ Harlow and about Zeitnot Industries and the Shimmers and all the thing we had seen, and I told her about the ghost and how he was a detective who was murdered on the streets of Chicago and how he promised to help us if we promised to help him solve his own murder.

Through all this, my mother wore an idiot smile and remained still, breathing easily. At one point, a nurse walked in. She looked at numbers and felt Mom's wrist and smiled at me and said that this was the best she'd been in a while. I thanked her for her service, like she was a waitress or a soldier, and told my mother more once the nurse left. By the time I left the hospital, I was satiated on my mother's companionship, and the sun still shone brightly, and the weather still felt pleasant. Still, to the North and to the West, I could not help but notice that a black wall cloud loomed, spitting lightning.

My phone buzzed again. I retrieved it and found a voicemail from Dr. Blake. Strange, I thought she was unreachable. Maybe she was back. We weren't scheduled for a session, but perhaps she wanted to meet up about matters more directly related to the PRI. I pressed play and held the cell to my ear.

"Adam. I need you. Please answer! You need to get the police... Send them to 827 County Road 5419. Hurry, Adam! I think I'm next. I think I'm—"

A scream. Other voices. The audio distorted. I called the sheriff as my ride pulled up. I had ordered an Uber with my home address, but as I climbed in the car I gave another.

"827 County Road 5419," and when he stammered, I said, "Please."

II

That morning:

The sun was rising above the eastern hills as Dr. Blake sipped her coffee. She was leaning on the hood of her car when her friend pulled up and stepped out of a Subaru Forester. During college, he'd been a tight end for the Razorbacks, but bad knees and a slow 40 kept him from going pro. He offered her a smile, which she returned.

"Treyvon Michaels, looking respectable," she said as he hugged her.

"You got to dress to impress," he said, stepping back and flashing his threads.

"How the fuck can you afford that suit on a social worker's salary?"

He shrugged. "I'm dating an RN. I could upgrade to doctor, though. Whatcha say?"

She slapped his shoulder and walked to the passenger side of his SUV. He liked to pretend he was a player, but Dr. Blake was sure he had never cheated, and she was sure she would never accept his advances, no matter if they were playful or not. He drove; he had asked her to join him, and he knew where they were going. They rode along, each sipping the coffee they'd brought from their respective offices, laughing about some joke he told her, catching up on lost times.

He said, "No, so how you doing, Sam?"

"I'm fine," she told him.

"New man in your life?" and when she said no, a bit sheepishly, he said, "All right, saving yourself for me," and he laughed and she laughed, and she sipped her coffee and he sipped at the nonfat mocha latte he'd spent eight bucks on.

"Am I stupid?" she asked. "For wanting something... real?"

"No," he said, and looked away from the road long enough to make eye contact, and then looked back. "No. We all want that."

"Even you, *playa*?" she asked, grinning.

"No. I got that. She's good to me. She loves me. Says we'll get married."

"Good for you," she said, and turned to look out the window. A black crow, perching on a rotten stump, cawed at the car loudly, so that its carrion song pierced the window. Treyvon slowed to turn onto a dirt road.

"You'll find him," he said. She smiled to herself and thought of how she'd settle for a good roll in the hay.

She said now, business-like, "So what have they done?"

He nodded up the road like the family in question stood in front of them. All she saw were trees and overgrowth and inclining landscapes on either side of the two lanes.

"They don't have real neighbors, but there're people close who say their place stinks like rot. And their kids aren't going to school, so we're going to check on them, see if there's any abuse, see why the kids ain't going to school or at least enrolled in a home school program."

She looked out the window. "So why did you ask me to come along?"

"I thought you was free today."

She saw through his bullshit. They'd been friends long enough.

"You want me to diagnose someone."

"Just observe."

She shook her head and mumbled a curse. "I was offered the job at County Health, and I was offered good money."

"And you turned it down."

"I turned it down for a reason," she said, and then cracked the window for air.

"And?" he asked, when she didn't speak up.

"You believe in what you do, and that's great, and that's fine. I don't believe in it. I don't believe that some bureaucratic, red-tape-logged operation can enforce and correct and micromanage parenting decisions. I don't believe that spanking is all bad or that children should be forcibly removed from all houses that don't conform to specific guidelines."

"Children need protection," he said.

"It isn't black and white," she said. "DCFS is, at its best, a product of extremism, as is any bureaucracy, because a government agency can't function in gradations and be effective. And as such a rigid agency, it will not recognize when children truly need their help and when they just don't agree with tactics."

"Children have rights. A child has a mind and has opinions that need to be valued."

"Valued, yes, but they can't control the home. A child's mind is undeveloped, which means that it can't be held accountable for decisions. Children need boundaries and rules and they need to be told what is right and what is wrong, because they do not know. They cannot know. Brains don't reach maturity until, on average, age twenty-five, which means they can't be allowed to make rational decisions, especially life-changing decisions."

He didn't respond. He gripped the wheel and stared straight ahead and his silence ensured that the debate was over. This was not an issue of gender or race, but of one intellect matching another. More accurately, this was about politics. He was a smart man and an empathetic man who saw the good in everyone, but Samantha had been jaded, sickened by the red tape and bureaucracy that routinely tied her hands.

The old farmhouse had settled onto a plot of dirt surrounded by crabgrass and had been encroached upon by various trees and shrubs. A detached garage held a rusted-out Ford flatbed. The house itself, with gray slats cracked and weathered, had a crumbling chimney, though from it, smoke rose lazily, probably from a smoldering fire.

The social worker walked up the porch, careful where he stepped. The boards seemed loose or rotted, or both. He motioned for Dr. Blake to stay by the car, turned to knock and saw the door open. A lean boy in his teens or twenties, wearing suspenders to hold up his britches but no shirt, his face and hair scruffy and unkempt, stared out at the social worker.

"Pa!" he said. He was joined by a lean man, even taller, who used too much Dapper Dan's on his thin gray hair. The taller man — Pa — smiled at the social worker.

"What we got here?" His teeth were black nubs, and there was a meanness in his eyes.

The social worker started to introduce himself and Pa shushed him. From the trees stepped more men, sons of Pa or cousins or siblings of the boy, each carrying a weapon: a shotgun, a rifle, one a pistol in each hand. Another swung a machete in wide, careless arcs. They wore their father's dirty grin.

"We about to sit down for some dinner," Pa said. "We insist you join us."

~

Samantha wiped the vomit from her lips and crouched in the dark room. Maybe they didn't know what cell phones were. Maybe they didn't think it mattered. She had tried Marion and got no answer, and then she tried Adam. Somewhere in the house, Freddie Fender sang "Wasted Days and Wasted Nights" on an endless loop.

Still crouching, she listened to see if any of them were coming closer. They sounded preoccupied. *Oh God! What had they done?* She didn't want to think about it, and even now, as she heard them talk and laugh and chop, long after the screams had quieted, she could not help but picture what had happened.

"Have 'em for dinner! Pa, you a class act! You riotous!"

"Save me some dark meat!"

"Bubba, it's all dark meat!" Laughter.

"Quiet now! (this was Pa, she could tell). Go git your granny up. Tell her supper's almost ready."

Samantha felt like she'd vomit again and was sure she hadn't much left in her stomach.

"What about the girl?" one of the boys asked. She could hear it in his voice — the hunger.

"We ain't cooking her, if that's what you're asking," Pa answered.

She wondered if the one who asked was the one with the machete, the one who swung first when they were ushered into the house. He had laughed when the social worker spurted blood.

"What then?" Lascivious, hungry. It didn't matter which boy spoke.

"Relax," Pa said. "You'll each get a chance. We got to make sure the seed sticks. But y'uns need your strength. So go on and git your granny! I ain't gonna tell ya again. Dinner'll be ready in a half hour, and if we carved him

247

right, and you boys ain't too gluttonous, we might have enough vittles left for a week."

Desperately unsure of the time, but sure she was out of it, Samantha dialed her cell again, and started with a whisper that crescendoed to regular speech and then to a scream: "Adam. I need you. Please answer! You need to get the police... Send them to 827 County Road 5419. Hurry, Adam! I think I'm next. I think I'm—" as the boys entered. All of them.

She lay broken on the dirt floor, bleeding, tears scarring her cheeks, listening to Freddy Fender drone on and on. They'd hurt her. In fact, they had all stood around and had cheered each other on. It hurt and it kept hurting, and the hurt didn't abate but pierced her and reminded her that she was being violated. The harshness and the brutality and the pain lasted so long, and she bled and she hurt. She felt worse when she felt the first one cum and when the last one came, she felt deflated. Now, prostrated on the dirt floor, she clung to the soil and watched mealworms break ground and wriggle and squirm, and in the other room she heard them all smacking their lips and jostling each other at the dinner table. She heard their granny ask about the girl in the other room, and they laughed and their Pa said they'd get another turn after dinner.

The light gilding the lateness of the hour, the shadows on the lawn longer now than when she'd first arrived earlier that morning, they all returned to the room. Touch is fleeting, and the weakest of the senses. Touch disappoints the most. Touch is a pariah, and they say — whoever *they* are — that touch is the last sense to leave the dying. So touch is the cruelest of the senses. Touch lies to you. It lied to Samantha.

Afterwards, crumpled and broken on the floor, she heard their short conversation. The boys asked if they'd know who was the father and Pa said "No," but said it didn't matter, that they all should remember a time when him and his brothers took care of them, and they all called each other brother and he was sure he wasn't biologically all their fathers, but that's how they were raised, anyway.

"Cause when it comes down to it," he said, "family is all of it. Family is all you got. And don't you boys forget it."

III

Chris stared out of the black pane of glass that did little to reveal his location, his new world, his security. The black was tenuous and pulled at his soul.

"I'm not safe here," he said.

"This is a hospital." The nurse had been checking his vitals but stopped when he spoke.

"You're very pretty," he said.

She smiled and said, "Thank you," and she blushed a bit.

"I don't need to be here. I don't want to be."

"What are you afraid of?" she asked.

He sighed. "That I won't see my brother again, to tell him that I love him, that I don't blame him. That my mom will die before I get back to see her. That I..." he thought of Dr. Blake and how pretty she was.

"That you...?" she said, with her eyebrow cocked.

"I would like to come home, to pull into a driveway... in a Beemer, the drive of an old Victorian in historic Fayetteville, and my wife would meet me at the door with my three boys and our one girl..."

"One girl?" she asked.

"One," he said with a laugh. "I can't handle more than one."

"And what if I want three girls and one boy?" she asked and squeezed his hand, but Chris ignored the question and stared off out the black window, seeing nothing. Somewhere in the blackness he thought he heard a crow.

"What if I don't get that... that normal life?"

"Tell me more about this house and Fayetteville," his nurse said. She offered him a smile, but Chris could only return a frown.

"I live in Fayetteville, but the house, the wife and kids, it's all a pipe dream."

"Tell me about your dreams," she whispered.

In his ear, through a Bluetooth device she couldn't see, he heard a voice say, "This is Bob Link and I'm here with Ernie—" *Christ, the goddamn journalists. Who else did Marion give the number to?* "— and Agent Case. I'm sorry. He needs you. We think he's dying. He's been injected with something. Some kind of nanotechnology."

"I'm tired," Chris said to the nurse. "I feel like people only want me for what I can do for them."

"They can depend on you. They see that."

He shook his head. "There are times when I don't want to do anything for them. Any of them."

She patted his arm and she offered him a warm smile. Then she checked the nonexistent watch on her wrist, and she said, "I've got rounds."

"Will you come back and sit with me again?"

"The drugs I gave you should help you sleep."

"I don't sleep. Will you?"

"Perhaps," she said coyly.

"Please," he said, and to that she could not argue.

"Okay," she said. "I promise."

When the sounds in the hall faded, Chris pulled himself out of bed and hobbled for the door. When he opened it, he found the hall empty and quiet. He returned to his bed and tapped his imperceivable earpiece.

"I'm in. What does he need?"

IV

Marion's eyes flitted open. Looming over him were blurred images of the journalists Link and Quill, and his old friend, ADA Tom Builder.

A halogen flickered as Marion sat up. He gave the three men a reassuring smile as he winced at the residual pain. Ernie Quill brought him some water, and they let him drink before Bob Link spoke for the three of them.

"Nanotech," he said, not sure of what Marion remembered before passing out. "The doctor injected you with this hardware. Tiny, tinier than would have been possible ten years ago, probably still impossible now. It — you have to understand the strangeness of it — it has biological components. It can replicate itself."

"And how do you know this?" Marion asked.

"Journalism isn't about writing," Bob said. "Writing is a craft; it is something to be learned. A good journalist learns a subject — politics, biology, chemistry, literature – and applies his writing skills to the subject he's mastered."

"And what did you master?" Marion asked.

Bob smiled so wide his mustache resembled the flexion of an eagle's wingspan spreading across his face.

"Drums, guitar, bass, biology. I went to school for biology. Everything else was personal."

Marion frowned. "Nanotech is small, computer chips. How the hell can it replicate?"

Bob shook his head. "No, this uses something more like stem cells, but it responds to commands from an artificial source — in this case an iPad. The stem cells can turn into anything."

"How can stem cells respond to computer commands?"

Bob shook his head again. He was getting frustrated. "The delivery system is organic — a stem cell — but the liposomes that were used incorporate dendrimers and phospholipid compounds, complete with a hydrophilic electromagnetic chain to carry the messages; so some stem cells become nerves. We have nanofibers and a construction similar to a neuron. It's like the internet. Over the air... like Wi-Fi. What we have to do is reprogram the nanotech, but we can only do that by reprogramming the iPad as the delivery mechanism."

"So can you reprogram it?"

Bob shook his head. It was Tom's turn to speak up. "We know someone who can, and you know how to find him."

Marion said, "No. If we go, it could compromise what he's working on, and I'll never get Mr. MITS."

"If you die," Ernie Quill said, "you won't get him either."

A flight brought them closer, and the rental car delivered them to the hospital's doorstep. Marion had slept for a lot of the flight, feeling weak, and ran a low-grade fever. Bob had driven the rental, with Ernie riding in the back, and Marion (Tom had returned home to his wife — men in positions of power were piece movers, not pieces themselves) drifting in and out of sleep for most of the drive.

"I hate Florida," Ernie said. "Anna wants to retire here. I'll smother from the humidity."

"You can't retire. You'll break up the partnership," Bob said from behind the wheel. They both looked expectantly at Agent Case.

"Fellas," Marion said. "I got this." He smiled weakly. And with that, he hobbled into the hospital.

~

"You look like shit!"

Marion grimaced. "Can you help?"

Chris smiled. He was laid up in bed, still wearing his hospital gown, with an IV in his arm and his body weak from the drugs and whatever treatments they were performing, but still he thought he looked better than Marion.

Chris took the laptop he'd bought with the nurse's help (he was a *technogeek*, he told her, and he needed to work; he had money and had been brought in without his computer — but with hers he could access his bank account and wire her the money, and any would do — he could make any laptop work) and began to work. Marion felt useless just standing around, unsure of what to say. Despite all the sleep, he was still exhausted. He'd identified himself as Ben Schubert, here to see about his mother, of whom, of course, they didn't have a record. He was persistent, in a non-threatening way, and had dressed out of character so as to not draw attention. So far, he hadn't seemed to alert any security.

Chris paused, then said, "This tech is amazing, really. It receives coded messages via electromagnetic means from the iPad. The trick is duplicating the messaging system from the iPad and then retraining the tech. It appears that to recreate this kind of entity, I'm going to have to program duplication orders and orders on what cells to target and how to target them. It's going to be difficult."

"Can you do it?" The desperation in Marion's voice countered Chris's calculating tone. Neither man liked how the other sounded.

"I can," Chris said. "I can retarget nanotech, but I can't get it out of your body. I can duplicate the iPad programming language, and I can lock out any other programs that might try and counter what we're doing. That'll have to be enough."

It took him three hours. Marion looked on until he got bored. Then, he checked the hall, and scouted out the rest of the building briefly for a better understanding of where Chris had been brought, even exited to update the reporters on how things were processing. The facility wasn't as heavily guarded as he feared, and from the street it looked like any other research hospital. Marion had just returned from updating them when Chris said he was finished.

Marion asked Chris what he'd done, specifically, but he didn't understand the details. Chris explained again that the nanotech could not be extracted, but he thought he'd reprogrammed it sufficiently so that it wouldn't hurt him.

"You think," Marion said. "But you can't be sure."

"I did the best I could."

"You ready to leave?" Marion asked, looking toward the black window. "I shouldn't have asked you to... if you want, we can..."

"No," Chris said. "I'm not sure what the doctors are doing here, but I want to know. Mr. MITS has come here for some kind of treatment. I'll call you when I'm ready."

Marion looked doubtful. "You sure?"

Above them, something jostled loudly in the air vents, drawing the attention of both men. After a moment without further sound, Chris offered him a tense smile. There was still a lot to work out between them.

"I'm fine, Marion. Really. I'm good. You asked me to do this. For Adam. I'll stick it out."

"You don't have to."

"I want to."

V

As I drove to the location Dr. Blake had given me in the voicemail, I reached out to ADA Tom Builder, then I phoned Colonel Hamilton, and then I reached Marion, finally. I made calls to Fayetteville Police Chief Willy Prader and to the Washington County Sheriff and to the Arkansas State Police. As the house came into view, I ordered the Uber to pull over, and I

253

exited. I crept over a ditch and whispered a call-out to my dear dead friend, another ally I hadn't seen in a while.

The woods were dense; brambles and vines tried to ensnare my footing, and I wondered what less-natural booby traps lay out here for trespassers. Wherever Dr. Blake was, the people in the house at this address didn't seem very trusting.

I drew my gun and crept through the sliver of wood that separated the county road from the house, keeping my head down and my eyes sharp for any weird bulges or trip wires. In the light of the day — fading but still good — I avoided several hazards, but focused as I was on those, I missed the three men that approached from behind and either side. They caught me up before I could draw a bead on any one of them.

"Pa!" one of them called out. "We got another'n!"

"You horded them last set of vittles," responded the old man as he stepped out on the porch. "Aw, he stringy. 'Fraid we won't get much meat off'n that one."

I struggled against all of them, but I didn't find ground to break their grips until the wail of sirens split the hillside air: help had arrived. From around Pa spewed a bat's legion of boys and young men, each with guns of various calibers and sizes, and a wild-looking one with a machete still doused in blood. My thoughts went dark. Fearing for my doctor, I pushed one man and squirmed out of another's grip. Snatching my gun from the third, I dispensed with all three as expeditiously as possible. Maybe I didn't need requalifying after all.

Gunshots echoed all around me as screams and cries responded from the house. Next to me, the chief approached, patting my shoulder. He was a short, fat man, always hungry. At my other shoulder, the ghost detective appeared. Cops swarmed the woods around the house.

"You're all hungry," Ba'al said, inside my head. "I can smell your hunger."

"God, I am hungry," Chief Willy Prader said. The uniforms were putting down the family, handcuffing some, checking the vitals of others. "Want to grab a brat and a beer after this?"

"I just want to make sure she's okay," I said.

Uniforms emerged from the house. Some escorted further family members — disheveled young men and boys ranging in ages from eight to around sixteen, and others called for medics, for ambulances. A female officer led out an old lady who cussed like a sailor. Two more officers walked out slowly, their arms around a gray blanket that shrouded a petite frame — I rushed across the yard and embraced Dr. Blake. I hugged her tightly and she let me, not returning the embrace but just resting her head on my shoulder. I rode with her when they loaded her in the ambulance.

At Northwest Medical Center in Springdale, she awoke in the bed to find me at her side, sipping water. I found it weird, our roles reversed, and leaned to her and took her hand.

"How are you?" I asked.

She'd been cleaned up a bit after the examination. One eye was purpling and swollen and there was a cut on her left cheek, scrapes up and down her arms, and the beds of her nails were dirty. Still, I thought Samantha was somewhere under all of that horror. I hoped she was.

I thought she was disappointed in me that I hadn't arrived sooner. I said, "I'm sorry it took me so long."

She nodded. Didn't respond. It was like she was trying to see something in front of her, the way she stared. The blankness in her eyes. Perhaps she was angry, and I'd let her down. But I had tried. I had tried to save her in time. Marion would have saved her in time. Chris too. Hell, if the detective was alive, she'd have never been... "I'm not unrepairable, Dr. Blake. There are good things with this, and there's beauty in the ugly too." I was thinking of my momand of myself and how I wanted to be better.

She tried to stop herself, but she began to cry. She wiped furiously at her tears, but she couldn't look away far enough for me not to see her.

"I wish I could believe you," she said.

Chicago—

She walks home after her shift at CVS, and she eats a sodium-loaded frozen dinner, because she can't cook and her husband did all the cooking and they're separated. And besides, he's dead. She watches television — which is to say she has the TV on while she stares at Facebook on her phone and checks her email — something that doesn't require thinking: *Dancing with the Stars* or *The Voice* or something to do with the Kardashians. Bunch of white people flouncing around on the boob tube: that's all there ever was.

She showers and brushes her teeth, but gets tired earlier and earlier. So she sleeps longer. She likes the feel of the mattress, of her hypoallergenic pillow, of the window open and the fan on cool. Likes the shadows and the dark and the cool; they mesh well together.

She tries to close her eyes and feels the first tears of the night. Staves them off for as long as she can, which is longer than she'd previously managed. She weeps into her pillow and bites at it and cries, afraid that her torment is lessening, and when it is gone, he'll be gone for good. She doesn't want to be separated and she doesn't want her husband to be dead. She needs him next to her.

No one can understand the pain a wife feels when she loses her husband, so no one can appreciate her grief and her tears. That weird white guy who came to her store a while back… he had answers, but no one can understand. But she thinks he — that I — might be of some help.

"Leo," she says, weeping… no one can understand a widow's grief.

She looks up. A shadow flickers — a familiar shape. She rears up.

"Leo!"

Nothing. Shadows. Cool. Her comforting environment. She's lost him. She can't see him for the shadows, the darkness…no one can understand a widow's grief, but Leo tried, he later told me, as he explained where he'd been when I, and Samantha, needed him most.

… He stands in the corner weeping silently. He isn't able to touch her or to reassure her. He isn't able to tell her that it will all be okay, and he isn't sure that it will be anyway.

13

A LATE INTERLUDE

I

The businesses on Dickson Street were an artsy mix of the eclectic: variegated bars and culinary delights and boutiques built for coed fashionistas. The bar in which Dr. Samantha Blake sat was cold and dark, mundane in décor and clientele and drink specials. She sipped on a Miller Lite and stared darkly at her reflection in the mirror and thought: *traitor*. She should have insisted they kill her. She should have fought them. Why hadn't Marion answered his phone?

"Fuck him," she said to no one in particular.

"My thoughts exactly," came the voice from the stool next to her. It belonged to a handsome young man in hipster clothes, thick plastic spectacles, tall and thin. His dark eyes exuded shrewd intelligence, like conversation was a chess match he had to win.

"And what are your thoughts exactly?" she asked, wearing a smile.

"Whoever he is, if he makes you that angry, then fuck him... metaphorically, of course. You don't want to give him the satisfaction."

She laughed. It wasn't particularly funny, but then, she was on her third beer. And she was, as the stranger on the stool next to her noted, "a waif of a thing."

"I run," she said.

"So that's—" he pointed to the half-empty beer, "—your... what... third, fourth?"

She snorted. A bit of beer foam bubbled out of her left nostril and popped, and she spewed a third of what she'd just drank. He offered to "get that" and wiped gently at her mouth and nose with a napkin. His fingers under the soft paper of the napkin caressed her flesh. This was his right hand. His left braced himself on the bar. She saw it and said, "So, your wife's not with you tonight?"

He smiled and retracted the napkin.

"Poets don't make much money, I'm afraid. So she's out earning our rent. I know, hearing that I don't make a lot of money is kind of a turnoff," he said, faux-apologetically.

Humility must be another of his sexual ploys.

"Not as big a turnoff as the wedding ring," she countered. The bartender brought her another beer and she faced it, prepared to give it her undivided attention. It was a short walk to her house. Hell, it was a shorter walk to my apartment, if need be. Crashing at a patient's place was not going to warrant board discipline. Not if they knew about her other adventures with that same patient.

She said into the mirror — because she could feel his eyes on her — "So tell me a poem."

He recited something that sounded sexual but said was about a teacup.

"Teacups don't have nipples," she said.

"If you think it was sexual," he said, "then your mind is elsewhere."

Her good judgment told her to finish her beer and get up and leave. She was still bothered by his left hand (or more accurately, what he wore on his left hand), but she caught another glimpse of her traitorous reflection and allowed it to ask, "Would you like to take a walk?"

Of course, he said yes.

They walked down the slope of Dickson and, at the railroad tracks, he nonchalantly took her hand by brushing his fingers against hers. They walked south, down West Street, and soon they were at the threshold to her house.

"Would you like to come inside?" His left hand snaked around her waist to the small of her back and pulled her in tight. Samantha's words were less a question than a statement of fact, perhaps better phrased by switching the order of 'would' and 'you,' with no inflection at the end.

He answered with a kiss to her lips, as gentle and soothing as his fingers, as his words. She led him inside.

They kissed again, their lips barely apart, their eyes open and reflecting their visages into the other's pupils. They began to undress each other, and she thought how black his pupils, how smooth his jaw, how muscular his lips and tongue. She thought she could get lost in his eyes, and then remembered that old saying about staring into the abyss too long. She felt Pa and his hillbilly boys pawing at her. She heard them laughing and could smell their sex and their body odor — their sweat and their musk, like sewage mixed with cum mixed with rot — and relentlessly they pressed against her and they grinded and pulsed and she could feel their sex pulsing. She looked up, pulled herself out of the abyss enough to see that it was not Pa or his boys but this married poet, his hand groping, his body eager and thrusting.

She pulled away violently, falling backwards onto the couch; she covered her face with her arm and a throw pillow and wept. She could feel him staring at her, unsure of what to do. Without looking up, she screamed *"Get out!!!"* but the pillow muffled her voice some and waited for the sound of the door to slam (she had to scream once more, and thought afterward she heard him mutter, "Crazy bitch!"). The door slammed. Samantha wept.

A couple of nights later she awoke instantly, shooting up off her sweat-stained pillow, screaming. After a few minutes of heavy breathing, frantically searching around her room for moving shadows, she resigned herself that this would be yet another sleep-deprived night.

As sleep refused to come, she went for jogs earlier, and she drank her coffee earlier and dressed and readied earlier, she went to her office earlier. But deprivation catches up sooner or later, and by the afternoon, she felt disconnected. She listened to her patients as a matter of habit. She felt cut off from her coworkers; she was.

When she ran out of things to do at her office, she went home and locked her doors and checked her windows, then checked her doors again. A locksmith installed added locks and she checked them all three times every evening. One night, after slipping into a bottle of wine, she picked up her cell and dialed six of the seven digits that would connect her to her favorite patient.

The next day, she canceled all her appointments and returned to the gun shop in Springdale, where she'd just been seven days earlier after her release from the hospital. The clerk said her background check had come back clean, and she completed her transaction and took her purchase home. She locked and then double-checked the locks on her doors. She sat on her couch with her gun in her hands and stared at her front door. When her cell rang, she jumped.

"Hello?" It sickened her how frail her voice sounded, how weak, how trembling.

It was the Washington County Prosecuting Attorney. "They can't bond out, Dr. Blake. They are going to go away for a long time."

She didn't respond but gripped the gun harder. She'd yet to load the shells into the chamber; perhaps she lacked the courage of that finality. What did it mean, to load a gun? Was it preparation for what could come, should any of them get out — despite all assurances that they wouldn't? Was it fear that they would realize the fruits of their labor? Or was it something more permanent, her locked doors there to ensure that no one could get in to stop her from... no. She scoffed. No, she wasn't suicidal. She was scared.

"Can you promise me that?"

"We have a lot of evidence," the prosecuting attorney said. "But it always helps... to have a voice. Listen, I can't imagine what you're going through, but juries are so fickle nowadays..."

"I'll testify," she said.

"I'll make it as easy as possible on you," he said.

She hung up the phone and began to load the clip.

II

Marion sat on the sofa in Samantha's living room and watched the steam rise from his cup of coffee. He could hear her puttering around the kitchen. He'd asked her if she had needed his help, but she'd replied with a curt and clipped, "No," so he sat on the couch and watched his coffee and thought about the nanotech replicating inside his body. She walked back in with her own cup and some shortbread cookies on a plate, which she sat between them.

"I don't fully understand, honestly," she said, standing above him. "You can't duplicate a microchip, but the neurons coupled with the stem cells act as relays, not dissimilar from how a microchip can retrieve signals. I just don't understand how the dendrites and other cellular components can duplicate that. It's like they have a Wi-Fi antenna that transmits the orders into code that tells them how to manipulate the stem cells — perhaps a string of proteins that can duplicate Wi-Fi receptors?"

"Bob Link was saying something similar," he said. "He was concerned about this receiver signal, and about the ability to change the stem cells into... whatever they needed to be changed into." He didn't tell her about Chris trying to reprogram the signal. He wasn't even sure if Chris had succeeded.

She reclined in an adjacent lounge and relaxed her neck till her eyes focused on the ceiling. She looked pale and scared and fidgeted like she was preoccupied.

"What's wrong?"

She didn't respond right away. Her eyes narrowed, her lips pursed.

Marion didn't need his classes in behavioral training to tell him something was wrong. He reached out to her, a slow, open hand that he meant to only touch her shoulder consolingly. His fingertips barely grazed her blouse when she jumped up and retreated toward the kitchen, a fire in her eyes that burned, "Don't touch me!"

He recoiled, snake-bit.

"I'm sorry," she said finally.

He tried again, this time pulling a few Kleenex from the box on her table, offering them to her. She dabbed at her eyes, thanked him and took a seat next to him.

"I don't know if I can treat him anymore," she said.

"What happened?" Marion asked.

Reluctantly she told him, because she needed to tell someone. She'd tried to tell her preacher, but he'd offered her disconnected scriptural platitudes, and asked leading questions in the most innocent of disguises, but implications that still stung. "What were you wearing that day?" And, "They had probably been following their moral imperative as set forth by the Bible. No women but their grandmother... they were sheltered."

"It was like he was finding a reason to excuse their behavior," she said of her preacher, and, of me, "He was defending his own sanity." She sounded disgusted by both, like she wanted to scrape our names off her tongue with a razor.

"You said yourself Adam doesn't always understand how to react in certain situations," Marion tried.

"He knew what I'd been through!" she snapped. "He knew what they did to me. He's not a fucking robot. He knew! And he...." She couldn't complete the thought. She let her words trail off, so Marion could find his own meaning.

"You told me once, when he was in the hospital, that his affect would be different. He cares, Samantha. In his own way."

She bit her lower lip and stared at the baseboard by the television. "I'm sure he does. But I can't take all of this. I can't take his brand of caring."

A few deep breaths for composure; it was important to maintain team morale. He sipped his coffee, wishing it were a beer.

"Neither Adam nor the PRI led you to that house. Is it possible that you're redirecting your — albeit justifiable — anger?"

She didn't respond but broke down weeping in his arms, burying her face, and it wasn't till she managed, "He was my friend," that Marion realized she was mourning not just herself, but also her murdered coworker.

"I'm so..." he wanted to say *sorry* but found it trite. "I wish you would've called me."

"I couldn't."

"I know you don't trust me," he said.

"I'd like to, someday. I'm not there yet..." Her voice trailed off.

"But...?"

She looked at him out of the corner of her eye. "I'm trying. I'm growing."

"I want to be there for all of you, not just Adam."

"Me? Chris?" The notion seemed to be alien to her. She pulled away at arm's length.

He sighed and tried to nod reassuringly. "I promise we'll find Chris," he said, but he could tell this didn't reassure her. He'd already let her down and more than that, even now he was lying to her, and that made him feel like shit.

Later, back at his hotel, Marion would flip through his channels and try to sleep, and he'd think about Samantha Blake and wondered if she shouldn't have let her in on the big secret, that he knew where Chris was being held. She was in a state that wasn't good for a person. He didn't feel good about leaving her, though she'd insisted.

14

SOLOMON'S HEIR

I

TEXAS

Five in all, so far. LaShawn Grady, 8, vanished at the bus stop one cloudy spring afternoon. The bus driver swore the kid got off at the normal stop, a block from his house, but he never made it to the door and no one saw anything out of the ordinary. When Jenny Tremblay, 9, wandered away from her friends at the neighborhood park, again no witnesses came forward. Not even her friends, who thought she had just been standing with them. Marco Acacia, 7, had gone with his older brother to the comic book store. He'd walked around to examine a life-size statue of Darth Vader while his brother perused the latest issues of Captain America, but when the brother looked up, Marco was gone. The bell over the door hadn't rung, and no one in the small but packed store saw anything. Then, brothers: Derek and Donald Reynolds, 8, vanished right after their soccer game. No parents, no coaches, no kid on either team, saw anything. In a month's time, this small Texas community had lost five kids, but the worst was yet to come.

Law enforcement agencies in the area increased patrols in the areas where children frequented, and they vetted teachers and daycare workers and healthcare workers and church officials. Citizens locked doors and increased neighborhood watches. Still, four more kids vanished, all within

264

the last seventy-two hours. A few citizens began to whisper a horrible word—*serial*—and the cops did little to diffuse the talk.

When Pythia called me, I was making French toast and listening to a haunting duet by Nick Cave and PJ Harvey about a serial killer. She said I needed to join a conference call with the Colonel. When I skyped in with Colonel Hamilton, I thought he was checking on my progress for his little favor. This made me nervous: I had found some resources for him, but due to the nature of the request, I was still hesitant to acquiesce. It relieved me some when he brusquely got down to business.

Two days after the twins disappeared, Derek's body was found in a ravine. On account of decomposition, the coroner couldn't readily attest to the cause of death, but it was odd that after only forty-eight hours, the body was in a condition that would normally take a year to achieve. That, in and of itself, was enough to warrant a call to the PRI, and for them to call me.

"How soon can you be up in the air?" he asked. He didn't wait for me to answer. "Agent Case will meet you in two hours. You'll take the jet into Dallas. From there, it's a two-hour drive."

It felt like forever since I'd seen my friend, and I so desired to see Marion again though I wish it were under better circumstances. I would feel just as joyous to be reunited with my brother, but the thought of him only worried me.

The colonel said, "Adam, did you notice anything about the case file?"

"I did," I said, glancing at the chair. "The remains of PJ Harlow's familial home are in one of the nearby towns."

"And Mrs. T— has been seen there, nursing a bandaged shoulder," the colonel said. The woman from Tennessee who PJ had possessed... I wondered why that tidbit was left out of the file sent to me.

After the call, I prepared an overnight bag, and within twenty minutes, Dr. Blake was at my door to drive us (Dr. Blake, Leo, and me) to the airport. I noticed in her a change, which I feared would be permanent. We didn't talk. She seemed tired, exhausted by life, her complexion pale and waxy, her eyelids heavy. I could almost see the dark cloud following her. Marion was already on the jet as we boarded, and stood to offer me a hug and shake Dr.

Blake's hand. I saw the slightest of twitches in him, that he too had noticed something was wrong with her. Presently we were in the air, flying south once more for Texas. I asked him how the investigation had been going, and he repeated the cases of the missing children, the states of decomposition that conflicted with the known timeline. I considered asking him about the nanotech, his other investigation into the activities of Mr. MITS and the shady doings at the PRI, but as we were on their plane, I thought better of it, and knew he wouldn't say too much anyway.

Sometimes, I think, some people look at my condition as an indication of my intellect. This isn't intentional, but usually a subconscious response to my affect and other outward symptoms. They forget about my advanced degree, about my conviction rate at the FBI, about my deductive abilities. Marion was well aware of what I was capable of, and even he had such moments. He and I knew of only one person capable of such advanced technological reprogramming, and he had been last seen in the company of my old partner, before he mysteriously vanished.

I changed the subject. "I got the strangest call this morning." This piqued Marion's interest. Dr. Blake's and Leo's, too. In fact, Leo had been there for it, but I feel like he was ready to judge my retelling, to in fact judge me on how I was processing the call myself. It was, in fact, the second I'd received, and I realized that it wasn't a telemarketer. "After I hung up from Pythia, an Italian priest called my cell — like, really Italian, with the dialect and all — and asked for me by name. He asked if I was tired of pretending to be sick, and if I wanted to battle the Shimmers once and for all."

"How do you know he was a priest?" Marion asked.

"He told me."

Leo said, quite unrelatedly, "In that body, the souls are still battling. You wounded her, Adam. But she getting stronger. I think I might have a way. But no one else can know about it. You hear me?"

I nodded like I was responding to Marion, who apparently had just asked me if I wanted a club soda. He handed me one, and as I didn't want to be rude, I choked it down.

I said, "He didn't give his name, but said he was part of a special tribunal created by the Vatican Investigative Unit." The aftertaste, like fuzzy saltwater.

The priest had said something else, something that had given me pause. He said that not many people knew of the investigative unit, or the things they searched for. Things like what the PRI went after. I didn't disclose this to Marion.

"What did you say?" Marion asked.

"I thanked him and hung up."

He studied me for a minute. Leo continued to talk about his plan, and I could hear it in his voice, how nervous it made him, and finally I thought: *There are lives at stake, Leo. You will do what you need to do.*

"What do we know?" Marion asked. "Why the kids?"

"Same reason Countess Elizabeth Bathory bathed in the blood of virgins," I answered. "The youth. The vitality. They believe this is the only way to truly gain immortality. The scary thing is, PJ might be right, which means more kids are in danger, and if she accomplishes what she's setting out to do, and restore her life, even more people will be in danger."

As we landed in Dallas, I considered my psychiatrist again. She had avoided all contact on the flight down, barely acknowledged Marion, and didn't seem interested in our conversation or the case at hand. I had thought, meanly—the blotchy cheeks, the erratic movements—that she was hungover, but quickly realized that she was merely ill. She vomited three times in flight to Texas, but swore that she felt better as we disembarked from the plane. She leaned on Marion as we made our way up the tarmac, a simple act, but seeing them, their arms around each other, her head on his shoulder, seemed more intimate to me than the situation itself suggested, and I wondered if I were seeing something of which they weren't even aware.

II

How many more lives did she need? How many more children needed to die? Because of these questions, I delved into as many occult references as I could find. I'd downloaded many volumes from the PRI to my e-reader, and I had several more grimoires scanned in my laptop. I busied myself with these as Marion and the local PD and sheriff went over files. I was close enough to listen. Dr. Blake tried to assist me, but was sweating profusely, her face pale, her eyes half-open.

I said, "How are you?"

She shook her head. "Probably food poisoning, a stomach bug." I couldn't help but suspect the witch, but I dare not voice that opinion aloud and risk upsetting Dr. Blake anymore.

I reached over and took her hand. "No. How *are* you?"

Our eyes met. I saw hers well up. I thought she'd pull her hand away, but rather she squeezed my fingers and forced a smile.

"I'll be okay. Thank you for asking."

She shook her head and lowered it till her cheek touched the table. She offered up a great sigh and a loud burp, and punctuated that with a quick rousing to see if anyone else but me had heard. She shot me a sheepish grin then composed herself and patted her sternum with a hand.

"Adam." Her voice was low, a whisper nearly, alert to prying ears. "Could she...? ...Do *they*...?" Her rational mind was struggling still with everything she'd seen since this had all begun.

"I think yes," I said slowly, contemplating what she was asking. If PJ Harlow could have made them forget about me, and if she could make the winds whip around a barn — if she could play with the elements and light and shadow, and if she could change her own appearance with a glamor — if she could die and possess another soul, then yes, she could make someone physically sick so as to incapacitate them. But why Dr. Blake? Why parcel her off from the rest of us? The only thing I could fathom was that PJ had plans for Dr. Blake, but before this case, there was really no indication of this. Unless PJ had set her sights on her when we were in Kentucky. This idea was reinforced by what I discovered next.

Marion walked over and dropped two property deeds in front of me. The warehouse up north — now a burned-out shell where we'd thought PJ had died — was one property, and the other was a classic shirtwaist style mansion here in this small Texas town. Both were deeded so many years ago to a Miss Julie Fell. He then showed me an old black and white photograph, who I assumed was Miss Fell. According to what Marion uncovered, she had been PJ's grandfather's mistress. She was very elegant, pretty and blonde, and even in the black and white picture, I could see her eyes were light. But that was superficial; she bore an uncanny resemblance to my good psychiatrist.

"We have Dallas SWAT, Texas Rangers, and the patrolmen from three counties ready to descend on this house with our command. We ready?"

I looked to Dr. Blake. "I want a dozen officers to stay here and watch her."

"I'm fine, Adam," she protested.

"I have to go with you," Marion said.

She assured me she would be fine, and so I left. I wasn't satisfied with the security detail left behind, a few armed patrolmen, but the truth was I wouldn't have been satisfied if it were a whole damn battalion.

III

The residential house still stood structurally, but its interior had rotted away, the plaster in strips as if chewed, the glass shattered in some windows, opaque with dust and grime in others. Things other than human had lived whole lives there. Some had died, as evidenced by the smell. . The house stood as a horror monument in a small town, the source of the town's urban legends and its campfire stories. The walls were still sturdy, though many of the floors had weakened to crumbs. Most of the damage was internal, eaten away from the inside out, like a cancer: a metaphor for the Harlow family if ever there was one. The house's structural integrity, load-bearing walls, and subflooring were all still intact.

A two-story house with gables and steep roofs, its magnificence had long since been compromised by rot and vacancy. The house, with its empty windows and electricity cut, stood black against the street. As long as the house had been abandoned, neighbors had crossed the street to pass it, so that its sidewalk remained relatively untouched. So the law enforcement and our PRI unit were the only people in years to consciously and willfully cross the perimeter, to walk up the front path to the front door of the house. Marion stayed back, listening as the snipers and SWAT scanned the house with thermal imaging, verbally reporting their progress. They detected a body upstairs.

Marion said, "Hold your fire."

I fell to the ground, unconscious and unresponsive, as soon as we entered the house...

Marion shouted into his mic. He bent to tried to rouse me, checked my pulse and respiration. I hadn't forewarned him about Leo's plan, sure that the more people that knew, the easier it might be for the witch to discern what we were up to. I was simply asleep, near as he could tell, but he couldn't have known that my consciousness was gone. I'd been reciting a spell our entire drive over, just under my breath, much to the chagrin of my partner and to the bemusement of the officers riding with us. I'd been searching for it ever since Leo had described the details of his plan, and finally found it in the digital copies of the grimoires on my computer back at the sheriff's office not long before we left. Used by Tibetan mystics and Kabbalah priests, the spell meant to help the user transcend to another level. He nodded to the patrolmen and motioned to me; they seemed to understand that they should stay by my exposed form. Marion ascended the stairs alone.

The woman whose body PJ had hijacked lay crumpled in the corner of a small bedroom down the hall. Only from messages through his earpiece did Marion know where to look. He kicked open the door with the toe of his left wingtip, then aimed his gun and Maglite toward the dark corner. The figure rocked inconsolably, her knees drawn to her chest and hugged tight by pale arms, long, wet and curly hair like a shroud covering her face. She refused to raise her eyes to him, even when she spoke.

"They are here, flittering about like butterflies. Can't you feel them, the two men — the ghost detective and your partner? They want her."

He didn't lower his gun. "Want who?"

"The witch," she said, and looked up, with a look like he ought to have known the answer. "Oh, my husband? Oh, God! My daughter! My daughter!" It was as though she was just now allowed to remember. She stood. Her face contorted as her arms extended and she rushed for him as quick as a leopard at a gazelle, her nails like claws that he wasn't prepared to defend against; he didn't really believe she'd attack with a gun pointed at her. In this moment a bit of his inherent chauvinist reared its ugly head, and he thought, "This petite thing couldn't hurt me."

She tackled him to the ground and slammed his gun-wielding hand twice against the floorboards. The gun went flying to a dark corner, and the Maglite rolled under the bed; its beam cast ineffectually against the window.

"I'm tethered to her, don't you see? I don't want to die!"

He resisted against her, trying to catch her flailing arms by her wrists, but found that her manic gyrations overpowered his strength. She meant to bite him — she bared her teeth and snarled and lunged with her jaws for his face, but he tore one hand away and pushed her chin up even as her free hand swiped at his chest. She grabbed his head and slammed the back of his skull against the floor.

A shot rang out. It sounded like an explosion, really, right above his head. The woman fell backward, spread-eagled across the floor, motionless. Marion looked up. A patrolman shook nervously in the doorway, his gun still aimed, the barrel still wafting smoke. Marion rose slowly and pushed the gun down. He patted the man's shoulder and said, "Okay, okay."

They walked downstairs to find the other patrolmen standing around me. One cradled my head as I convulsed. Marion rushed to my side. He called out to me, but I wasn't there.

IV

The ether was bluish and hazy. I know, not terribly original, but it is true, which must validate all the witnesses to the phenomenon. Leo stood beside me — or my spiritual me — and here he looked more complete even as I was out of my body. I felt air swirling around us slowly, brumous roiling; we weren't alone. She was there too, formless, omniscient... or so she'd have liked us to believe. Around her, tied to her like tethered balloons, the cries of the various children she'd taken, fade and crescendo, like drawn out moans. This was all that was left of their souls, their energies, and ultimately, it would be all we'd ever find of any of them save the boy Derek, as she had consumed every ounce of them. Destroying her, I realized (and Leo must have already known), would mean destroying what remained of them.

The particulate collected toward a single mass, darkening to near pitch,

271

as around us the landscape transformed, more definable house in which we entered, and more specifically, the unfinished boards and beams of an attic, with a lone door and no windows save a slotted vent. Reality existed in shadow, which cast its pall over everything even as the figure took form and revealed herself to us.

She glowered at us. I took a step back toward the door. I had come to fight, but I knew from the literature that if it didn't go our way I'd need to get back to my body or risk being stuck here permanently. I'd already died enough at the hands of this woman.

"There is power in the Shimmers," she said. "We could share."

About us, the shadows moved, and it was this movement that drew a concerned look from Leo. We both realized that we'd never been alone with her, but had always been surrounded by the seven princes of Hell, each waiting to laud the victor.

"They won't intervene," I said to Leo.

"But together we could harness them. If there were any two people on earth who deserved Solomon's inheritance, it is you and I, Adam."

"No one deserves any more or any less than what they get in life," Leo said, which brought out of her a snort of laughter — a derisive, haughty sound — and she turned her fierce gaze upon my dead friend.

"With their power, Detective Knight, we could restore your life. We could reunite you with your wife! We could make you a hero again!"

"Then why do you want Dr. Blake?" I knew why. I wanted her to say it. "Do you think if you get her sick enough, you'll kill her and be able to take her body?"

PJ looked at me, confused, with a cock of her head. "I'm not making your doctor sick," she said.

I felt her thoughts intrude my mind as she lunged and the haze swirled around us, and I was certain we'd suffocate in the consuming fog. Leo exploded in a blast of light—I cried out, horrified that she'd beaten him, as I struggled against the fog and fell prostrate on the attic floor. The fog retreated and I realized the witch and the ghost were fighting and thrashing. They crashed into walls, into the unused detritus that might have once

272

functioned as something utilitarian in a home, but now gathered dust. Real-world objects smashed and shattered, and dust flew as the amorphous masses collided. They rolled over me toward the door, knocking me against its jam, the boards searing me as though I'd touched the gate to Hell itself. The lone door in the attic flew open, and I realized with growing horror that it wasn't an escape, but an endgame from which nothing returned. It wasn't hell or heaven or an extension of the ethereal, but nothingness. Any soul that entered it would cease to exist.

Leo and PJ, still battling, took form again, broke apart, and saw that they were equally matched. They hunkered, heaving with breath, appearing beaten. I felt Leo in my own consciousness. *There's only one way*, he reminded me. We had discussed this, though I still didn't know his complete plan. I hadn't fully grasped how far it must be taken.

She rushed. He rushed. I heard a terrible sound — like clothes being rent off a penitent's back, but with a sound like leather splitting — followed by a howl of pain that I knew belonged to PJ Harlow. The pieces that were once her image fired as if in a chute straight into the blackness on the other side of the door, and as it consumed her into its nothingness, so also did her voice fade; I saw the Shimmers in the periphery grimace and recede into the darkness. At that moment, just as Leo reappeared to me, I closed my spiritual eyes and blinked: Marion and the other patrolmen hovered over me.

V

I needed a moment and could only nod when they asked if it was settled, if it was really finished. I stood slowly, and Marion helped me outside, into the fresh air. A deep dusk had settled over the area, and a cool plains breeze blew up to the porch. I let my vision settle and sat on the chilly porch while my stomach turned. I wanted to vomit, but had nothing to heave but bile, and gagged once or twice in reflex.

"What happened?" Marion asked me as Leo reappeared. How could I tell him what I'd seen? As horrible as she was, as much pain and death as she'd dealt out, I'd hoped that even for such a lost spirit there was a solace in death, a chance for redemption. I'd never once dreamed that a spirit could die into nothingness and lose all hope for salvation, lose all awareness.

"So she's gone?" I said finally.

"I thought that's what you said?" Marion asked.

"She's gone," Leo said. I looked up to my old partner and nodded.

We returned to the station with no more words except a few reassurances from me to Marion that the witch would no longer bother us. We found upon arrival that Dr. Blake lay sleeping in an empty cell, pale, trembling and sweating, covered up with a blanket. I awoke her and supported her as we walked out to the car.We returned to the airport and boarded our plane, and she slept most of the way home.

"I hope she feels better," Marion said to me, looking at Doctor Blake's curled and silent form, his voice low so as to not wake her. "I can't imagine what she's been through."

"I can't either," I said.

"You think it could have been the witch? PJ making her sick?"

I shook my head. "No, this isn't the effects of any spell."

When he asked me what I thought it could be, I just shook my head. Third-party conjecture was just gossip, and I couldn't do that to her.

Marion disembarked with us at XNA and we got her home. We went to my apartment next, where Marion rummaged through my fridge and found us both something to eat. The ghost was sulking in the shadows as I realized I needed to tell him that I knew there was no other way. She would not have stopped until we were all dead, or worse, the whole of humanity would have been in jeopardy.

Marion said, "Tomorrow we need to fly up to Chicago and debrief." I nodded; I was familiar with the procedure. "You think she's okay?" he asked.

"If she's still sick in the morning," I said, "she should see a doctor."

It would be a long time before I learned of her actions that night, that not long after we tucked her in, she rose and dressed and drove to an all-night pharmacy, returning home with a simple test that showed her exactly what was making her sick. She did not sleep the rest of the night, but held the device in her hands as she sat on the edge of her tub, her handgun within reach, and she cried.

~

Chris awoke and flexed the fingers of his right hand, unsure anymore of the day. Dr. Green stood over him, smiling. He asked how Chris was feeling. There was something reptilian about him.

"I'm..." Chris raised his hand and stifled a scream. His thumb was his own, but the index, middle, ring, and pinky finger belonged to at least one other person. Still they responded to his desire to curl and extend them, each a shade darker than his own flesh and separated from his knuckles by a ring of stitches.

"Successful transplantation!" the doctor said gleefully. "Not just of the flesh, but of the carpals and metacarpals, the nerves and muscles. This gives us very high hopes."

He noticed a stitched X on the back of his right hand, and suddenly felt as though he stared at something alien, a parasite that had attached itself to his body and would slowly take him over. He could no longer contain his scream. Calmly, the doctor pressed a button and, as several nurses entered, he injected a syringe into Chris's bicep. Chris's world slowed and melted to tranquility.

The doctor pulled up a chair and gently slapped Chris's cheek. "You must understand, Mr. Richardson, why we need you."

"Zeitnot," Chris muttered.

"No. No, we are a small research hospital, privately funded by the new CEO of that conglomerate, for sure, but our benefactor has intentionally kept us separate. He is very interested in our research, mine and my colleague's. We have taken two very different courses, mind you, but if we are both successful, our research could go hand in hand." He laughed at his little pun. Chris groaned.

"We've made some progress. But the nervous system presents a special obstacle that is not easily overcome. I did consider using you for parts, but we risk then losing that marvelous brain of yours. You must be wondering what we've been doing this whole time. Well, we've been finding out how best to incorporate you into our research, and we've been taking steps to ensure we don't lose your mind. I insisted on this, but others were

275

skeptical, till you marvelously reprogrammed that nanotech in Agent Case." He cocked his head and mocked a frown. "Oh, you thought you two were acting clandestinely? How misinformed your little group is. You don't realize the importance of your roles in all this."

"Tell me."

The doctor removed the communication device from Chris's ear and stomped on it.

"Okay. We are going to keep experimenting to make you... even better. We've got the best parts of other people and we are going to make you great. Sadly, you probably won't survive the process, but we will learn a great deal, as with your fingers. It always starts so small, doesn't it?"

Chris's world darkened. The words he spoke and heard were heavy and vacuous. "What about my marvelous brain?"

"You have been subjected to at least ten MRI's since your arrival, and we've got three more for you tomorrow. We're scanning your brain and we're monitoring it continuously. Our hope is to recreate it through fresh AI and an encoded 3D image, then scan it into a mainframe. If my theory is correct, your consciousness—your 'marvelous brain'—will survive even if your body doesn't."

"Oh, God!" Chris said. His communication device was gone, his nurse was missing, and Marion had no way of knowing what they were doing. He should have taken the offer to get out of there when Marion visited recently; however, something told him they wouldn't have made it.

"I'm the closest thing there is, Christopher, and you will be my finest creation."

Chris succumbed to the injection and drifted to sleep.

15

AMBLING REPOSE

I

We were under a severe thunderstorm warning the night Dr. Blake arrived at my home and drove me to her office. She gave little explanation, other than we were meeting a friend. I was not entirely surprised to find Puck waiting for us. I'd met him once before during the incident with Hilbert, but I hadn't had the opportunity then to get to know her childhood friend.

He sat in her office, in the dark, so perfectly still that when she flipped on the light and we saw him there, so alive but so motionless, we both jumped.

"I did not mean to startle you," he said, and rose to tower over us, maintaining the most amicable of expressions. "But I have news for you of the utmost importance."

He studied me like a cocker spaniel might study a baby. Blinking, as though with fresh tear film, he saw the world anew.

"Six months ago, fearing another economic collapse prompted by yet another housing bubble, a bipartisan midnight session of high-level government officials met with the incumbent president in hopes of staving off another Great Depression. This classified meeting has both socioeconomic and militaristic implications and has become known as Operation: Home Tract."

I said, "We don't know anything about you, Puck. We don't know who

277

you are. We don't know what your intentions are, where you're from. Your people."

He blinked. "The government approved the loans and provided welcome gifts, tailored for the new homeowners, all of whom had credit scores below subpar for standard mortgages. The men got three-station gas grills with a lifetime supply of propane. The women received a monthly basket of bath oils and soaps. Where there were children, the gifts were age and gender appropriate. Teddy bears and cell phones and GI Joe and Barbies."

"What do homeowners' gifts have to do with a secret political agenda?" I asked.

"The gifts were the delivery method." It felt like talking to a robot. He looked to each of us and blinked, but his facial movements were minimal and he spoke as if it were a recorded message he were replaying, rather than partaking in a conversation.

"What were the government doing? What did they hope to accomplish?"

"They had four objectives: 1) Wipe out subprime loans by targeting at-risk credit scores with loan offers they couldn't hope to repay; 2) Stimulate the economy with that promise of new loan money; 3) Unburden the stress on the already over-stressed prison system; 4) Test a weaponized biochemical agent that could be introduced to foreign insurgent populations so as to tear said insurgents apart from the inside."

"What was their delivery method?" Dr. Blake asked.

"How do you know about this?" I asked.

"The delivery method varied, depending on the gift. The military learned a lot from this exercise."

"Who are you?" I asked.

He blinked at me as if he didn't comprehend the question. "I'm Puck."

"How do you know all of this? How do you know about this case, about us, about her?"

As I pointed to Dr. Blake, she sat at the edge of her desk, clutching her stomach, exhaling forcefully.

"She is sick," he said.

"I'm fine."

"How do you know?" I repeated. I knew Dr. Blake trusted him. I knew she wanted me to trust him too. They had some kind of history together, but I just couldn't. Not until I knew more about where he came from.

He took a deep breath and looked to the lamplight. "I and my people have a name, given to us by your people. Dearest Samantha came closest to guessing my identity when she named me."

"Puck," she said.

"Fairies?" I said. "Puck was a fairy in Shakespeare's *A Midsummer Night's Dream*. But he was also a mythological figure, also known as Robin Goodfellow. Another name for the devil."

"I'm not one of your Shimmers."

This snapped Dr. Blake out of her stupor. "Adam, only you can see the Shimmers. Everyone can see Puck."

"But you're like them," I said. "You reek of them."

"The military learned that, with these residents, inhalation proved the best delivery method, the most direct to the bloodstream. But absorption through the skin also proved an effective method. This is how they transformed the residents of Ambling Repose."

"Transformed them? Into what?" Dr. Blake asked.

"What are you, really?" I asked. I felt like a broken record.

He regarded me for what felt like forever, and then did something human, something that seemed totally out of character for him. He sighed. "Several months ago, a man, his wife and their little boy died in a house fire, and a sheriff was murdered. Just prior to that, the little boy had been taken aboard UAP — unidentified arial phenomena. Your partner, Mr. Richardson, investigated the abduction. Was there when the boy was returned, in fact. Everyone, including your partner, believed the boy was taken by some evil force, but let me ask you something, Mr. Richardson. Do you think your little brother is evil? The way he treats women? How put out he acts with you and your mother?"

"Of course not." Talk about opening a can of emotional worms.

"Then I can't believe they are evil either, though we might differ on certain points. My people are called the Alcheri. We have been called fairies or fair folk or the Fae. We are related to the same individuals who took that little boy up in Wisconsin. We, and they, are the reason that after Marion left, The Man in the Suit returned to the little town, killed the boy and his parents in the house fire, and shot the sheriff."

"Can we trust you?" I wanted to. I needed to. I was tired of being misled. Dr. Blake touched my arm. "I trust him." That was enough for me.

"Then tell me all you can about Ambling Repose."

II

FLORIDA

We split up upon arrival: Marion and I headed on to Dade County Correctional Facility, and Dr. Blake headed for the Dade County Sheriff's location nearest to Ambling Repose. We'd been called when the whole community was put on lockdown after an 'incident.' There had been a death in the neighborhood. A Sheriff's deputy had been attacked, and about that same time the FBI received a letter from a prisoner charging abuse by the guards and local government agents that had been populating the local correctional facility. What struck us—what struck Pythia, who notified us, was the nature of the neighborhood itself. It had been declared a financial failure and had been abandoned, with every unit in the gated community condemned.

A red bell sounded an ear-piercing alarm as we entered the visitation room at Dade County. In front of us sat the letter writer in an orange jumpsuit, a young Latino, shaved head, covered in tattoos. He looked angry and despondent, scared. Mostly though, despite his tough exterior and his machismo, he looked scared.

"We got your letter," Marion said.

The young man stared at some interesting flash of mold on a tile on the wall and blinked, like he didn't understand English. Marion and I took our seats across the table.

"We aren't going to insult you," Marion said. "Neither of us speak Spanish, so we aren't going to throw a few phrases at you to pretend like we do just so you'll talk to us. You sent the letter, Javier. We know you did. So why don't you just tell us what you're afraid of."

He still refused to look at us. "And what if I did? Write that letter?"

"We aren't the enemy," I said.

"You spoke about abuses in this facility. You may not believe this, but we're here to help you. Tell us what's going on."

I saw a tear in the corner of his eye, this tough guy covered in tattoos, arms folded across his chest. He still wouldn't look at us. Machismo meant pride and meant staying strong, despite all the walls crumbling down. But speech is both above and below machismo.

"They take us out of here," he said, his throat seizing up. "The guards and the other government men — sometime like cattle."

"Where?" I asked.

He shook his head vehemently, nearly ready to scatter his tears.

"None of them ever come back. No one they take out ever comes back. Except last week, it was my turn and I was on the bus, and one of the guards got bit. And that guard hasn't been seen since. But they sent the rest of us on the bus back. For now, they said."

"Where did they take you?" Marion asked.

"Ambling Repose." He bit his lip and hugged himself. "There's talk from the guards... what they got there... they... they..."

"What's there?" Marion asked.

The prisoner looked positively horrified when he answered. "They got monsters there."

The Black Ops Team was strapping on gear when we pulled up. As we exited, the squad leader approached. The hair was shorter, but followed the same arc over the scalp, the eyes the same shade of hue, the build identical to that of my partner's. Marion noticed the squad leader and flinched. He looked Marion up and down but said or acknowledged nothing. I could not reconcile the likeness between the two men, but nothing was verbally addressed either between Marion and me or anyone else. Still, he and I exchanged a glance.

"What are we walking into?" Marion asked his doppelganger.

Another Black Ops team member handed us our bulletproof vests, which we strapped on.

"Death," the team leader said. Around us, the team readied their assault rifles. Marion and I had service weapons— his a .357 and mine a 9-millimeter — we felt exposed and outgunned. The team leader said the Miami gangs had moved in. Cheap housing appealed to the Cuban and Puerto Rican population, and with them came their undocumented family members, including those involved in local gang activity.

"Is that who's in there now?" Marion asked. "What we're about to face?"

A deputy was attacked, we were told. While the majority of the neighborhood had been cleared of innocent families, it was suspected that the gangs still ruled the streets of Ambling Repose.

"They're out of control," the Black Ops team leader said. "We are to clear the entire community by arrest or terminal force."

I turned away. Marion followed me as the Black Ops team performed self-checks. Out of earshot, we debated our calling here. The PRI would not have been brought in for a gang-infested neighborhood cleanup. And then there was what the prisoner had said.

We opened the gates and filtered inside, guns drawn. I chose this Hooters song on the iTunes app on my phone, and Marion snapped "Turn it off!" We followed the squad to the first house, where they kicked the door open. A shadowed figure staggered forth, I heard a snarl and a gunshot, and the figure fell to the floor.

I approached as the Black Ops team dispersed to make their way to the next house. I knelt and examined the fallen figure, a woman with long dark hair. Her skin was gray, like clay, and refrigerator cold. The next two houses showed signs of an intense fire. I overheard one of the team say "Controlled burn" to Marion.

The next house offered a sound, like a scuffling, and by the time I arrived, the Black Ops team had dragged out a gangbanger and surrounded him in the yard. The questions came fast: "Where are your friends?" "How long you been in here?" "Where are the occupants of the house?"

The boy was whimpering. He said that his friends were all dead, and

282

he'd been here since the night before. He said he had been chased by the homeowners and had locked them out the previous night, along with their daughter, before they could... here his words faltered.

"Before what?" I asked, kneeling down in front of him.

"Before they could eat me."

Over my shoulder I heard the cock of a gun; the team leader said that they couldn't leave witnesses to what happened here. We heard then more shuffling and turned to see a man and wife and a little girl lurching toward us. Their skin was pale and crusted with blood. The little girl's ulna had snapped awkwardly out of her forearm, and there was a large gash in the man's neck. The gangbanger screamed. The trio stared at us with cataract eyes, moving clumsily, as though they had forgotten how to walk. The Black Ops team drew their guns and fired in triple taps, shots to the head that dropped them all. When we turned back, the gangbanger was gone.

"Nearest perimeter fence, eight hundred yards," the team leader said. "Watch for amblers."

Another man pulled out a remote and hit a button, and we heard a sound, the buzz of a fluorescent, echo from all directions. The gangbanger wouldn't get out now, he said, even as we heard a gate swing open. Another ambler stumbled out, drawn to us by either by how loud we were or the smell of our flesh. Another Black Ops team member fired his weapon.

If it had stayed like that, we might have had a chance, but the Black Ops team had opened doors and gates throughout the community and soon all the amblers were shuffling toward us, salacious, arms outstretched. They walked from every street and cul-de-sac, down the pavement and the sidewalks, across yards, from every direction. There were sixty-five houses in the subdivision with an average household occupancy of 2.75 people per house, and another sixty-five to seventy people if you counted the prisoners who'd been bitten—we were surrounded by about two hundred and fifty denizens of Ambling Repose, dead but still hungry.

There were seven Black Ops team members, Marion, and myself. Each Black Ops guy held a Barrett Rec 7 with five 30-round clips, and a P226 MK 25 service pistol. Marion and I held three magazines each on our person for our respective weapons.

We all began firing. Rounds missed. Magazines were reloaded or changed out. The amblers pressed on, some dropping like flies, some inching closer.

III

The deputy who had been bitten had been quarantined at the local station after the attack; the other officers locked him in a cell until a doctor could arrive. Two deputies accompanied Dr. Blake into the cell, where the deputy lay under a blanket, shivering violently, ashen in color and unresponsive to commands. He sweated profusely and was cool to the touch. Dr. Blake heard the radio from the lobby. "Time of the Season" blared from the speakers.

She sat next to him on the jail cell cot and patted his forehead comfortingly. He whipped his face toward her with unseeing eyes and snarled. One of the guards reached for her shoulder, to pull her out of the way. She checked the deputy's respiration and his blood oxygen level with a pulse-ox and asked about the attack. No one really knew. He'd been on patrol in Ambling Repose and had seen someone breaking into houses. He had radioed in to report, but when he left his car to investigate, he had been confronted by someone, who subsequently attacked him.

"Was it the guy breaking into the houses?" Samantha asked.

The overly-cautious officer shook his head. "No ma'am, he was very adamant about that. This individual came out of a house. Besides, the guy wasn't breaking in exactly. Guess I misspoke. He was going around opening doors, but not going inside. Just opening them."

"So how does he know then? Did the person say anything?"

The deputy shook his head. "No ma'am. Just attacked him. But he could tell it wasn't this other fella. Said the other guy was dressed like a gangbanger."

She was about to ask him for the description of this gangbanger, to text the information to Marion, when the sick deputy began to convulse. She reached out to stop him but the other deputies stepped in and pulled her away. As quickly as it started, the thrashing stopped, and the man settled into his mattress, his muscles and body sagging into death. Samantha pulled away from the guards and approached the dead man. She meant to raise her fingers to check his pulse, for final confirmation, but as she did, the dead man's eyes opened and he lunged for her as if to bite her. Before she could react, a gunshot reported through the concrete cell walls, and the deputy fell back against his pillow, lifeless.

IV

Working as a cohesive unit with the Black Ops team, we cleared a path down a side street that allowed us room to run. Marion and I paired up, split off, and hoped to find the gangbanger before the Black Ops did. We disposed of a few straggling amblers, and kept searching, until in a gangway beside a garage we heard a commotion in the shadows and found the gangbanger cowering behind some trash cans. He stood when we coaxed him and looked all the more scared, his gaze shifty. It was then we got a text from Dr. Blake saying the deputy was dead.

"Why were you letting them out?"

He wouldn't look me in the eye. "We was paid. We was told to come and open the doors to all the houses. Said to do it before you got here today. Seems someone knew you was coming."

"Did they tell you what you'd find?" Marion asked.

"If they did, I wouldn't be the only one left."

"Who paid you?" I asked.

"Some doctor a few hoods over. Swanky place. Worked for one of the research hospitals in the area. But wasn't from here."

"How could you tell?" Marion asked.

"Accent. Like Haitian or something. He said when y'all come, to give you this," and he handed over a business card with the doctor's name and his home address. "He's expecting you," he said.

I pocketed the card as a two-man patrol of the Black Ops team rounded the corner and drew their weapons. Marion and I moved to shield the banger and drew our guns as well, sure this was how it would end, in a firefight between supposed allies; perhaps that was why we were asked to join the search, so then it could look like friendly fire, executed on Mr. MITS's orders. I began to fire, had begun to squeeze the trigger, when a

285

half dozen roving amblers emerged from the shadows and attacked our would-be assassins. I wanted to help them, I'm sure I did, but I retreated with Marion and the banger in the other direction, the sound of gunshots to our backs as we headed into the shadows.

We were trapped. If the two survived, they would report to the others that we were helping the banger. If they didn't, our progress to escape was still impaired: the neighborhood fence had been electrified, and if I was right about the duplicitous nature of our investigation, it would be only a matter of time before we were followed.

"If we can't get past the wall," the gangbanger said, "how we getting out of here?"

"We could go under it," I offered. "We can see if Dr. Blake can access the sewer system."

"I don't think a suburb's sewage line is large enough for grown men," Marion said, then looked up to the perimeter wall. He looked back to the nearest house, calculating. "We'll go over it," he said.

But as he began calculating the physics of propelling us over the wall from the rooftop, the Black Ops squad found us and opened fire. We attempted to round the corner, to escape through another backyard, but found our path impeded by a dozen more amblers.

V

The MRI scan lasted nearly four hours, which was half as long as yesterday. They had scanned his entire brain and subsequently had been performing scans on each section, getting more and more detailed. The process seemed to take forever. But as sick as he was from the magnets tugging on the iron in his blood, on his mind, and on his soul, he could not take his focus off his hand. He was missing part of himself and feared for what they planned to take next.

Dr. Green entered, staring at his chart on an iPad, as pedestrian an entrance as entrances go. When he looked up, he forced an unnerving smile. His words ripped through Chris like shards of ice.

"I think we'll try a bit more today," he said optimistically. "We'll go for your left leg below your knee. You'll be prepped for surgery within the hour.

Good day."

16

THE WITCH DOCTOR'S DAUGHTER

I

How did I get here, on the terracotta floor of an entry hall in a house two neighborhoods away from Ambling Repose, breathing in tetrodotoxin, grasping at my ever-tightening throat? Leo looked over the shoulder of a Haitian knelt over me, wearing a smoker's jacket and lounge pants, puffing on a Cuban cigar, his hair in dreadlocks. He said, "I have heard of you, *Shimmer Man*. You see the demons," laughing, adding, "You should have brought your partner, I suppose" — How did I get here without Marion?

Well. I'll tell you.

We had shimmied up the gutter of a perimeter house via its air conditioning unit and a drainpipe. Marion was clipped in the right triceps by a bullet, but he successfully secured the gangbanger and me over the fence before hurling himself over after us. We noticed the gangbanger wince as he landed. Marion ripped off the man's jacket to expose his left forearm, where a large bite mark appeared, infected and throbbing.

"Who bit you?" Marion asked, as I examined the wound.

"I'm cool, man," the banger said. "Let's just...."

Marion aimed his service pistol at the gangbanger's head. I asked him to take a breath, at least see if Dr. Blake couldn't find a cure. Slowly, Marion agreed, and we all breathed deeply, to relish in the night air. I moved out of the path between Marion and the gangbanger and began searching my contacts for my doctor's name when, in the sudden silence, we noticed that the fence had quit humming. But I hadn't enough time to run, or even to suggest we run. The gangbanger lunged for me hungrily, but a shot rang out from overhead that dropped him in his tracks. It hadn't come from Marion; he looked as surprised as I. The Black Ops team had scaled the fence, and one soldier with a smoking assault rifle perched on top, staring at us.

They had been a squad of eight, but only four joined us now. Not one of them was my partner's doppelganger. I started to ask where the others were—out of habit—when Marion reached for my shoulder and gave it a squeeze. One look at him told me the answer. Really, I should have already known. I noticed something in him then, that moment when I saw his realization that the squad leader hadn't survived, a moment of loss, a furrowing of the brow, like a jigsaw piece of his identity had been swiped before he could even begin to assemble the puzzle.

"You didn't have to shoot him," I said.

One of them answered. "We did. We deciphered a few methods of successful delivery of the toxin. One is through direct delivery to the respiratory system, not secondary transmittal. It must be functionary. Key here is transmittance. Blood to blood—a bite, an open wound."

I looked down to the dead gangbanger. He was pale and unmoving, but his eyes were half open and stared up, vacantly, past my shoulders to the stars over the tree line.

I said, "With all the possibilities for infection, what if one of us has been infected and doesn't know it?" We undressed and examined each other for any exposed wounds then, satisfied, we proceeded on to the sheriff's department and to my good doctor, where I would uncover the lead that would lead me to the Haitian's house.

II

The dead had risen in front of her eyes, and Samantha sat contemplating how time often melded into one moment. The last time she'd experienced this epiphany was a few days earlier; she'd sat in the waiting room of her doctor's office, awaiting her name to be called. She stared at the paperwork on her clipboard, attached her insurance cards, and looked around the room.

She sat in the jail cell, staring at the body of the dead deputy, wrapped in a dark gray wool blanket as he was cocooned in his own prison blanket. She thought of the other people in the doctor's waiting room that particular afternoon.

A heavily tattooed woman in a skimpy outfit. A couple of nervous young kids still in high school. An obese chick screaming at the bunch of young'uns scampering about her feet and ankles. These were the people in the waiting room as Samantha sat, staring at her clipboard. When her name was called, she looked up with heavy eyes, full of longing.

For her life, before she met me. But that didn't deliver her far enough back, because of Puck, and what he was to her all those years in her childhood. He'd been there since her earliest memories, lounging on the oak tree limb outside her window, plucking at her mind, her soul.

III

There were eleven carbons, seventeen helium atoms, three nitrogen atoms, and eight oxygen atoms in each molecule of the compound streaming through my bloodstream. I felt myself gagging, but I felt myself salivating, also. I could see my dear, dead friend looking on pityingly. I realized then how ineffectual he was. Zombies were soulless, so it was as if we'd sent a dryer sheet to fight a shark. And the Haitian might have dabbled in removing souls, but his cauldron was a vat of chemicals, meant to act on my biology, dispensed via concentrated aerosol as I had snooped around his door. Leo couldn't help me; all he could do was flip a switch, or rattle a pan or fluff a drape.

But he was here. With me, unlike the others, whom I had ducked out on back at the station to follow up on this lead. Puck had sent Dr. Blake an email detailing the chemical compound used in the creation of the amblers. I'd called Pythia, who said that the compound was the product of an R&D department overseen by the PRI. She sent me the name of the doctor who supervised the project. While Marion was arguing with the deputies for letting Dr. Blake get near an infected person and with the task force for nearly getting us killed, I simply snuck out the back.

I felt my mind fleeting, my soul pulling away, leaving behind only black hunger. The Witch Doctor took my elbow and guided me into his living room, sat me in his velvet chair. He offered me a smile that may have been meant to be comforting, but seemed as genuine as a gator's grin, as he crouched beside me. I idly wondered if he weren't worried that I would lash out at him, but by now, I'd lost the ability to speak.

"The magics prevent you from harming me, your master," he said, as though this was meant to be a reassurance. But I felt myself going. Soon I was rising above, staring down at my body sitting in the chair, and I could see the Witch Doctor, who looked up at me as though I was a kite drifting and keyless, unanchored by gravity, just floating higher and higher. The Haitian followed my soul's progress with a smile, before addressing my body again with a pat to my forearm. Leo watched me, his eyes wide, his mouth agape. He reached up for me, mouthing the word "No," but in this state, I heard nothing.

But still I was connected. One foot in the world, so to speak. I saw Leo leap to the chair and disappear into my form, and then I heard the Witch Doctor say, "You will not suffer anymore. My medicines and those of Dr. Green won't allow your body to age. So you, my dear friend, will be able to roam free as a spirit, without concern for yourself or your loved ones anymore."

I stopped. I hovered. I willed myself down, and my biological head turned, powered probably more by Leo's conscience than my own. I imagined my spiritual foot attached to my biological shoulder as though my scapula were an anchor and drifted behind Leo when he sprang my body out of the chair and tossed the Witch Doctor up against the wall.

The Witch Doctor still smiled, but his lip quivered when he spoke. "You shouldn't be able to do that."

"Your zombies have no souls."

He shook his head. "Your soul is gone, Mr. Richardson."

Leo said, "I'm not Adam Richardson," with my lips, and snapped the Witch

Doctor's neck.

Leo doubled over, grabbing at his—at *my*—stomach, and spent several minutes violently wrenching as my body clung to the classical piano, the recliner's arm, the bookcase, then the drapes, which I yanked off the rod in a violent upheaval. Anything he could stabilize my body with as I still drifted in the ether, watching helplessly as my own body knelt and retched and dry-heaved, as yellow bile spilled from my mouth and nose. But by degrees, my vision began to fade. The image of my physical form dissolved, as did the living room and all it contained, till I floated in a sea of black tranquility that promised to sustain me till the end of days.

IV

I awoke in a bed, in a room I did not recognize. In the corner stood Leo, and kneeling in front of me, the Witch Doctor. Alive? But I had seen him die. How was he alive? The room was draped in paisley wallpaper and its frilly lace curtains blew in the wind. I looked at Leo and said, "This room is for a little girl."

Indeed, in another corner, an old-fashioned, multi-storey dollhouse measuring three feet high sat, covered with dust. Against the far wall, opposite the tiny bed in which I lay, a child-sized white vanity with a mirror matched the white dresser next to me, its drawer handles painted pink. It didn't seem large enough to fit adult clothes.

I felt discombobulated, either the effects of my soul again tethered to this reality or, more probably, my body recouping from the drugs and the violent expulsion and was surprised when the Haitian Witch Doctor cradled my right hand with both of his. "How are you...?" I began, but he just smiled at me, and I noticed for the first time that his teeth were rotten, and his eyes were jaundiced. When he exhaled, I smelled the burning plastic of chemicals.

"I am a minister of the soul," he said. "I deal in death. The spirit, once it attaches to a body, it doesn't want to untether. I thought you were just a cop bursting through my door, but when I *zombied* you, *Shimmer Man*, your friend took over your body and expelled my magics. And then he did a most... surprising thing. Do you know of this which I speak?"

My tongue like cotton, I managed, "What?" I clinched at the sheets and found my wrists bound. I wondered why Leo stayed so contently in his corner, looking at the floor. Instinctively, I pulled against the bindings.

The Witch Doctor smiled and nodded. "Relax. Precautionary, only. No. He gave up your physical form. He did this so that your soul might live again. I have never seen such loyalty."

I turned inward, quit struggling, and asked a question that surprised me. "So, he's real?"

I felt ashamed. I couldn't even look at Leo, and I noticed he refused to look at me.

"Oh, yes indeed," he said ecstatically, gripping my hand tightly with both of his own, squeezing down on my knuckles.

I said: "But he snapped your neck."

"There are many levels to zombification," he said with a hearty laugh, and threw his head back to expose a strange bulge to the side of his neck that threatened to poke through the flesh.

"You didn't just die when he snapped your neck, did you? You were already dead."

"I was diagnosed with cancer," he began after a moment. A melanoma had been found on the sole of his left foot that he hadn't noticed till he stepped down wrong one day while walking with his daughter to the market. He realized he couldn't leave her yet, and delved into the practices of his people. Such practitioners were easy to find on the island. Though there were fewer of them, he was able to seek one out who was willing to help, for a price. The Haitian was an exceptionally quick study and was granted a level of undeath by an ancient doctor that allowed him to retain cognitive abilities.

"The only real cure for cancer," he said.

I looked around his little girl's room, dusty from years of unuse. "What happened to her?"

"The priest, he wanted payment for his generosity to me, and I could afford nothing, so he took it, the only thing I had."

"Your daughter," I said.

"I swore revenge, but his magics were most powerful, and I was but a novice. I had no way to defeat him, until there came to my village a man in a suit asking for the secrets to voodoo."

At the mention of this man, both Leo and I perked up.

"He promised me great power. And he delivered. He introduced me to magics even more powerful than the priest who'd saved me and then killed my daughter."

He paused and took a breath. To reconcile a deal with the devil and admit to it out loud weighed on him. I waited patiently for him to continue, and I could see Leo was attentive as well. The Haitian had long since let go of my hands, and now rubbed his together nervously, wiping his palms and intertwining his fingers.

"I committed atrocious acts. I slaughtered my mentor, the priest. And when the man in the suit offered me a job at a research hospital, I took it. What kind of research hospital desired a Witch Doctor—this I did not know. But I went, and I felt my soul darken further. Hell is within, and for the zombie who meanders this world, hell is one's own mind.

"You never sleep. Your mind never quiets. There is always a hunger and there is always a buzzing, just a little louder than a fluorescent light. It muddles the sounds of voices and the sound of rational thought. It provides a kind of madness. It was selfish of me... to impose my abilities on her. She was my first resuscitation, still fresh, not long in the ground. I should have known she would never appreciate this room. She is not a girl at peace."

I swallowed hard. "Where is she?"

"The basement," he said. "Your gun is in the side drawer." He untied my hands.

I drew it and checked the magazine. I let myself out of bed and stood on uneasy feet, swaying a bit. I could feel Leo and the Haitian watching me, so I gave them both a solemn nod.

My gun in hand, I stepped out of the room and shook off the dizziness, found the wall for support as I made my way down the short hall to the steps leading to the first floor. Leo and the Haitian followed behind me, directed me to the kitchen and pointed to a door that opened to a set of steps that descended into darkness. Why did the steps always lead down?

The Witch Doctor reached past me to flick a light switch. The dim bulb hanging from a chain helped some, but the source of the shuffling and other sounds that echoed up the steps were still masked in darkness.

I took a few steps. My head bumped the lightbulb, and, on its chain, it oscillated, shadows dancing against the wall. Still, I could not see, but I descended further.

I could feel the cornerstones and furnishings of the basement all around me, smell the mold-caked cinder blocks, the old boxes and mustiness; with the blindness, I needed my other senses, and my internal monologue or loud thoughts were a distraction. I tried to rely on my ears, but the concrete warped the sounds. I jumped and aimed at every noise. I drew my Maglite and pointed it along the barrel of my pistol.

And then I saw her.

The thin beam scrolled over the basement trash, penetrating the near-impenetrable darkness, when I glimpsed a pale ashen foot scraping across the floor.

The child snarled at me. Her shoulders flexed and her fists clenched, but she hadn't the eyes of a child— more a caged, feral thing that lurked easily in the shadows and knew only hunger.

I fired my gun. The bullet hit her square between the eyes. Still, my hands shook. She toppled over backward, lay lifeless on the floor. Smoke from the barrel dissipated in the darkness. I lowered my weapon and waited for the reverberations to quiet in this enclosed room. I kept my Maglite trained on her, waited for her to move—just because she now lay lifeless mattered little: she was lifeless to begin with—but she did not stir.

When the room had silenced and I was sure all was still, I ascended the stairs. Harsh sunlight scattered mites of dust through the kitchen window, and a forlorn smile settled on the Witch Doctor's countenance. A tear rolled out the corner of his eye and slid down his cheek.

"It was hubris, *Shimmer Man*, thinking I could save her with magics."

"The man you describe, who owns the hospital, you said he wears a suit?" It was a piss-poor question. A lot of people wore suits. But it was the way he said it, as in awe of a powerful force meant to be feared.

"We were a part of the Zeitnot Industries, till recently, when we were shaved off like dead flesh, but the man in the suit came and assured us that he would continue our funding, as the new CEO of Zeitnot. We'd be a pet project, he said. He said he had a personal stake in our research."

"What stake?"

"This man stepped out of the ice machine at our facility."

I frowned. *What did that mean? He stepped out of the ice machine. Ice Machine? Ice... ice... medical research facility...* "Cryonics?"

He was studying me, my face, my aura, perhaps, or my mind. "The man in the suit. He is not of our time, monsieur."

My breath caught in my throat. I had to cough just to get out, "What are you saying?" but it was clear. I caught a glimpse of Leo. I never knew ghosts could be flabbergasted. We both could read the man well enough to know that he wasn't lying. His last reason to lie lay motionless at the bottom of the steps, and his other motivation, his revenge, had grown idle and cold with fulfillment years ago.

"Who is he?" I asked. My head was spinning. I needed to know everything about Mr. MITS, and the possibilities swirled around me, left me drunk with tangentially useless thoughts. The Witch Doctor stared down the steps to the darkness, so I moved in front of him, forced him to look at me. He blinked his jaundiced eyes and looked as though he saw me for the first time. I repeated my question, louder, and with more force.

"I do not know," he stammered.

"He's telling the truth," Leo said, but I ignored my dear, dead friend.

"You're lying!"

"No!" The man was nearly in tears. He tore his eyes away and looked to the stairs, began weeping. I looked, too, sure her corpse would be crawling into the kitchen, persistent, hungry, insatiable. But there was nothing.

I loosened my grip, and the Haitian sank to the floor, curling around his knees, and wept. The Voodoo, the zombification of his little girl, had just been a way for him to stave off his inevitable mourning.

"I do not know who that man in the suit is, but my colleague knows—Dr. Victor Green —and our hospital is the Green-Lifeway Research Facility here in Miami. Your brother is there, Shimmer Man. Now, I must ask you to put down one more zombie, if you can stomach it. Please. I just so desperately want to see my little girl again."

"This Dr. Green: is he involved in that cryogenics experiment from where Mr. MITS came?"

The Witch Doctor shook his head, and when he met my eye I saw such a look of fear. "No sir. He involved in much, much worse, and last I was there, your brother was his number one patient."

I chanced a look over to Leo, who appeared convinced, and so I drew my gun once more, and fulfilled the witch-priest's last request.

V

Dr. Green finished a thorough check of Chris's vitals and looked at the below-the-knee transplant. He smiled his reptilian smile, impressed with his own work, which did little to appease Chris, who shrank away, his own skin crawling.

"Do you know what is really fascinating?" Dr. Green asked.

"Plastic surgeons have been playing Frankenstein for years."

Dr. Green shook his head. "Such a blanket, disparaging statement when some have done some truly remarkable work. Lives have been saved. Faces have been restored, and you chalk them all up to a mad scientist.

"No, what is truly remarkable, my friend, is what we've accomplished with your brain. Countless MRIs, hours and hours of digital scans, and we've successfully mapped every wrinkle, every speck of that gray matter. We have sedated you and monitored your dreams. We have mapped your entire brain and recreated it with a reasonably accurate digital model."

"What do you mean, 'reasonably accurate'?" Chris asked.

"To be one hundred percent accurate, we would have to remove your brain, slice it into micro-thin cross sections that could then be scanned into the computer, but we aren't there, yet." Dr. Green readjusted his glasses and sat on the side of Chris's bed.

"Do you understand consciousness? We—I should admit—with no disrespect to you, have also desired your brother's brain, for his insights into his *Shimmers* may revolutionize consciousness. But there is an idea

297

that our consciousness experiences everything. When you lounge on the couch, you aren't *externally* feeling the couch, but the nerves in your back and legs are constantly receiving the information; they transmit that to the brain, which processes the information. Likewise, our eyes. We don't see television. Images—light—are processed by our eyes and sent via the optic nerve to the corresponding part of the brain that processes those images. Our brain processes what we see. Our brain processes all of our interactions with the physical world."

Chris looked at his hands and the false fingers. With but a thought, he could wiggle one of the alien toes on his new foot.

"We can't create that level of sensory input, not as accurately as the human brain," Dr. Green continued. "Not at an artificial level, not with microchips." He beamed. He flashed his pearly whites and his aqua eyes brightened. "Until now."

Chris met the doctor's steely gaze with silent contempt, an act of defiance.

"Microchips are the key. Currently, without getting too technical, microchips are large. The resistors they hold, the key to computations, are very large. The smaller the resistors, the more you can fit on a microchip, and the more computations you can do. Right now, we have resistors that are about ten nanometers wide. IBM and Zeitnot have told the public they are working on resistors seven nanometers wide. That is barely wider than a DNA molecule.

"But Chris, *we* have resistors *one* nanometer wide. We have duplicated your mind. Modern processors would require millions of terabytes to attempt to accomplish what we've done."

Chris wanted that to be all. But he understood the lingo. He understood bytes and scans and MRIs.

"What am I?" Chris asked. "What have I become?"

To this, Dr. Green smiled. "You are my creation. And your mind, your consciousness, will live on forever!"

17

ENDGAME

I

Months later, I would find myself in Europe, in various countries. While there, I encountered a being that I never thought I'd see again. It was dying, unable to sustain the life that had been given it. In the end, it gave me its journal, which I have decided to incorporate into my own writings, here.

I watch them, the men in black, with the handsome athletic man who looks like a hero and his friend with the strange affect and the pretty woman, enter the hospital to find my brother and my father. They have guns. Father taught me about guns. He taught me how they operate and how to disassemble them and how to aim them so that they are most effective. I have a gun.

There is a police force in the hospital—armed security guards. They will be no match for the men in black, but I will intervene soon, when the time is right.

One of the guards got a shot off on the one who seems to be the leader before being killed. The leader, the handsome man, his name is Marion; I learn this when the strangely-affected man screams his name. It is good to know names. Knowing the name of an enemy means you have power over that enemy. This doesn't appear to be the first shot to this area; he'd been favoring his right shoulder.

My father's name is Green, apropos since he gave me life and then turned me out into the world to learn, and green is the color of Spring, which is life renewed. I know languages and what words mean. I speak German and Spanish and English fluently. I have read countless books, everything in the local library. I even learned to enter the houses of others without detection. I learned, though, that I have no name. My father had a file on me labeled Trial 10-023B. I called myself Trial Ten for a while, and then shortened it to Triten.

I am not a monster. My father's work was seamless, and the donors who contributed to me were of similar flesh tones and in respectively agreeable stages of lifelessness. If anyone notices a scar, they assume (because a few have ventured guesses), that I was in some sort of accident. They do ask me why one of my eyes is blue and why one is emerald-green, and I tell them I have heterochromia iridum, but Father said it was not a mistake on his part, but an opportunity to give me character.

I asked him once why he made me. He said until his accomplishment, only God created life. I asked him if he wished to be a deity. He didn't answer right away, and he soon changed the subject. I resolved to learn all I could about my father from that point on.

I began with internet searches at the library. I learned he graduated medical school from the University of the West Indies in Mona, Jamaica in 2005. I learned he grew up in Virginia, his father the descendent of a plantation owner; my father's father was a tobacco farmer who raised his five children on that very plantation. It seems, from earliest inception, my father had been preoccupied with the creation and cultivation of life. How could such a man be vilified?

He was the second from the youngest, the youngest being a sister whom he lost when he was eight—she was five. A newspaper reported that she drowned in a pond in the field where they raised some cattle. My father's relationship with his family seemed to strain after that accident, and an investigation into the Green financials from that time showed ten years of tuition payments to a boarding school in France. I examined the roster; the student enrolled was my father.

When he was eighteen, he was cut off financially. His surviving siblings all had full rides to their respective degrees. And what a waste. One went to an agricultural school to learn the family business. Another went to business school. Another got a PhD in cultural studies. The one with the MBA backpacked through Europe and did humanitarian work in the Middle East until recently, when ISIS learned he was a Christian. There again God pops up. It seems life would be much better without such a being, but that would be like me unmaking Father. Try as I might, I cannot deny my creator. That humans can do this baffles me.

I know I am not human. I see it when I look in the mirror. There is no spark, no glimmer in my eyes, as I've seen in the eyes of others. Mine are dull, like unpolished marble. My flesh is dry and pale, ashy. If I were to remain still, you might think me dead.

I eat. My body does require nourishment; I learned of nutrition during my studies. I learned what it takes to make a body strong. I learned that I'm stronger than most men. Father made me stronger.

They are advancing. The guards have nearly been wiped out. Father is in his office, a gun in his hand. He seems to hear me, though. He keeps glancing up to the ceiling tiles as I scurry about. Still, he doesn't seem to be relieved to know that I am near. Apparently, they are more dangerous than I surmised.

II

Marion led us down a wing on a particular floor and opened a door, and Chris was there, sitting in bed. Half dazed from whatever meds they were pumping into his arm through an IV, he smiled a dopey smile at us as errant gunfire echoed in the hall and Dr. Blake slammed the door shut behind us. I rushed to him, hugged him, muttered how much I missed him, felt his arms wrap around me. I was only vaguely aware of a shuffling sound above, and out of the periphery caught a glimpse of dust raining from the ceiling tile. I was on the verge of crying, so that, as doped out as he was, as glad as he was to see me, it was Chris who was comforting me. I'm not ashamed to admit that without my brother, I would not be able to make it through life.

Marion approached, probably to tell us that we should leave, but stopped and said, "What the hell happened?"

I pulled away and saw he was looking at Chris's hand, and when my brother swung his legs off the bed, we caught sight of his leg as well. He'd gone as far as he could with the IV attached to his left bicep.

"Jesus," Marion said.

"I can walk on it," Chris said.

"If I'd have known," Marion said, but the words were stupidly ineffectual.

Still applying pressure to his right shoulder, he approached and shook Chris's hand as I unhooked my brother's IV. We helped him out of bed, and Dr. Blake helped him dress. He made googly eyes at her, but we all knew it was the medicine.

"We need to go, now," I said, the panic in my voice as footsteps and yelled orders closed in from the other side of the hall. Marion took off his jacket and his dress shirt, then rolled up his T-shirt sleeve and examined the wound. The most recent shot had grazed him enough that no slug was lodged, but there was a gash and plenty of blood loss, and it had reopened his earlier wound. He was growing pale. His eyelids fluttered, and he staggered and fell against a cabinet. Chris and Dr. Blake and I rushed to steady him.

Marion said, "Not yet. We have to find Dr. Green."

III

They are coming for you, Father. I watch this group shuffle intently toward your office.

I was not created with a sense of morality. My god delivered to me only one commandment—learn. I have learned by dissecting humans who resemble me. I learned to leave no trace, as I learned to enter the library after hours. Instinct tells me they should abandon the slowest so that the group could move faster. That they don't intrigues me. It makes me question morality, and it makes me question the report I read from when my father was a child. It came from a buried newspaper report, an interview with my father's mother. She said she didn't like the attentions my father paid toward his little sister. She called him sick.

My father had nine trials before me. The elusive elixir has always been life. How do you inject life into dead tissue? Popular science fiction has always suggested electricity, and so my father attempted to stimulate the nerves of the previous subjects. Voltage and amperage had to be just so. Not enough will barely make a bicep twitch, and too much will microwave the organs and muscles and turn the nervous system to bacon.

He learned it was both chemical and electrical. A concoction of amino acids and carbohydrates in liquid form needed to be injected, which he discovered after multiple tests on rats. At the same time, the amperage and voltage had to be just so, and specifically administered within minutes of the protein inoculation. Timing was crucial. A second off, the dosage wrong, the amps wrong or the voltage too much or too little, and life would be permanently denied. This is the proof that life is not an accident and that evolution is not random. The spark that I do not see in my eyes, that could not be duplicated by anyone other than God, is by design. For as random as it feels, life provides too specific creatures to have been left to chance by evolution.

IV

There are guns on you. I drop out of the ceiling into a crouch that will better allow me to lunge at my enemies, and they face me. The men in black round the corner and train more rifles on me. I do not care. I raise my gun level to the forehead of the one they call Marion. They all know that with one squeeze of the trigger I can drop him.

"He's my friend," the weird one says, as he steps forward to shield Marion.

I say, "What is this... you say 'friends,' that such a word should mean something to me. I have read about it, and I've seen it in others, but I have not experienced it. A man with the power to give life would have skill with his scalpel— enough to make his creation presentable to the world. And you, my brother, would rally against him?"

"He's committed crimes," Marion said. *This one is weak. He is fading, or seems to be, but I detect something in him, something he doesn't even register. He won't die today, and he won't die for a very long time.*

"He has turned you into me," I tell my brother. "He wanted me to have your mind."

"You call him your brother," the weird one says. "But he's my brother. He's my blood."

"The man who gave you life — Dr. Green," my brother says, and he looks disgusted, "stole from me. He stole my mind. He stole my soul."

"No," I said. "He allowed you to share it."

The weird one turned to my father and said, "Tell me about the cryonics project. Tell me about Mr. MITS."

"Who?" my father asked.

"Your boss! The man in the suit."

My father stammered.

I refocused my weapon to my father and pulled the trigger.

"What did you do?" the weird one asked.

I couldn't respond verbally. I had seen in my father's eyes the deception that he had practiced for so long and had hid from me. I had not learned of morality from him, but in the books I read and in others I saw. Bearing false witness bred distrust, and I saw they were right, and he was wrong. His eyes had revealed this to me.

A soldier in black fired his gun and hit me in the back. It didn't hurt; I don't feel pain as others do, and with my construction came accelerated healing thanks to the nanotechnology flitting through my bloodstream. Still, another shot came, and I realized that even I couldn't withstand too many more direct hits. I leapt; I felt the glass shatter and shards split my recycled flesh. The sun was bright, and the air was warm and it was a long way to the ground.

V

We returned home unsatisfied. I searched all I could about Dr. Victor Green but was unable to learn more about the thing he had built. It had looked so human, save for its dead eyes. Chris spent the night in a local hospital, as I slept by his side, and he was discharged in the morning. He asked me where Dr. Blake was, and I answered honestly that I didn't know. I was bothered by the fact that the creature couldn't be found after jumping out the third-story window. Black Ops thought it might have crawled to the sewer access fifteen feet away, slithered in and died; a blood-trail led in that direction. It seemed plausible. It seemed likely. Still, that night I felt a presence that wasn't Leo as I lay in bed and looked out my open window to the darkness and the rain. I thought I saw someone looking in. Used to be, I liked leaving the blinds up and the curtains tied back to see the rain and lightning as it fell. Gave me a kind of peace. But after I thought I saw that face, I never left them open again.

I rose and cinched my robe around me and padded out into the living room. The ghost sat brooding, as he often did. In my spare bedroom, my brother slept soundly, snoring a bit. The creature had tried to claim him at the hospital, had tried to say they were brothers. What if she came back for him?

304

Darmstadt, Germany—

Spring the following year—

I stand in the ruins of my ancestor's castle and look down on the ancient town (I speak out of turn; I'm not a direct descendent of the Frankenstein name, nor had my research indicated that Dr. Green can claim such lineage, but allegorically, I am also from Mary Shelley's imagination, inspired by the gothic ruins where I now stand).

I see the weird one. He is preoccupied with a new group, priests for the most part, and while he recognizes me, and seems alert to my presence, he does not come after me.

A caterpillar meanders up the brick face of a ruined wall at the castle. I flick it off and crush it under my boot. It begins to rain, but I do not desire to find cover as others in the area. I appreciate the rain, and I love the cool and the wet. I let my clothes and flesh get drenched and I laugh.

18

AMEN

I

Colonel Hamilton dropped his keys in the dish on the table by the front door and walked to his liquor cabinet — a designated cupboard in the kitchen — where he filled a tumbler with ice cubes and then with Scotch, took a sip that maybe once forced a shudder out of him back when he was less conditioned to it, savored it, and licked his lips. He stared into the dark recesses of his apartment and thought of demons and ghosts, of the monsters of all types that he'd seen. He didn't sleep much anymore, but only because his bed, his home, was empty. There was no one left for him to save from the monsters. God and country were not enough after God took his family and the country didn't give a shit. The ice cubes jingled, his tumbler a miniature tambourine as he walked into his bedroom, turned on the overhead light, and began to undress. He planned to wash his face and brush his teeth after another snoot of Scotch, down some mouthwash, and go to bed till five the next morning. He planned to live out the next day as he lived out the previous.

Peripheral movement turned his attention away from his state of undress. The man in the suit stood in the doorway to the bedroom. Held a gun on him. The colonel had a piece in his dresser, six steps away. He took a crab-step toward it, not taking his eyes off the man in the suit.

"I'd hoped you'd stay away," Hamilton said.

Mr. MITS smiled. "I got friends."

"You'll run out of friends eventually."

"Perhaps."

"You're a goddamn cockroach," Colonel Hamilton said.

Mr. MITS leveled his gun as the colonel took another step. If he extended his hand and opened the drawer, with a little luck, he could get a shot off.

"I really am," Mr. MITS said cheerfully.

"I know the truth. Adam Richardson and Marion Case know the truth. You're finished."

He took another step. Opened the drawer and reached inside.

"You'd think so, wouldn't you?" Mr. MITS said, and pulled the trigger three times.

Colonel Hamilton fell against the blinds in his bedroom window and slumped to the floor.

II

Chris was late, as usual, so I ordered him a local lite beer while I sat on the patio in the shade on Dickson. I watched a few people cross the street. One lady, jabbering on her cell phone, nearly walked out in front of a car. The driver slammed on the brakes and waved her on. She waved back and nodded, a scowl on her face like it was his fault when she was trying to cross against the light.

I sipped on a glass of water. An older, Mediterranean-looking gentleman in a priest's collar sat down, dressed in a polo and khakis. He'd walked up to my table with four or five younger guys who stood back and surveyed the scene like they were *Cosa Nostra*.

"You have time to think about my offer?" he asked in broken English, a strong Italian accent. "You think your government is the only institution with resources to combat such things. My institution is older than your government. We have more resources. Adam, we can help you fight the Shimmers."

I sucked the glass dry through the straw. The waitress set the beer meant for my brother in front of my companion and offered to refill my water. The old priest sipped on the beer and seemed to relish in it. I looked around for Chris but saw no one in the throng of pedestrians and early bar-hoppers of Dickson that resembled him.

I said, "King Solomon was a religious man who learned he could control the demons and used them to build the Temple." An odd statement, for sure. But I was thinking about the witch and her quest for power. I also was thinking about the Church.

"Hubris is our scourge," the priest said, and hung his head. "He had not the safety net of the new covenant to secure his piousness. None of us can claim such control. You are not crazy, Mr. Richardson, and we are not so proud that we would assume to take control of that which afflicts you."

The waitress sat more water down in front of me. She smiled at us, and the old priest praised her for the beer as though she'd brewed it herself.

He said, slurping it down more, nearly finishing it, "We are here for but a few more days. We will expect an answer by then."

"What have you told me?" I asked. "Nothing of substance that I may really consider your offer. You've given me no reason to trust you. To believe you can help. Why should my answer be anything other than no?"

He emptied the remainder of the glass down his gullet, tipping the base to kiss the sky, then stood and offered me a smile meant, I'm sure, to be reassuring.

"The Shimmers represent all we combat. We at the Vatican have more resources than your government, are operating with more knowledge. As for trust and belief — these are shadowed by the notion of faith. Now, I have told you all you need to contemplate the salvation of your own soul."

He walked away.

"You want more water, hon?" the waitress asked.

I handed her the bottle. "That wasn't who the beer was for," I said. "Will you bring me another?"

She glanced at the tabletop, smiled and said, "Sure." After she left, I followed her gaze, and saw a crumpled hundred-dollar bill in the center of my table. The priest, it seemed, had been sure enough to pay my tab and leave a healthy tip.

He had been right, though. I needn't more proof. Proof of what the PRI stood for existed in Mr. MITS, whom none of us trusted. Proof existed in the Black Ops team and Chris's abduction and in what we'd turned up in investigating Zeitnot Industries. And his statement that I wasn't crazy put me in a precarious position. If I believed that also, then I had to side with him, and he had to be telling the truth. But if I didn't, then I'd admit that I was crazy, which would mean my hallucinations were out of control, and I was probably... *actually*... strapped down in a padded room somewhere, hallucinating everything that had happened. Perhaps Dr. Blake was merely a recurring figure meant to check my dosages. Perhaps Chris only came to hold my hand with all his own digits and tell me stories that were more fiction than truth about our father and our grandfather—the exaggerated greatness that is the myth of most families. Perhaps Marion was permitted to visit me, and only whispered to me the mundane details of cases that I then transformed into this imagined world. Perhaps the ghost was just another figment of my imagination.

It was in this precarious position I found myself when Chris hobbled up and sat down, smiled lasciviously at the waitress as she delivered the new beer, and raised a hand with three bandaged fingers to deliver the full glass to his lips. Underneath the table, he rubbed at his leg, the leg that Dr. Green had ostensibly amputated and replaced with another. Either the graft wasn't holding so well, or my somewhat sedated state required another detail to keep me locked in this fantasy.

"Is this real?" I asked.

Chris smacked his lips and sat the glass down a little too hard. "Certainly fucking feels real." He squinted in the sunlight, seemed to remember something, then drew a pair of Ray Ban Aviators out of his pocket to shield his eyes.

"How are you doing?" I asked.

He didn't answer till after another satisfying drink. "I feel like I'm Frankenstein, Adam. We should go see Mom after this."

"Frankenstein's monster," I corrected. "Frankenstein was the doctor."

"Fuck," he said and laughed.

III

My old partner's arm was still in a sling when we met up with him at Midway Airport. He asked Chris about his injuries and Dr. Blake how she was doing, then led us to a car that drove us through Chicago traffic toward the federal building downtown. We sat in silence for most of the drive, with only the ghost to speak and only me to hear.

"You ain't seriously contemplating going with them. They can't be trusted, Adam. You can trust me. You know that." This was the gist of his monologue till I could stand no more. My compatriots only heard my end of the conversation.

"Yeah, I really am thinking about it. Can we trust the PRI? I think we've learned we can't. Yeah, I trust you, but you've been thrust into this situation like the rest of us. Here, we're pawns. What if there—what if we have actual control? Maybe he did, but it's no worse a lie than what the PRI told us. Don't give me that whole 'devil you know' crap. Maybe we can all go? He didn't say we couldn't. We are strong together."

He said, "You know they don't want us. They only want you."

Curiously, not my brother, my doctor, nor my old partner said a word during the one-sided conversation they overheard. But each seemed to hang on to everything I said, as though trying to decipher the full message to either gauge my lunacy or my intentions.

Our arrival at the federal building was unceremonious. We trudged up to the thirteenth floor, prepared to deliver our post-case notes to Col. Hamilton and a conference room of PRI agents and Black Ops. The colonel was not present with the remainder of the Black Ops team and the other PRI agents, but Mr. MITS had returned, as well as someone we did not expect: our old boss, Tom Builder, stood next to Mr. MITS, looking somber. Both Marion and I tried to attract his attention, but ADA Builder motioned to a few empty chairs, and Chris and Dr. Blake followed our lead to the seats.

The room murmured with unintelligible words, and I leaned over to Marion to ask if he had an inkling of what was going on, and he said, "No," a betrayed look darkening his eyes.

Mr. MITS stepped forward, capturing my attention and the attention of my team. The room quieted as we all looked up expectantly, and I'm sure I wasn't the only person in the room to notice the inauspicious absence of our PRI director.

"Earlier today, police responded to an address here in the city: shots fired, possible homicide. They found Colonel Hamilton in his apartment. Three shots, all center mass. Nothing wasted."

I'm sure to everyone else in the room, he seemed emotional. But his choking, his alligator tears, seemed manufactured to me. I did not consider my colleagues, but only thought of my own feelings. Surely Colonel Hamilton had been safe. But if he wasn't, then were any of us?

"Rest assured, we will find the killer," Mr. MITS continued, and I could all but hear the harrumphs and the cheers from the Kool-Aid-sucking bureaucrats of the room. "But in the meantime, we cannot forget our mission. We cannot ignore what has come for us, and we have to be prepared. Therefore, I would be honored to introduce to all of you the new director of the PRI, recently promoted from the position of ADA Supervisory Special Agent in the FBI—Tom Builder."

While the room clapped and cheered, I noticed Marion's frown. I knew not how to react. I had trusted ADA Builder; he had always been good to me, and so I wanted to be happy for him, but as he stood side-by-side with Mr. MITS, I felt only betrayal.

"Thank you all for your service," Builder pontificated to the gathering, but he settled his eyes on my old partner. "I am not a man who believes in rocking the boat — just ask my former agents. I will not change what is working." This seemed to draw the approval of those in attendance. Most of the PRI nodded. What remained of the Black Ops team stood at parade-rest, but I could have sworn I saw several of their shoulders relax at this news. Agents began to talk amongst themselves, and a general sense of ease spread over the room, underpinned by the news of the recent homicide. Though people had relaxed with Agent Builder's promise not to upset the status-quo, the other news sank in. Eyes moistened and cheeks reddened at the realization of Colonel Hamilton's death.

One agent called out to no one in particular, "Will we get to conduct our own investigation into the director's death?"

Mr. MITS yielded the floor to our new PRI director, and Tom Builder effectively quieted the room. "Please," he said. "I wasn't finished. Everyone. When things are working, I don't want to rock the boat, but things aren't working, are they? We have distrust in the unit, and we have lost over half the SPECWAR soldiers assigned to us, including your platoon lieutenant," he said, looking from them to Marion. I recalled the uncanny resemblance between the two men, and I shivered.

"With all due respect, sir," said one of the Black Ops, "we were only out there..."

Tom raised a palm, still looking at Marion. "We have had agents eschewing their caseloads to work on side projects completely unrelated to the task at hand. Because of this, lives have been lost. You are a better investigator than this," he said. "What happened?"

Dr. Blake stood up. She'd been sitting in a chair just behind Marion, so I caught her movements out of the corner of my eye. "With all due respect sir, I've seen Agent Case work. His tangential focus, while it might seem impertinent to the respective cases, has proven absolutely necessary in exposing these weak links in the department. Specifically related to—" but that, and her raised finger, both meant to indicate Mr. MITS, was as far as she got before our new director cut her off.

"I know a unanimous decision was made by the former director and his chief liaison to Homeland Security—" (Mr. MITS hung his head, feigning guilt)"—to invite civilians into this investigative unit, but I believe this is where the breakdown in functionality began."

Chris's chair shuffled. "Now wait a minute! You guys came begging to drag my brother back into this crap, after it was your investigations that nearly destroyed him. We came to watch out for him."

"And at what cost?" Builder said. "Experimental surgeries. Implanted chips that could kill a strong agent at any minute. A witch who left more dead in her quest for power..." He turned his gaze on my psychiatrist. "What did you suffer, Dr. Blake? What horrible things did you experience unnecessarily because you followed Adam Richardson to the PRI?"

Her face wrinkled to an expression of rage, but her ghost-tight lips expressed no sound, and a solitary tear rolled down her cheek. She allowed Chris to put a comforting arm around her, and though she tried to speak up, the words failed her, and, eventually, glaring at the director, she allowed Chris to lead her out of the room.

"Adam, you need a solid, stable partner here at the PRI."

I rose to my feet and shook my head. "You can't."

"I am." He looked at Marion. "Effectively immediately, Agent Case, you are suspended pending an internal investigation into your recent activities. You will answer for your actions, Agent Case. I brought you here for a chance to excel, for a chance at redemption after the debacle that nearly cost us Agent Richardson's mental stability. You have failed. The outburst from your team, which has kept me from doing this in the privacy of my office, where this matter should have been handled, is only further evidence of how you've mishandled this situation."

He looked around to the rest of the room. "Obviously, I have some matters to attend to. I am going to review the personnel files of everyone here, and I will be keeping a close eye on each of your cases. Agent Case, if you and your team will accompany us to my office, we'll conclude the matter there."

Marion stood and stalked out the door. I followed closely behind, and we caught up with Chris and Dr. Blake at the elevator. They read the scowl on his face and noted his silence and looked to me for interpretation.

"He was fired," I said. "I think we all were."

"Officially, I was suspended," Marion said. "They still want you."

The elevator doors opened. We entered and turned back to see through the open door of the conference room. Agents refused to look at us, and Black Ops soldiers stared us down coldly. Mr. MITS and Agent Builder seemed to be looking over a case file, but when both looked up to watch the doors close on us, I saw Mr. MITS smile.

IV

The private jet rolled more smoothly than the PRI's chartered carrier, or maybe I just told myself that as I sat in my own compartment, away from the old priest and his entourage, with only my ghost to accompany me. Leo entered without saying a word, appearing with a sanctimonious scowl on his face and didn't say anything for the longest time. When he finally did speak, he avoided the subject.

"How's Chris?"

"He's in love," I said.

The day before, Chris and I had lunched on Dickson, soaking up the afternoon sun, though he'd barely touched a bite. He'd barely even tried his beer.

He had said, "She was so upset yesterday. But when we got on the plane, she wouldn't sit near me. She wouldn't say anything."

"You don't know what she went through," I said.

"I asked her. She wouldn't tell me."

I shook my head. "Don't look at me. It isn't my place."

He took a sip of beer. Used to be, for Chris, a sip meant parting his lips and opening his throat so that the ale could cascade for several seconds down his esophagus in one gigantic gulp, but now the beer barely kissed his lips. "I should go see her. I should go check on her."

I related this.

Leo said, "Does he know you're here?"

"I left him a note. I don't know when he'll find it. I think he was going to her office this morning or for lunch or something."

"She won't be there," Leo said, closing his eyes like he was concentrating. "She's caught a flight. She's closed her office for a few days."

"Where?" I asked.

He opened his eyes. "It ain't you, my man. I trust you. I don't trust them. I get it, though. The PRI is powerful, and they are the enemy, and we need something just as powerful to combat them. But you got to be careful what you wish for. And you can't trust someone just because they have a collar. Some dogs come with collars, and those dogs would bite your hand off in an instant."

"And if they can help me beat the Shimmers?"

"What if the Church is like the witch, only they've had centuries longer to get it right?"

314

"Get what right?"

"The quest for power," he said.

I let that resonate with me. Outside, the gilded ocean reflected small whitecaps, and I sat hypnotized by them as I contemplated my own fate. I was setting off on my own journey and my friends must be content to live out the lives the witch had teased them with. I pushed play on my iPhone, put the headphones in my ears and listened to Hozier's "Take Me to Church." Out my window, I saw nothing but the endless ocean.

V

I wouldn't learn until later that Marion was listening to the same song on his satellite radio and examining his bullet wounds, which were basically non-existent after thirty-six hours. Outside, lightning flashed, and thunder echoed between the Chicago buildings, and rain pelted the tin roof. He ran his fingers over the tender, pink, rippled flesh where there should have still been an open wound stitched closed— but he hadn't even needed stitches. The wound had sealed under the bandage, and just a day or so later, pink flesh had latticed over the scar. Hell, at this rate, there may not be much of a scar after it was all said and done. *Wounds don't heal this fast,* Marion thought. And then he thought about the nanotech infesting his body, and how Chris had reprogrammed them. *What had he done?*

A knock sounded at his door. He stood as the rain intensified, a thousand needles a second on tin. He opened the door and was not as shocked as he should have been to see a soaking wet Dr. Blake standing in his doorway, staring up at him. He should have asked her what she was doing there. She should have told him. But neither spoke. Instead, she stood on her tiptoes and put her arms around his neck. She kissed him, and he kissed her back, and they stumbled back into his apartment. She slammed the door shut, and he peeled off her wet clothes and she ran her fingers over his healing wound and, still kissing, they tumbled backward embracing to his bedroom, then to his bed. And the rain beat on and lightning flashed and the thunder rolled. And somewhere else in the city, Mr. MITS watched them through the lens of a hidden camera. And Hozier was climaxing and finishing his song.

Amen.

—

My name is Adam Richardson. I was once a promising young FBI agent. Since I was diagnosed paranoid schizophrenic, I was relieved of my duties. But I'm not someone you should be afraid of. Occasionally, I see things most people can't see. Most of the time, these are hallucinations of my illness. Occasionally, they prove to be real. Some of what I see are good, but most aren't. I want to stop the frightening things.

I'm going to stop them.

Made in the USA
Middletown, DE
07 April 2022